The Art of Pokémon The First Movie™

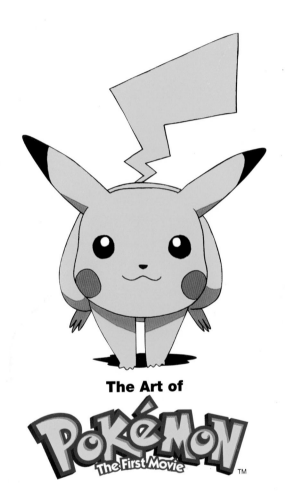

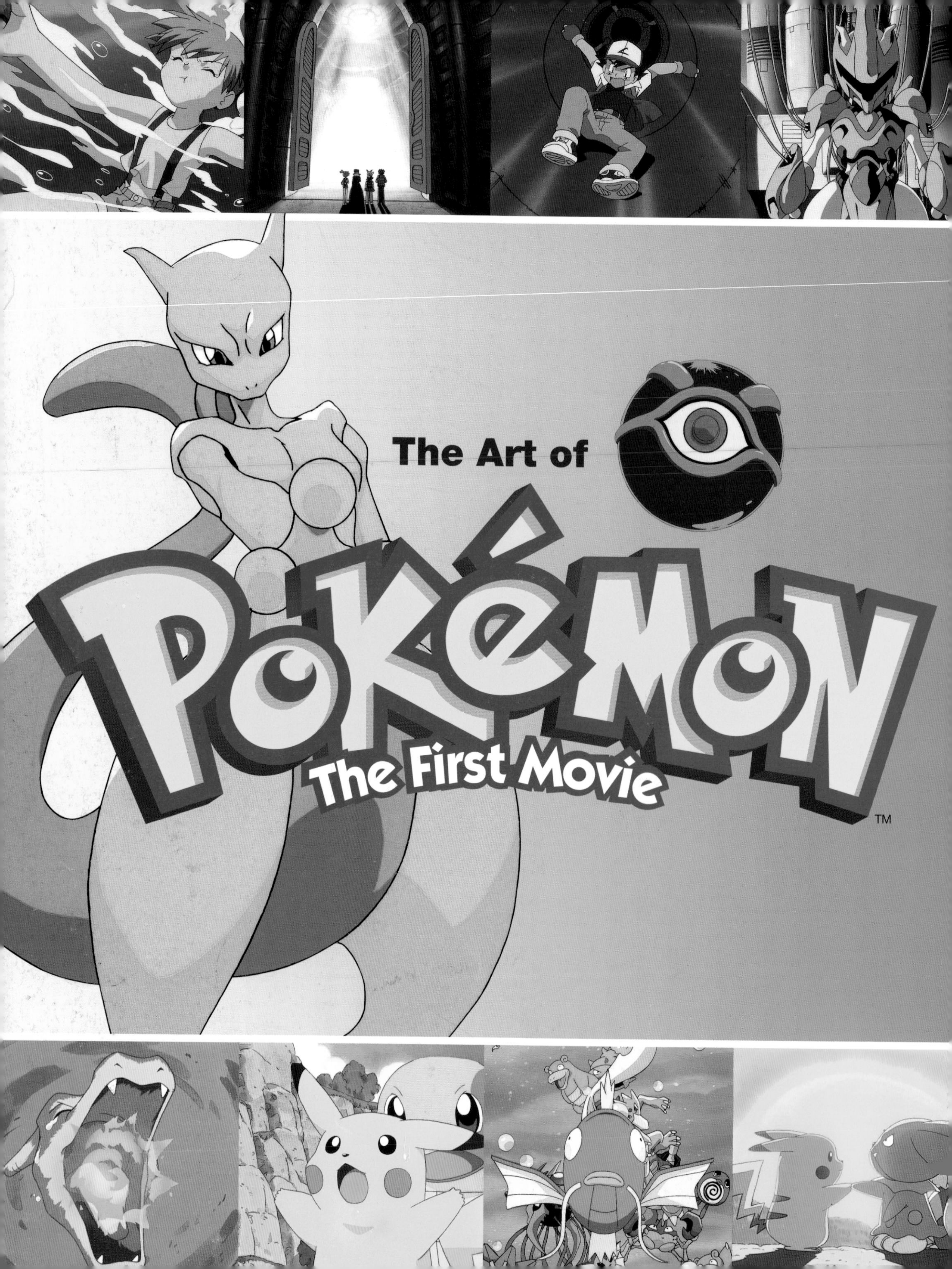
The Art of
POKéMON
The First Movie
TM

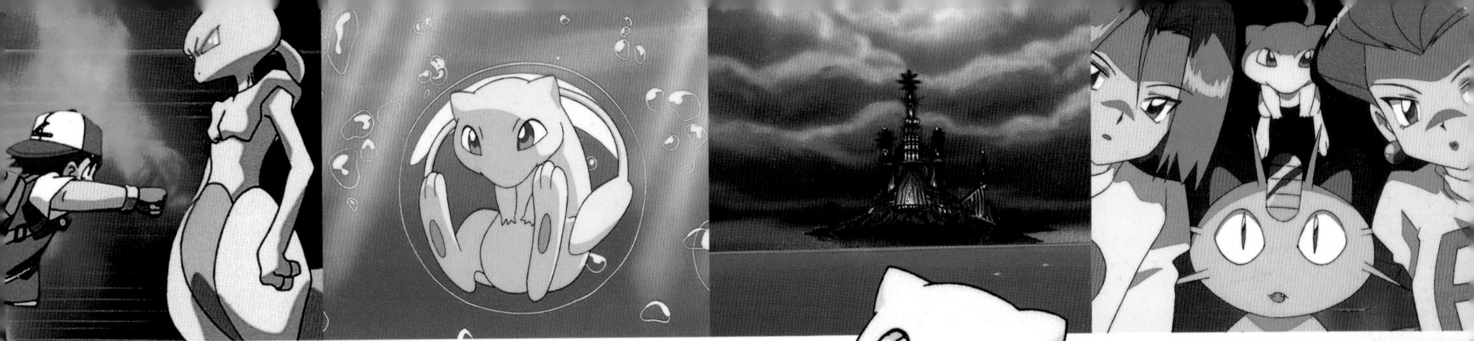

Mewtwo Strikes Back

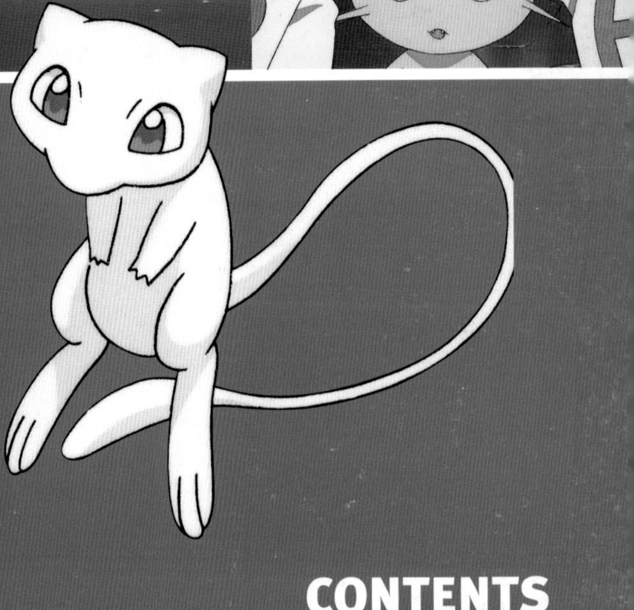

CONTENTS

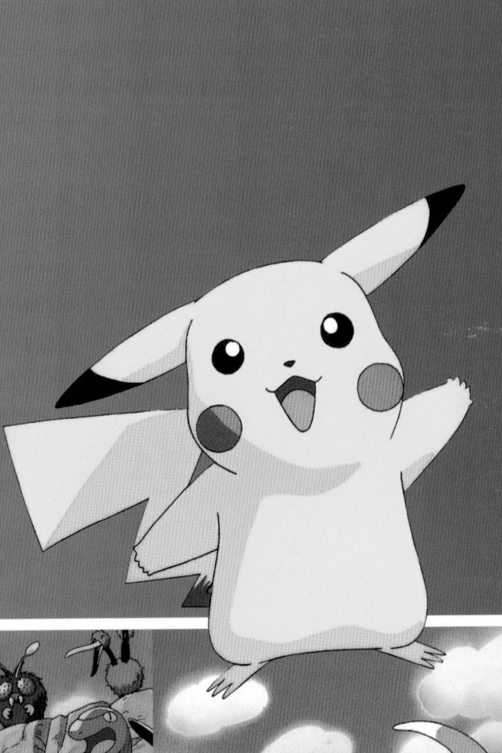

Pikachu's Vacation

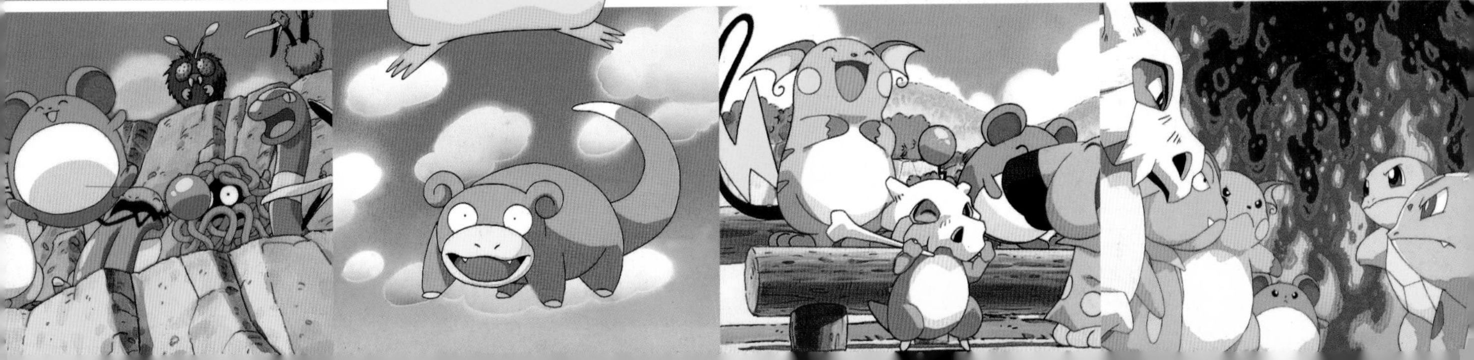

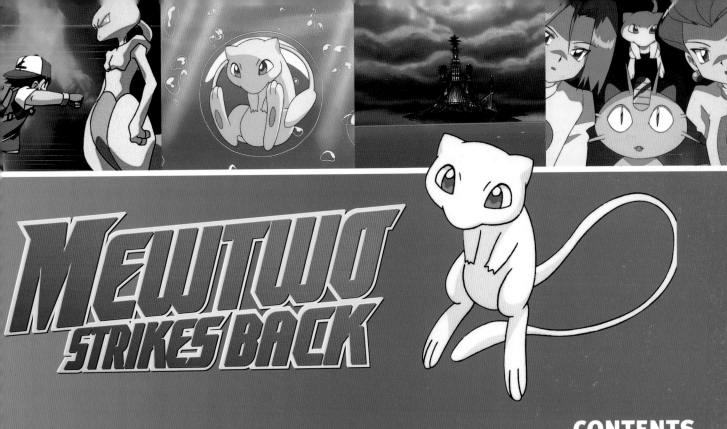

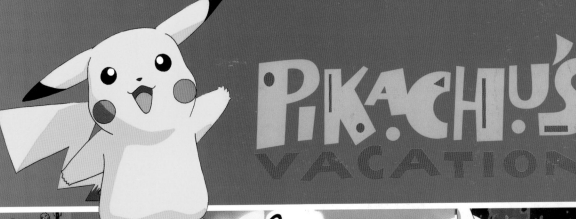

MEWTWO STRIKES BACK:
CAST OF CHARACTERS

FERGUS

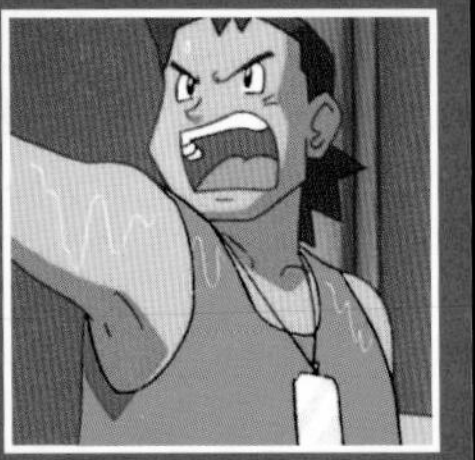

Trainer Fergus, who specializes in Water Pokémon, has a Goldruck and a Tentacruel. His most powerful Pokémon is a Gyarados.

BROCK

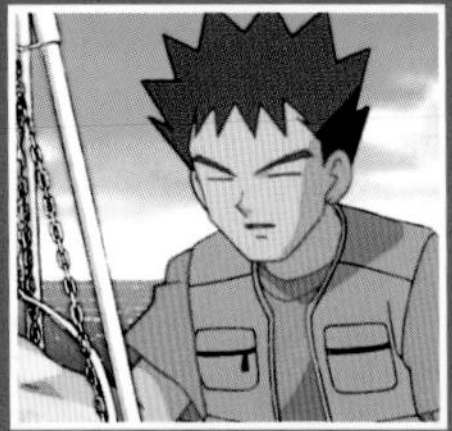

Pewter City's Gym Leader Brock, who specializes in Rock Pokémon, has trained an Onix and a Geodude. While journeying with Ash, Brock also trains a Vulpix and a Zubat.

COREY

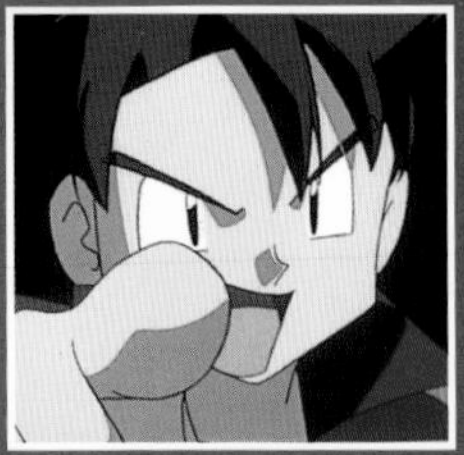

Corey flies to Pokémon Palace on Pidgeot's back. Although he specializes in Flying Pokémon, Corey also trains other types, including a Venusaur and a Scyther.

PIRATE TRAINER

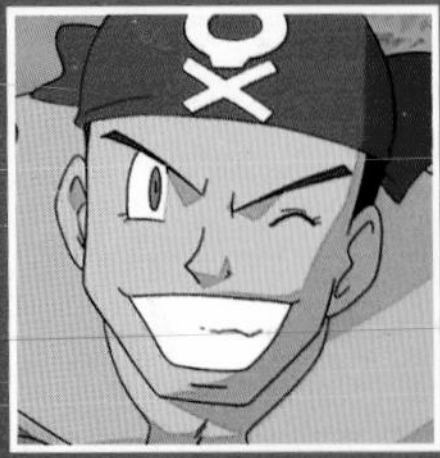

This pirate trainer collects exotic Pokémon, such as Machamp and Donphan, but he doesn't train them thoroughly. He seeks out Ash to challenge him.

MISTY

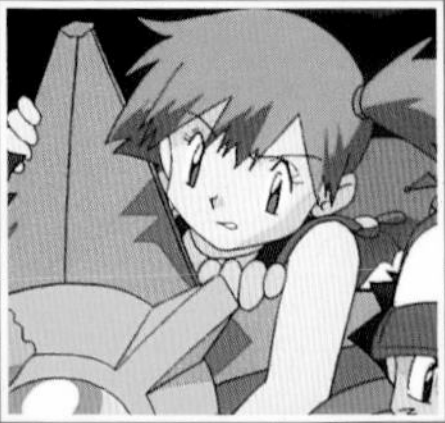

Cerulean City Gym Leader Misty specializes in Water Pokémon. She often relies on Staryu and Goldeen, and is currently attempting to train a difficult Psyduck she caught through sheer luck.

NEESHA

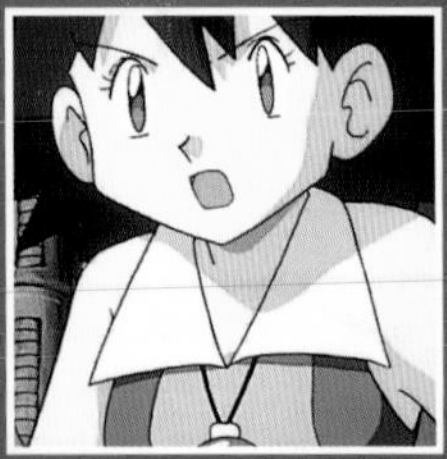

Neesha arrives at Pokémon Palace astride a Dewgong. She collects cute Pokémon, including Ninetales and Wigglytuff.

ASH

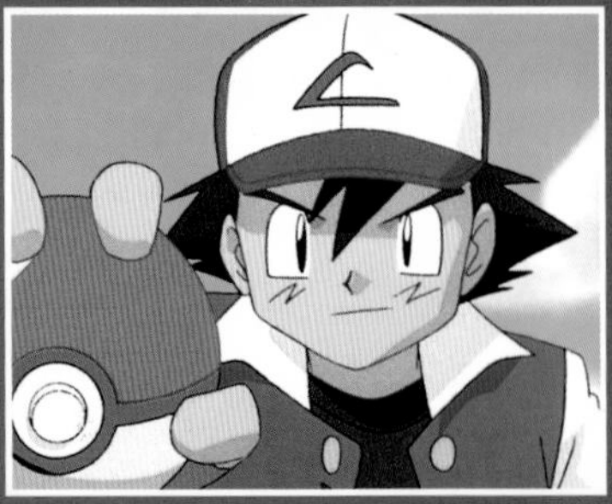

Ash is eagerly training as hard as he can to become a Pokémon Master. Born in Pallet Town, he is currently on his training journey accompanied by his friends Brock and Misty, as well as his Pokémon Pikachu. When Ash starts a Pokémon battle, everything else slips his mind, even his growling stomach! Pokémon are Ash's life.

THE PROFESSOR

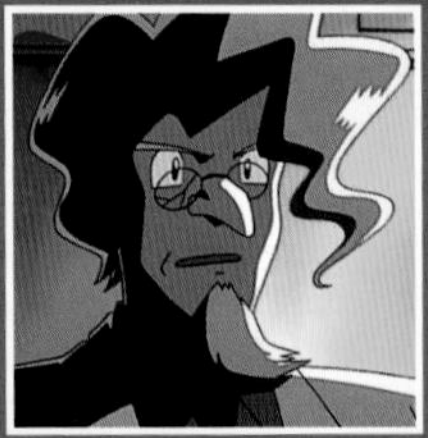

The leader of the scientists, the Professor creates Mewtwo from the fossilized remains of Mew's eyelash. The Professor is thrilled by Mewtwo's power, but fears its dark side.

TEAM ROCKET:
JESSIE & JAMES

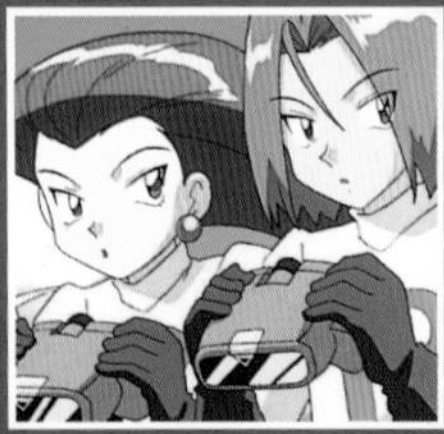

In yet another attempt to steal Pikachu, The clutzy human duo of Team Rocket pursues Ash and his friends right into Pokémon Palace!

GIOVANNI

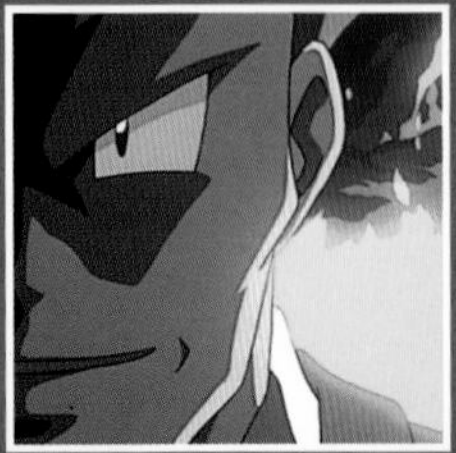

Team Rocket's foul-ups are a constant source of aggravation to Giovanni, Team Rocket's boss. Giovanni schemes to use Mewtwo's awesome power for his own evil ends.

MIRANDA

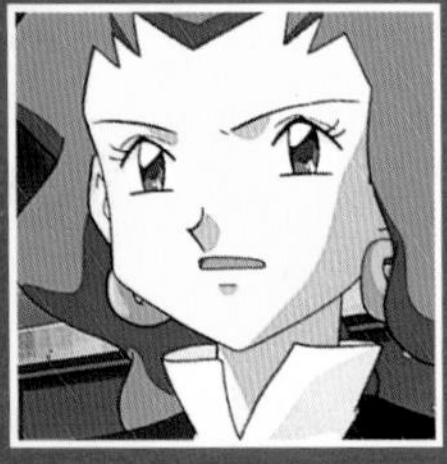

Miranda, the harbor master, forbids travel across the bay due to the dangerous weather conditions. But when Ash and his friends disobey her to get to New Island, Miranda hopes they have a safe passage.

JOY

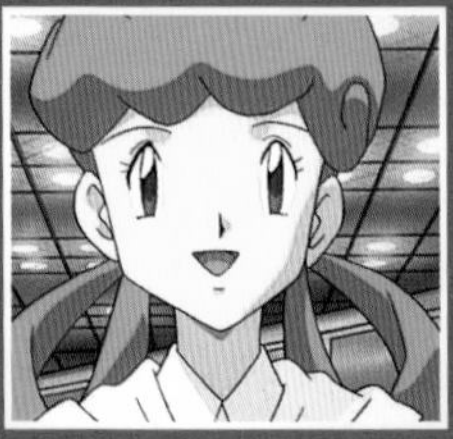

Mewtwo takes over Nurse Joy's mind to use her knowledge and skills to carry out his revenge.

JENNY

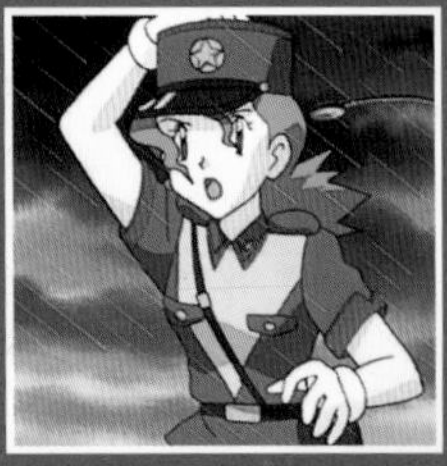

Policewoman Jenny tries to stop the Pokémon trainers from taking boats out into the bay during a fierce storm.

MEWTWO STRIKES BACK

Written by
Takeshi Shudo

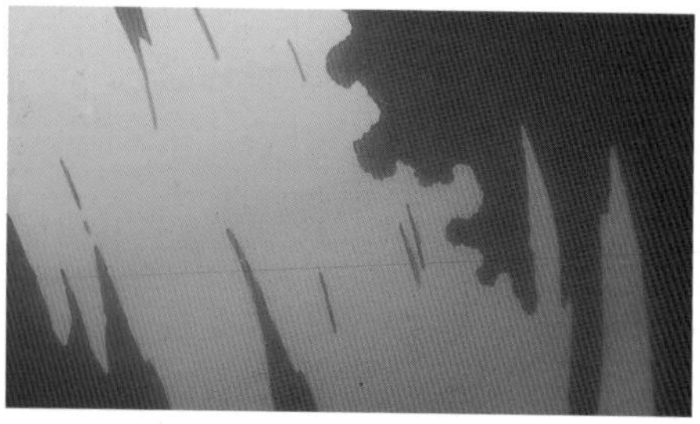

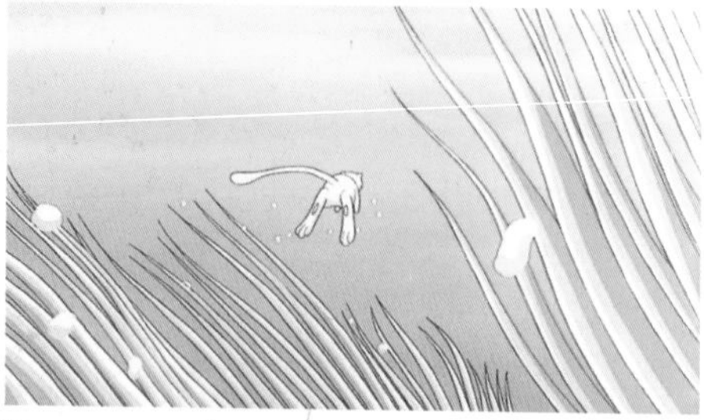

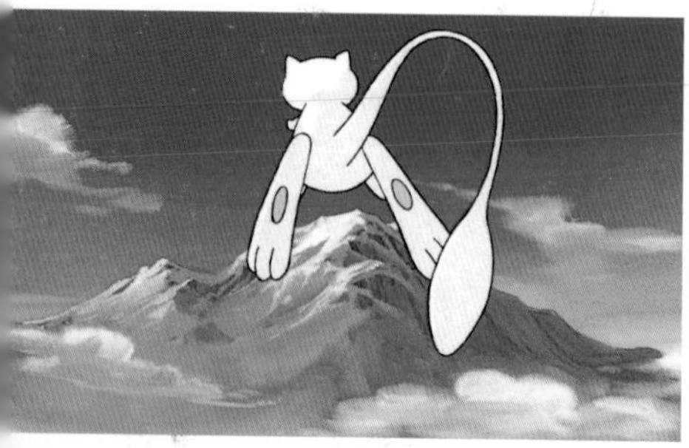

Growing in a glass tube, Mewtwo wonders, "Who am I? Why am I alive?" Mewtwo's dreams are filled with crystal clear water and swaying sea grasses. A shadow passes overhead.... It's Mew! Mew's presence is somehow comforting.

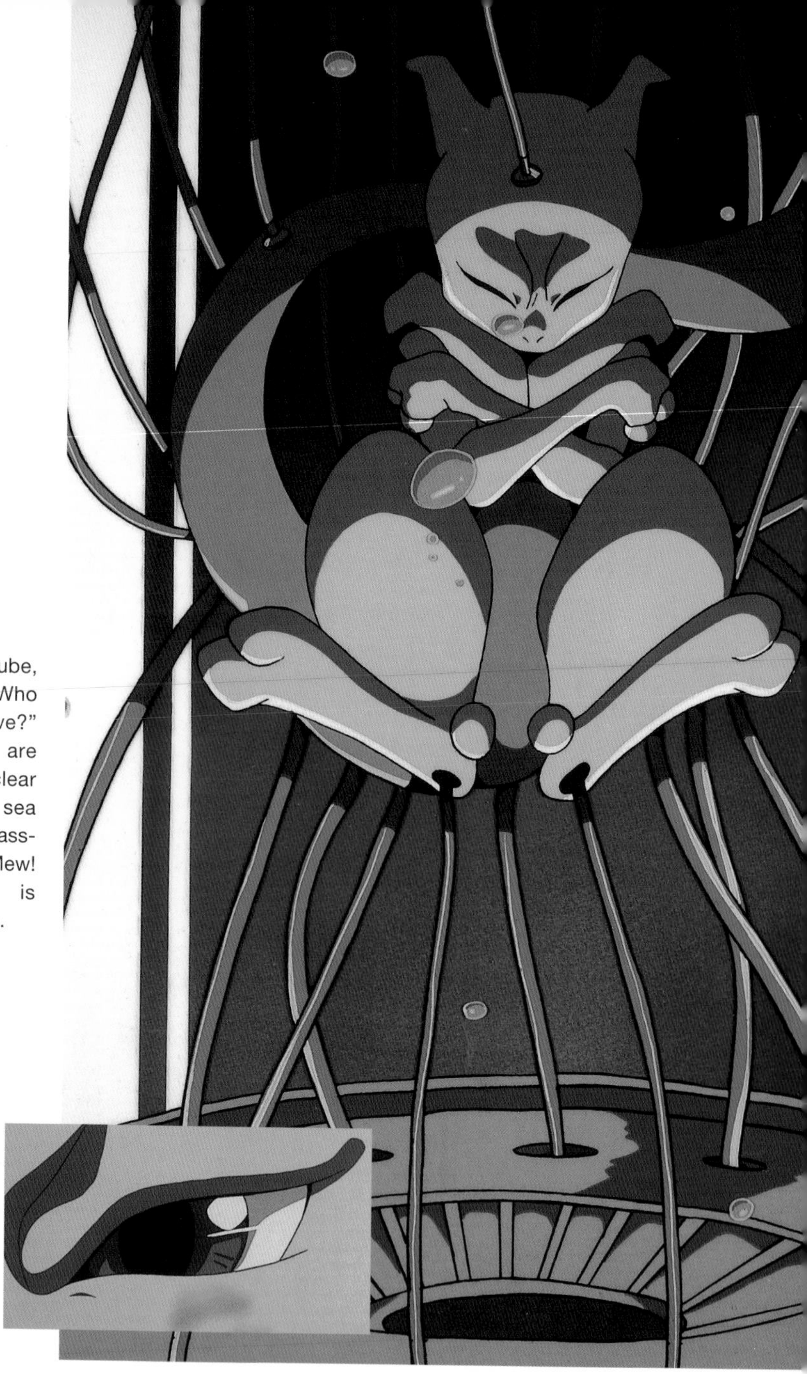

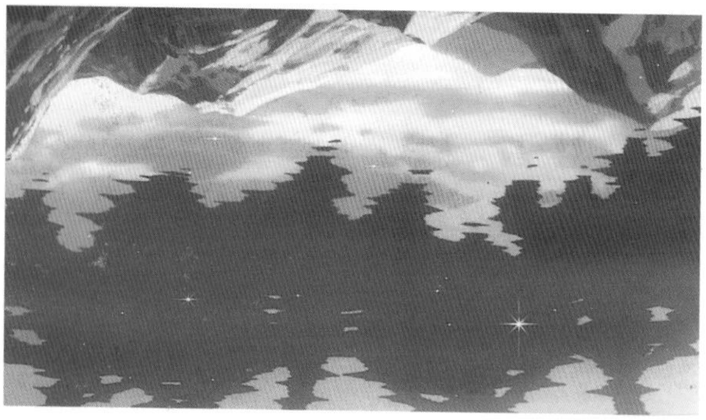

The Creation of Mewtwo

"Who am I? Why am I alive?"

In a secret laboratory somewhere far, far away, scientists create a Pokémon that has never existed before. Its name is Mewtwo. While it grows in its glass womb, Mewtwo asks the same questions over and over again.

"Who am I? Why am I alive?"

As it sleeps, Mewtwo dreams—always the same dream, a dream of crystal-clear, blue water and, just out of reach, of Mew, swimming, a strangely comforting presence.

"Tell me who I am," Mewtwo begs the dream Mew over and over again. But the dream Mew never answers—just keeps on swimming, just out of reach...

"Why won't you answer me?" cries Mewtwo.

Mewtwo's brooding gradually grows into an intense rage, a whirlwind of fury that shatters the

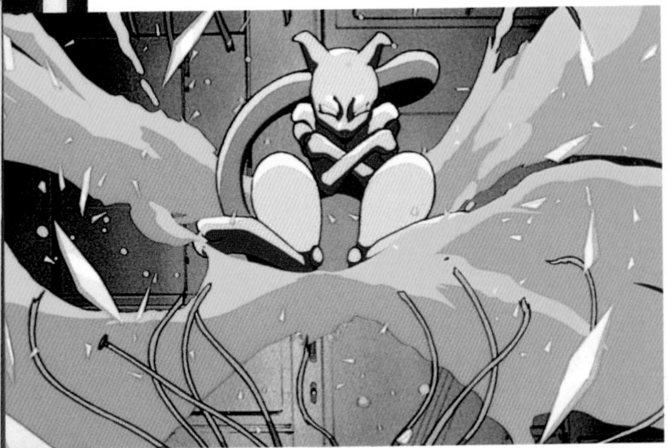
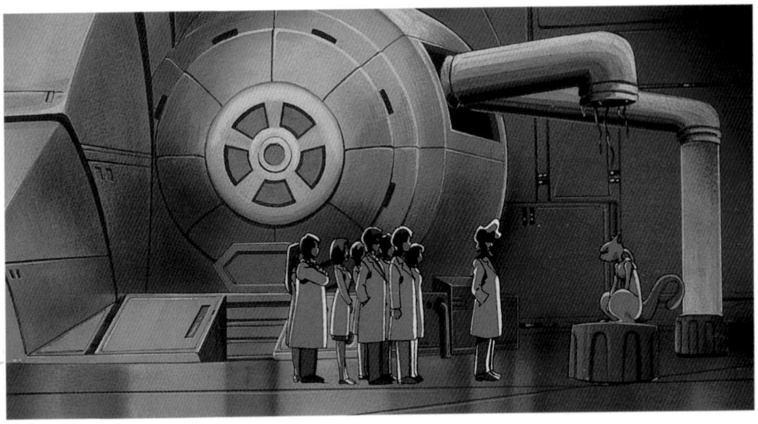
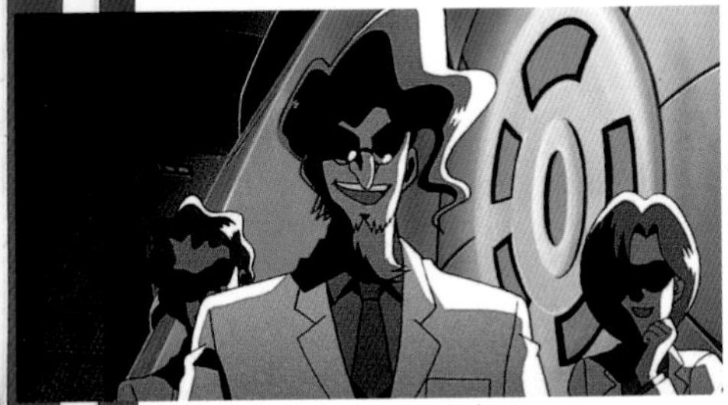
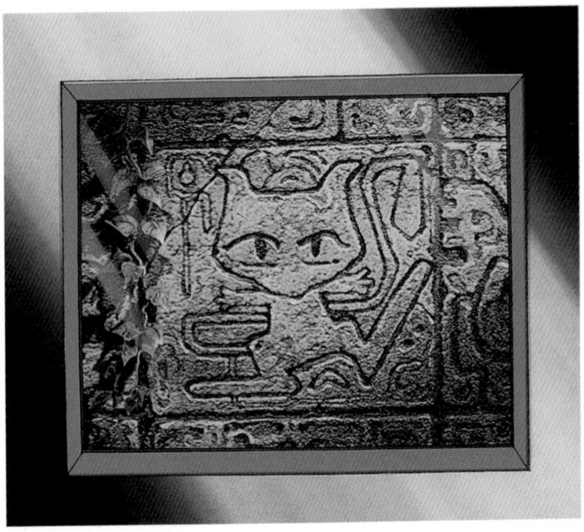
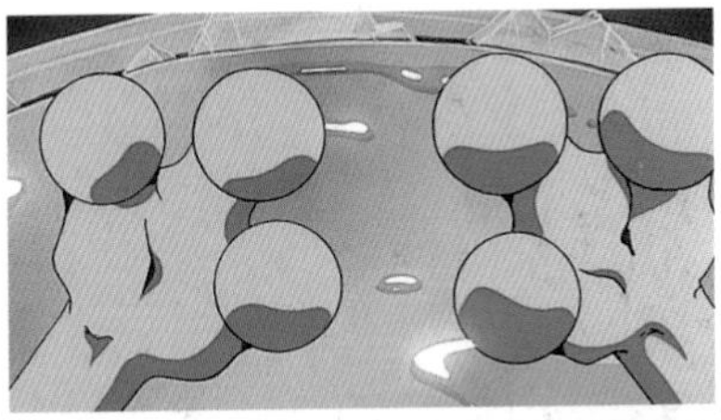
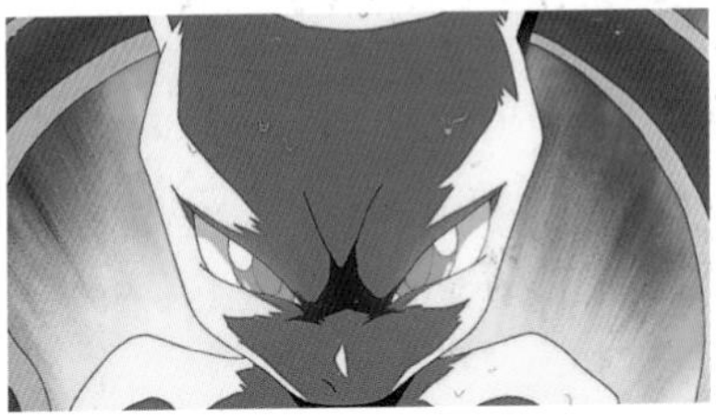

Mewtwo awakens to find itself surrounded by the black shadows of scientists. They created Mewtwo with the help of a glyph of Mew carved into an ancient stone tablet. Mewtwo's anger explodes in a great burst of flame.

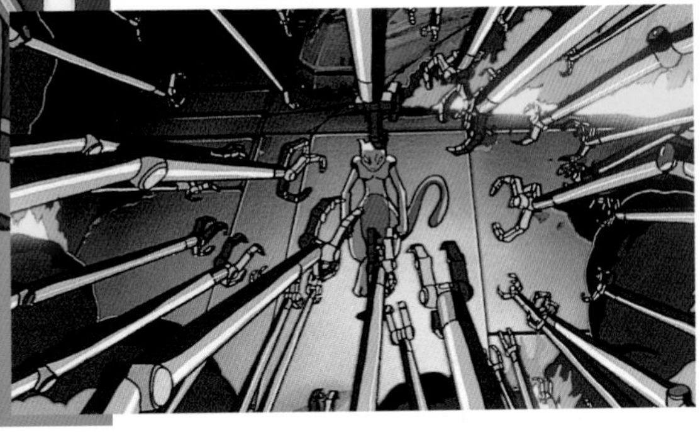
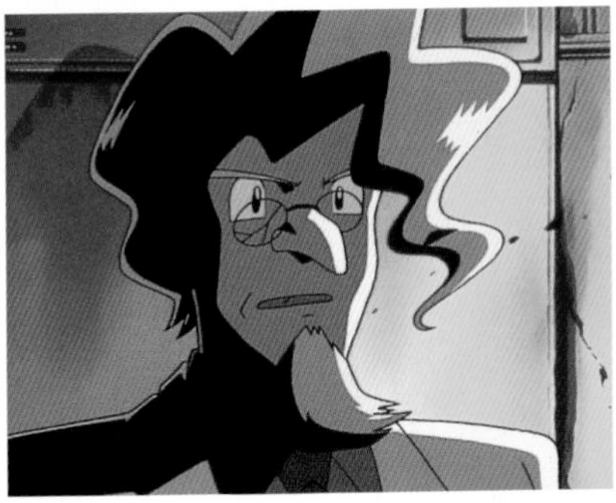
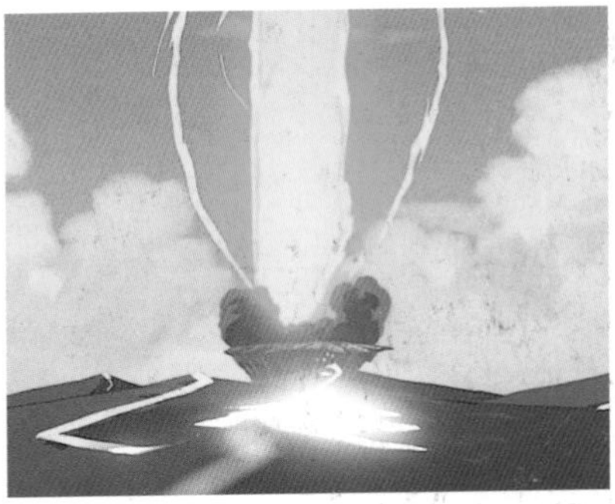

glass tube around it.

"We did it! We created Mewtwo!" The scientists in the laboratory are ecstatic. They have invented a brand-new Pokémon from the genes of the very rare Mew.

"Humans created me. But they are not my parents!" This makes Mewtwo very angry. Its fury explodes in a huge ball of fire that engulfs the entire laboratory in a pillar of flame. Mewtwo didn't know it had such power!

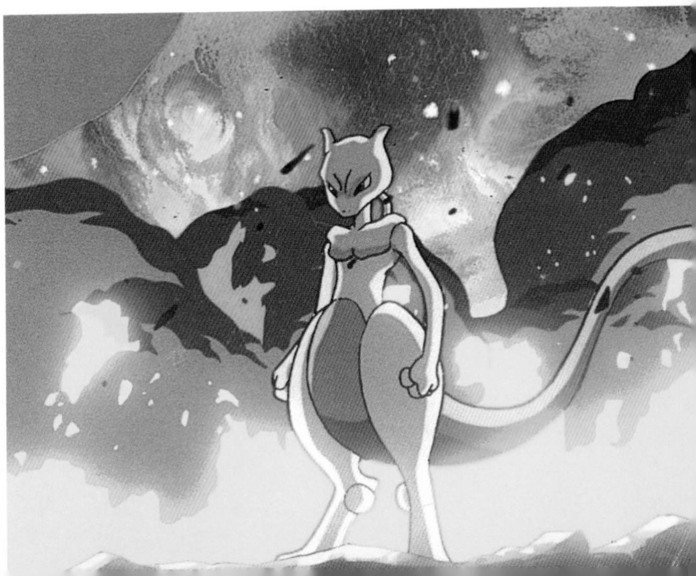

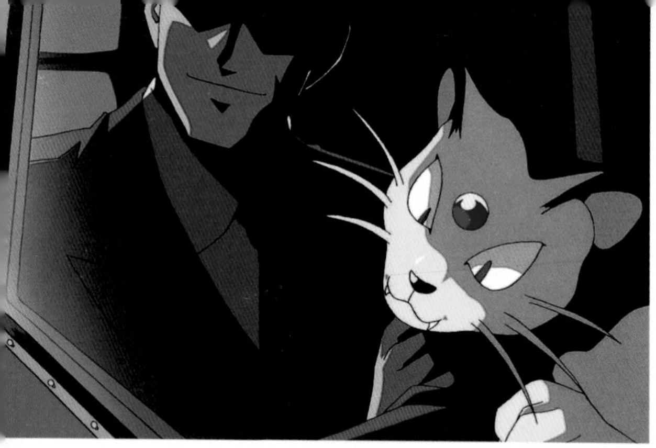

Giovanni intends to use Mewtwo's incredible destructive energy to take over the world!

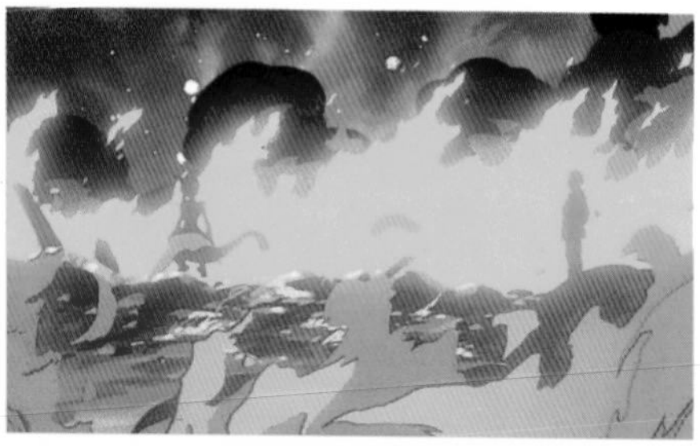

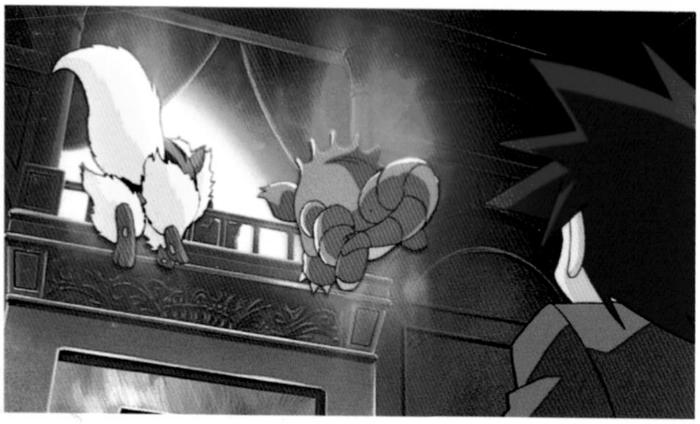

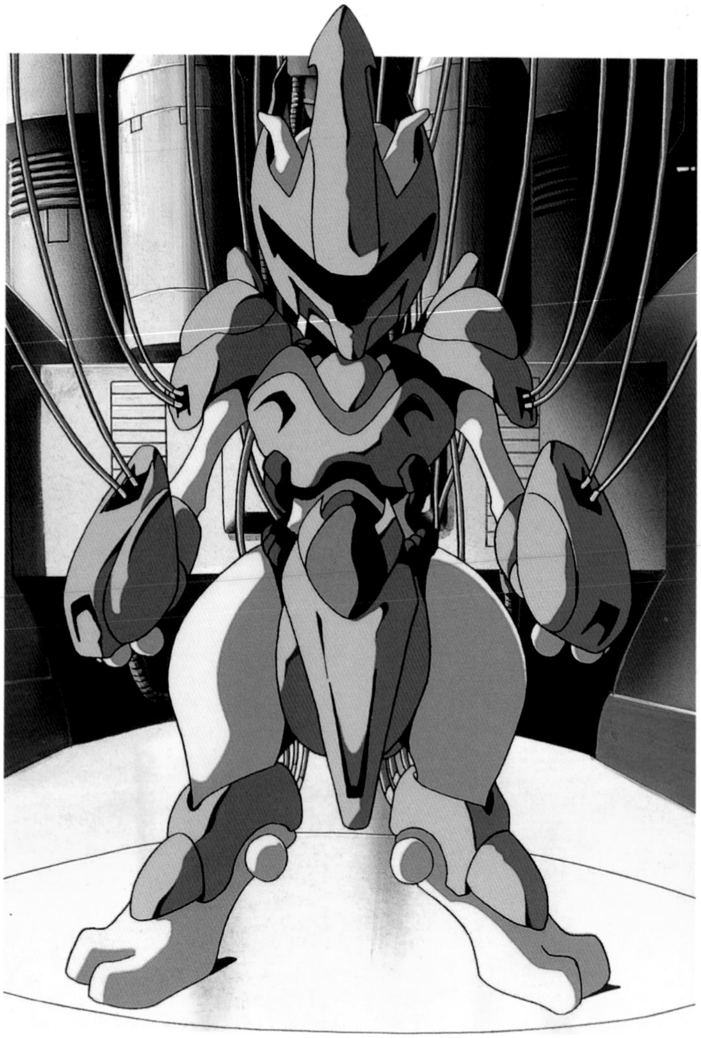

Although wearing armor to control its enormous power, Mewtwo is still strong enough to defeat every other Pokémon.

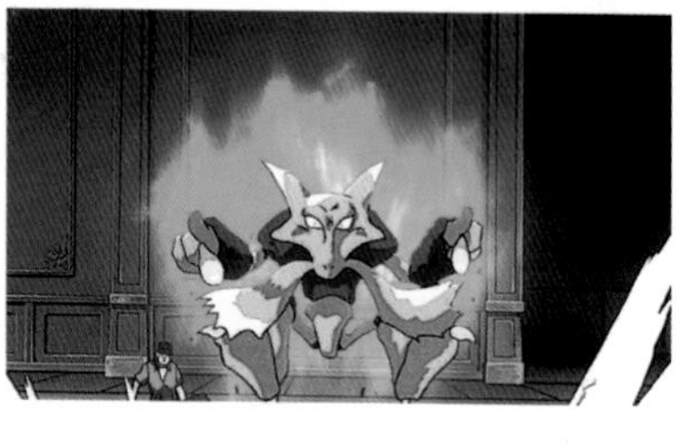

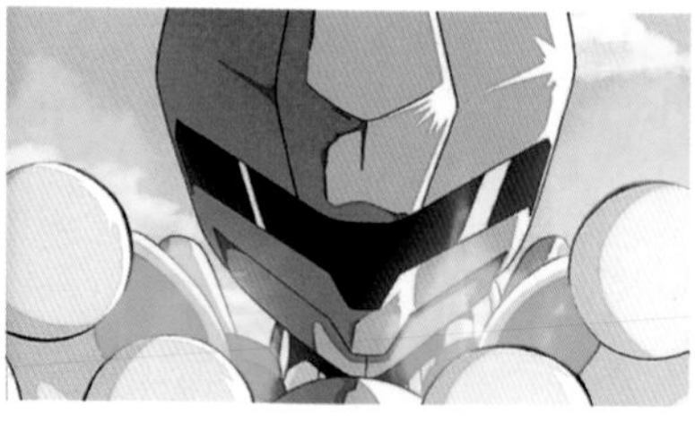

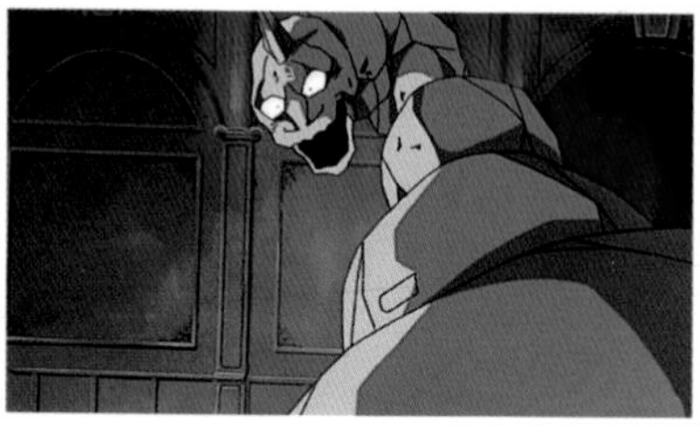

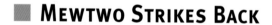

Mewtwo Strikes Back

When Team Rocket's leader, Giovanni, learns about Mewtwo's awesome power, he invites the new Pokémon to join him.

"With your power, we can take over the world!" Giovanni proclaims.

Mewtwo is fitted with heavy protective armor to dampen and control its power. Giovanni trains Mewtwo. Mewtwo defeats one Pokémon after another in battle, but all Mewtwo's victories don't ease the vast emptiness it feels inside.

"What is the point of all this fighting?" Mewtwo wonders. "What is the purpose of my existence?"

"Humans created you to serve them! That should be your only purpose and your only desire! Beyond that, your life is worthless!" Giovanni spits.

Mewtwo glares at Giovanni. "My life is worth-

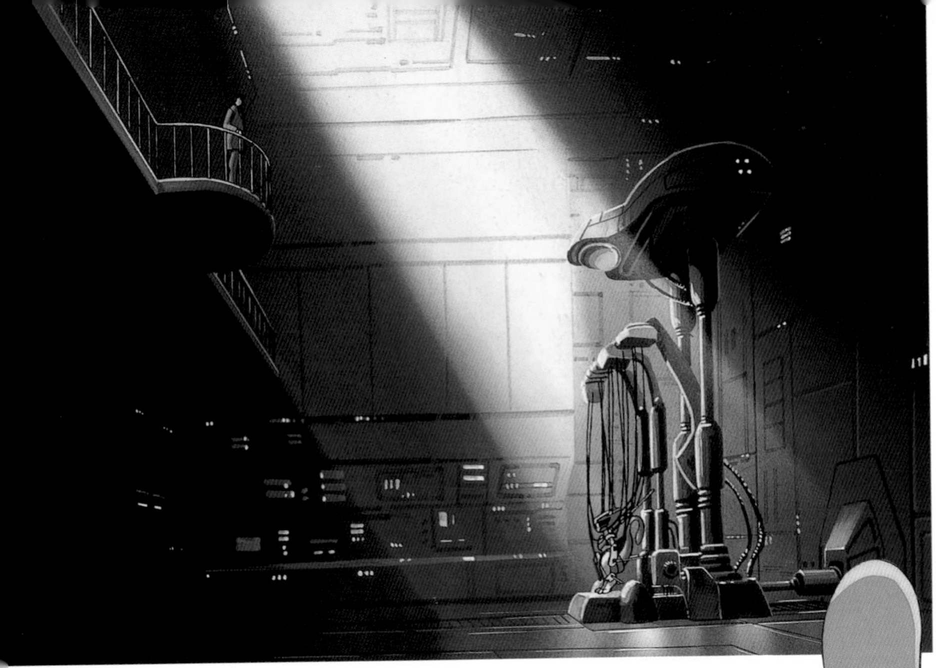

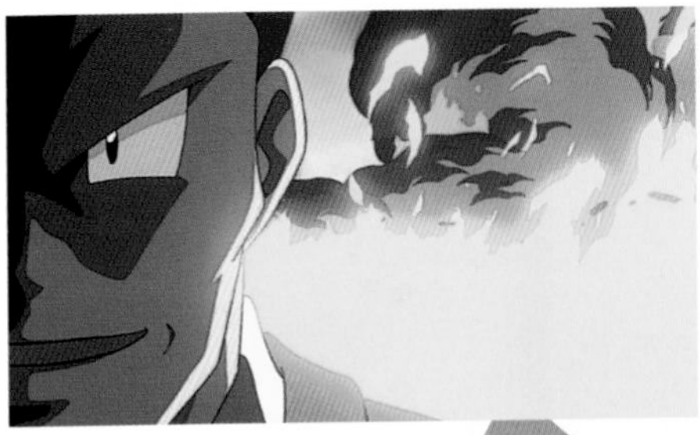

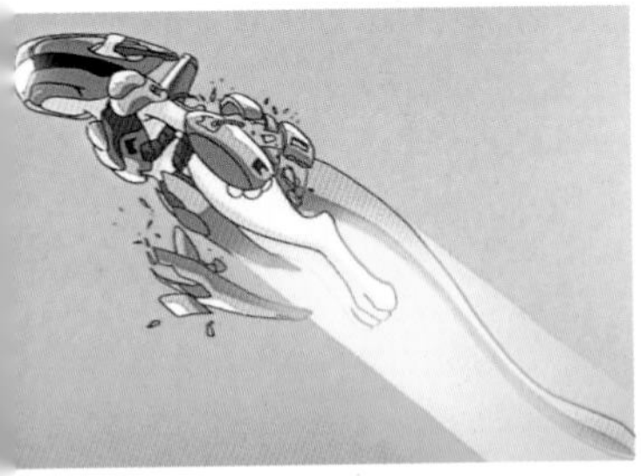

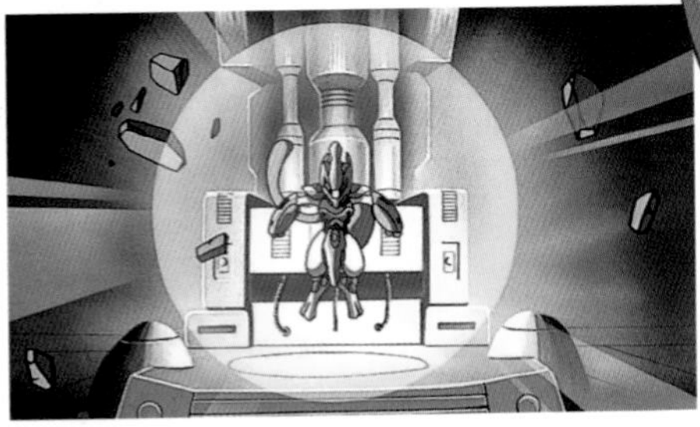

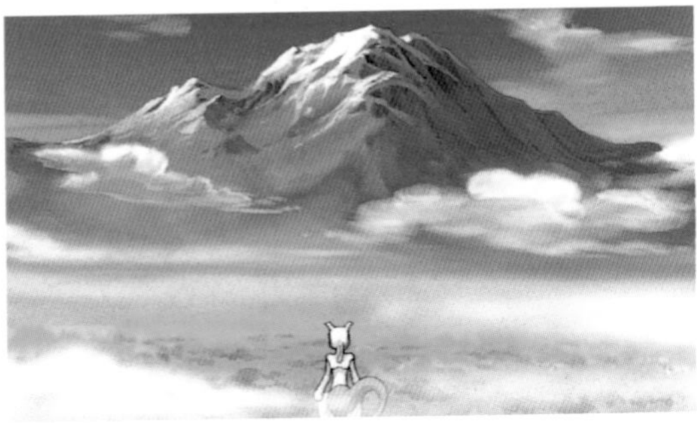

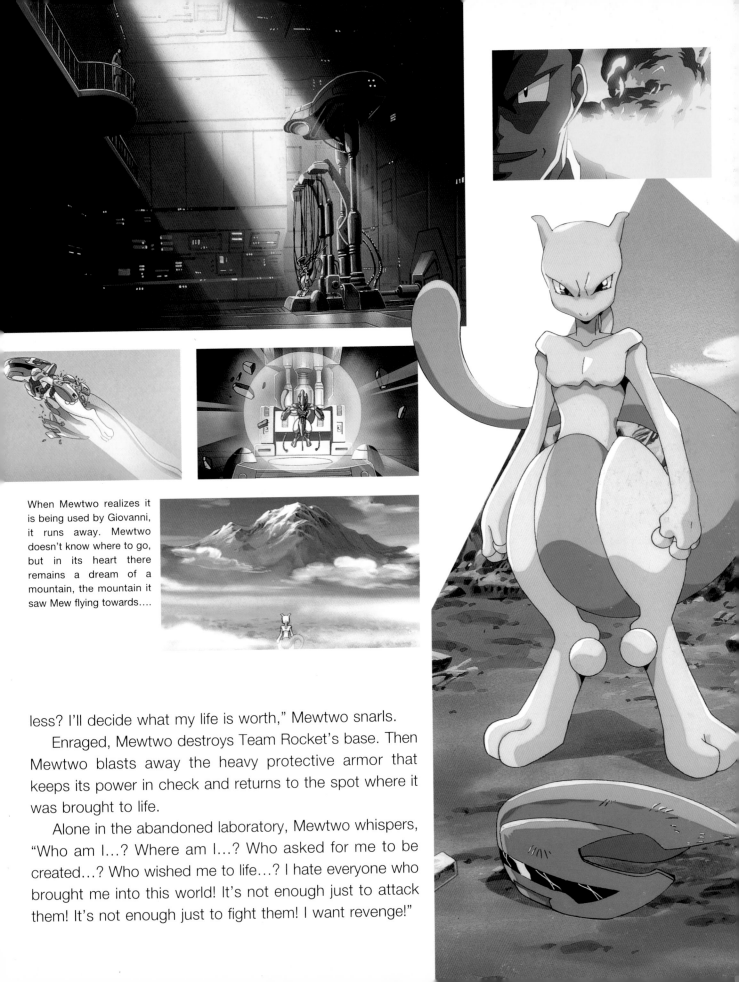

When Mewtwo realizes it is being used by Giovanni, it runs away. Mewtwo doesn't know where to go, but in its heart there remains a dream of a mountain, the mountain it saw Mew flying towards....

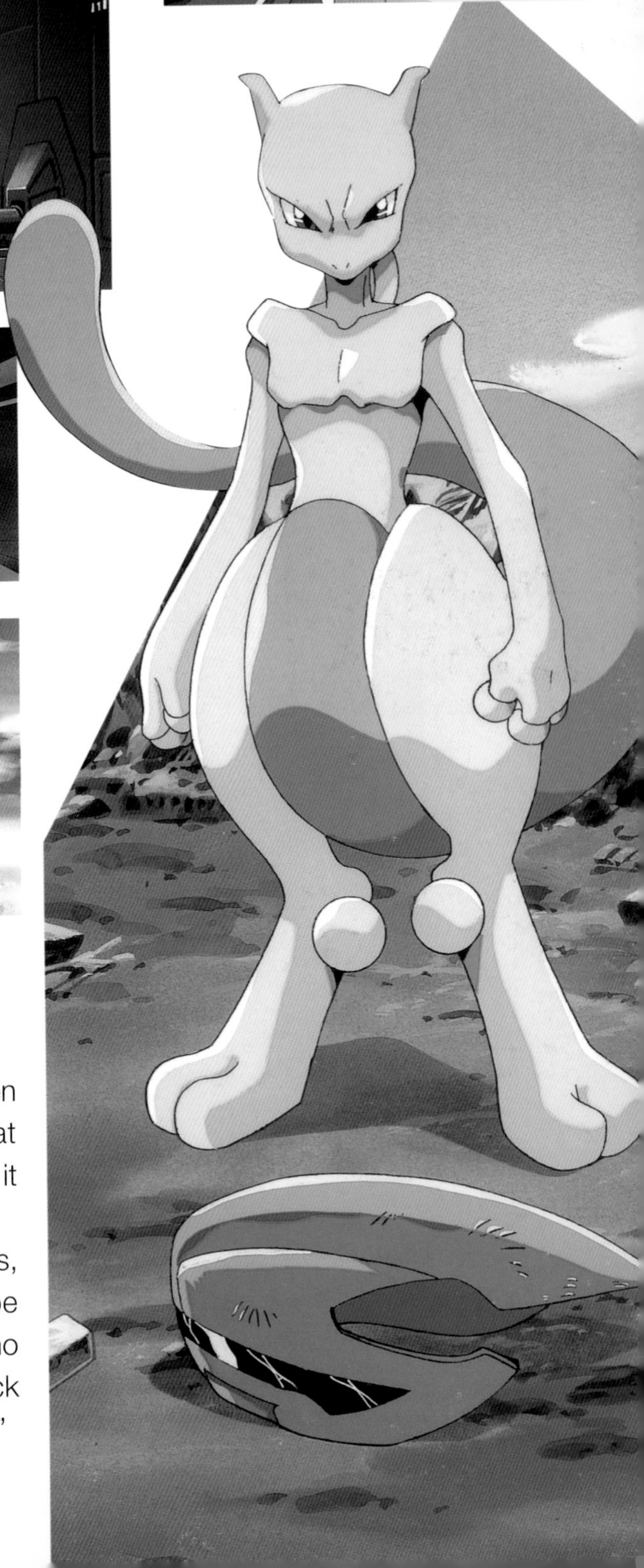

less? I'll decide what my life is worth," Mewtwo snarls.

Enraged, Mewtwo destroys Team Rocket's base. Then Mewtwo blasts away the heavy protective armor that keeps its power in check and returns to the spot where it was brought to life.

Alone in the abandoned laboratory, Mewtwo whispers, "Who am I...? Where am I...? Who asked for me to be created...? Who wished me to life...? I hate everyone who brought me into this world! It's not enough just to attack them! It's not enough just to fight them! I want revenge!"

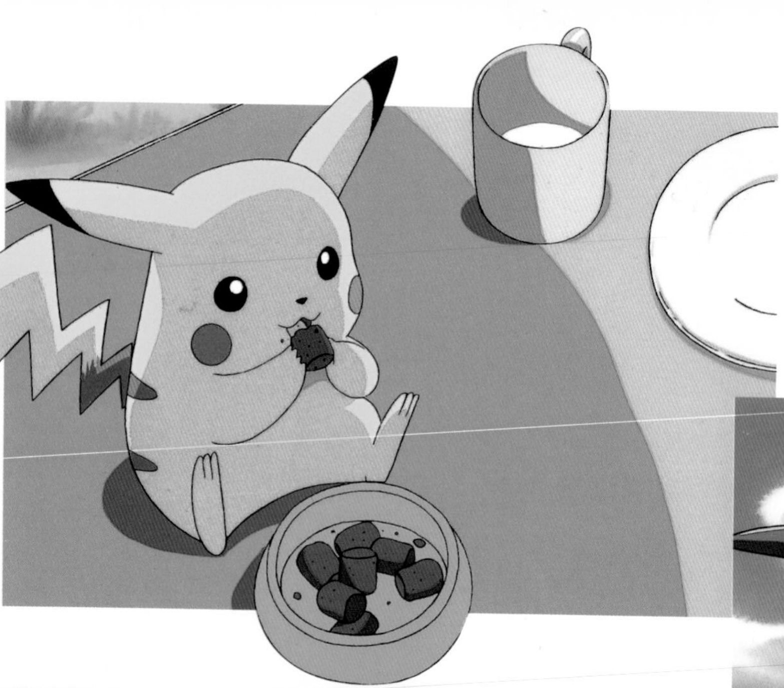

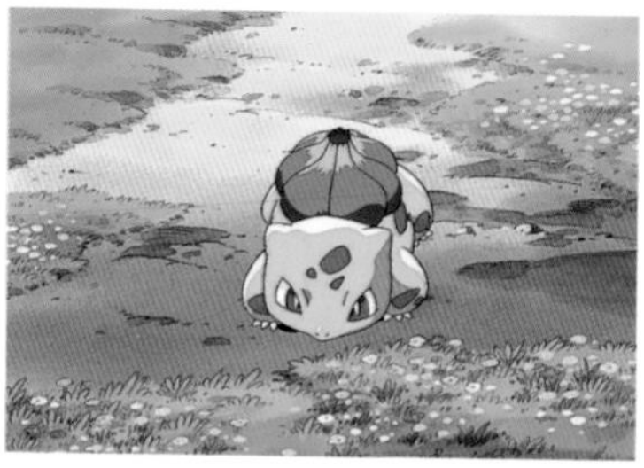

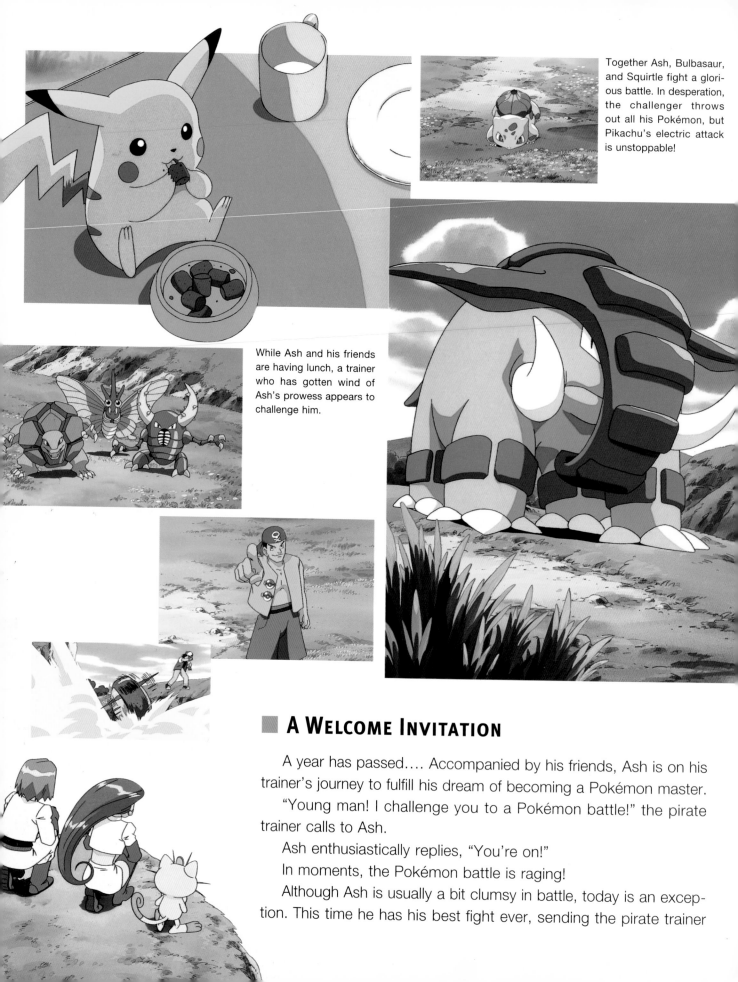

Together Ash, Bulbasaur, and Squirtle fight a glorious battle. In desperation, the challenger throws out all his Pokémon, but Pikachu's electric attack is unstoppable!

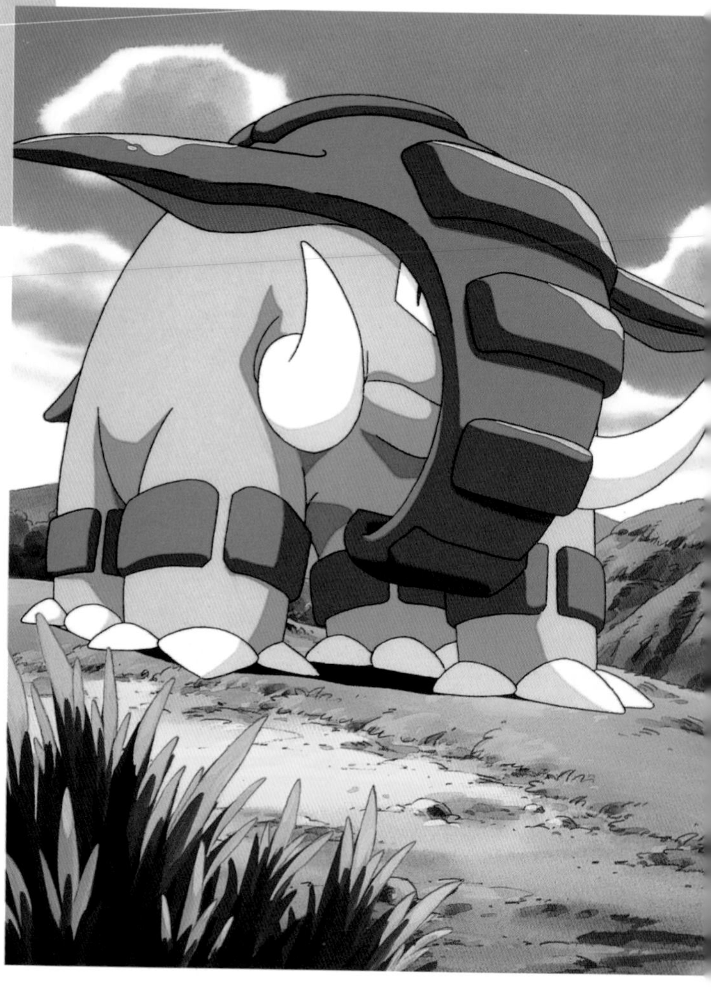

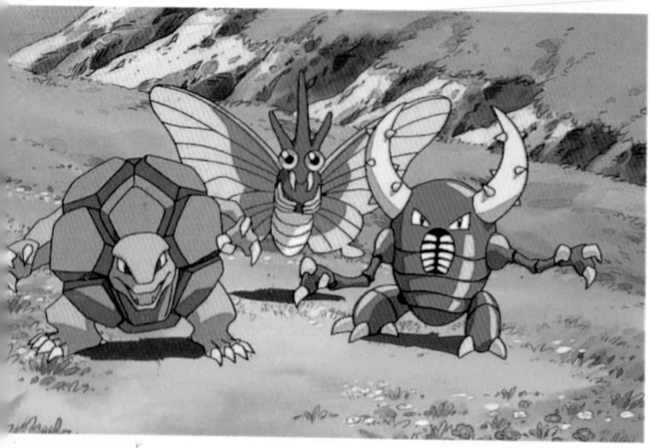

While Ash and his friends are having lunch, a trainer who has gotten wind of Ash's prowess appears to challenge him.

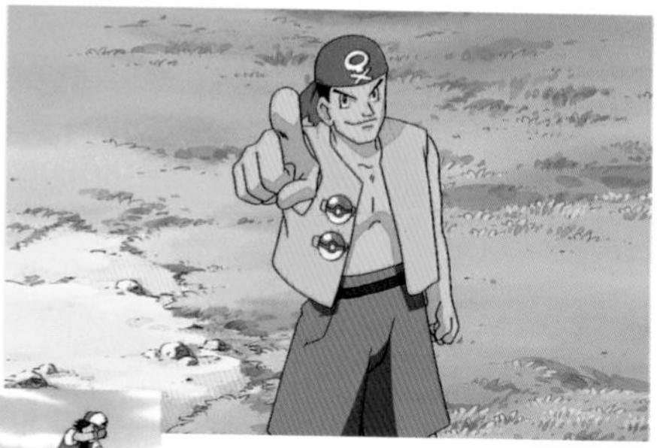

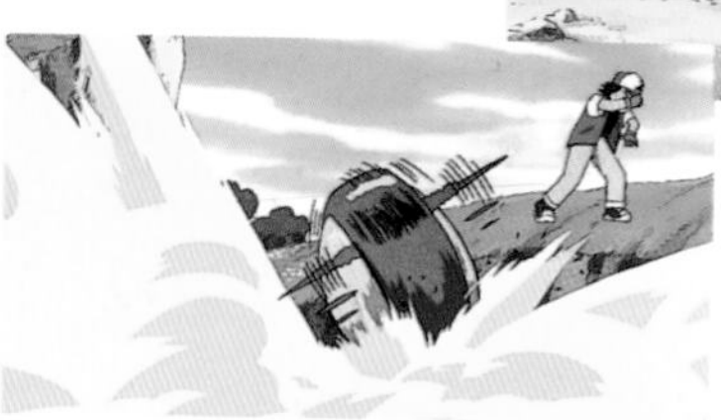

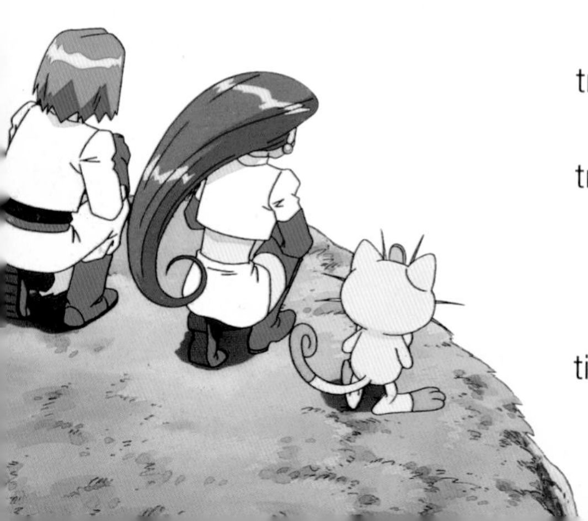

A Welcome Invitation

A year has passed.... Accompanied by his friends, Ash is on his trainer's journey to fulfill his dream of becoming a Pokémon master.

"Young man! I challenge you to a Pokémon battle!" the pirate trainer calls to Ash.

Ash enthusiastically replies, "You're on!"

In moments, the Pokémon battle is raging!

Although Ash is usually a bit clumsy in battle, today is an exception. This time he has his best fight ever, sending the pirate trainer

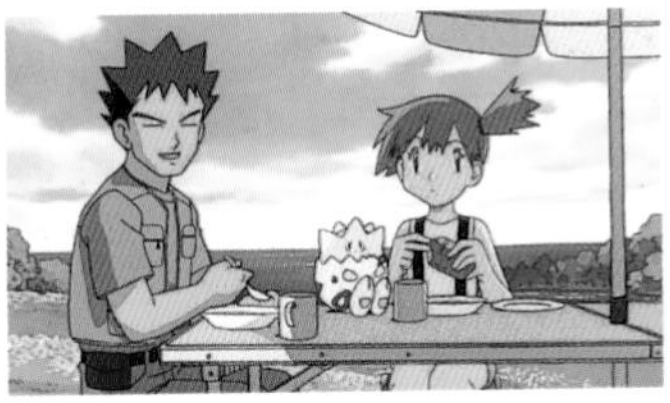

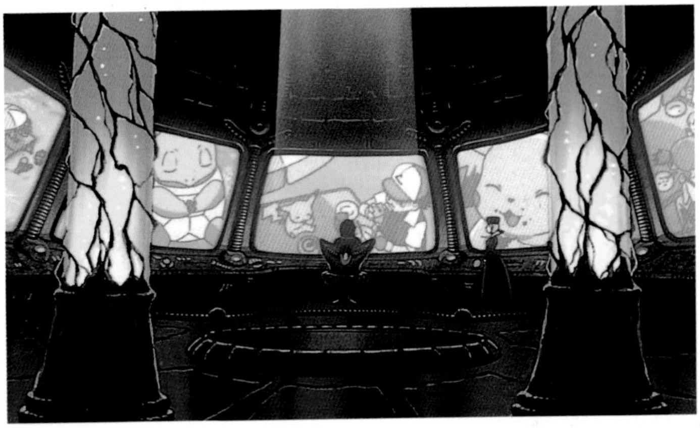

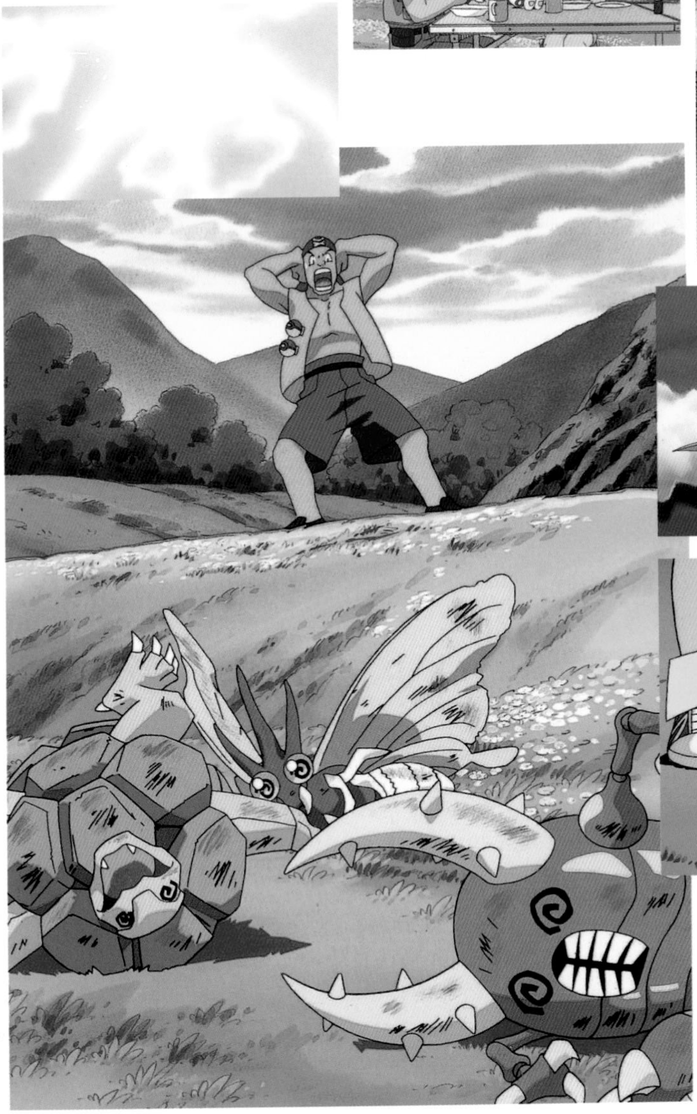

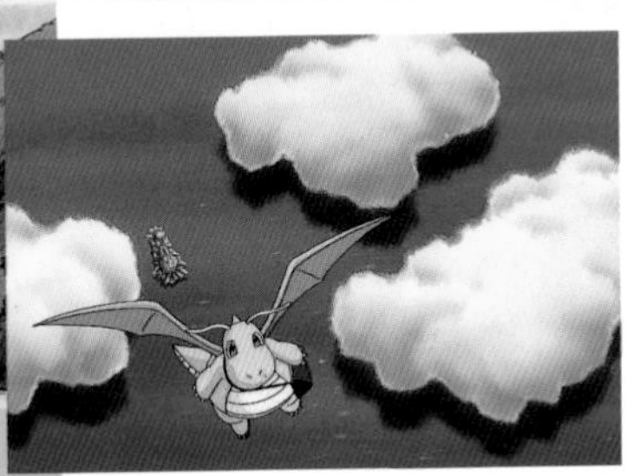

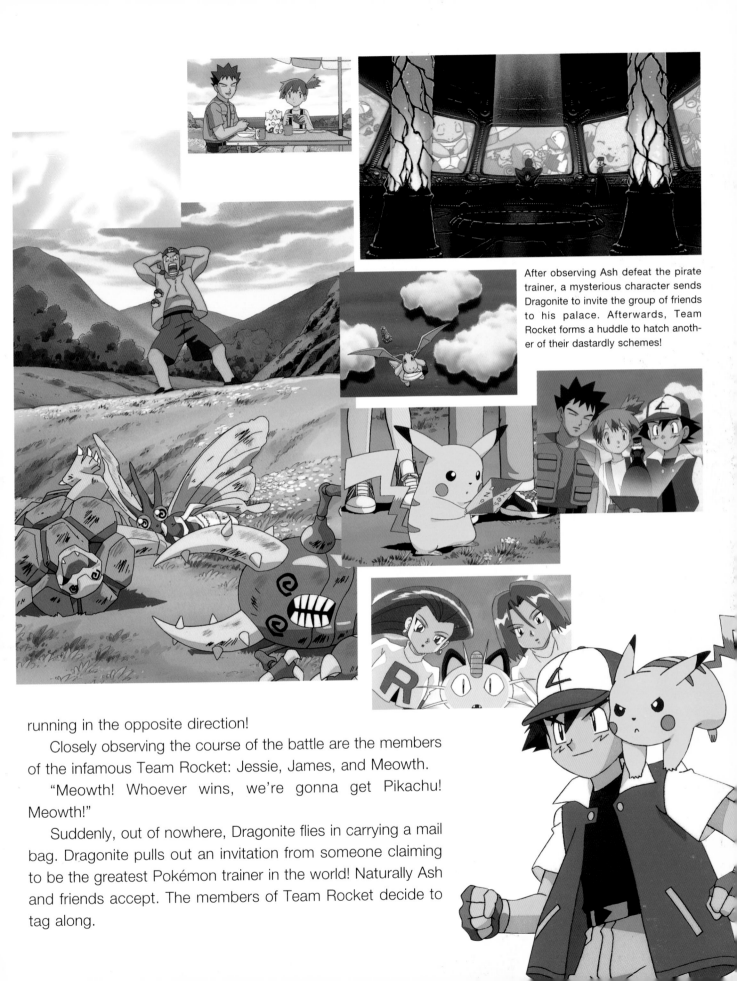

After observing Ash defeat the pirate trainer, a mysterious character sends Dragonite to invite the group of friends to his palace. Afterwards, Team Rocket forms a huddle to hatch another of their dastardly schemes!

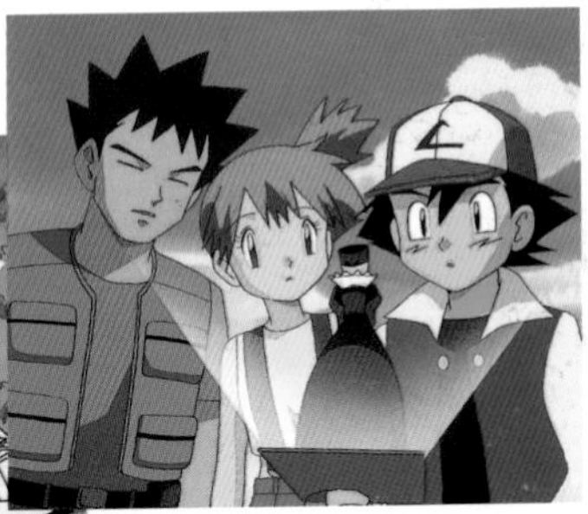

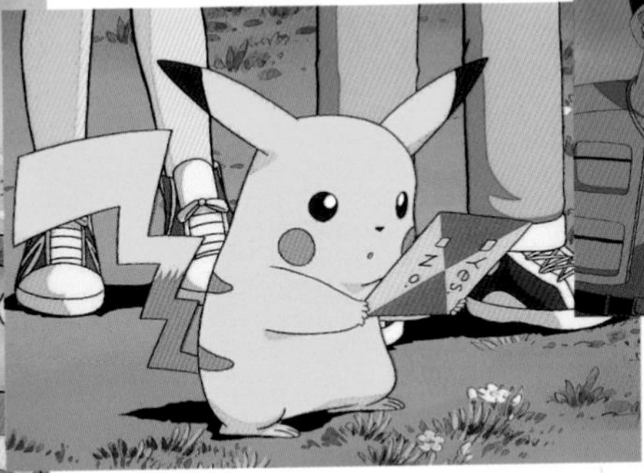

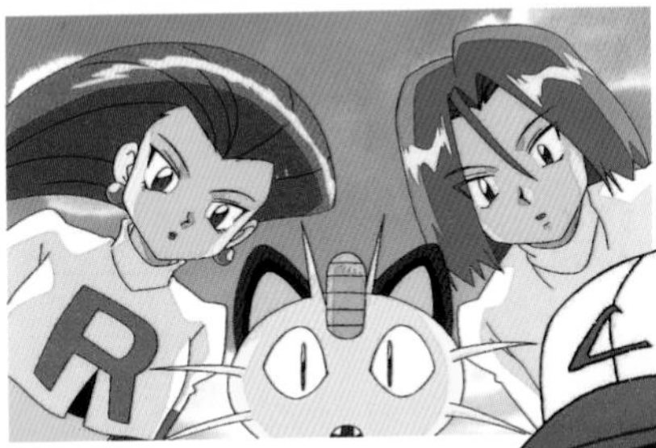

running in the opposite direction!

Closely observing the course of the battle are the members of the infamous Team Rocket: Jessie, James, and Meowth.

"Meowth! Whoever wins, we're gonna get Pikachu! Meowth!"

Suddenly, out of nowhere, Dragonite flies in carrying a mail bag. Dragonite pulls out an invitation from someone claiming to be the greatest Pokémon trainer in the world! Naturally Ash and friends accept. The members of Team Rocket decide to tag along.

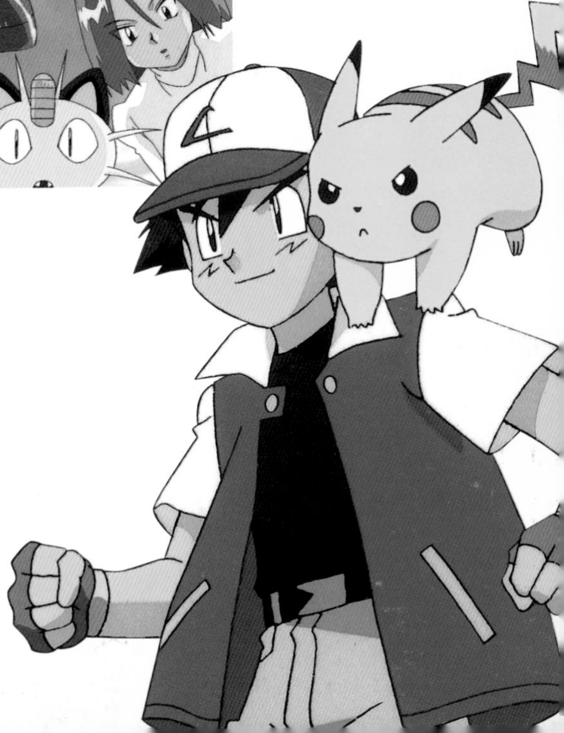

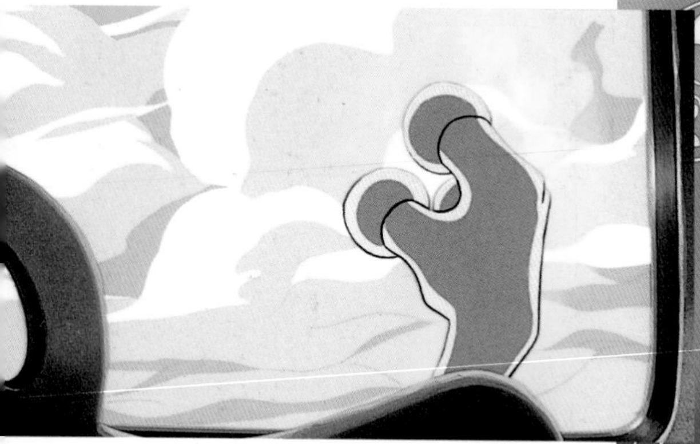

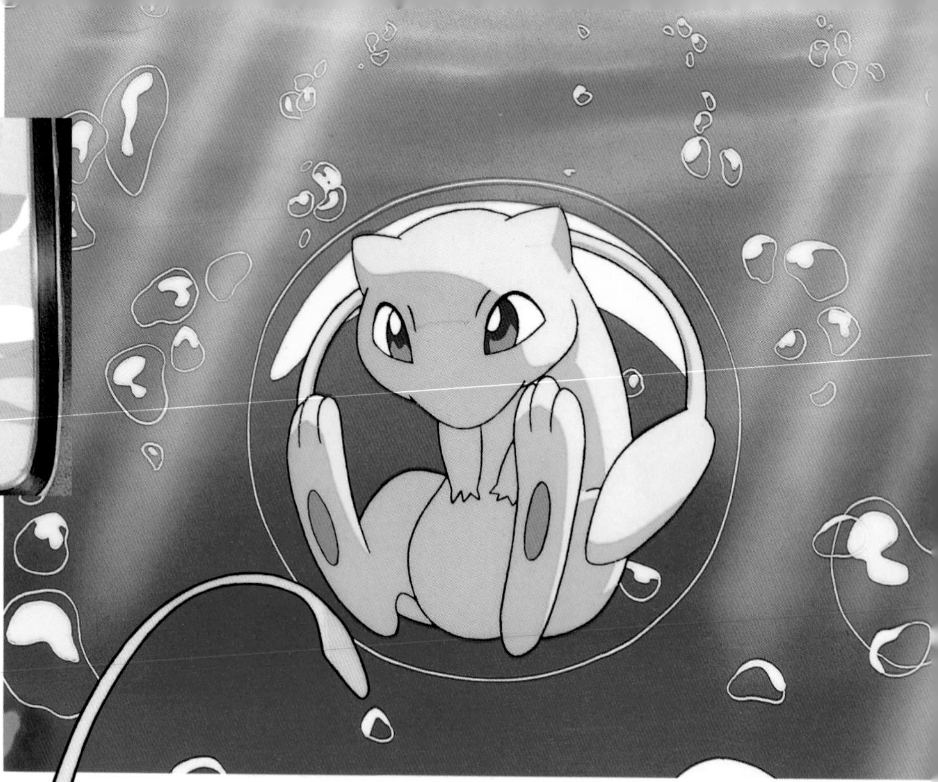

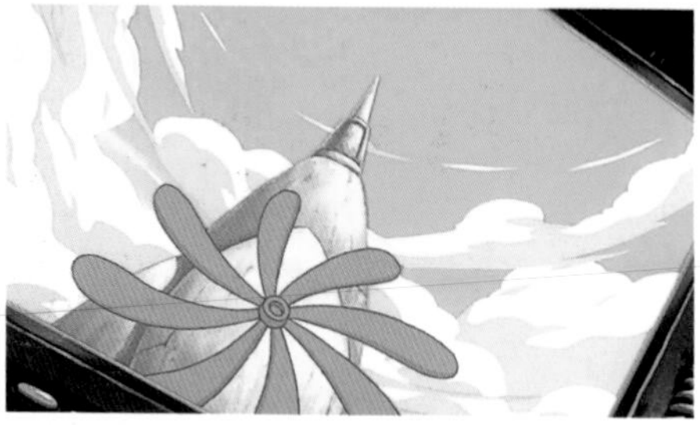

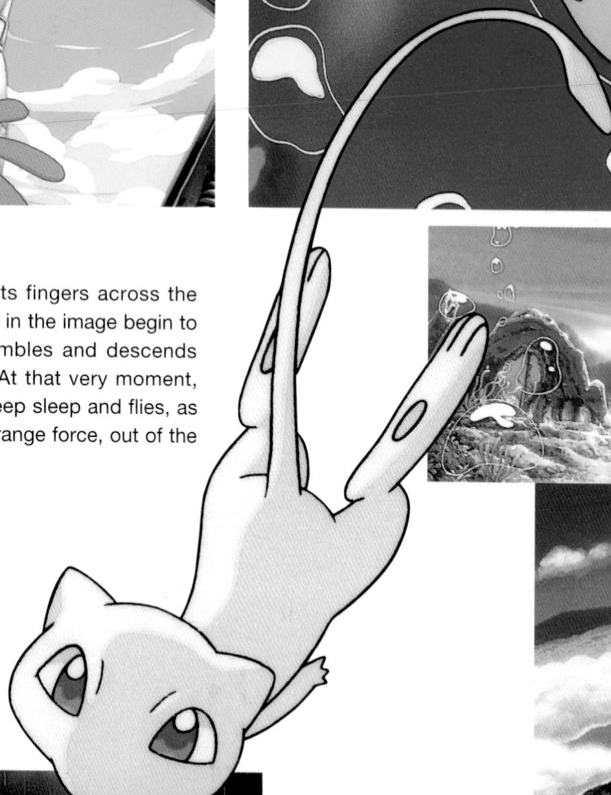

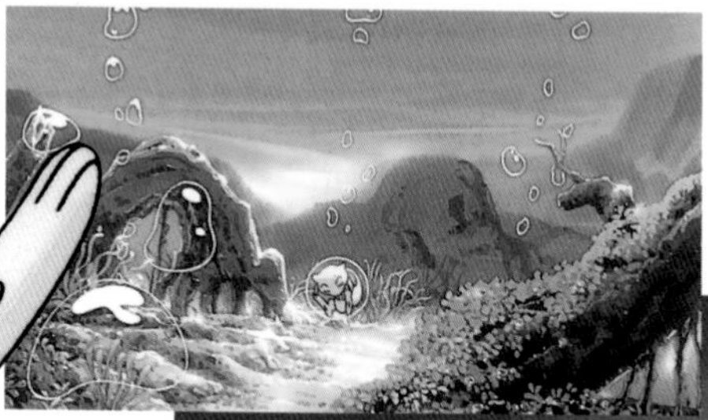

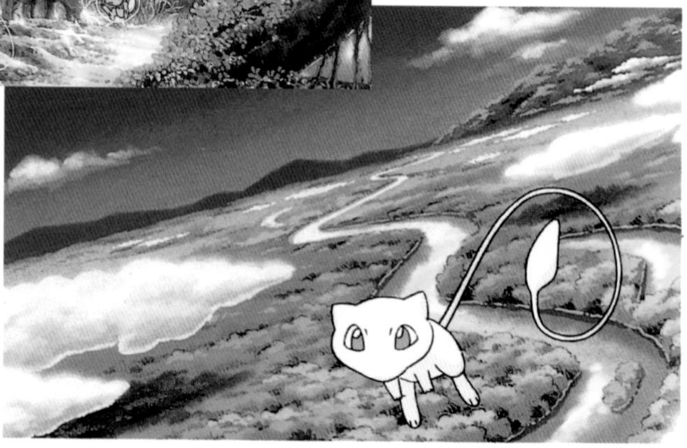

When Mewtwo moves its fingers across the video screen, the clouds in the image begin to move! Then the sky rumbles and descends over Mewtwo's island. At that very moment, Mew awakens from a deep sleep and flies, as if compelled by some strange force, out of the depths of the jungle.

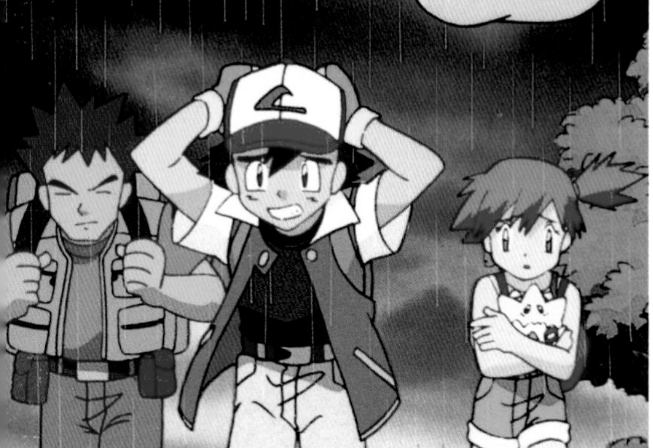

As Ash and his friends begin their journey to New Island, a terrible storm hits.

Across the Stormy Sea!

A finger points toward the sky....

The finger belongs to Mewtwo. As Mewtwo's finger circles, so do the clouds in the sky. In moments, the sky grows dark and foreboding. A great storm begins to brew....

At the same time...somewhere far, far away...a white Pokémon floats peacefully amid the bubbles of a crystal clear lake. Slowly, it awakens. The white Pokémon is Mew!

Bursting out of the water, it flies up into the sky, as if

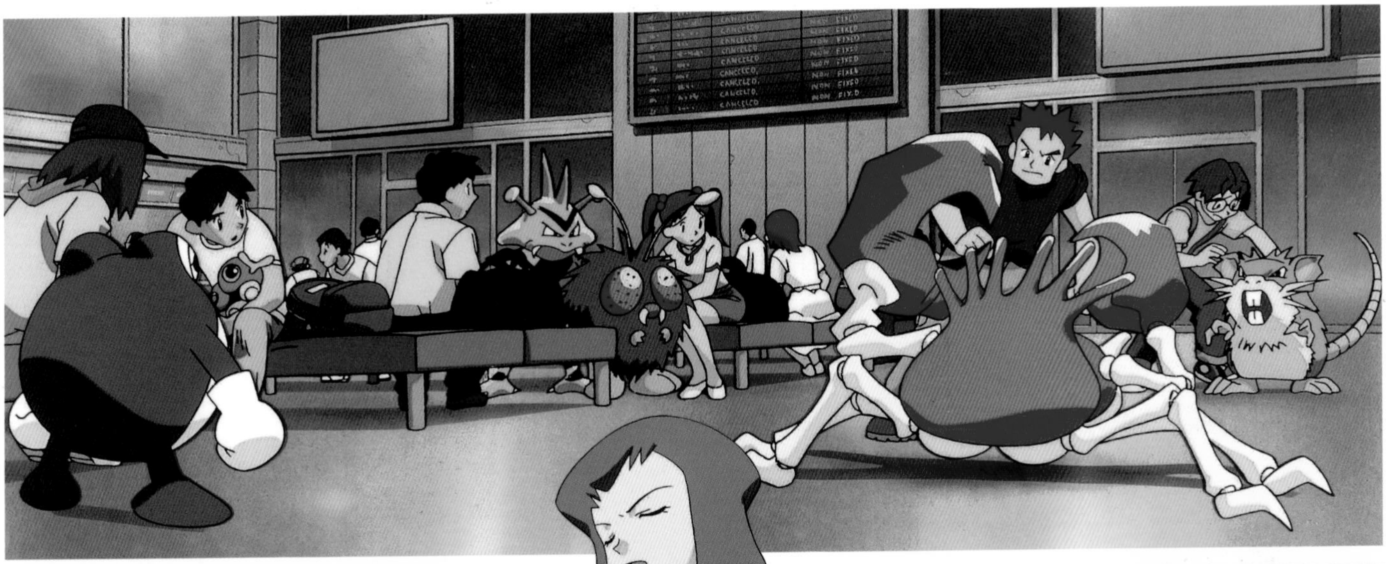

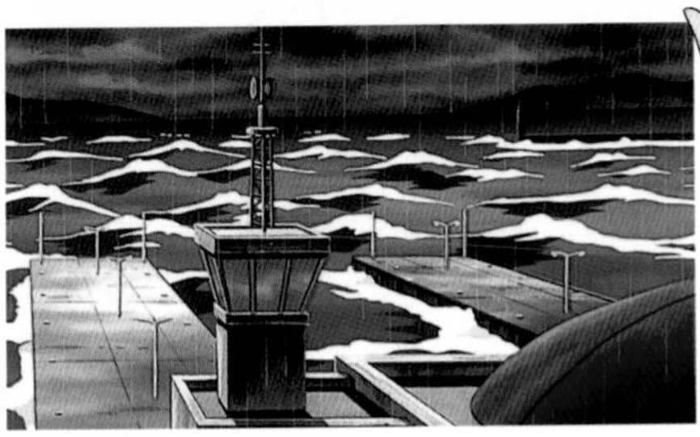

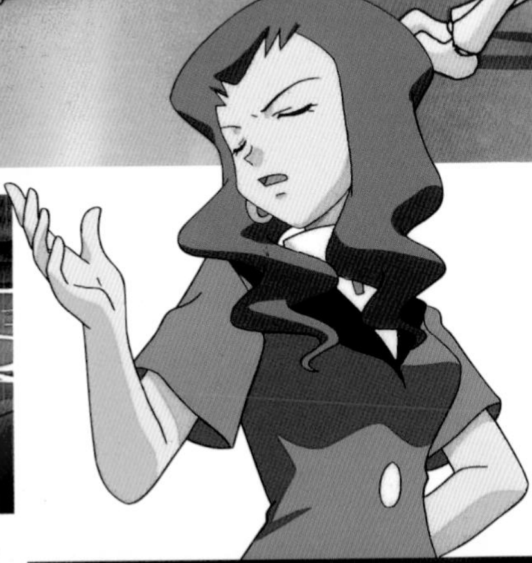

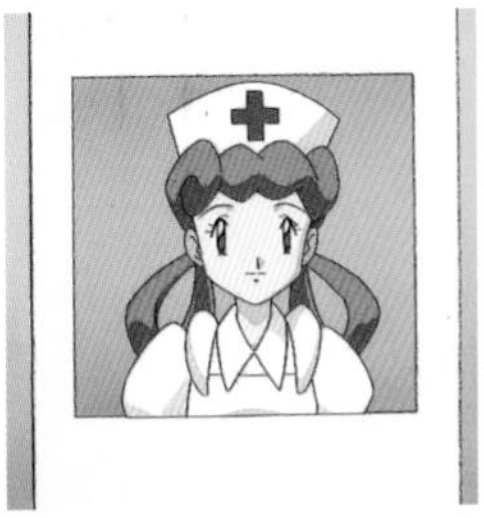

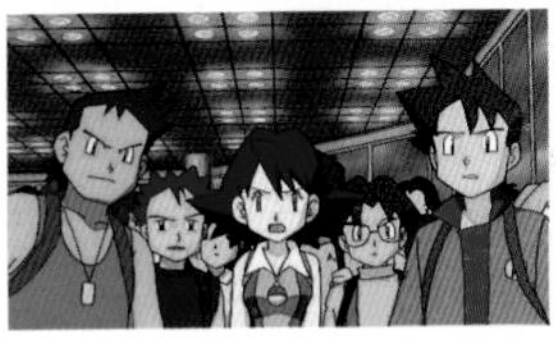

With Nurse Joy missing, no one dares take any risks.

The harbor is taking a real beating from the storm. The waiting room is full of trainers who have been invited to the island. The bay has never been hit by such a wild storm before. It looks like no boats will be able to leave the dock.

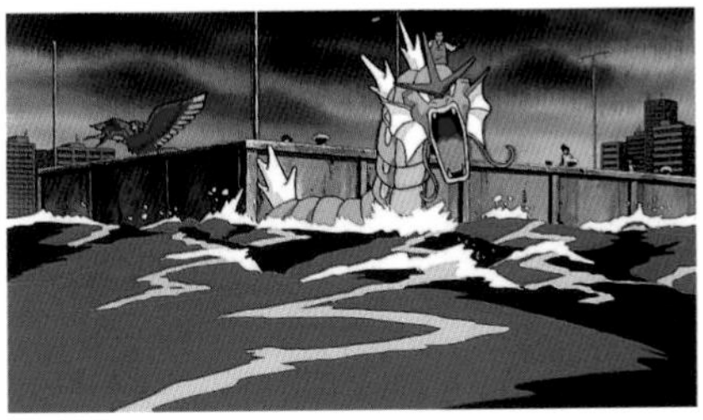

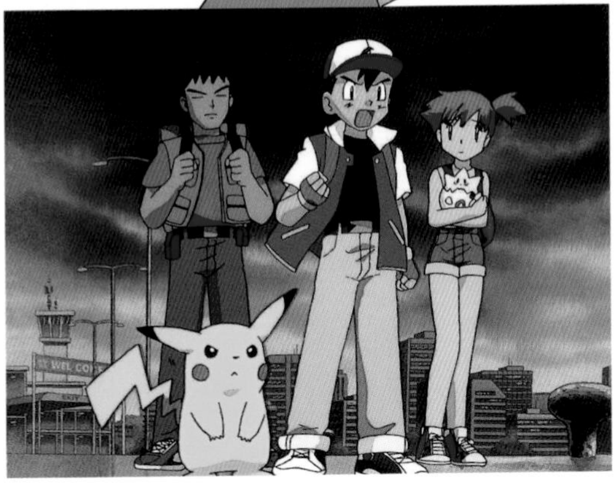

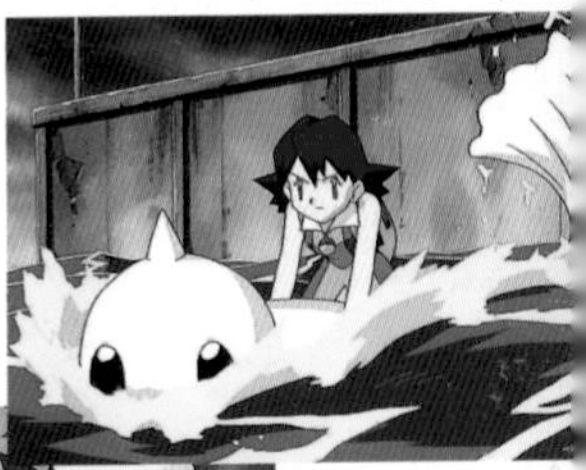

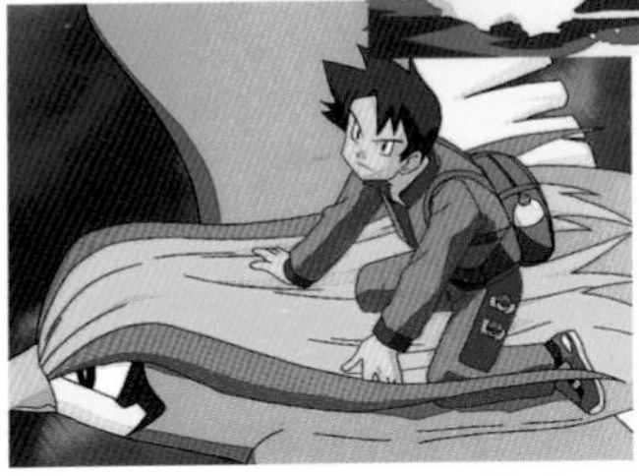

compelled towards a destination....

Getting soaked in the pouring rain, Ash and friends look out to sea. “Wow, what a storm!” Unfortunately, Pokémon Palace is located on New Island, surrounded by water.

When Ash and his friends arrive at the dock, they find they aren’t the only ones invited to the palace. The harbor director is also there, trying to prevent anyone from going out to sea. “The eye of the storm is located right above New Island!” she warns. “I can’t allow any boats to sail! Our hands are full trying to find Nurse Joy from our Pokémon Center! If anyone gets injured in this storm, she’s the only one who can help!”

But her warnings don’t discourage the trainers. Many of them jump onto their Water or Flying Pokémon. “Cross the sea? No problem!” they shout as they take off.

Ash is determined to go too. “I have to get to that island!”

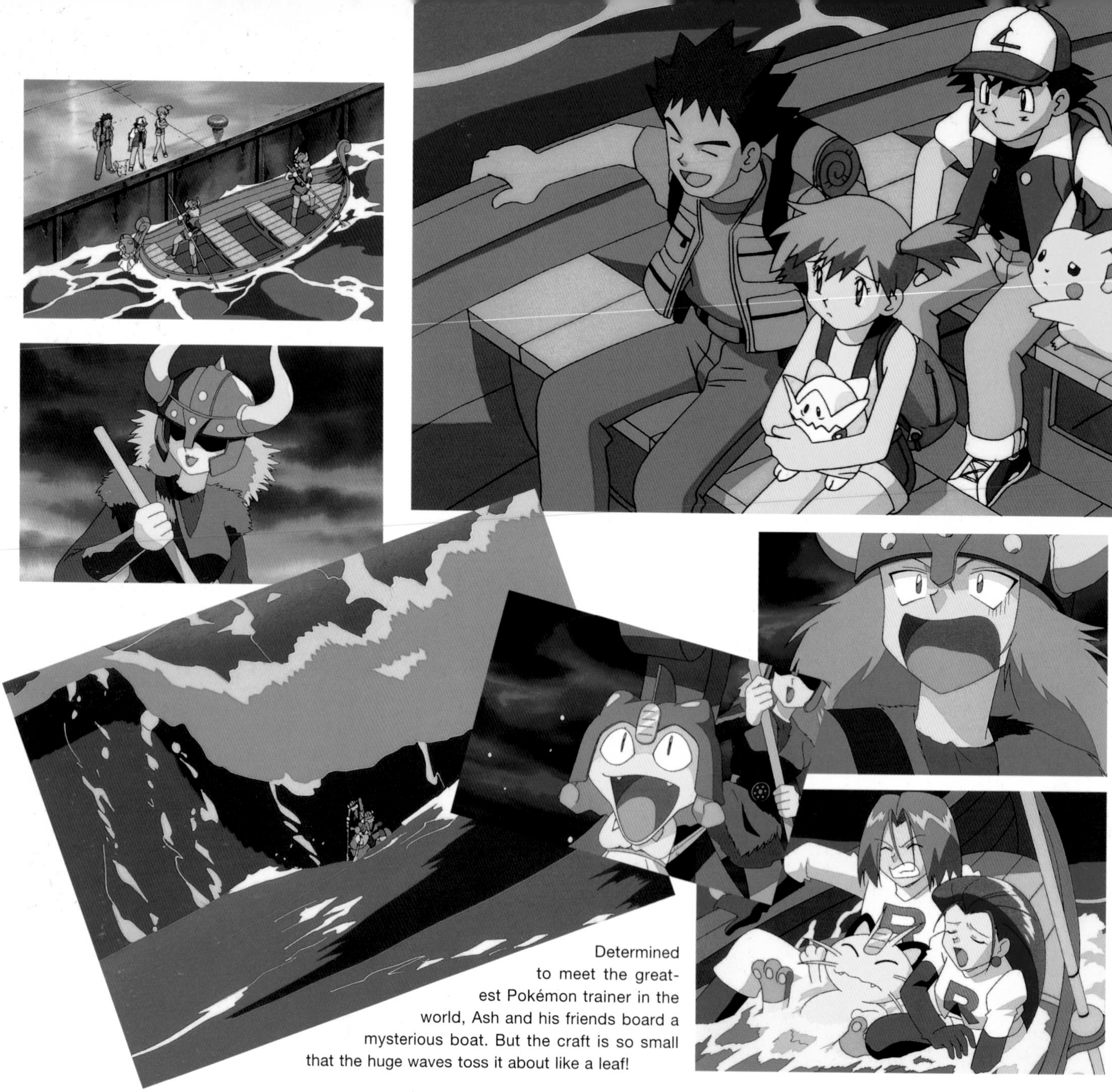

Determined to meet the greatest Pokémon trainer in the world, Ash and his friends board a mysterious boat. But the craft is so small that the huge waves toss it about like a leaf!

The three friends' Pokémon aren't strong enough to carry them through the storm across the raging water. But suddenly, a peculiar duo in a peculiar boat appears. "Want a lift," one of the the strange people asks.

Ash and his unsuspecting friends are thrilled. "A boat!" But soon, their enthusiasm wanes.

"Whoomsh! Splash! Boomsh!" Huge swells pound their little vessel. And what's this? The strange rowers turn out to be the members of Team Rocket! But the storm leaves no time for an argument!

Unable to hang on any longer, Ash and his friends are thrown into the raging sea. Relentless waves almost swallow them, but Staryu and Squirtle help them escape the terrible storm. When they reach the surface and catch their breaths, they are greeted by an eerily calm sea and the ominous shadow of New Island.

When Ash and his friends fall into the sea, Misty quickly calls out her Water Pokémon Staryu!

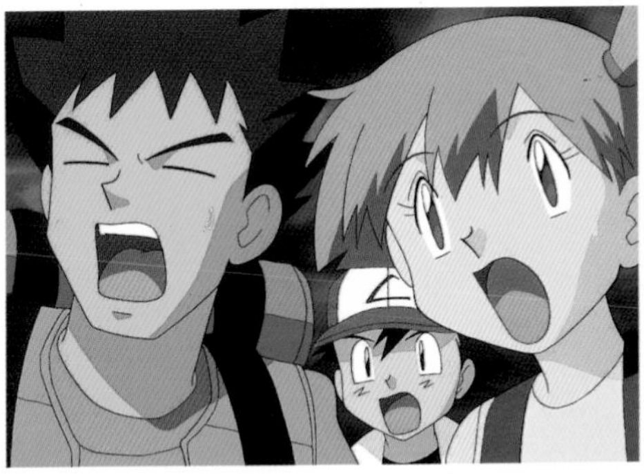

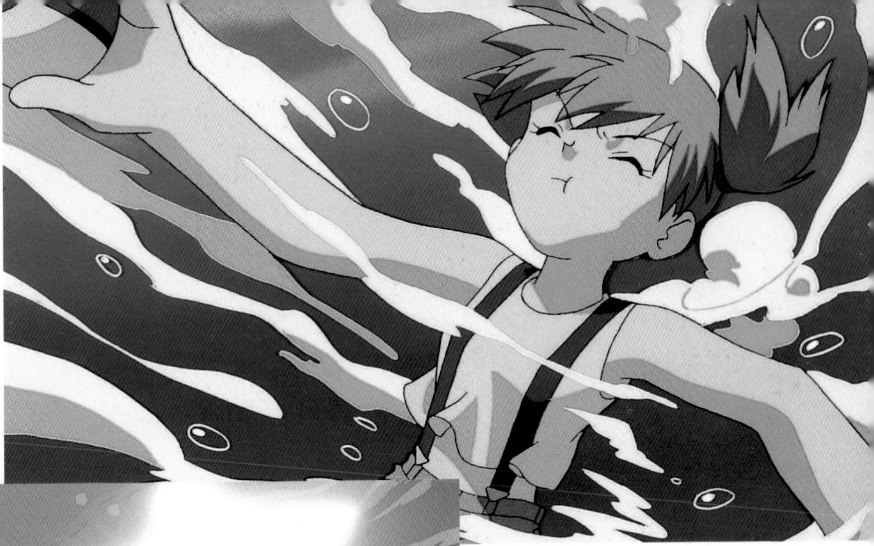

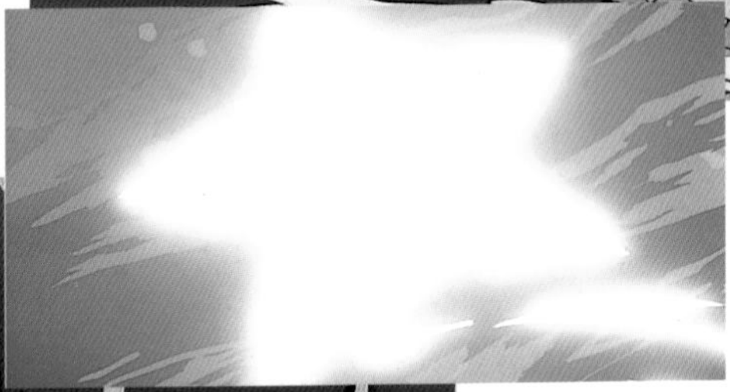

Ash brings out his Water Pokémon Squirtle and joins hands with Misty, who grabs Brock. Together, the three ride out the storm. Squirtle and Staryu bravely swim on through the raging sea.

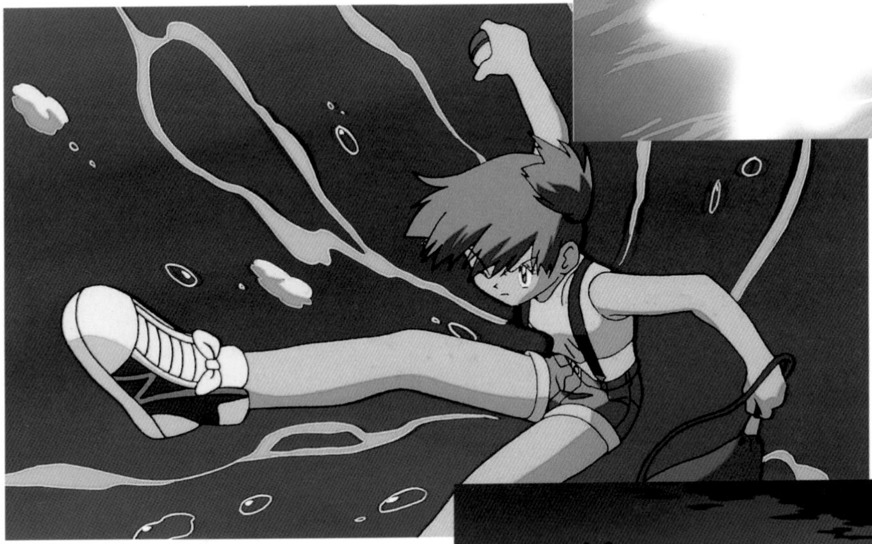

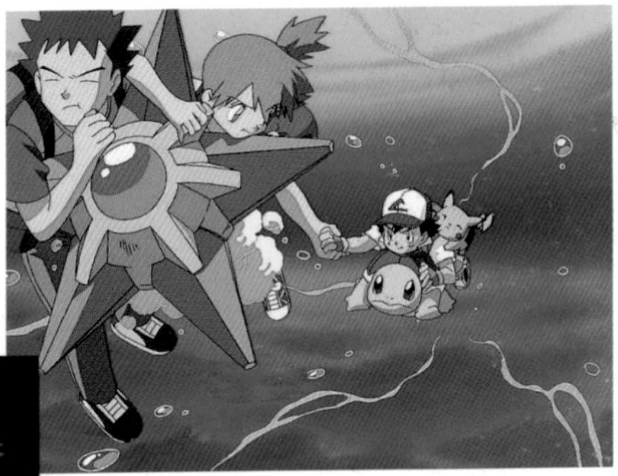

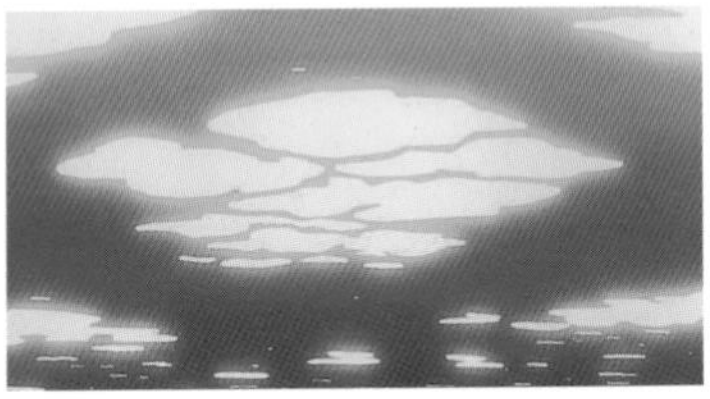

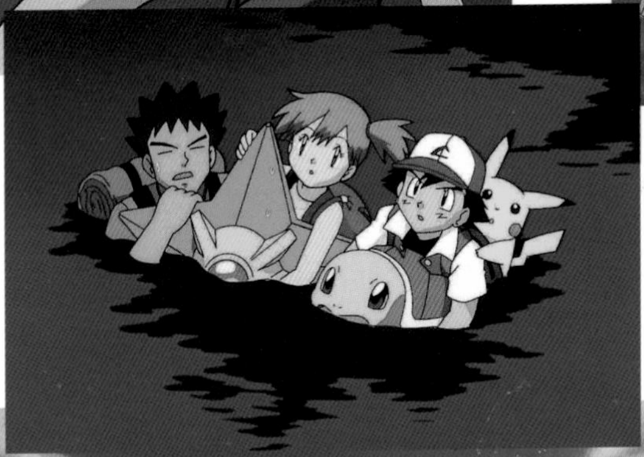

When our friends dare to rise to the surface to get their bearings, they find themselves in the calm eye of the storm. New Island casts an eerie shadow over them.

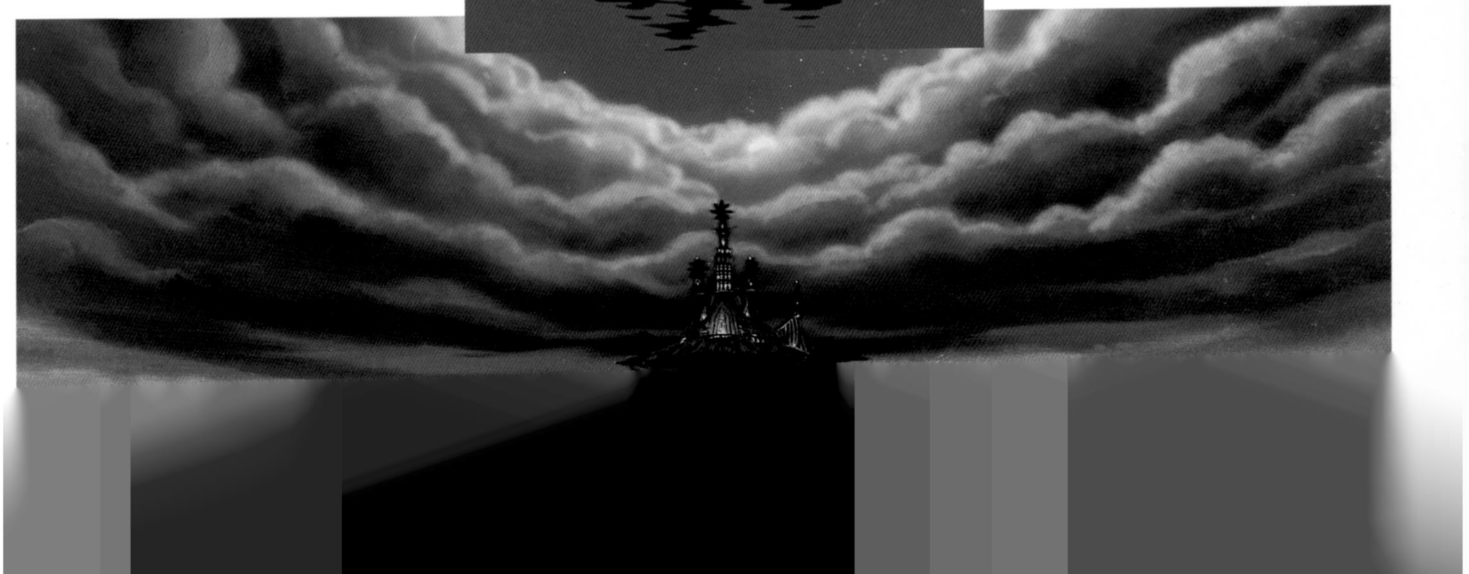

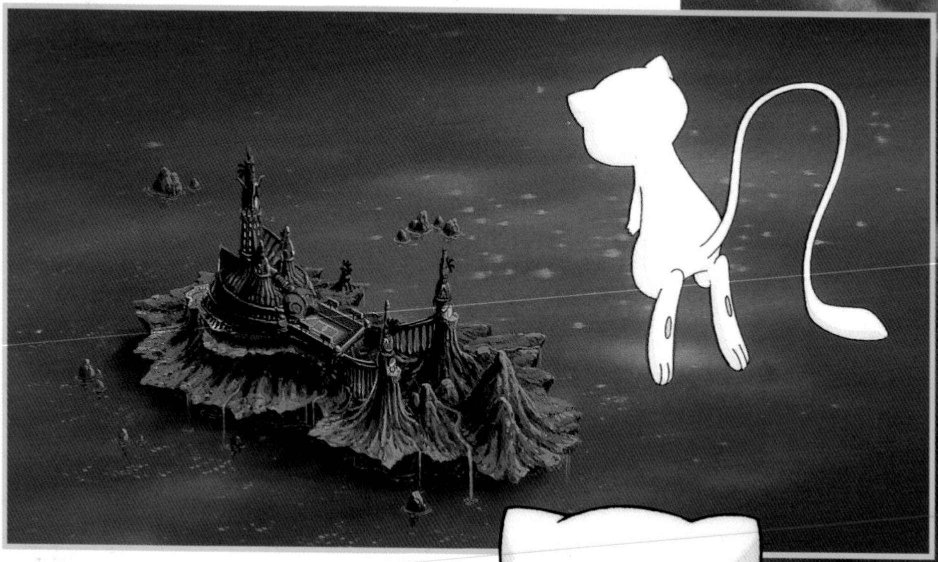

As if compelled by some unseen force, Mew heads directly for New Island. When Mew arrives, it follows Team Rocket into Pokémon Palace.

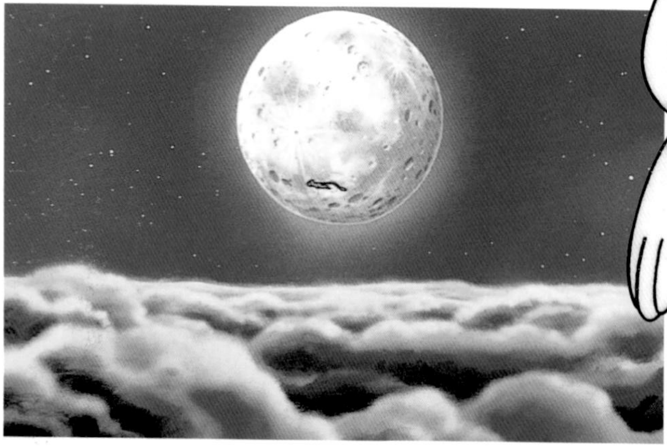

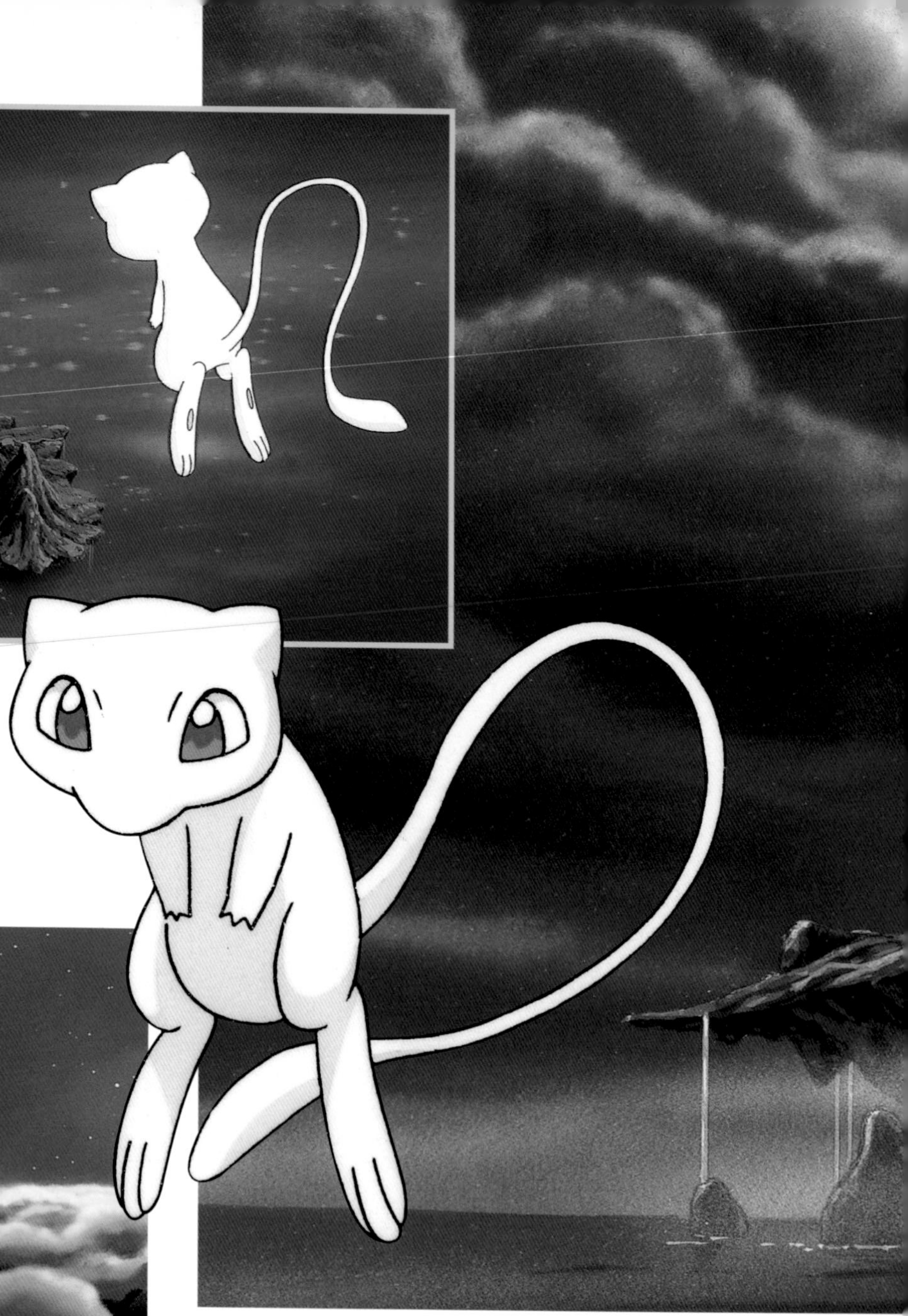

Pokémon Palace

A bright flash streaks past the glowing moon and dives through the boiling clouds. What is soaring through the raging storm? It's Mew!

Mew comes to an abrupt halt when it sees the ominous silhouette of Pokémon Palace. "Mewww!" it cries and speeds towards it.

Meanwhile, Ash, Brock, and Misty arrive at the island's dock, where they are greeted by a mysterious, cloaked woman.

"May I see your invitation?" she asks.

When Brock glimpses the woman's face, he exclaims, "You're Joy, the missing woman from the poster!"

The others also see the resemblance. But the woman is perturbed by Brock's outburst.

"You must be mistaken," she says. "I've had the good fortune to live on this island and serve its master all my life. Now, please come this

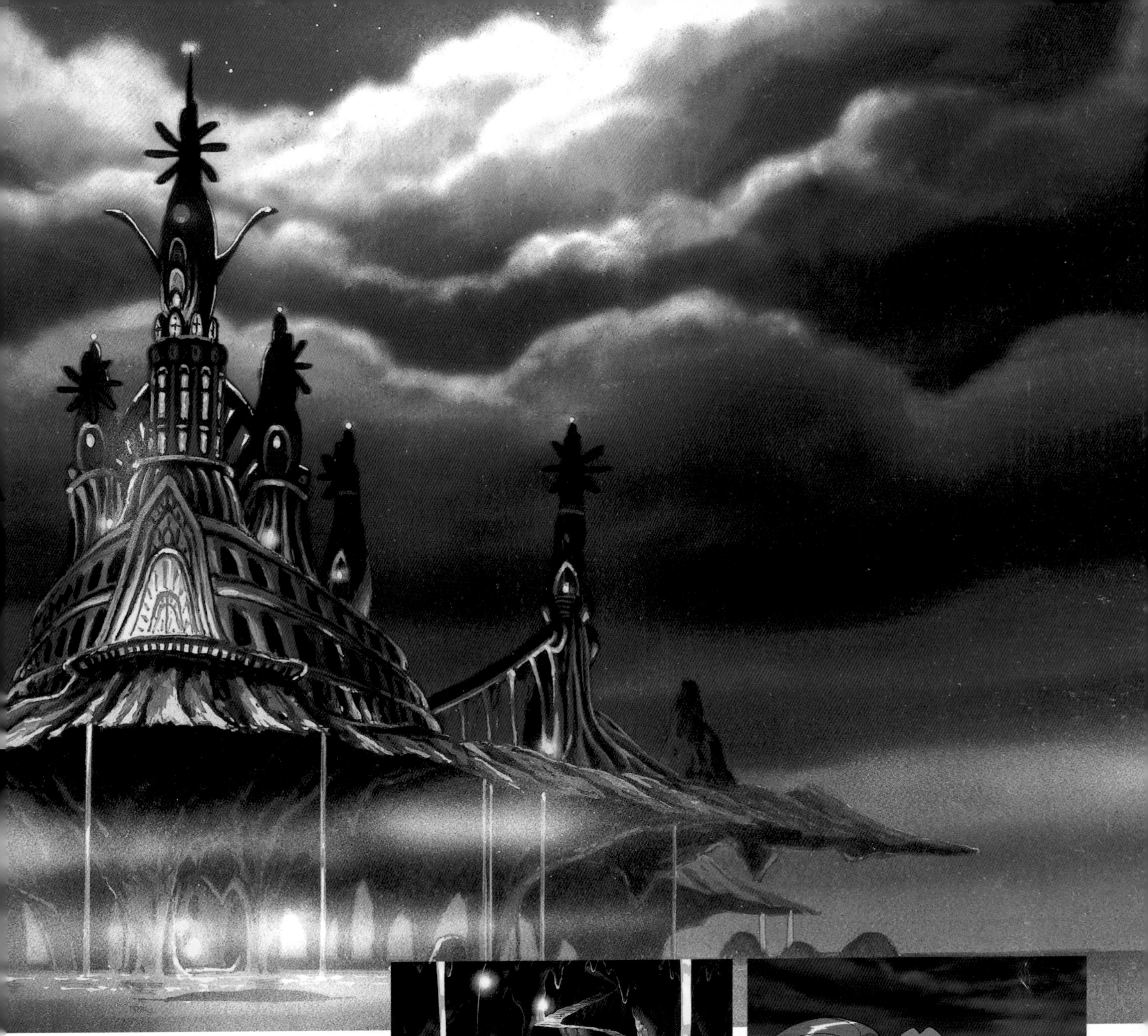

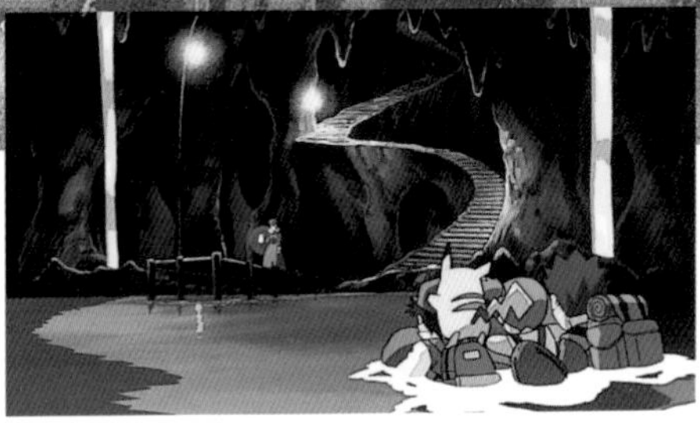

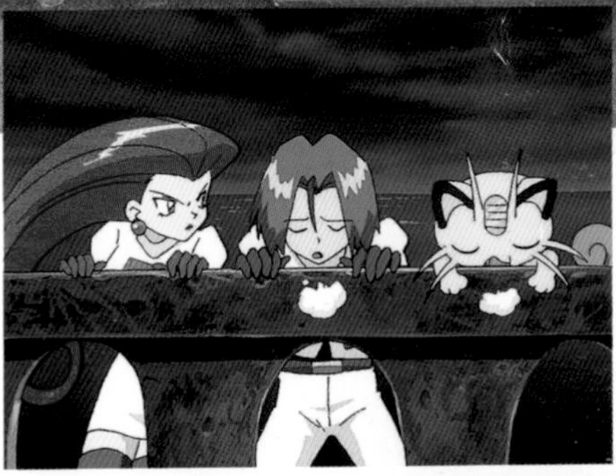

way. The others have already arrived." And she leads them into the palace.

As for Team Rocket.... Somehow they manage to make it to the island as well. As they watch the others enter the palace, James thinks for a moment. "Hmm. We don't have invitations.... So we'll just have to go in the back way!" he decides, pointing to a sewage drain.

Meowth gags. "Yuck! Meowth ain't no sewer rat! Meee-owth!"

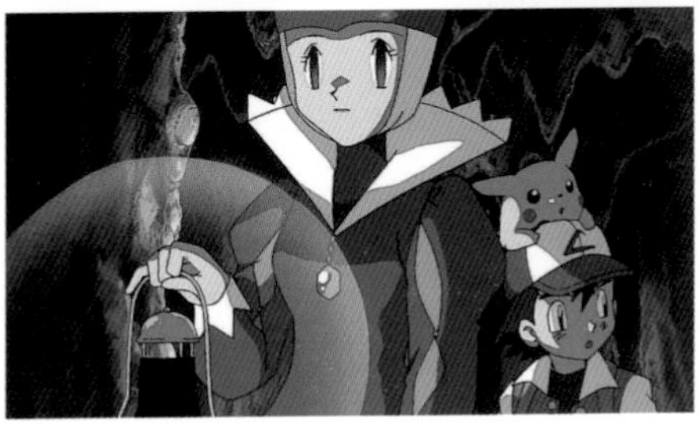

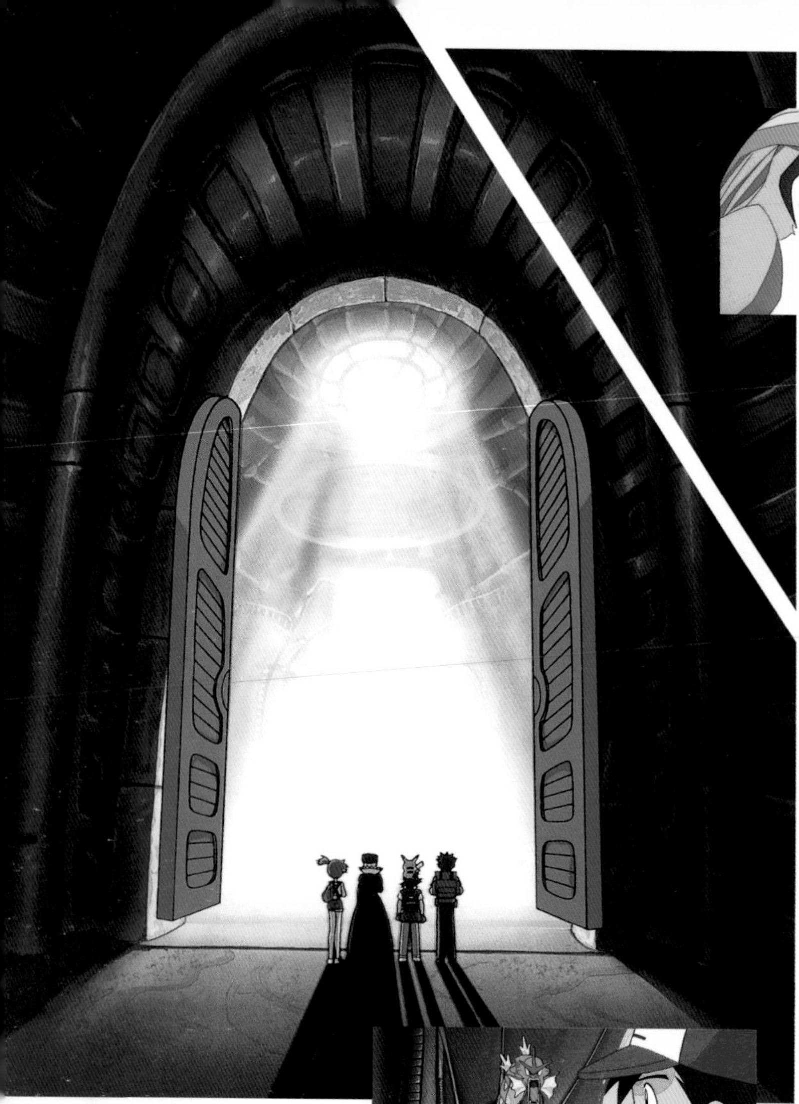

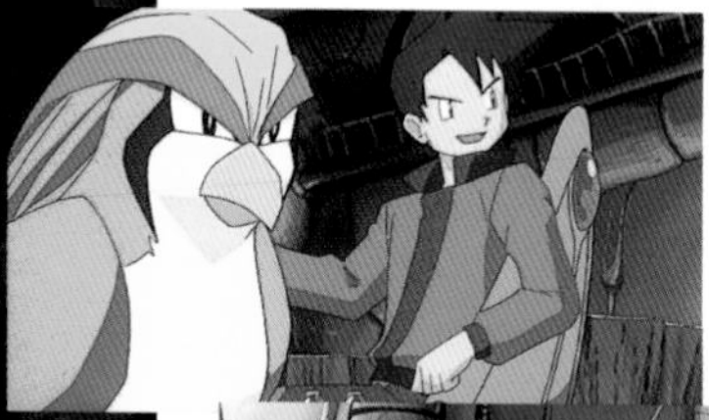

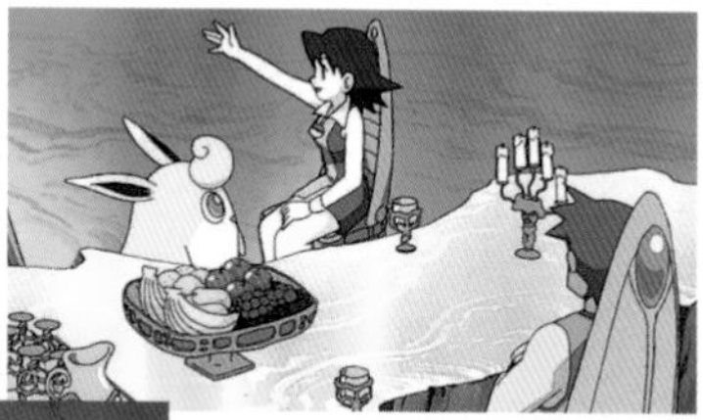

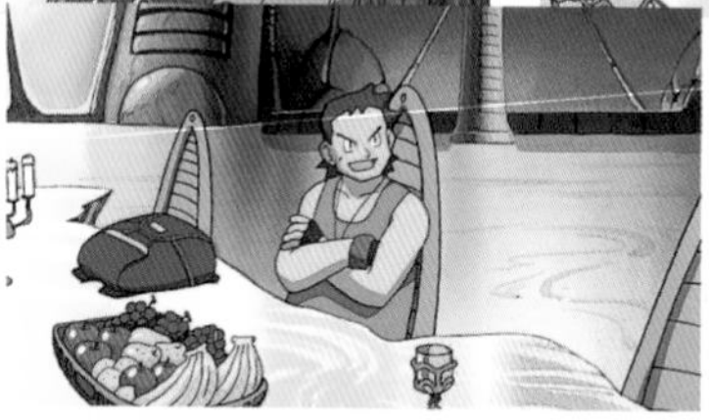

Corey, Fergus, and Neesha were carried through the storm by their favorite Pokémon.

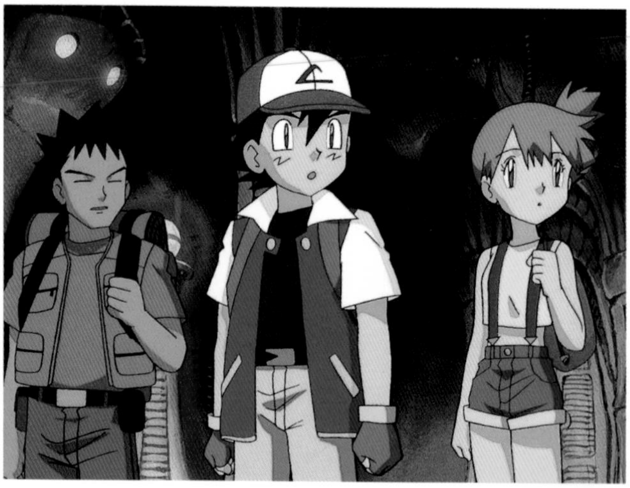

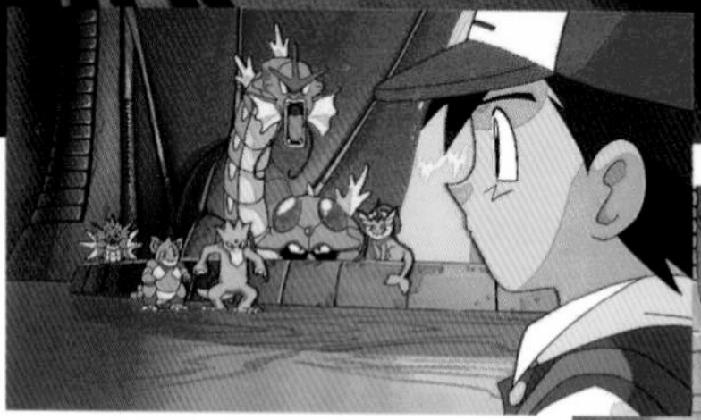

Ash and friends are shown to the great hall by the cloaked woman. There they are surprised to find only three other trainers, relaxing around a large table.

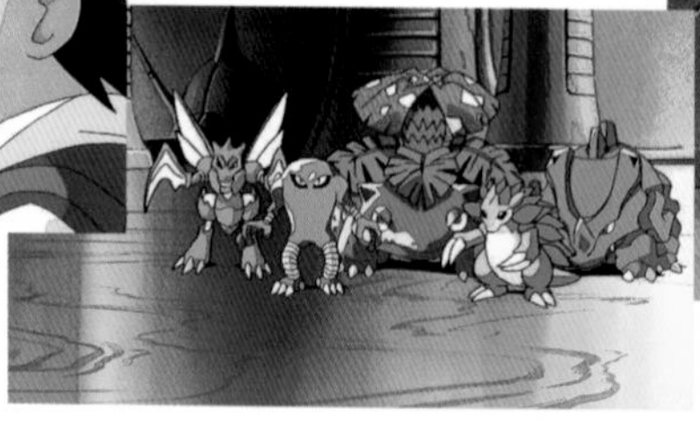

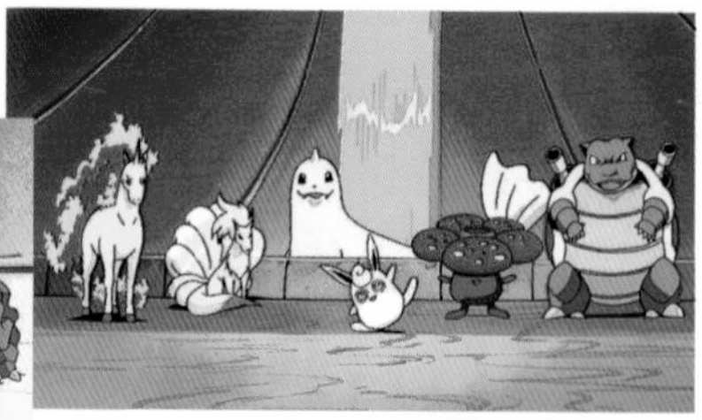

Mewtwo's Arrival

"C-c-creak..." Slowly the imposing Pokémon Palace doors open and Ash and his friends enter. "The other trainers who came for the tournament are seated over there," the mysterious woman tells them.

The three friends are surprised. Out of all the trainers that packed the waiting room at the harbor, only three other trainers have made it to the island!

"That's it?" Ash asks.

"Trainers who can't travel through inclement weather are of no use to us," the woman answers. "I'm sorry, but the storm was actually your first test. You are the select few who passed. Now, if everyone would please show us your most powerful Pokémon...."

Suddenly, a great fanfare fills the great hall!

The cloaked woman calmly tells the trainers,

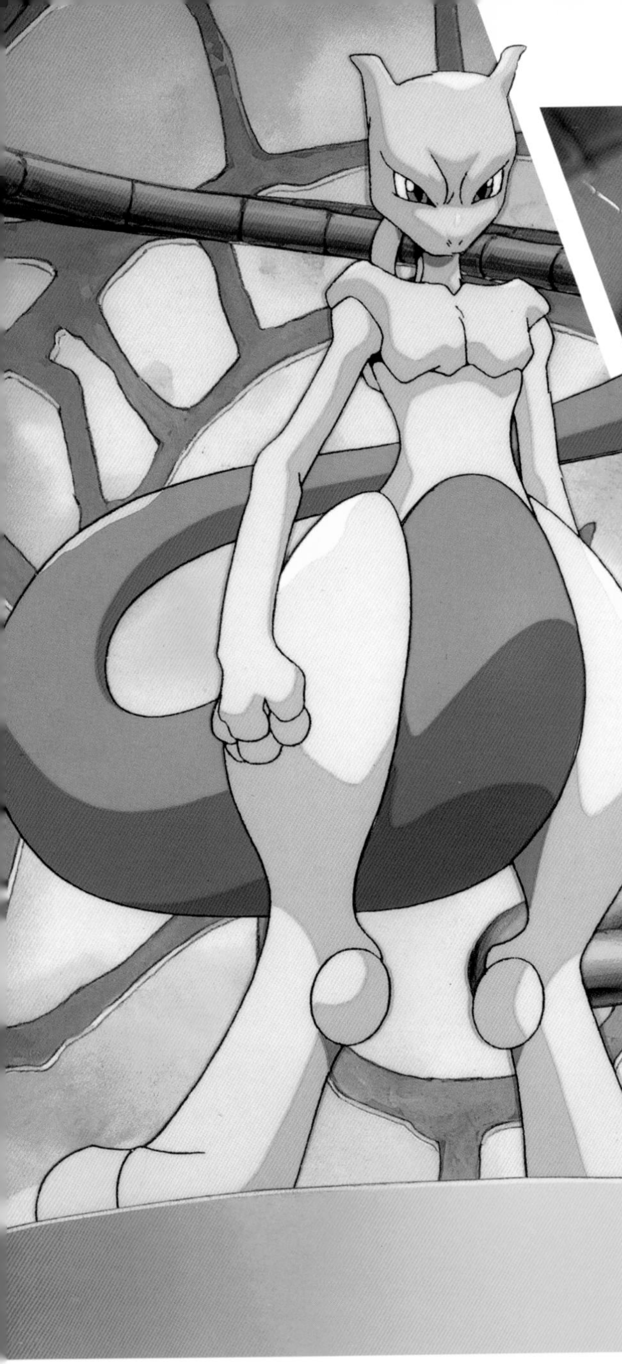

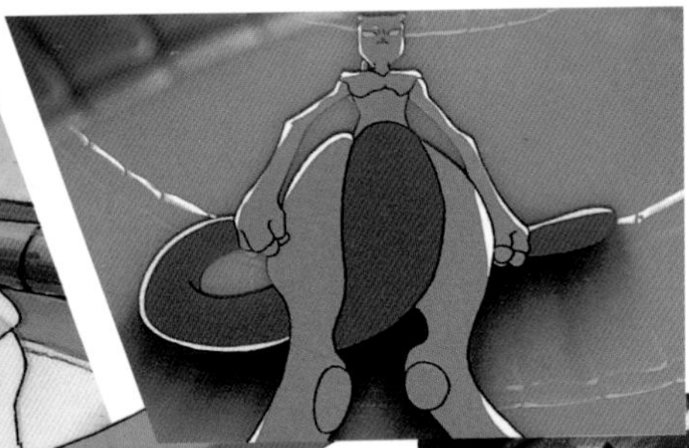

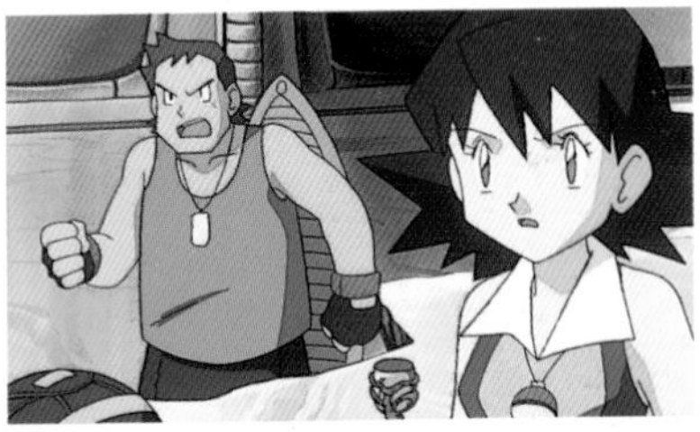

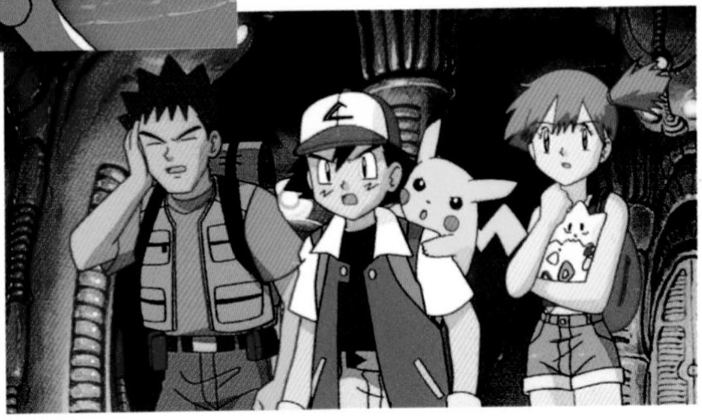

Mewtwo appears in front of them, bathed in light.

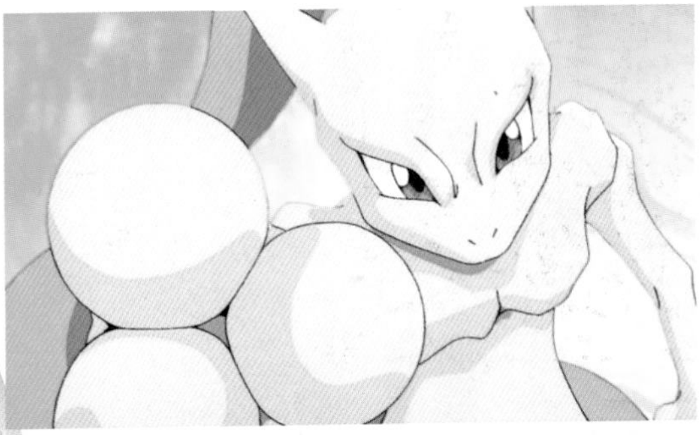

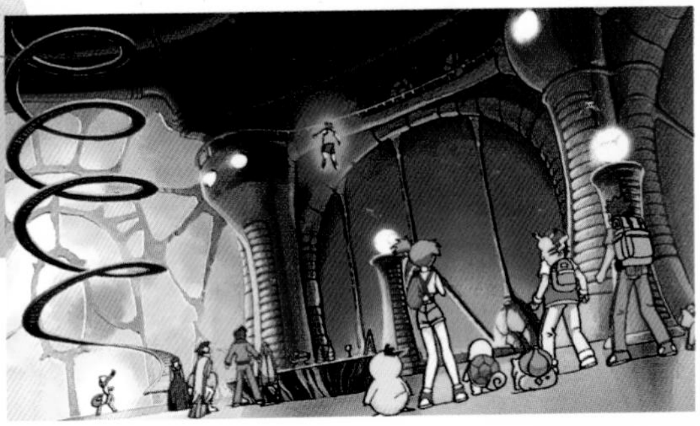

"Thank you for your patience. In a moment you will be introduced to the greatest Pokémon trainer in the world."

Suddenly all the lights in the hall go out. Then, on a stage at the top of a flight of stairs, a spotlight blinks on.

"Meet the greatest Pokémon trainer who ever lived! I present to you, Mewtwo!" The spotlight shines directly on Mewtwo.

One trainer blurts out, "A Pokémon trainer who's a Pokémon? That's ridiculous!" Mewtwo responds with a display of power, flinging the trainer up into the air and slamming him down on the floor.

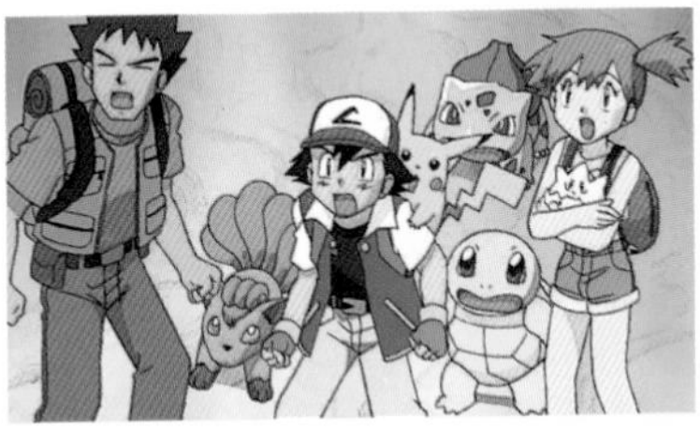

When Fergus refuses to accept Mewtwo as a Pokémon trainer, Mewtwo puts him in his place.

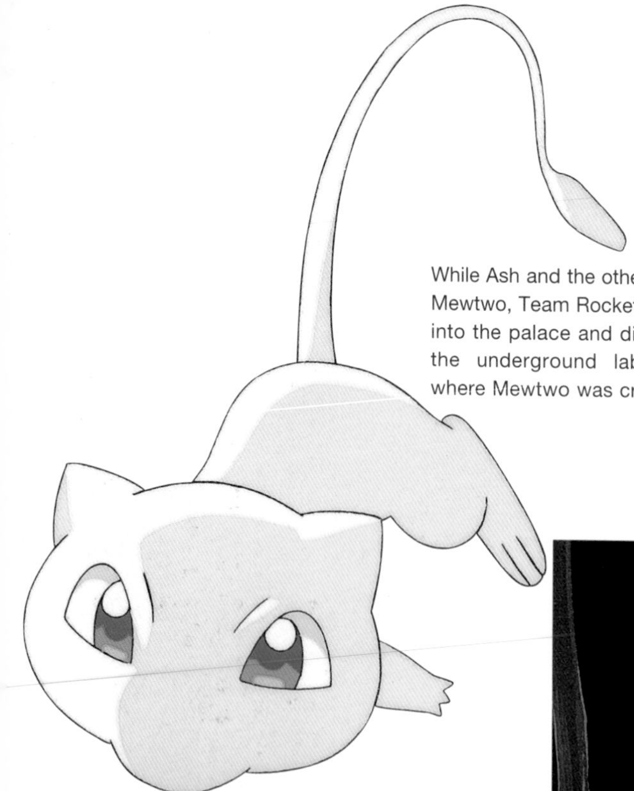

While Ash and the others meet Mewtwo, Team Rocket sneaks into the palace and discovers the underground laboratory where Mewtwo was created.

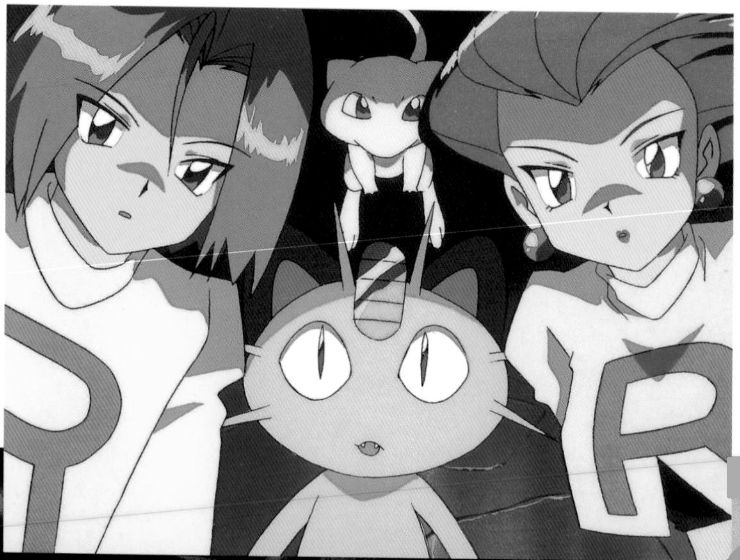

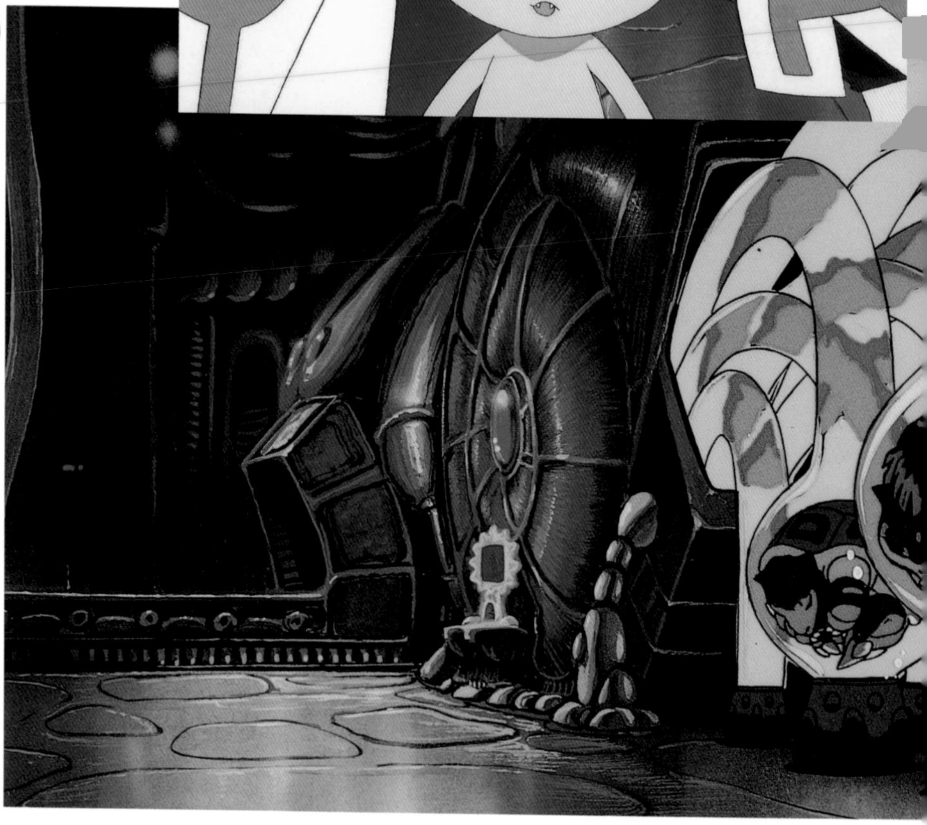

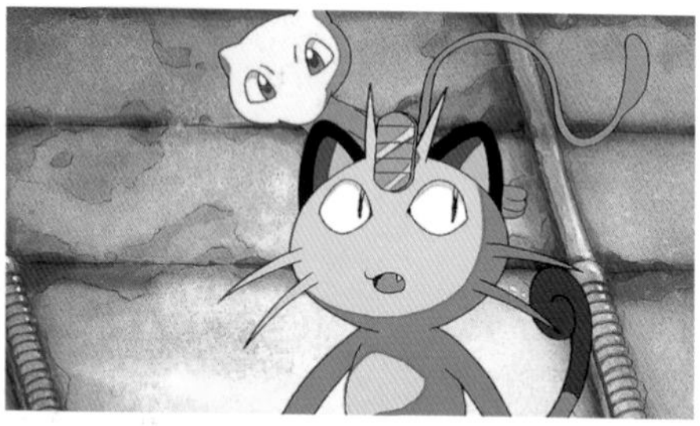

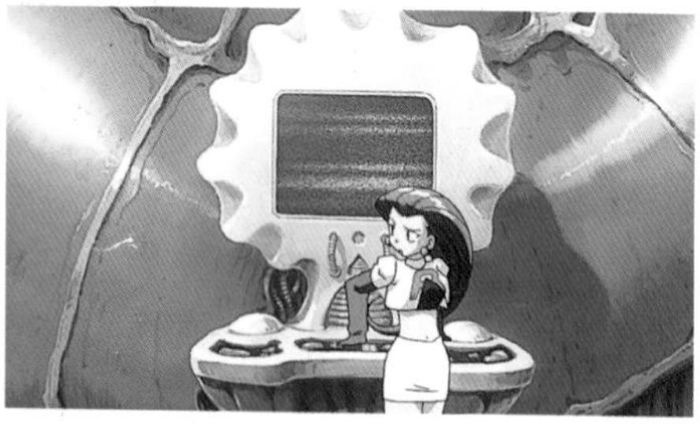

The Underground Laboratory

"Meowth! Where are we?"

Having sneaked into the palace through the sewage drain, Team Rocket stumbles upon an underground laboratory filled with machines, instruments, and large glass tubes. Curled up asleep in each tube is a different Pokémon! Jessie accidentally touches one of the machines, which sets off a recording.

"This is a Pokémon Duplicating Machine. From the smallest sample of any Pokémon, this invention can create an exact duplicate. But we have taken this process one step further to create something extraordinary! By recovering the DNA from a fossilized hair of Mew, one of the most elusive and rarest Pokémon in the world, we created the greatest Pokémon that ever lived! But our creation rose up against us. And now our laboratory is doomed, and we with it."

A scratchy video tells the secret of Mewtwo's creation.

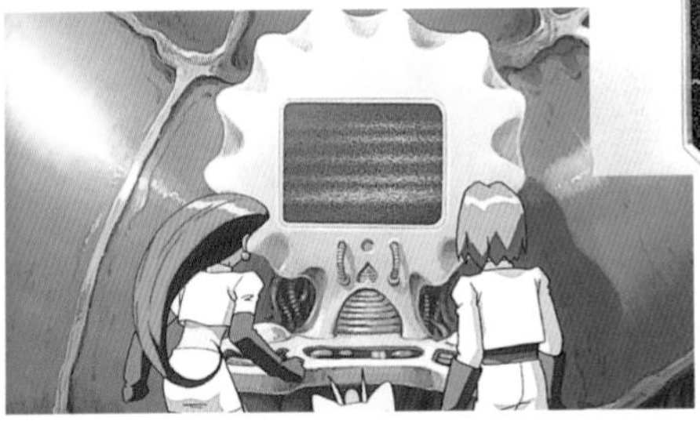

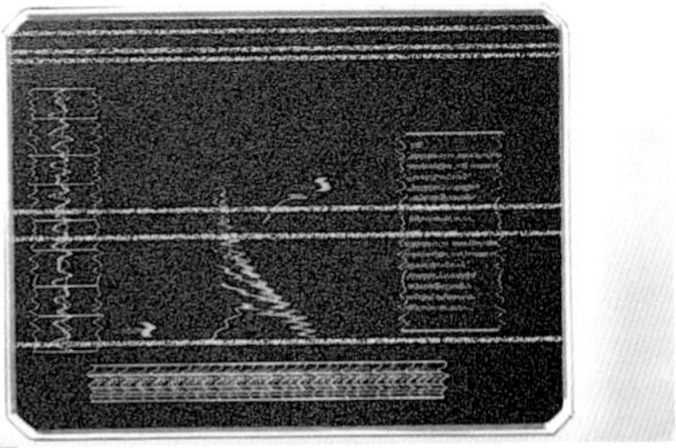

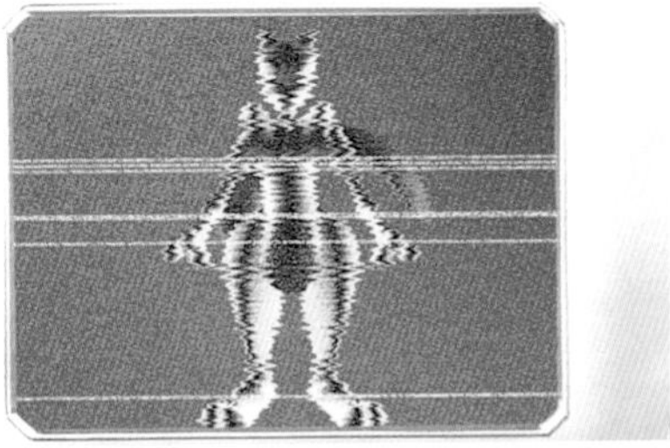

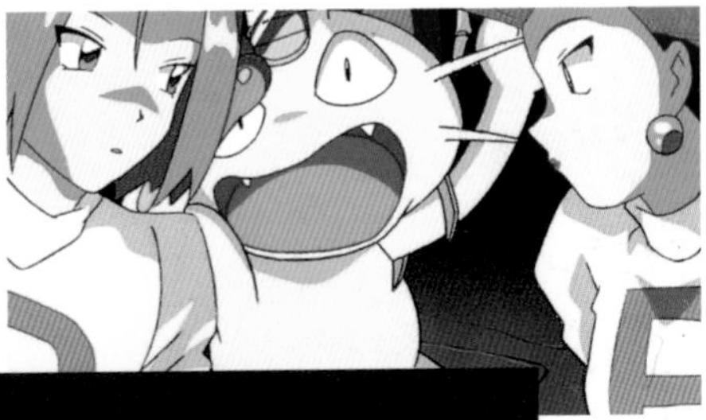

The instant the computer claims it can duplicate any Pokémon, it creates an exact replica of Meowth from a hair it pulled out of Meowth's tail!

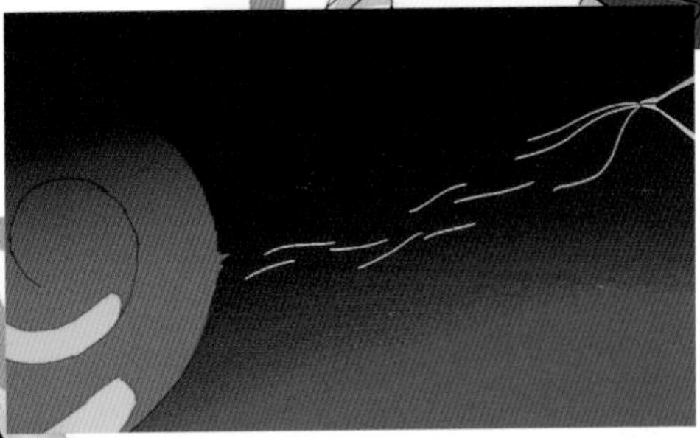

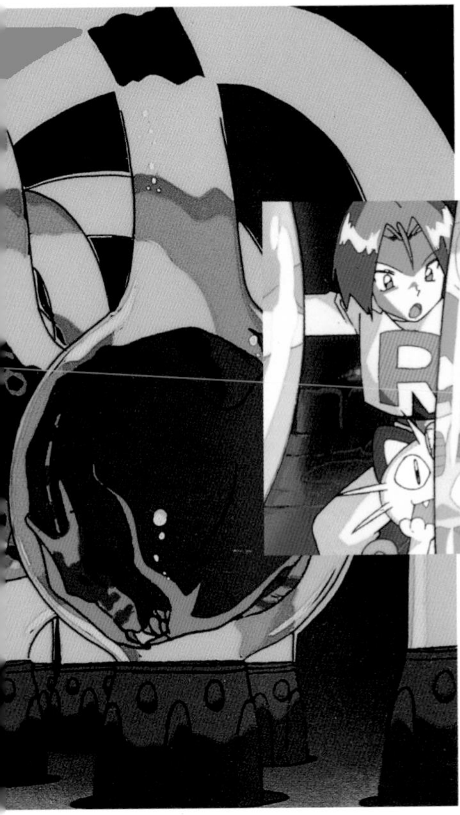

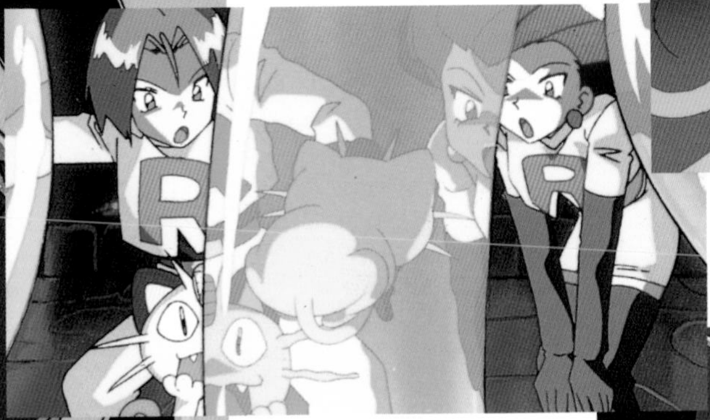

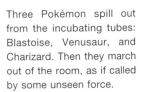

Three Pokémon spill out from the incubating tubes: Blastoise, Venusaur, and Charizard. Then they march out of the room, as if called by some unseen force.

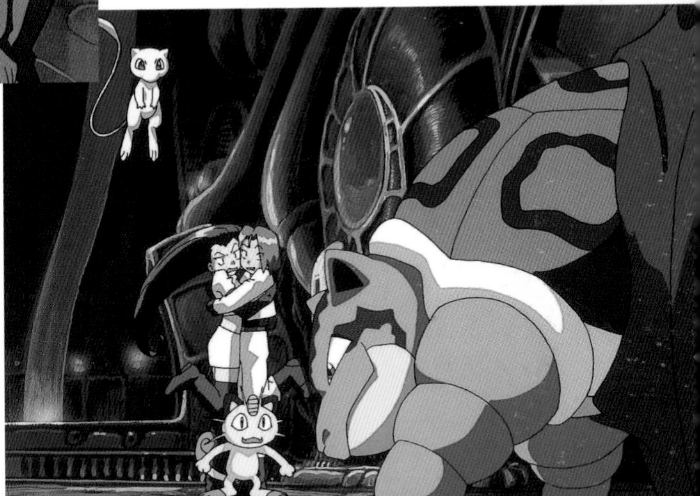

The screen goes blank.

"Is this the same laboratory?" Jessie wonders.

At that very moment, a Pokémon curled up in one of the tubes begins to glow brighter and brighter. Suddenly the end of the tube expands and the Pokémon inside slides out at their feet!

Jessie and James shiver. "This place gives me the creeps!" whimpers James.

As the two clutch each other in terror, out pops Mew from behind them!

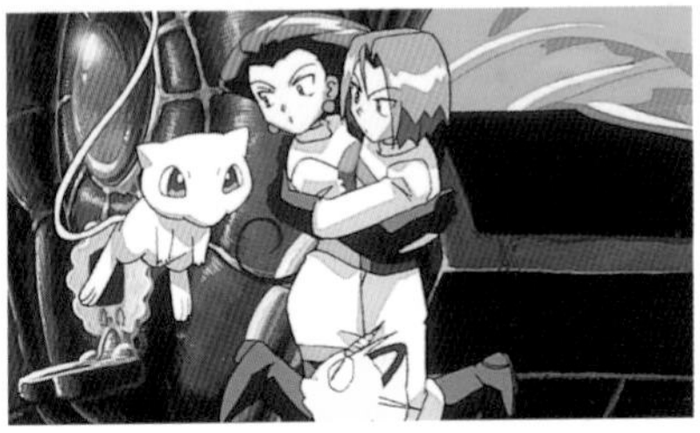

Mew follows the three new Pokémon out of the laboratory.

Flung to the ground by Mewtwo, Fergus commands Gyarados to attack. But Gyarados's "Hyper Beam" is ineffectual against Mewtwo, and as quickly as the battle begins, it is over.

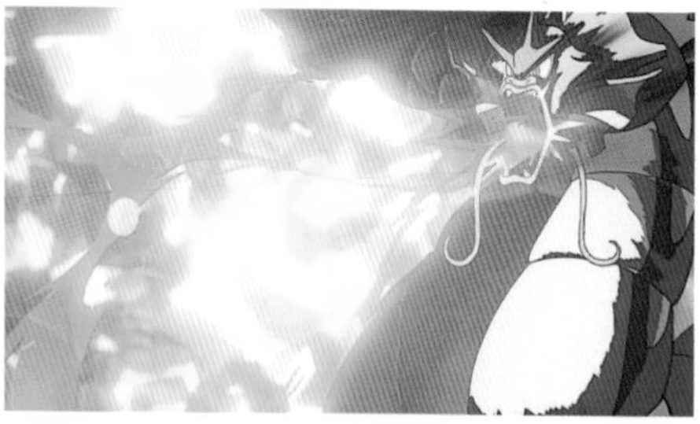

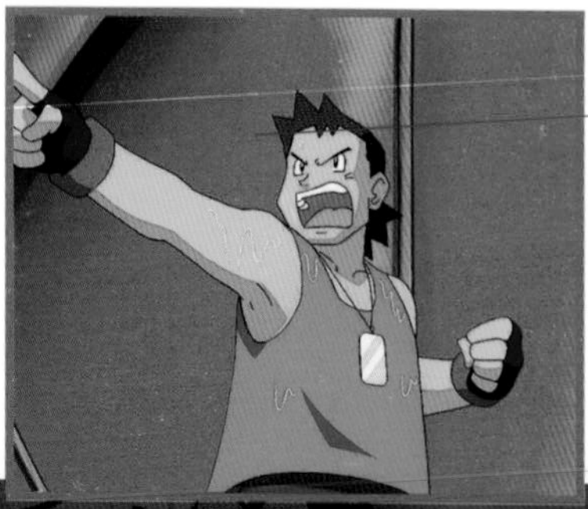

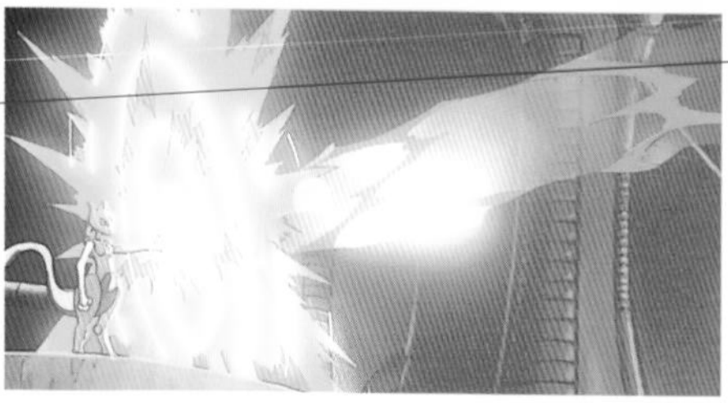

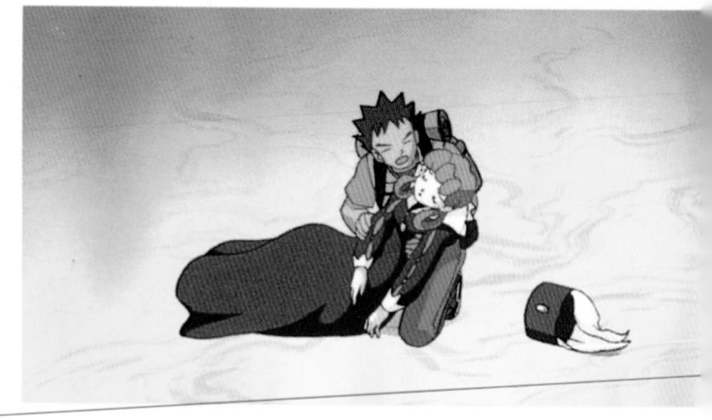

The mysterious cloaked woman indeed turns out to be missing Nurse Joy. Mewtwo has taken over her mind to make use of her extensive knowledge of Pokémon physiology.

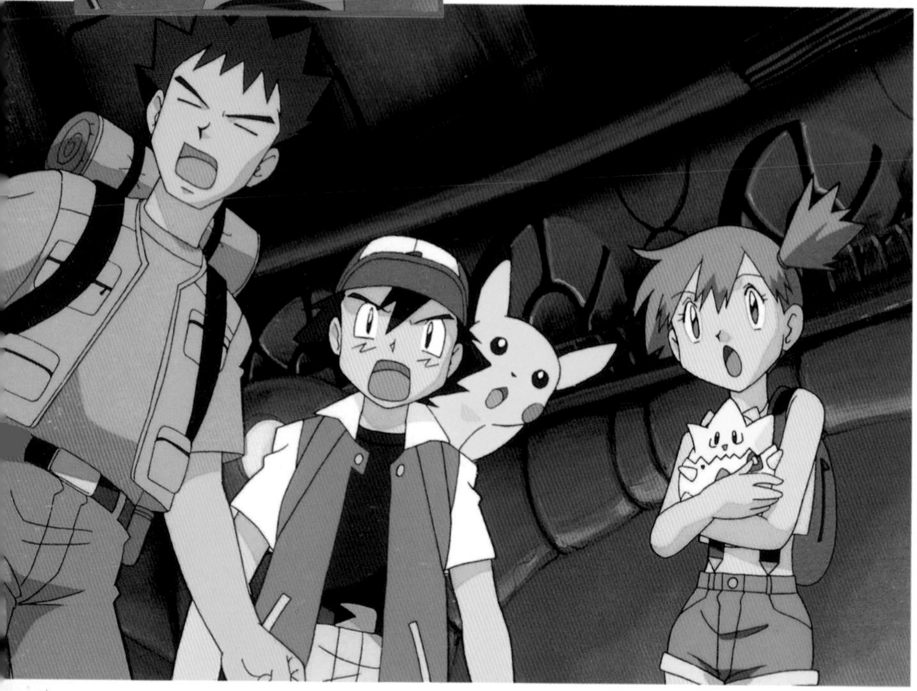

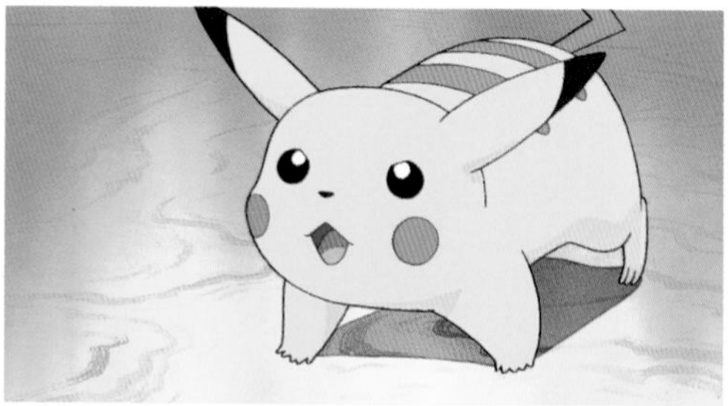

Pikachu disapproves of Mewtwo's hostility.

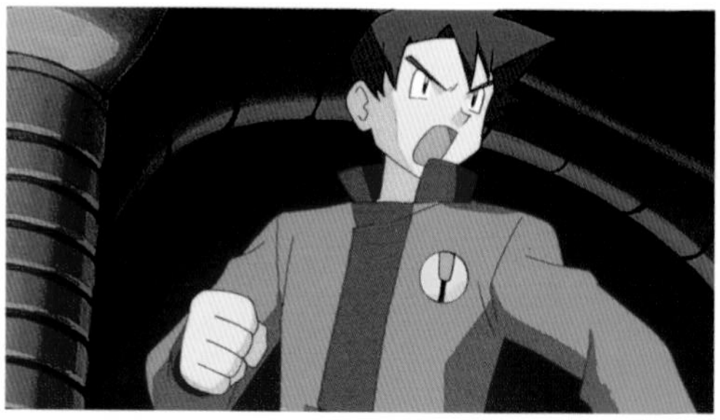

"There isn't a Pokémon alive who can't be captured!" Corey shouts with determination.

The World's Greatest Pokémon

Mewtwo tells Ash and the others, "Once I still had hope for the human race. But no more. Humans have shown themselves to be pitiful creatures, far inferior to Pokémon. If beings such as these are permitted to rule the earth, we are all doomed!"

"So you're saying Pokémon should be in charge?" Brock asks.

"No," Mewtwo replies. "Not Pokémon, either. They are the ones who allowed humans to take over. In fact, some Pokémon live only to serve humans!"

Pikachu argues that Pokémon aren't humans' servants, and the reason Pikachu is with Ash is because they care about each other.

But this only angers Mewtwo all the more.

"Living with humans is a grave mistake," Mewtwo spits. "The weaker the Pokémon, the

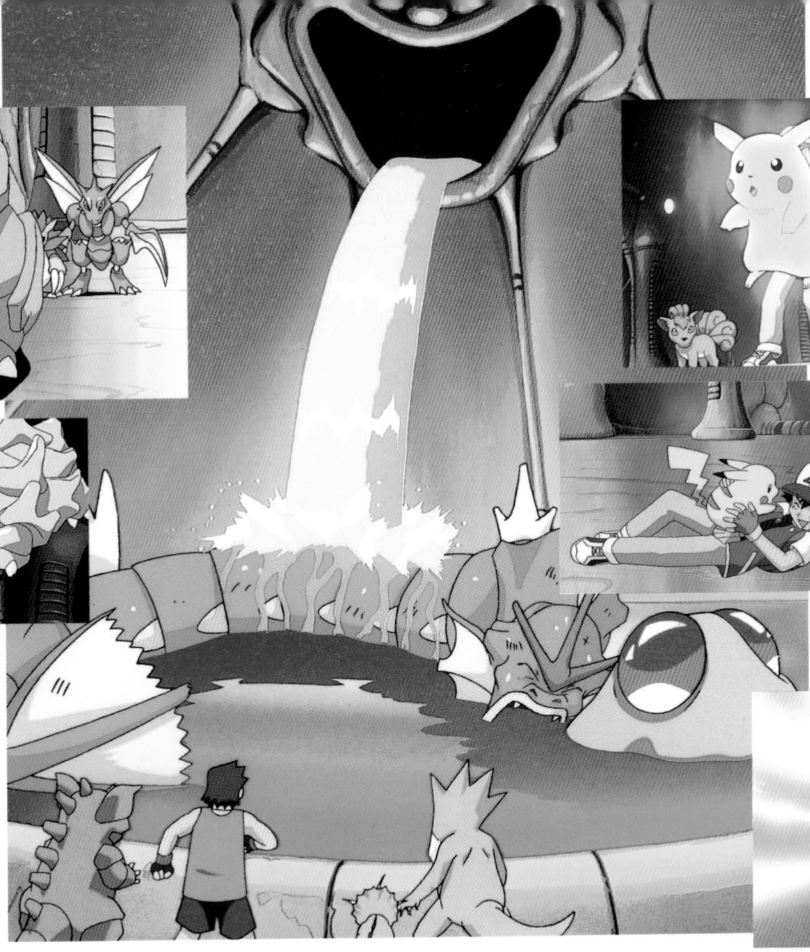

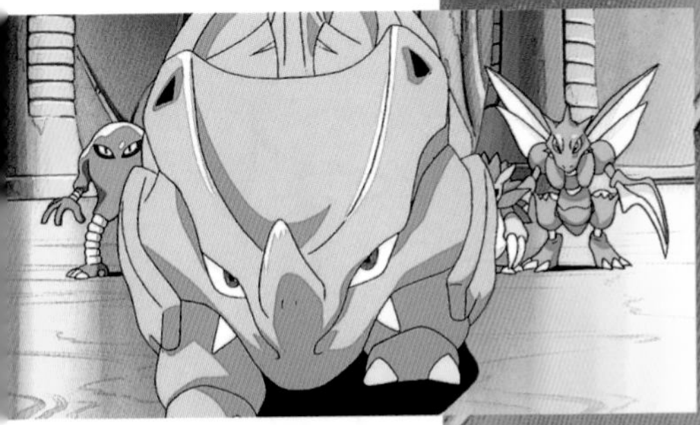

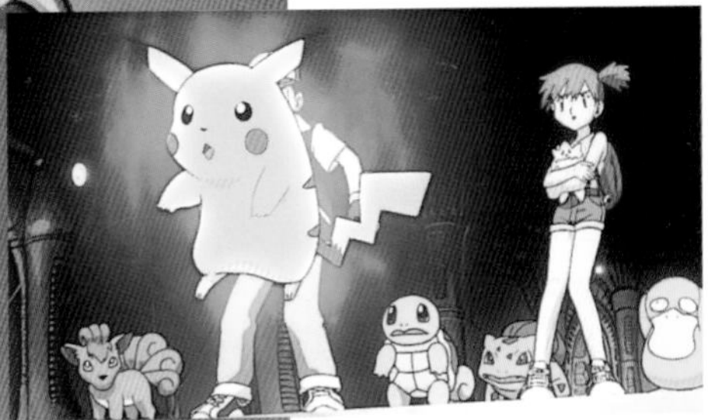

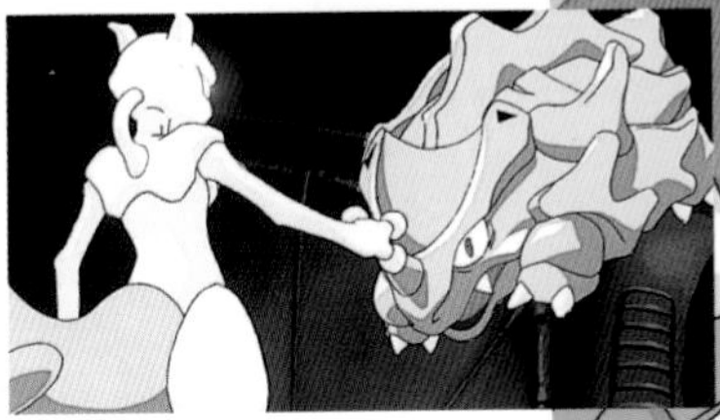

Ash catches Pikachu to break his fall. "Give up," Mewtwo commands.

Corey commands Rhyhorn to attack, but Mewtwo effortlessly flings Rhyhorn aside with one hand.

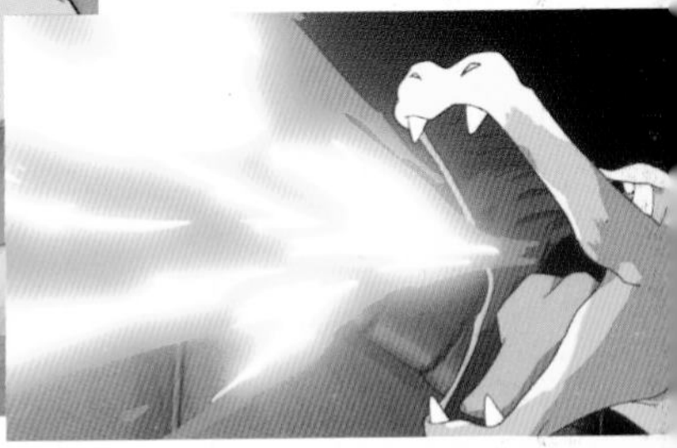

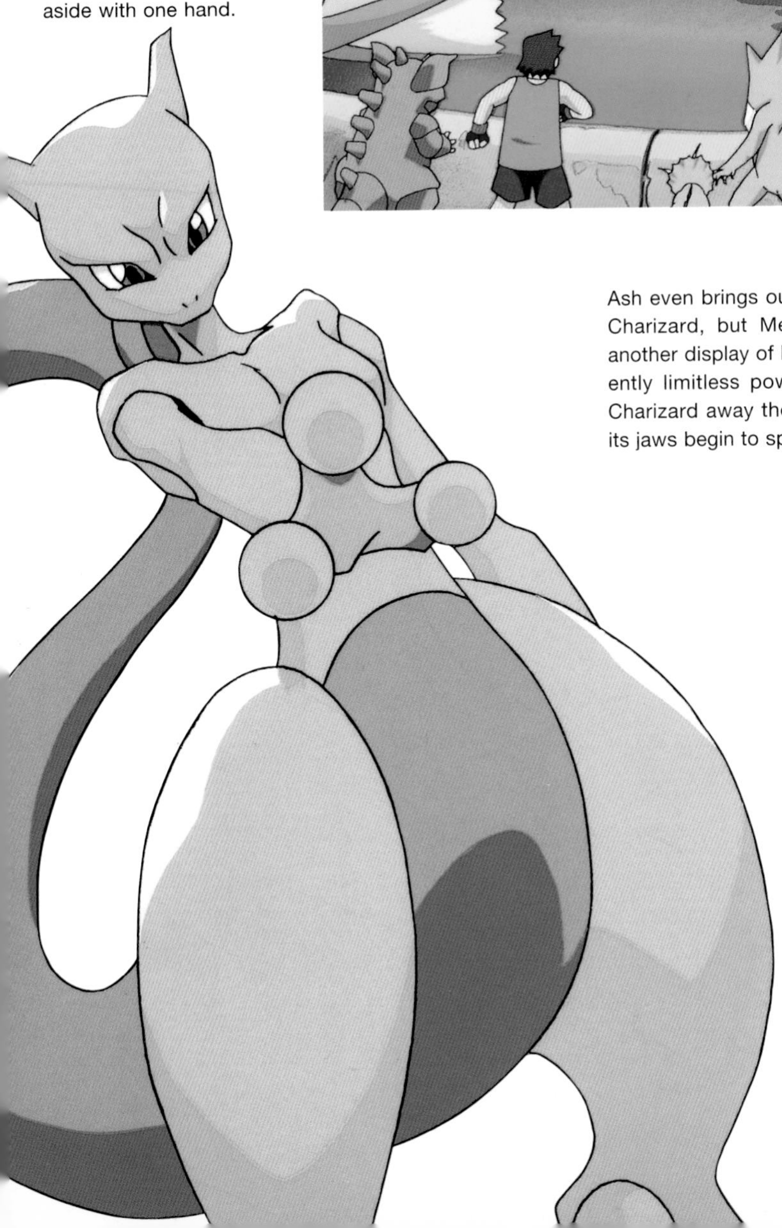

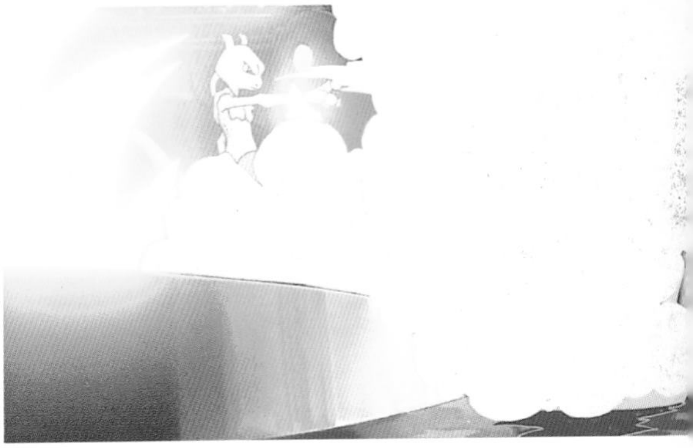

Ash even brings out his wild Charizard, but Mewtwo, in another display of his apparently limitless power, flicks Charizard away the moment its jaws begin to spurt flame.

more dependent it is on humans." A blast of energy from Mewtwo's fingertips tosses Pikachu aside.

Ash is furious. "Why you—! How dare you treat my Pikachu like that!"

The other trainers shout louder than Ash. "There isn't a Pokémon alive who can't be captured!" But none of the trainers or their Pokémon stand a chance against Mewtwo.

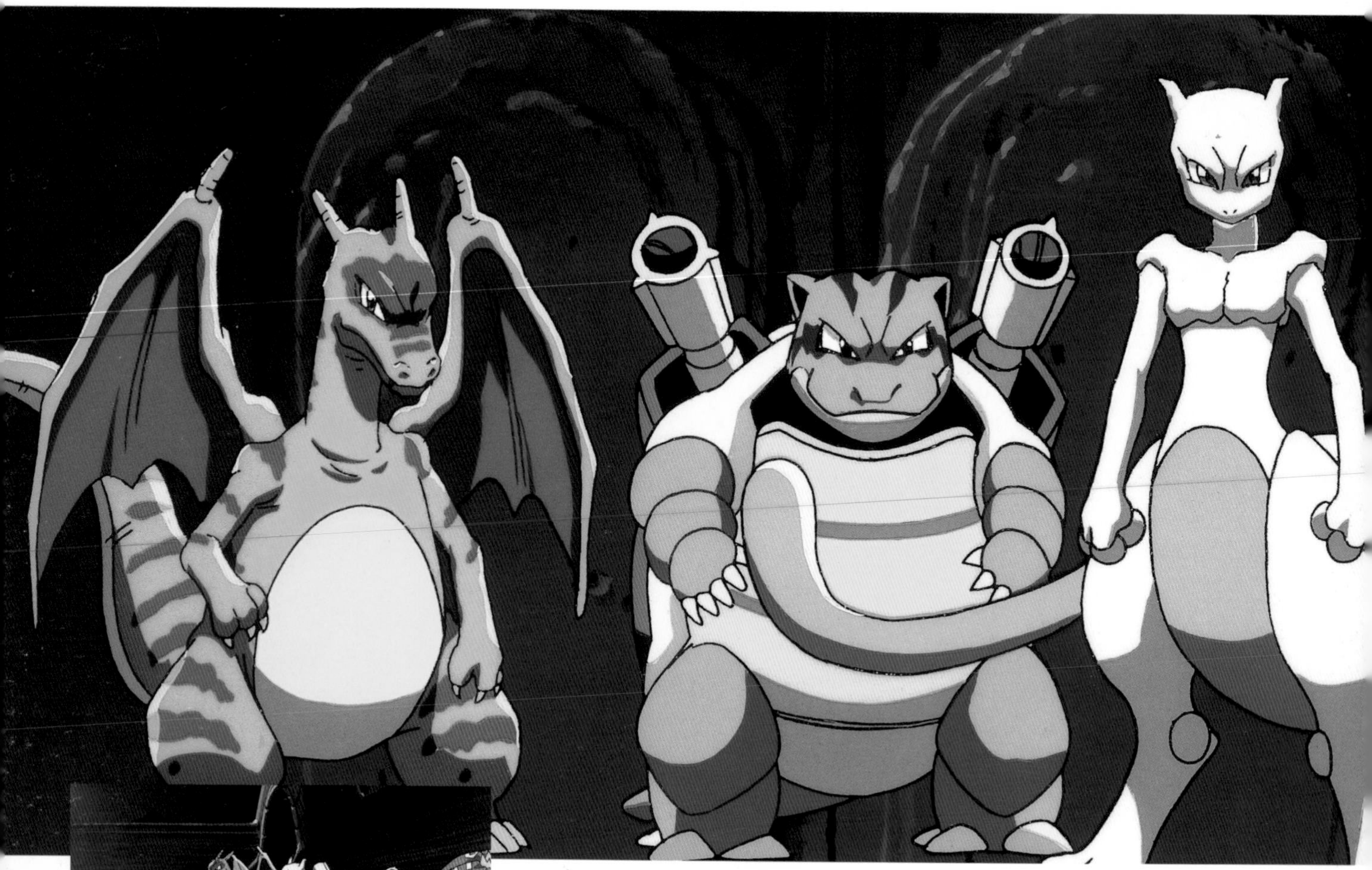

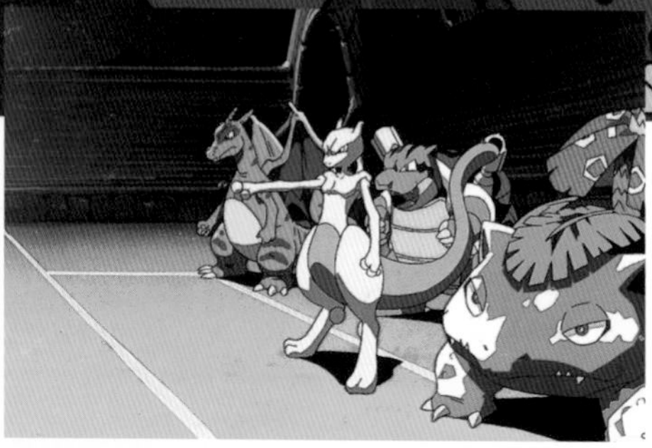

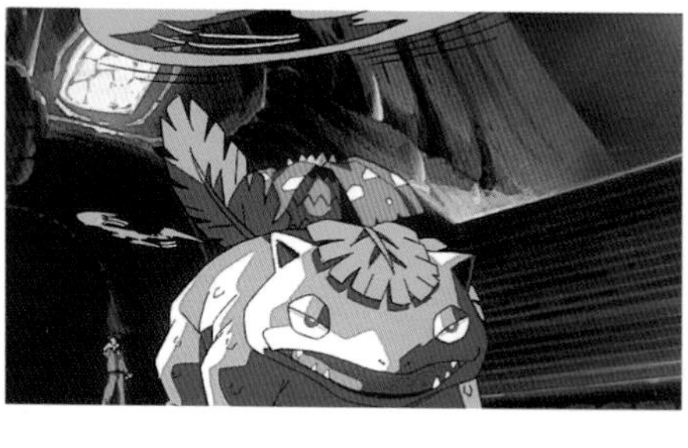

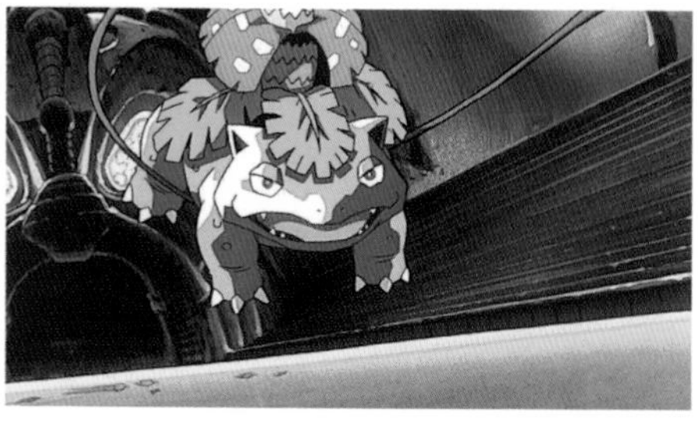

Corey's Venusaur tries a "Leaf Cutter" attack but is defeated by the "Vine Whip" from Mewtwo's Venusaur double.

Pokémon Battle Royal

Mewtwo boasts, "From the moment of my creation, I have been more powerful than any Pokémon on this planet! And I command Pokémon far better than any Pokémon trainer in the world!"

Ash finds all this hard to believe. "You'll have to prove it!"

"Is that a challenge?" Mewtwo sneers.

Mewtwo raises its arms and the three Pokémon from the underground laboratory—Charizard, Blastoise, and Venusaur—appear.

"The first Pokémon a trainer receives are Charmander, Squirtle, and Bulbasaur.... Here beside me are duplicates of the most highly evolved stage of those three Pokémon. Now who will be the first to challenge me?"

Corey's Venusaur faces Mewtwo's Venusaur double, Neesha's Blastoise challenges Mewtwo's

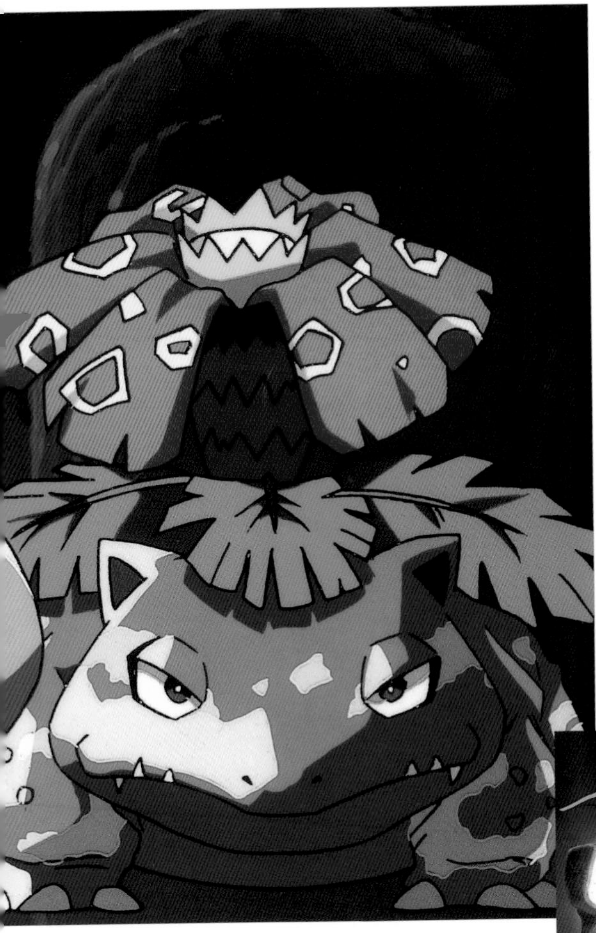

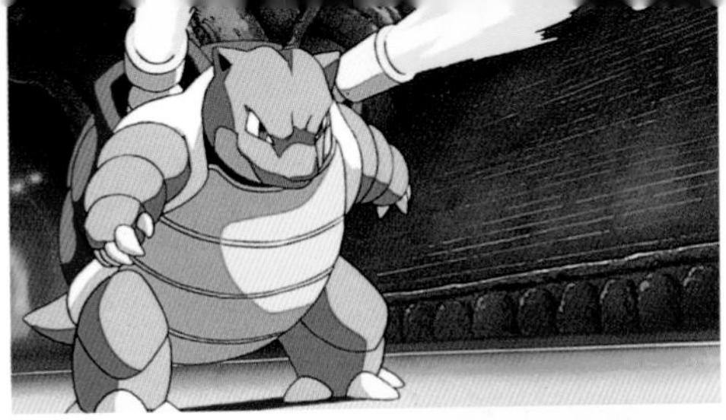

Neesha's Blastoise confronts the Blastoise double. "Attack!" Attempting to finish the battle in the first move, Blastoise launches a "Hydro Pump."

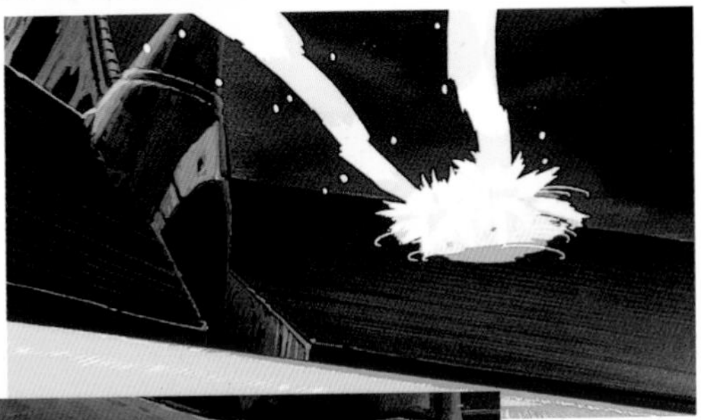

Dancing around the "Hydro Pump," the Blastoise double throws its whole body into a "Tackle." After the attack, Neesha's Blastoise faints.

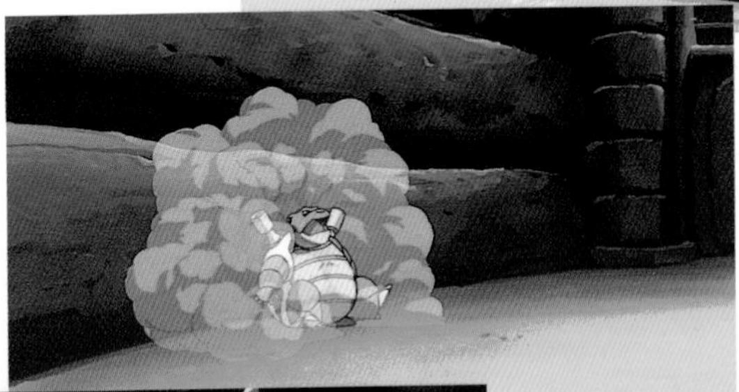

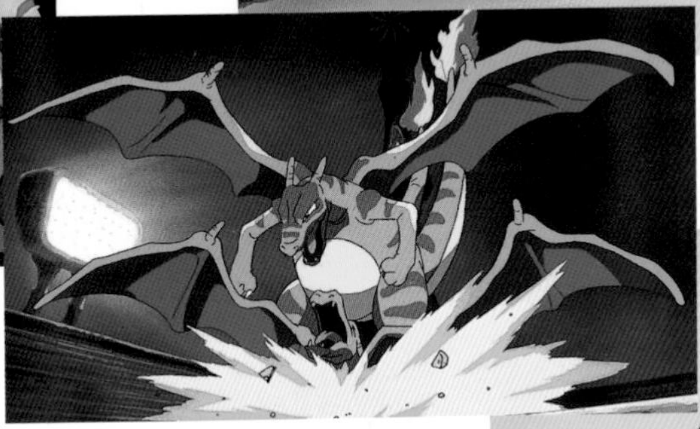

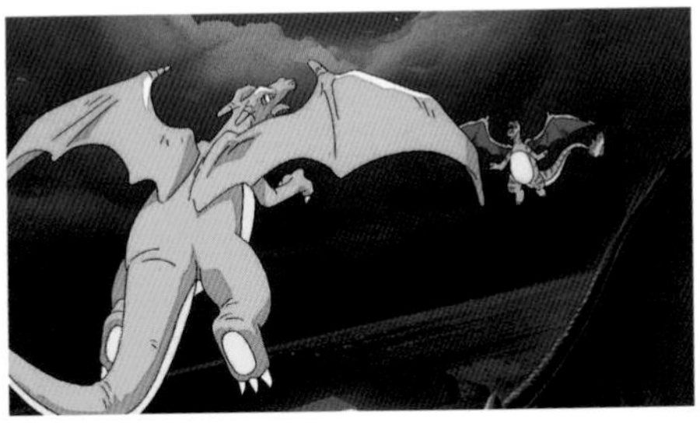

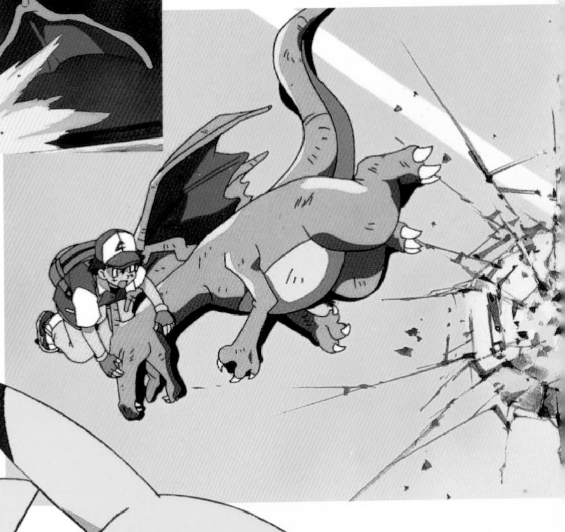

Ash, the third challenger, advises his Charizard to use its speed, but the super-speed of the Charizard double is even faster. Ash's Charizard is smashed into the floor by the earthshaking "Seismic Toss." Ash runs to Charizard, who whimpers with pain as it hits the ground.

Blastoise double, and Ash's Charizard tries to stand up to Mewtwo's Charizard double.

All the trainers' Pokémon use their strongest attacks and cleverest tricks, but against the enhanced duplicates, their best efforts fall short. Even Ash's powerful Charizard is pounded so hard into the ground that it can't get up.

Watching the raging battles unfold, Pikachu is amazed by the Pokémon doubles' skill and power.

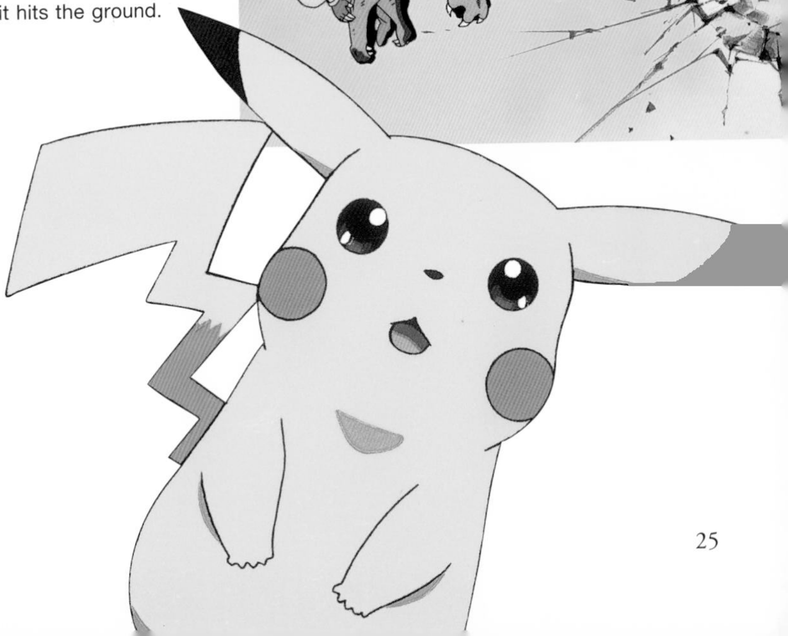

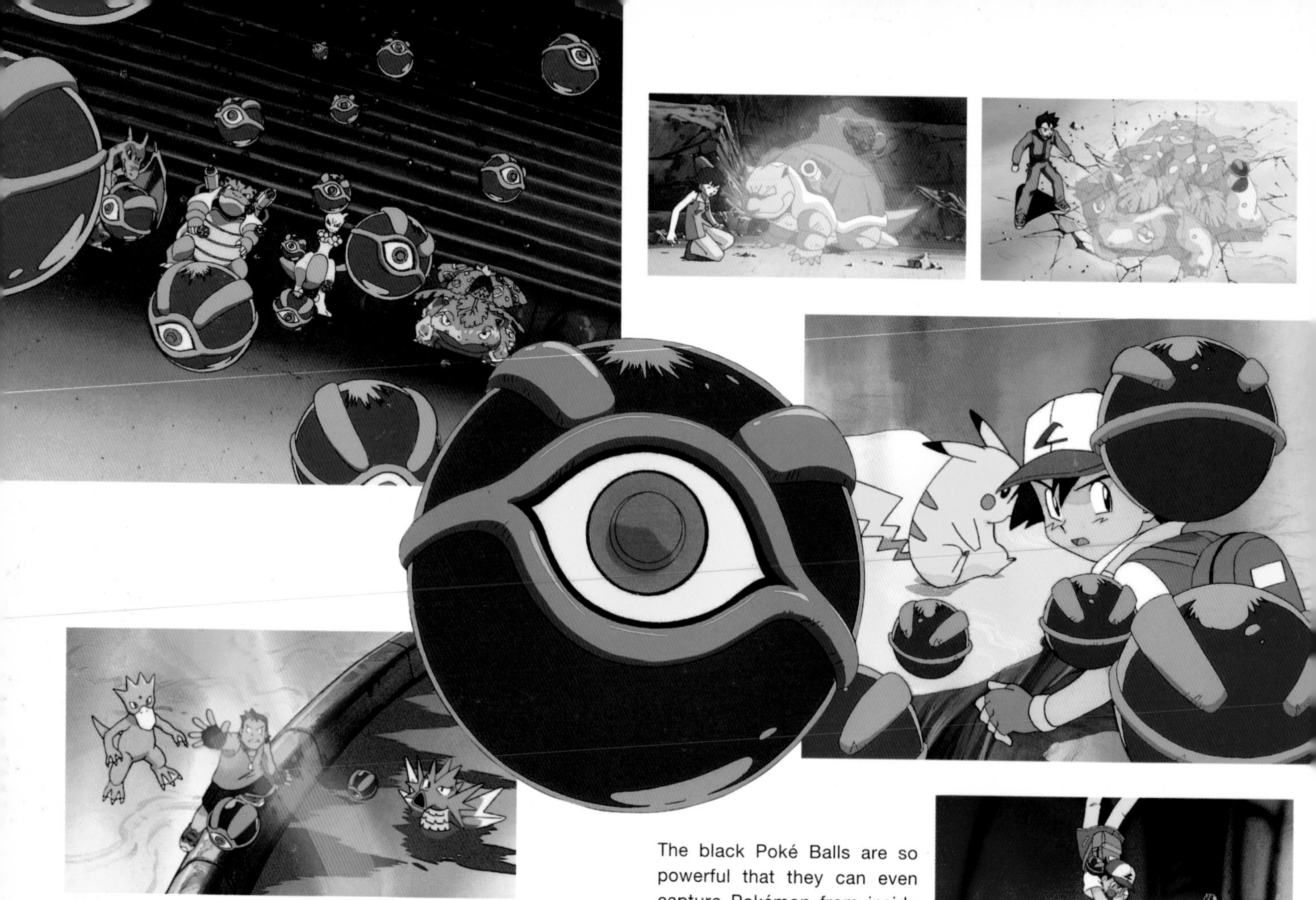

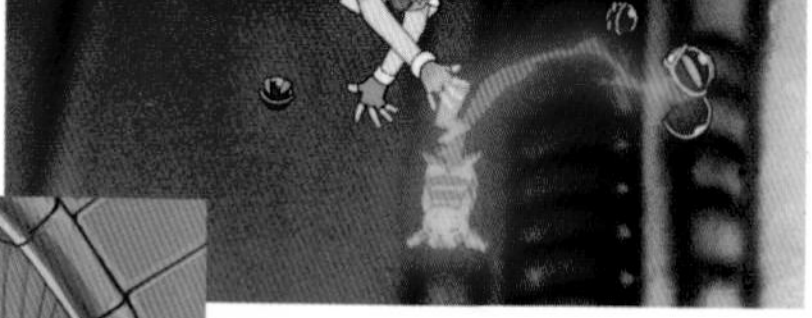

The black Poké Balls are so powerful that they can even capture Pokémon from inside their own Poké Balls. Ash gives his all to save Pikachu.

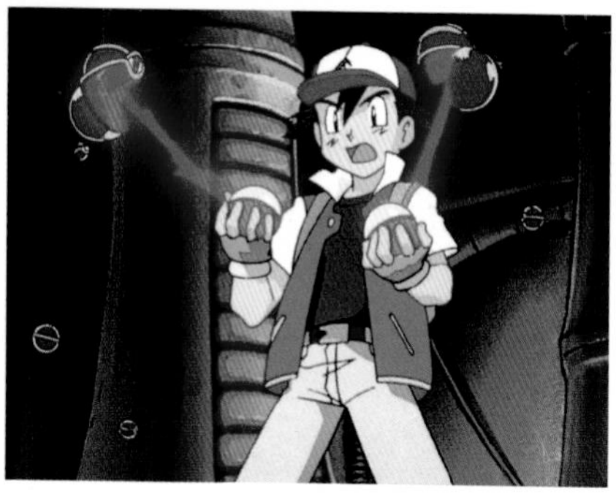

"I'll make duplicates far superior to the pitiful Pokémon you trainers are so proud of," Mewtwo declares as the air fills with hundreds of black Poké Balls.

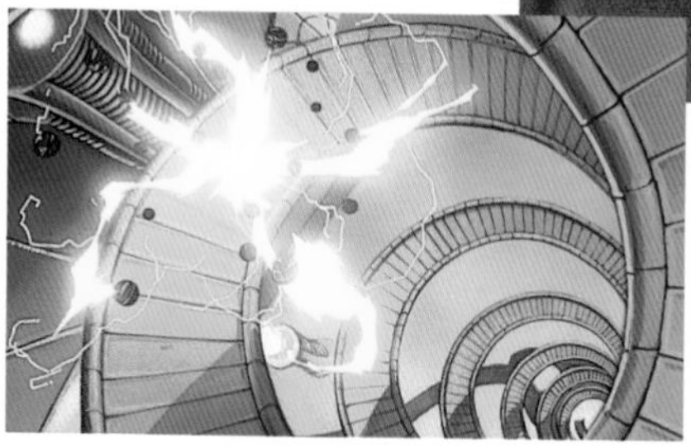

Weakened by its electric attacks against the black Poké Balls, Pikachu plunges down a spiral staircase. Ash dives after his Pokémon, but he's too late, and the Poké Balls gobble up Pikachu!

The Black Poké Balls

"See how powerful my Pokémon are?" Mewtwo gloats. Then suddenly a barrage of black Poké Balls fills the air and begins capturing the other trainers' Pokémon, one after the other.

"Stop it!" Ash protests. "That's against the Pokémon League rules!" Capturing another trainer's Pokémon is not allowed.

Mewtwo brushes Ash's accusation aside. "I make my own rules."

The Poké Balls shoot towards the Pokémon like black rain. They do their best to escape, but one by one they are sucked into the balls.

"Run, Pikachu!" Ash shouts as the Poké Balls zero in on the last remaining Pokémon....

Pikachu bravely tries to fend off the black

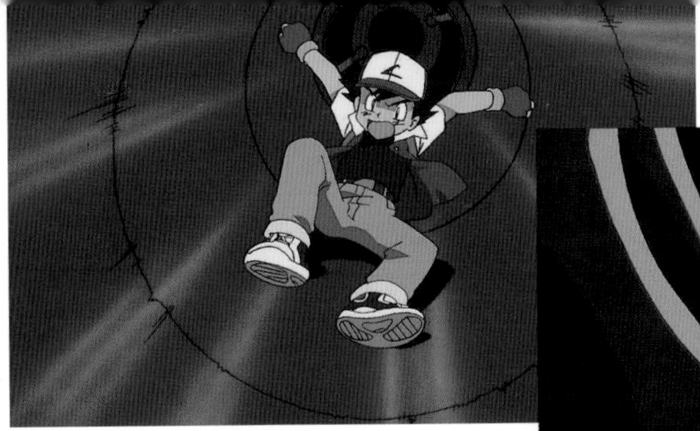

Racing after the Poké Ball that captured Pikachu, Ash dives into a chute and slides down into the underground laboratory, where a copy of Pikachu is already being made. Jumping inside the machine, Ash manages to free Pikachu.

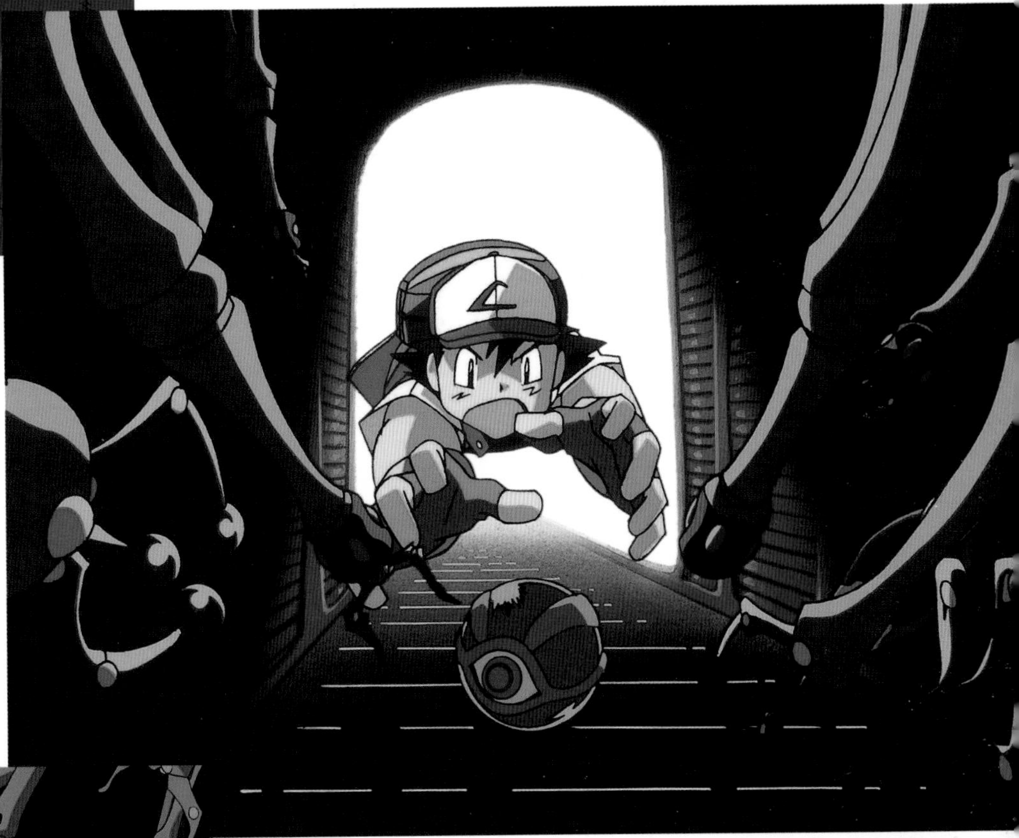

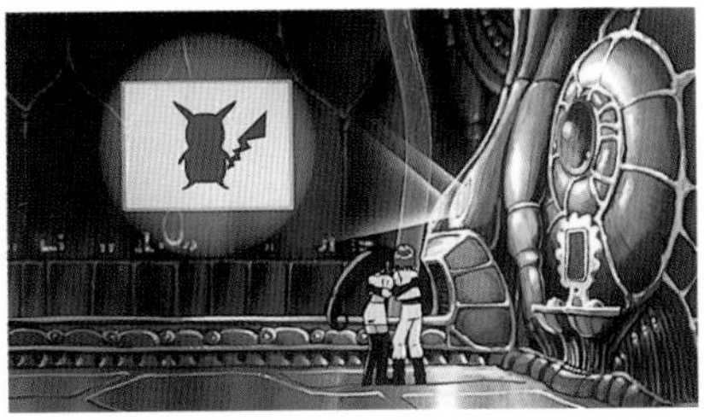

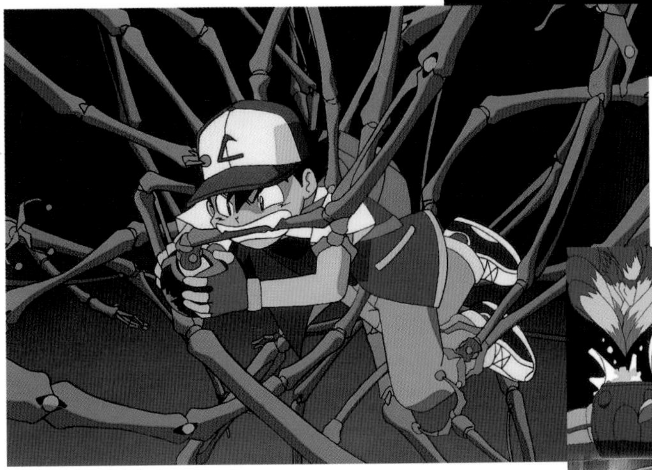

After pouring out the duplicates, the machine explodes with a big bang.

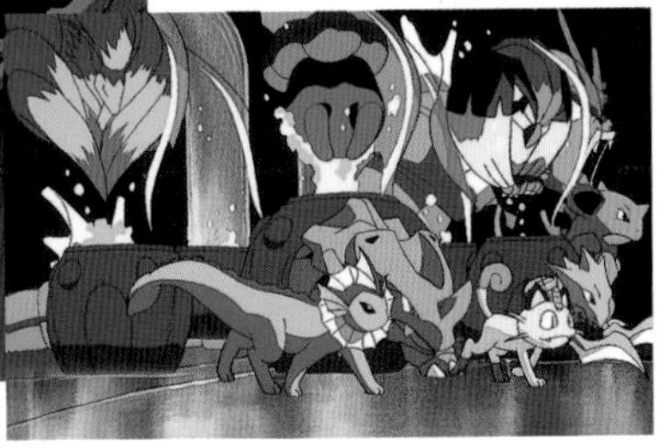

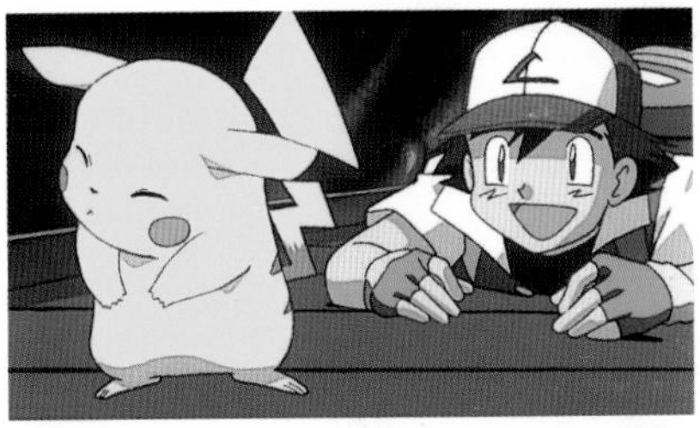

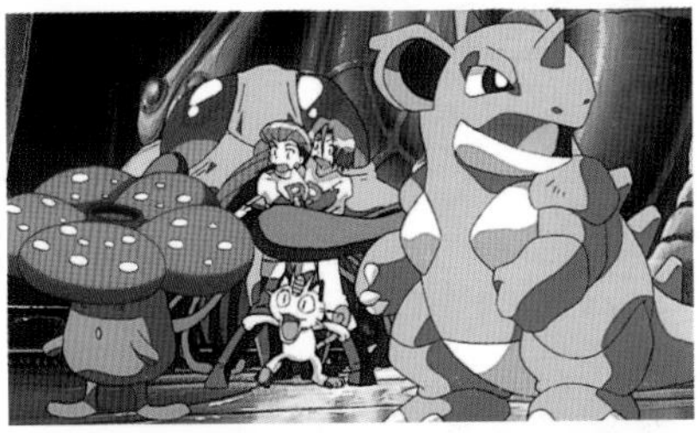

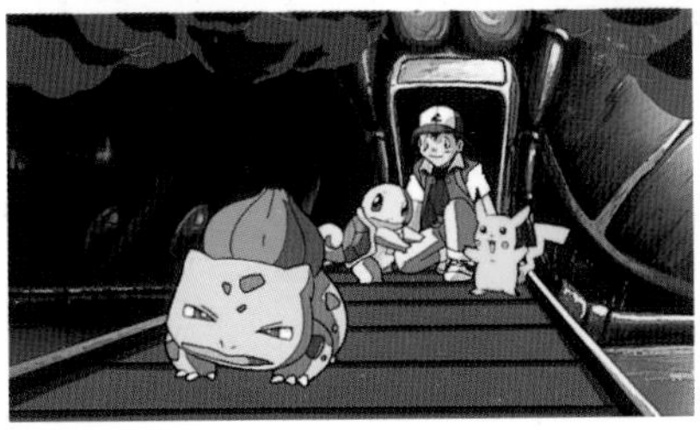

Destroying the machine frees the captured Pokémon.

Poké Balls but, overpowered by their sheer number, Pikachu's electric attacks gradually weaken. Finally, out of energy, Pikachu collapses and is swallowed up by a Poké Ball.

In hot pursuit of the Poké Ball that caught Pikachu, Ash dives into the Pokémon Duplicating Machine. Inside, Ash wreaks havoc with its hardware. Finally, the machine breaks down and all the Pokémon duplicates inside it come pouring out—along with the original Pokémon captured by the Poké Balls!

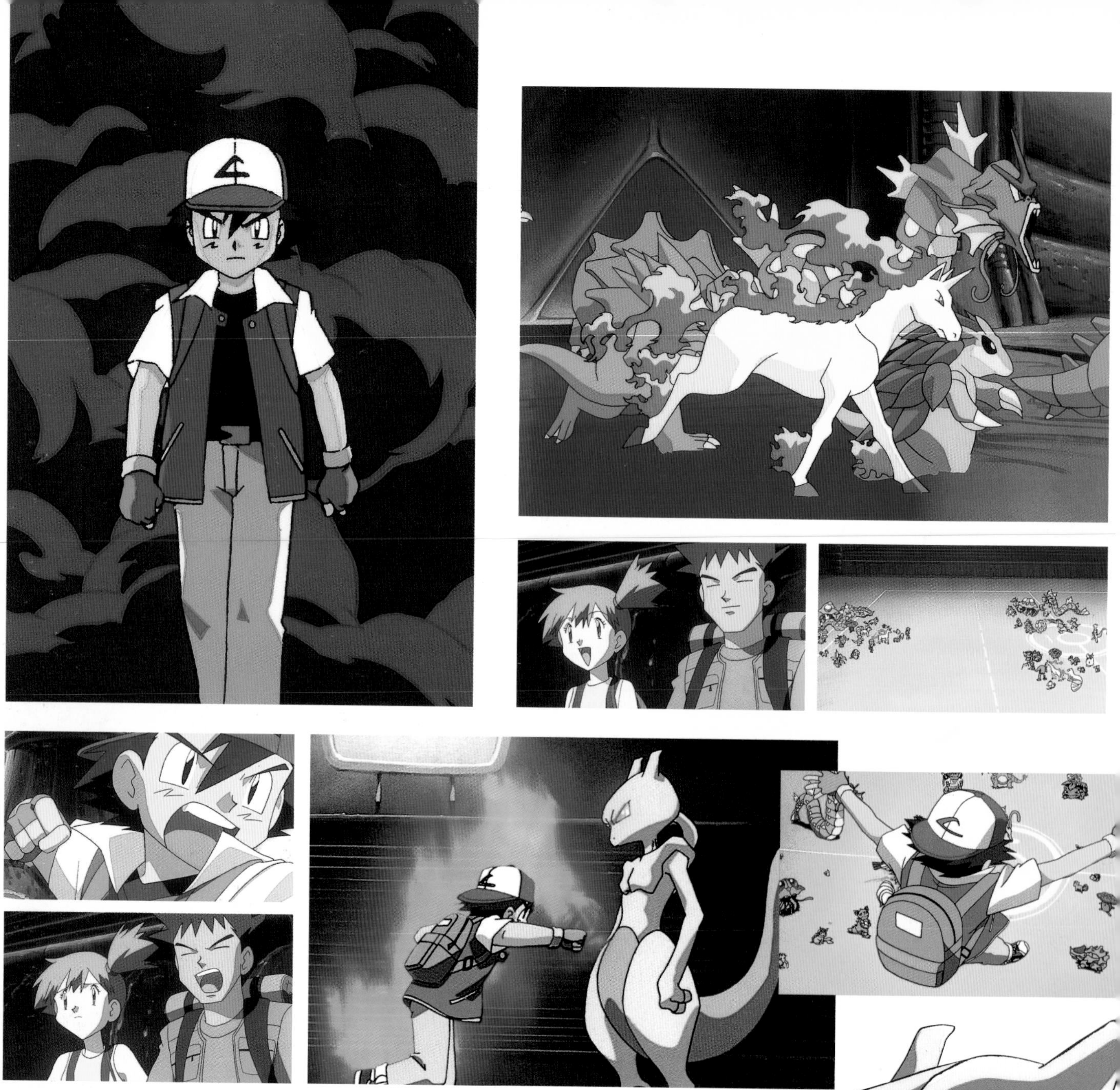

Mew vs. Mewtwo

"I will not take your worthless lives, humans! But you must leave this island at once—if you can get through the storm, that is!"

Just as Mewtwo finishes his victory speech, the floor of the arena splits open and all the duplicate Pokémon pour out, followed by a huge black cloud of smoke. Ash emerges from the smoke, furious with Mewtwo. "This is unforgivable!" he shouts.

Ash is followed by the original Pokémon, who race back to their trainers.

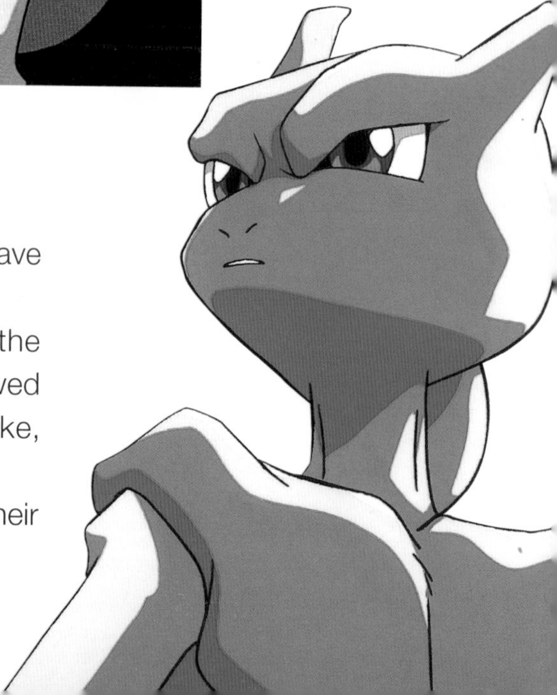

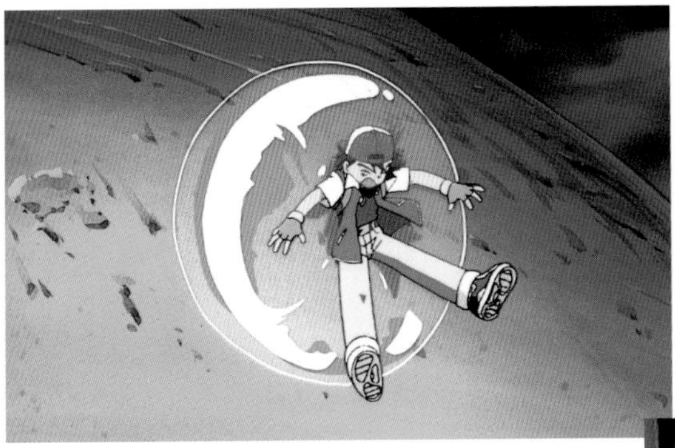

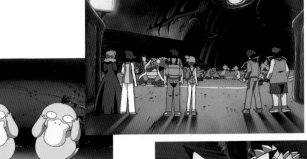

As if this is all a game, Mew floats playfully around on a bubble.

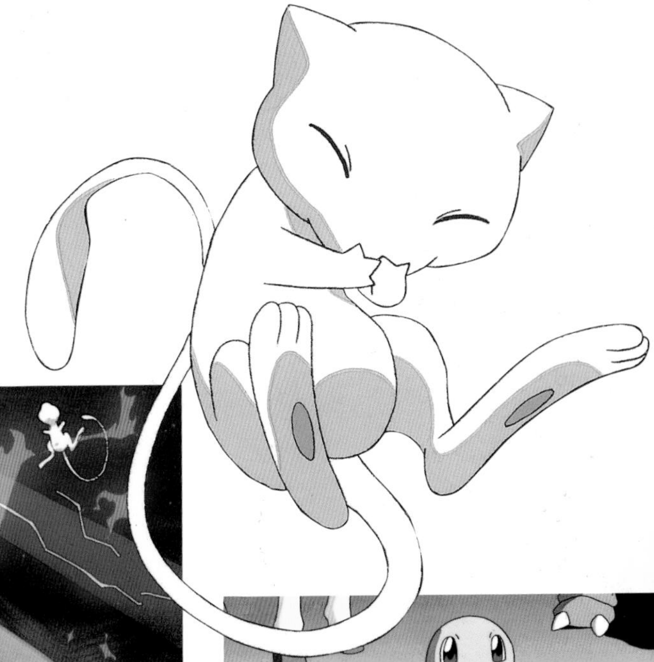

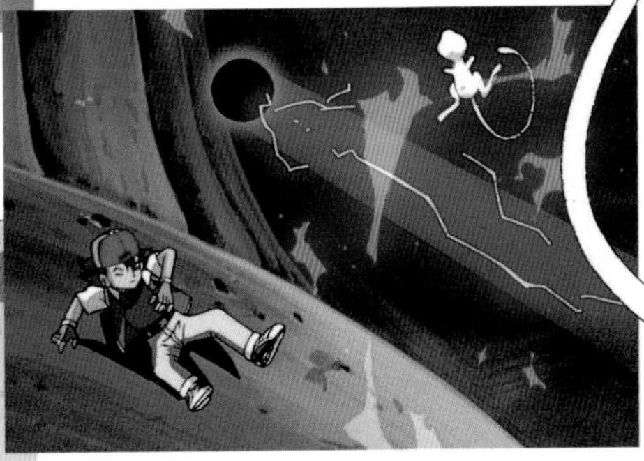

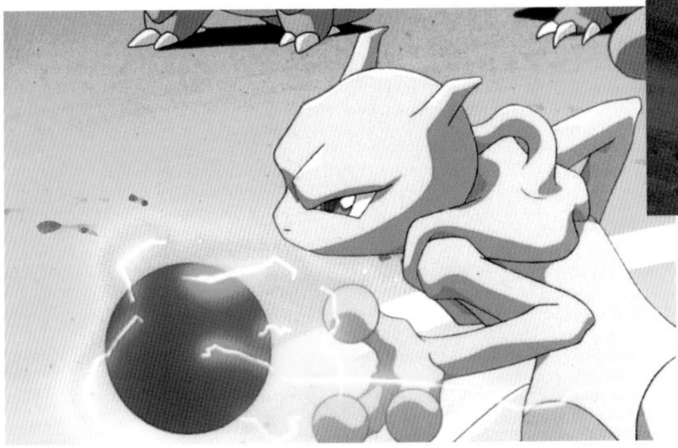

Mew's lighthearted manner irritates Mewtwo. But as they fight, Mewtwo is shocked to discover that Mew's power rivals its own!

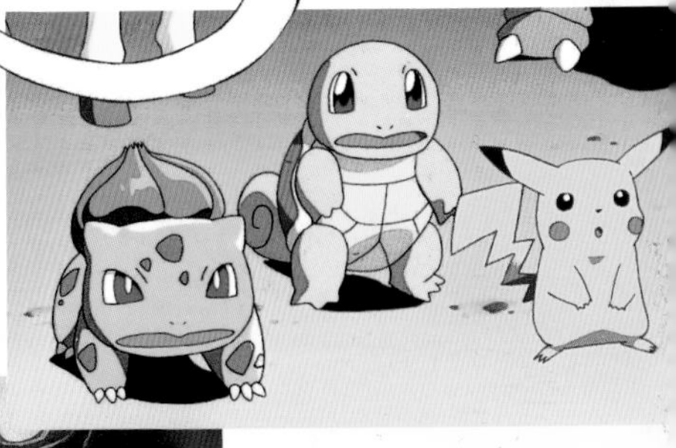

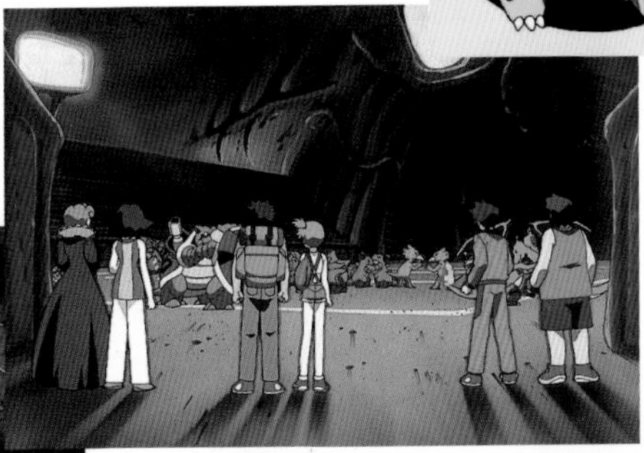

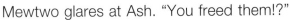

The trainers watch helplessly as the conflict between Mew and Mewtwo sets off a battle between the Pokémon and their doubles.

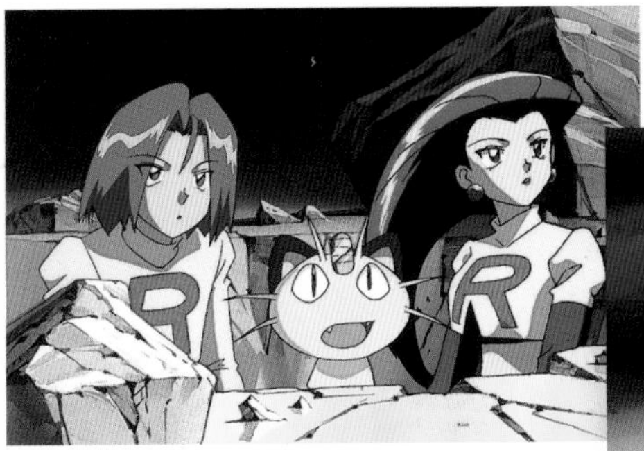

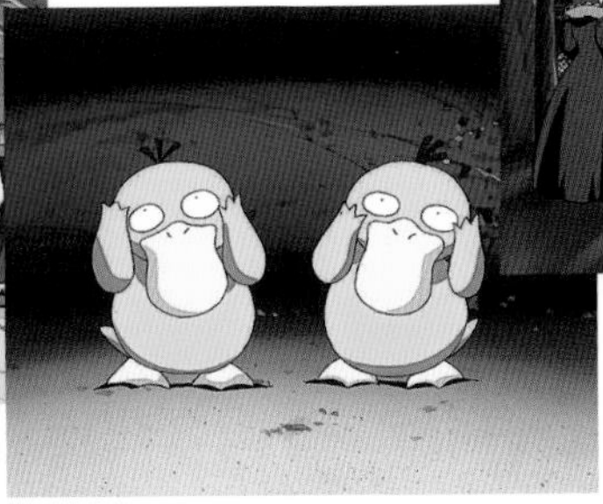

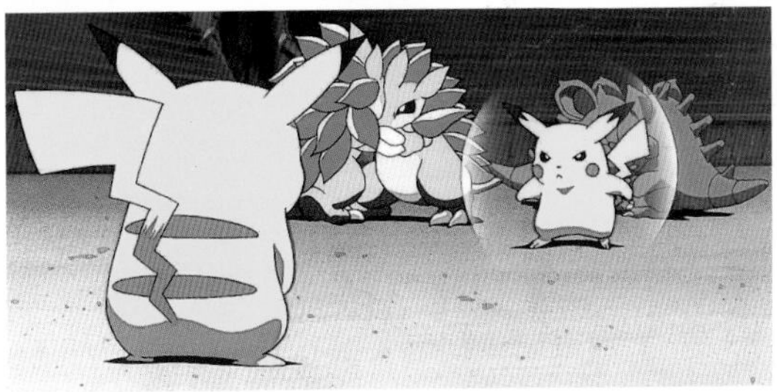

Mewtwo glares at Ash. "You freed them!?"

"Yes! And I'll do everything in my power to protect my Pokémon—my friends!" Ash charges Mewtwo. In a fury, Mewtwo swipes Ash off the ground and flings him at the wall with all his might. But just as Ash is about to smash into the wall, some mysterious force cushions the blow. Everyone stares in amazement.

Just above the arena floats a glowing white Pokémon. It's Mew! Mew saved Ash!

Mewtwo turns to the white Pokémon. "So you're Mew.... From you, I was created. But I am stronger! I challenge you to a battle to the finish to determine which of us is the most powerful! You or I! Your Pokémon against mine!"

With that, Mewtwo attacks Mew. Mew counterattacks. As if that were a signal, all the Pokémon and their doubles begin to battle each other.

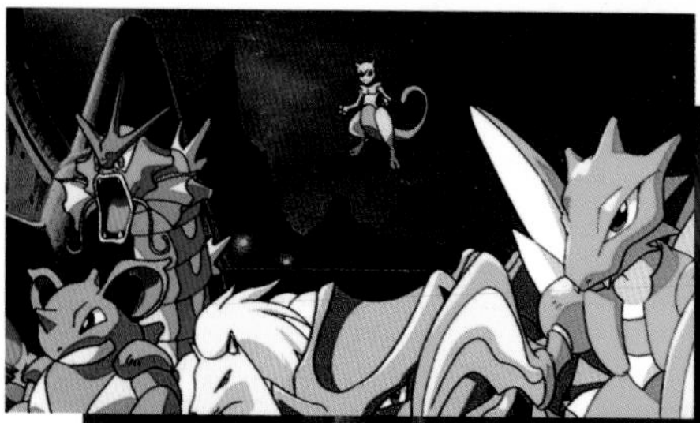

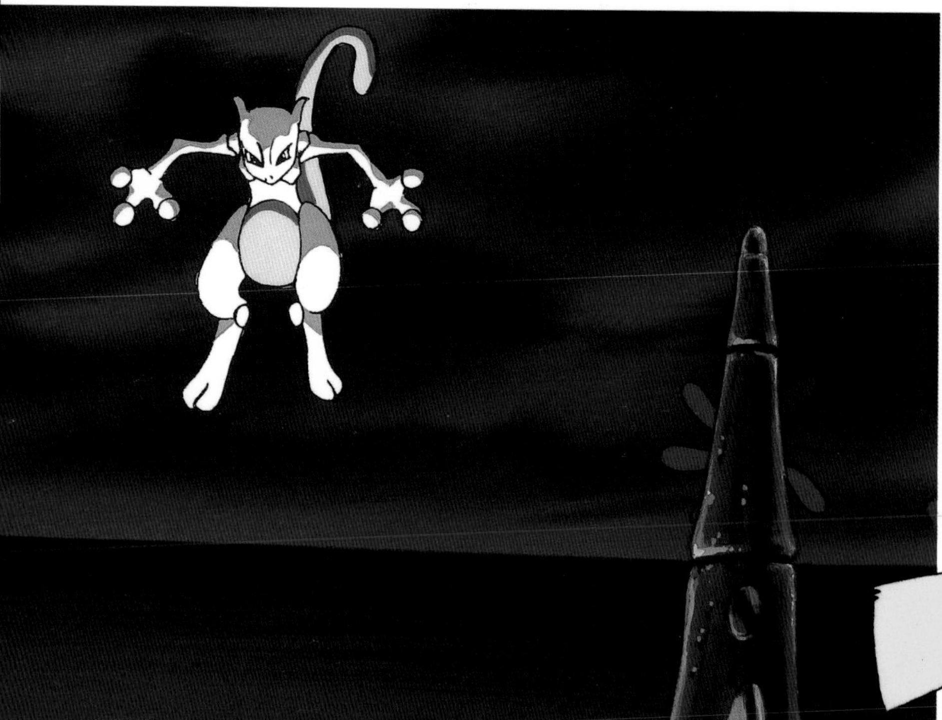

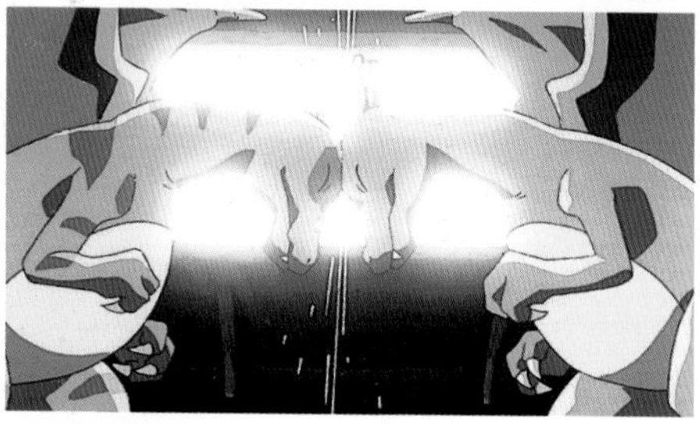

The duplicates feel compelled to protect their territory by chasing off the originals, but as they fight, they hurt themselves, too. Both the originals and the duplicates are living beings; only the way they were brought to life is different.

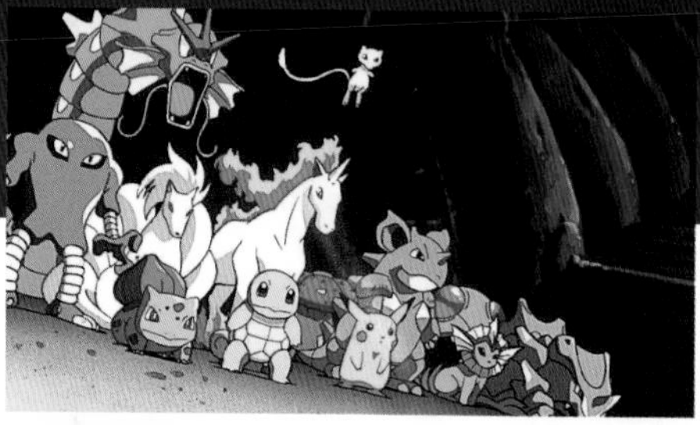

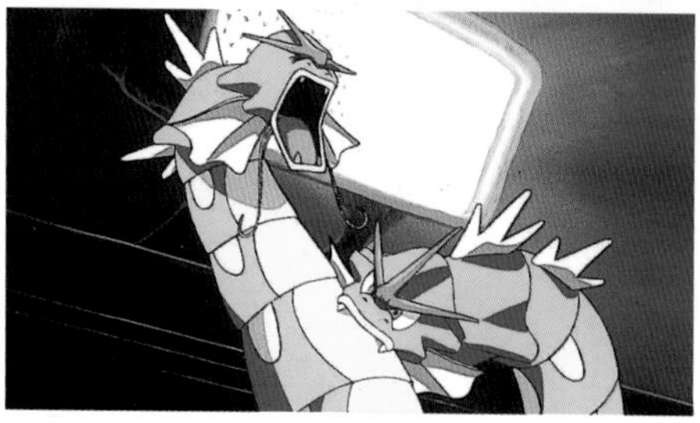

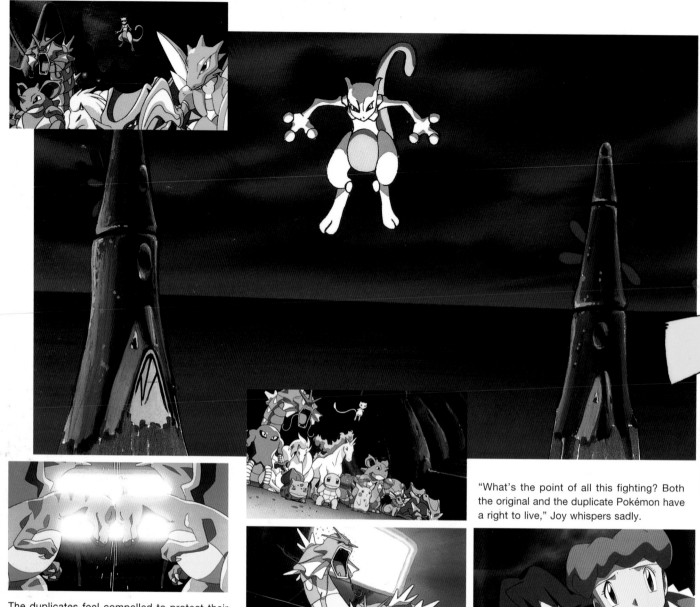

"What's the point of all this fighting? Both the original and the duplicate Pokémon have a right to live," Joy whispers sadly.

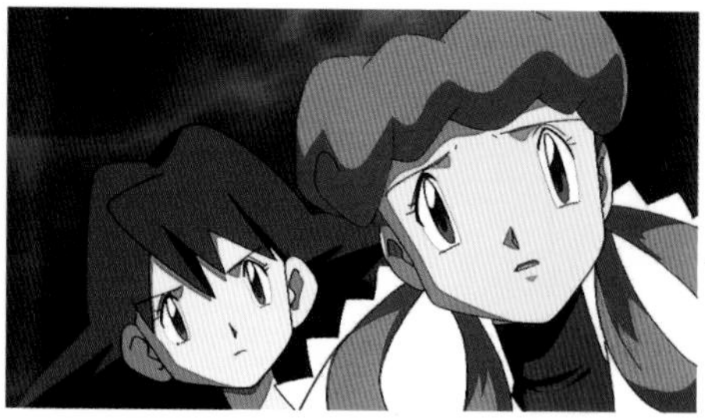

A Tragic Battle

The battles continue without a respite.

The Pikachu double shocks poor Pikachu relentlessly. But when Pikachu's double hits Pikachu, the double winces too, as if its attacks hurt them both!

According to the Encyclopedia of Biology: "An individual of a species will not tolerate another of the same species on its territory. That is the nature of living things."

Mewtwo was manufactured, but now it is a living thing. All the Pokémon, both the originals and the duplicates, are living things, unable to tolerate each other's presence. They fall to the ground in exhaustion, but they continue their feeble battles....

The battle between Mew and Mewtwo rages on and on. It looks as if the fighting between the original and the duplicate Pokémon can't stop

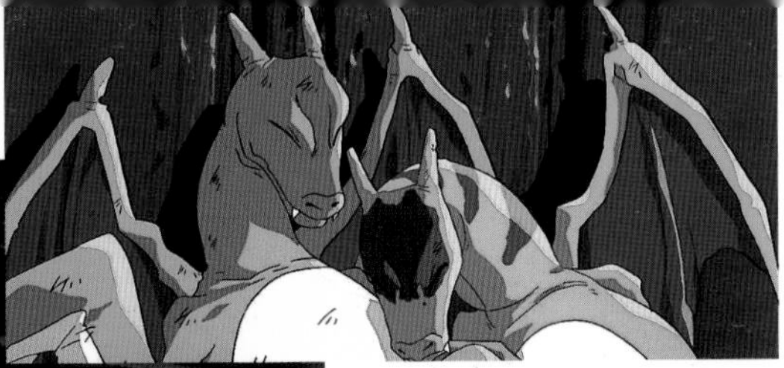

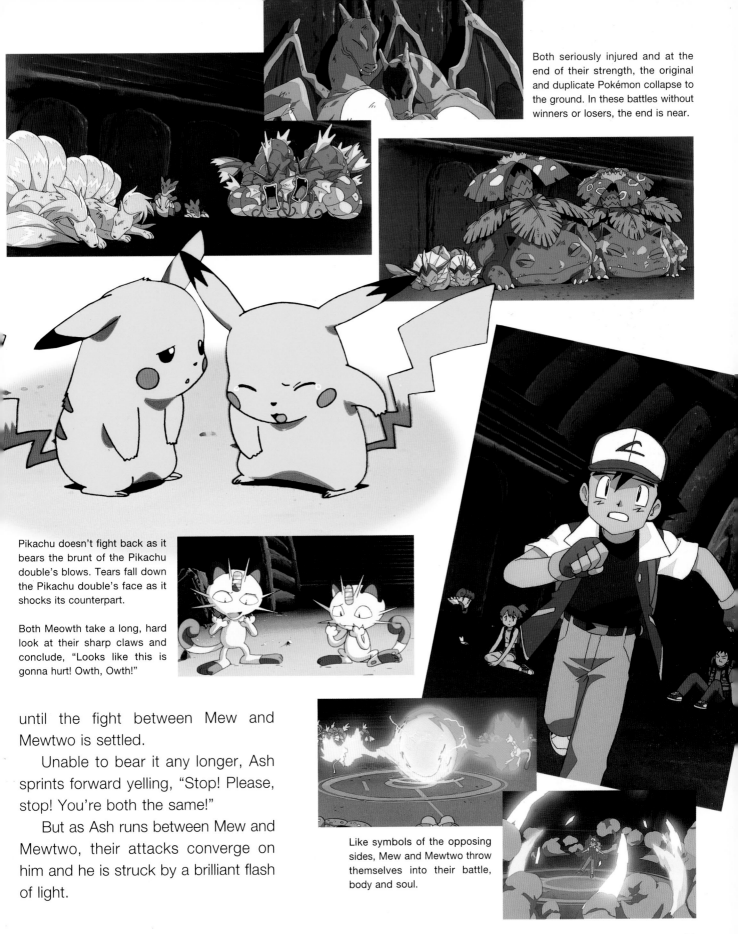

Both seriously injured and at the end of their strength, the original and duplicate Pokémon collapse to the ground. In these battles without winners or losers, the end is near.

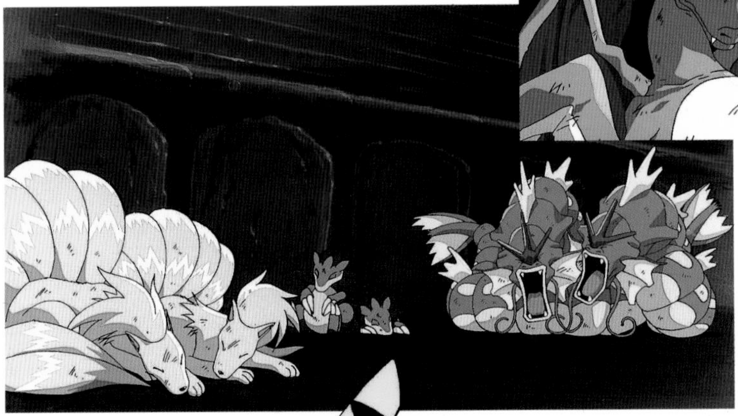

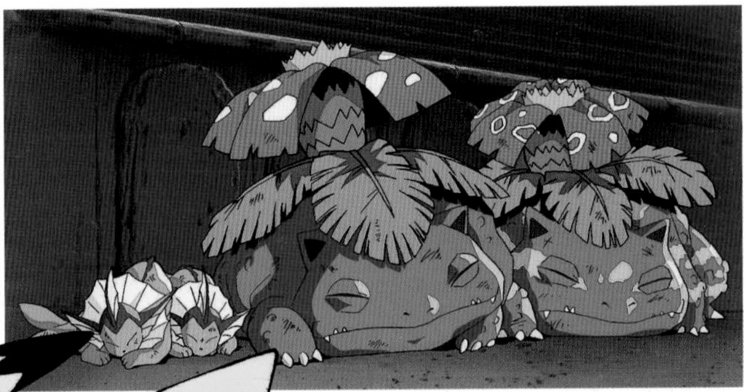

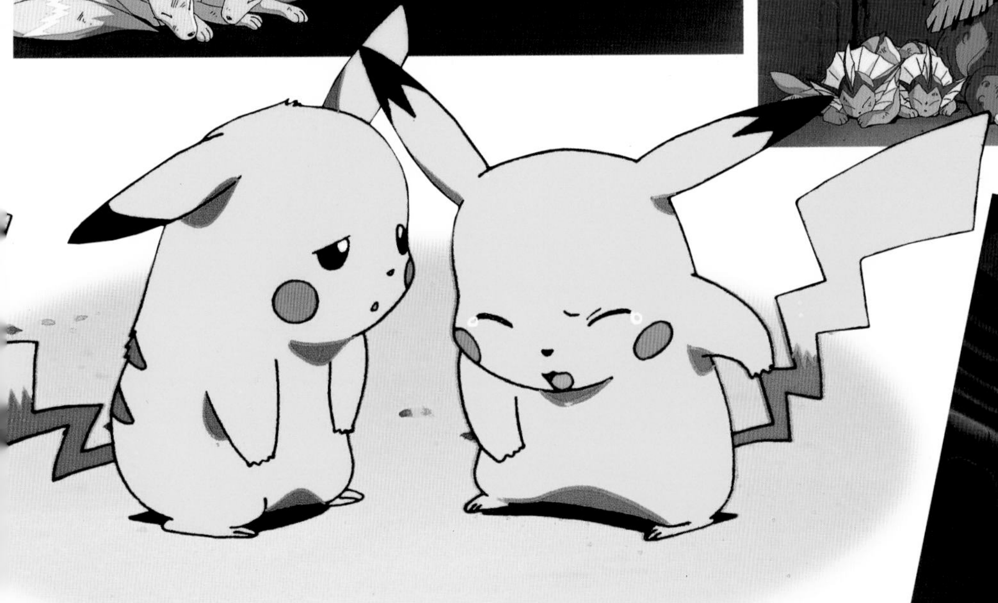

Pikachu doesn't fight back as it bears the brunt of the Pikachu double's blows. Tears fall down the Pikachu double's face as it shocks its counterpart.

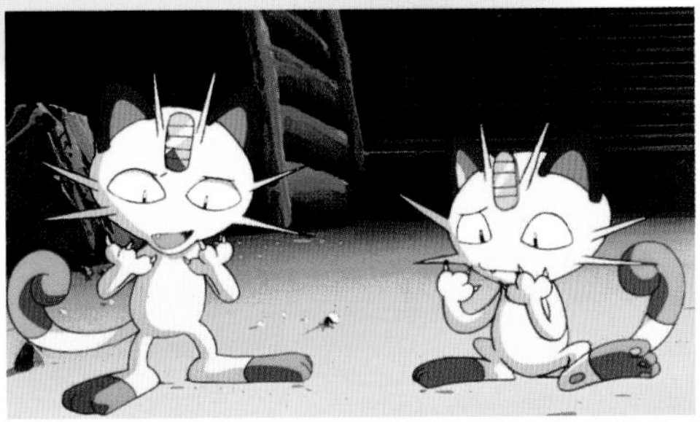

Both Meowth take a long, hard look at their sharp claws and conclude, "Looks like this is gonna hurt! Owth, Owth!"

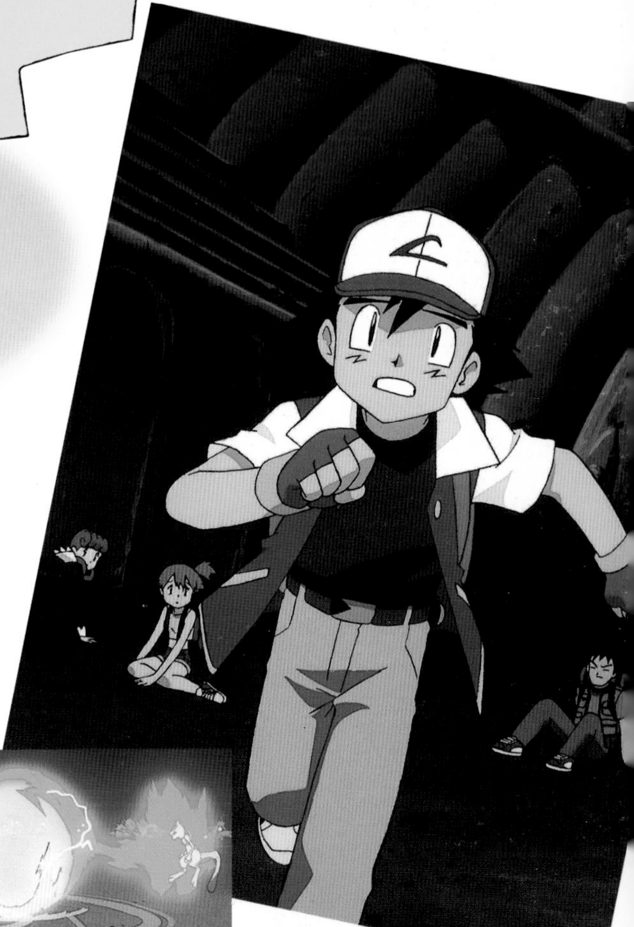

until the fight between Mew and Mewtwo is settled.

Unable to bear it any longer, Ash sprints forward yelling, "Stop! Please, stop! You're both the same!"

But as Ash runs between Mew and Mewtwo, their attacks converge on him and he is struck by a brilliant flash of light.

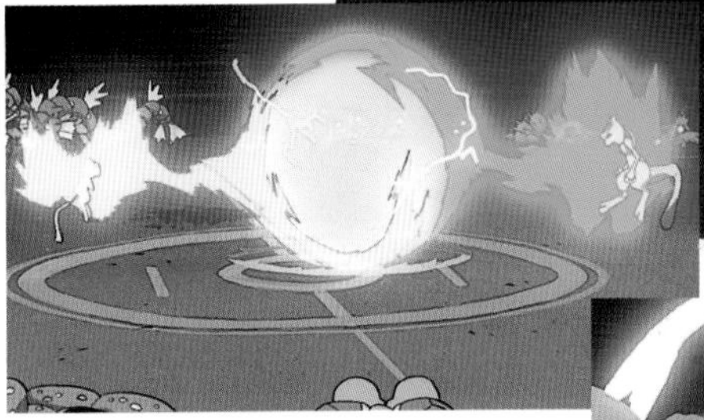

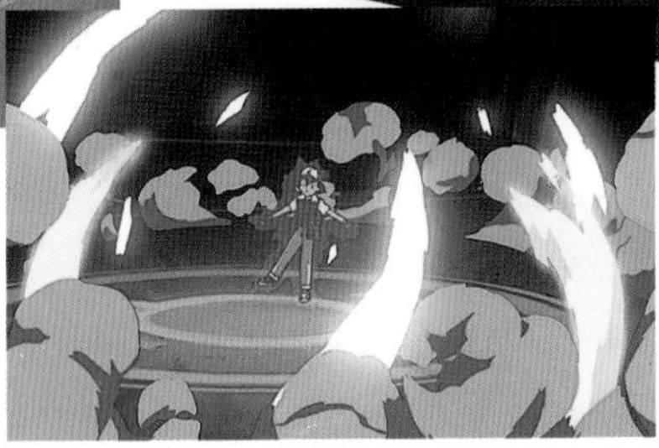

Like symbols of the opposing sides, Mew and Mewtwo throw themselves into their battle, body and soul.

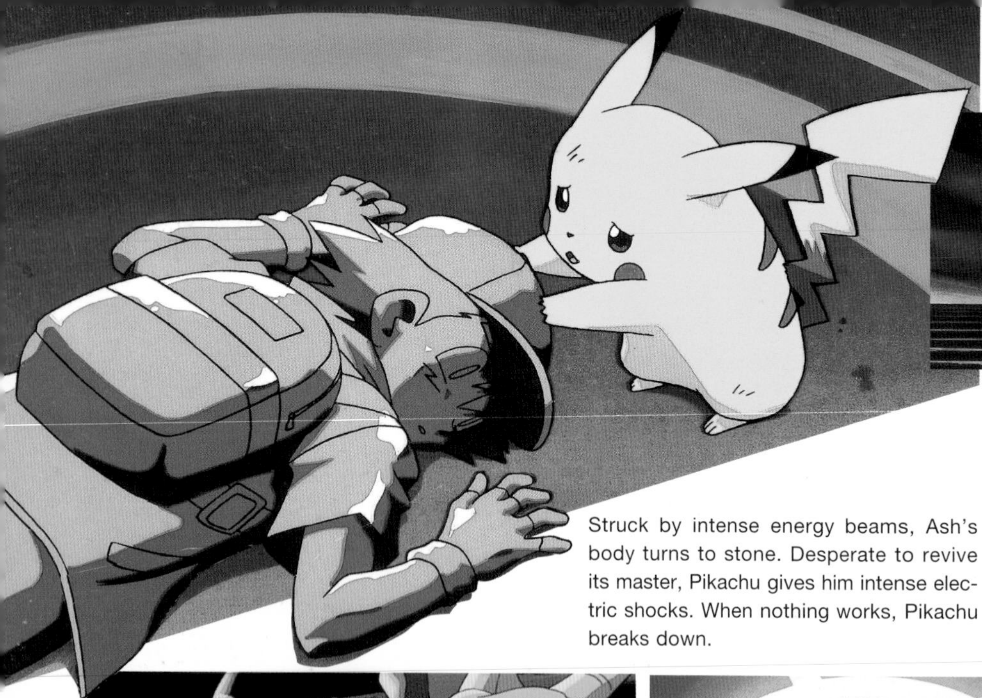

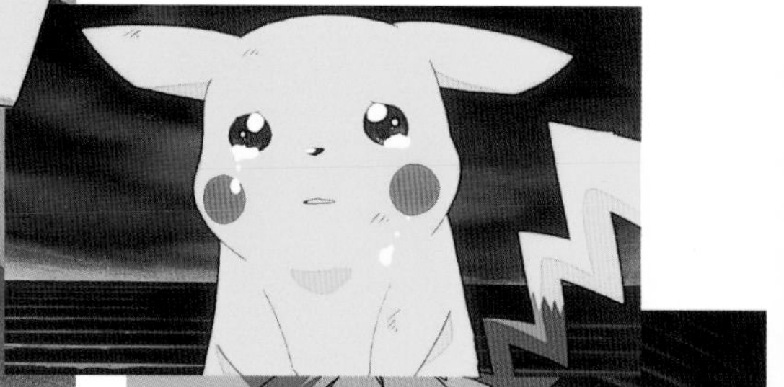

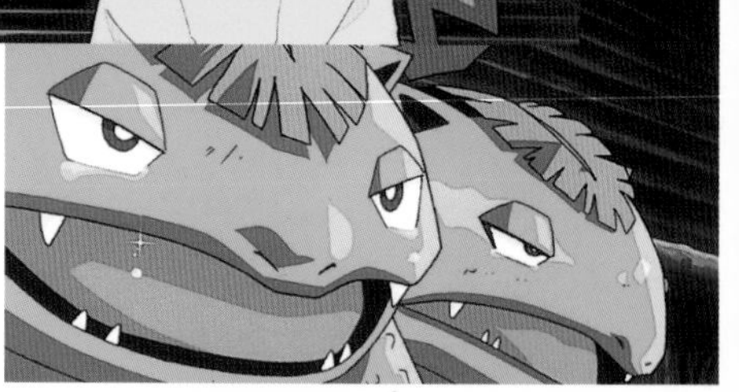

Struck by intense energy beams, Ash's body turns to stone. Desperate to revive its master, Pikachu gives him intense electric shocks. When nothing works, Pikachu breaks down.

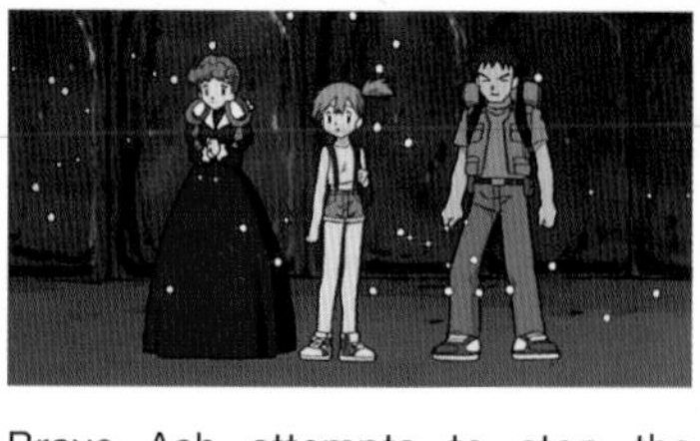

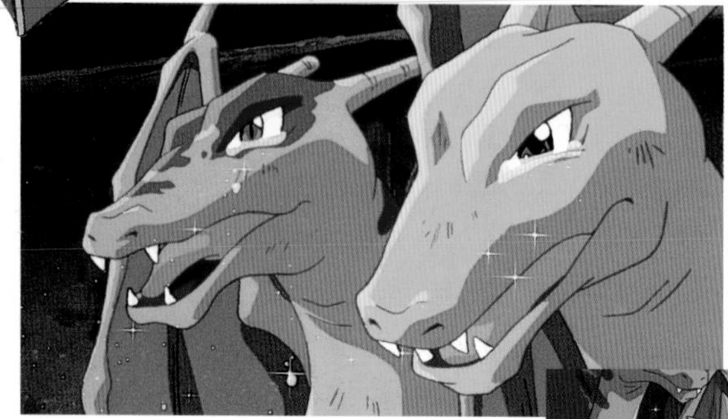

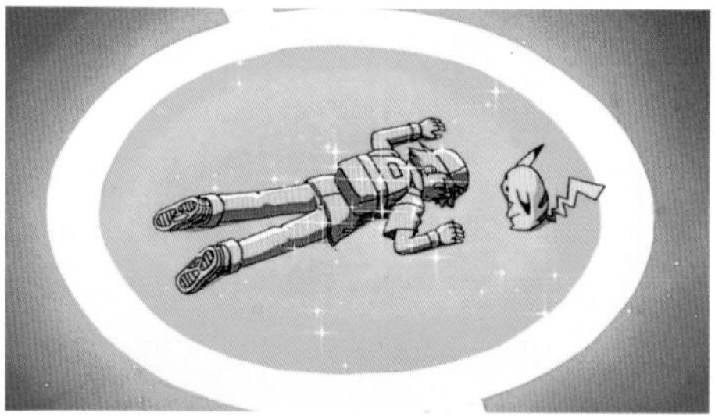

Brave Ash attempts to stop the senseless battle. Pikachu's grief moves the other Pokémon to tears. Miraculously, the Pokémon's tears transform into glimmers of light that gently surround Ash's body.

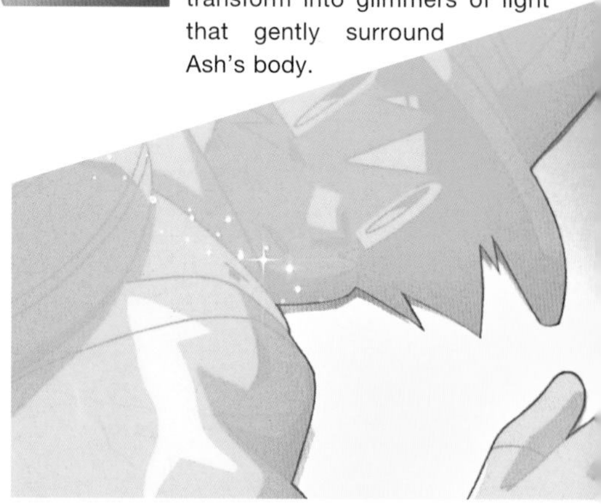

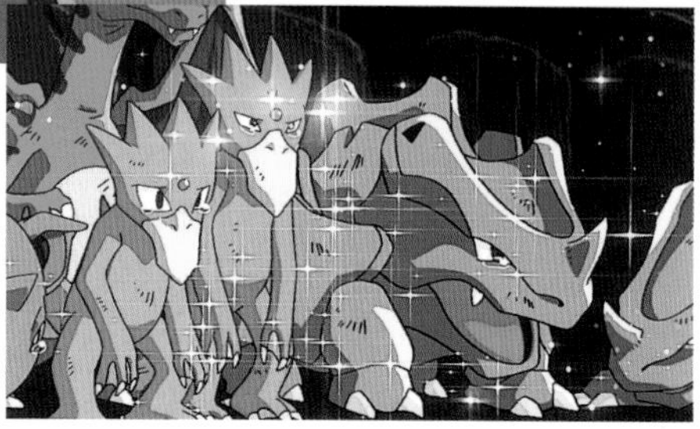

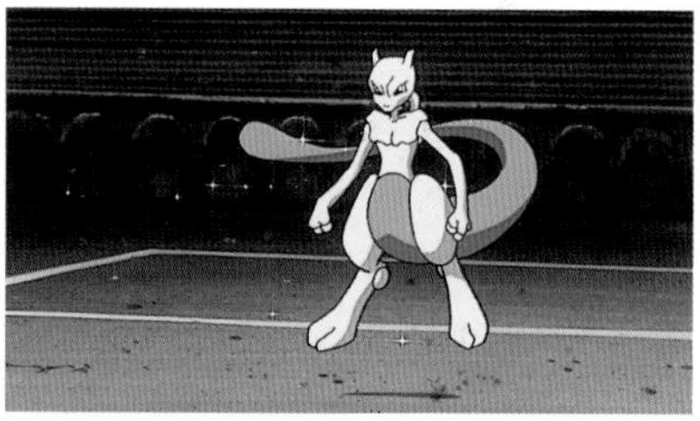

Somewhere in the World...

The bursts of energy turn Ash into stone and he falls to the floor with a sickening thump! In shock, Mew and Mewtwo stop fighting.

"Unheard of! A human attempting to stop a Pokémon battle!" Mewtwo exclaims in disbelief.

Pikachu rushes to Ash. "Pikapi... Pikapi..." But Ash doesn't answer. Pikachu tries a "Thundershock" and a "Thunderbolt" to jolt him back to life, but Ash doesn't move a muscle.

Tears begin to fall from Pikachu's eyes. Watching Pikachu at Ash's side, all the Pokémon stop fighting. Then they begin to cry, their tears glistening as they roll down their faces. Miraculously, the tears sparkle, rise up into the air, and swirl around Ash's still body.

Mewtwo is amazed. "Pokémon shedding tears over a human?"

When the glow surrounding Ash dissipates,

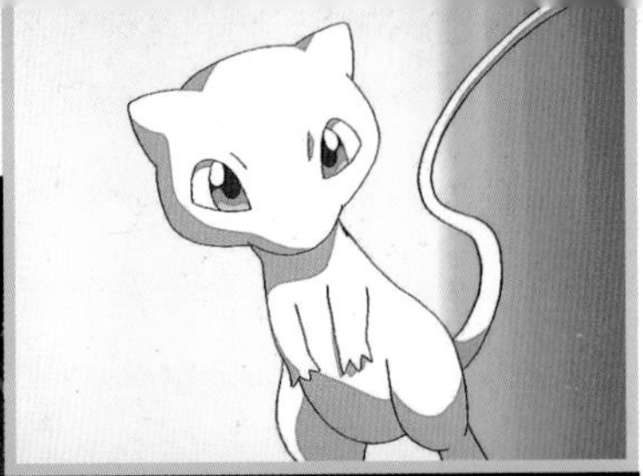

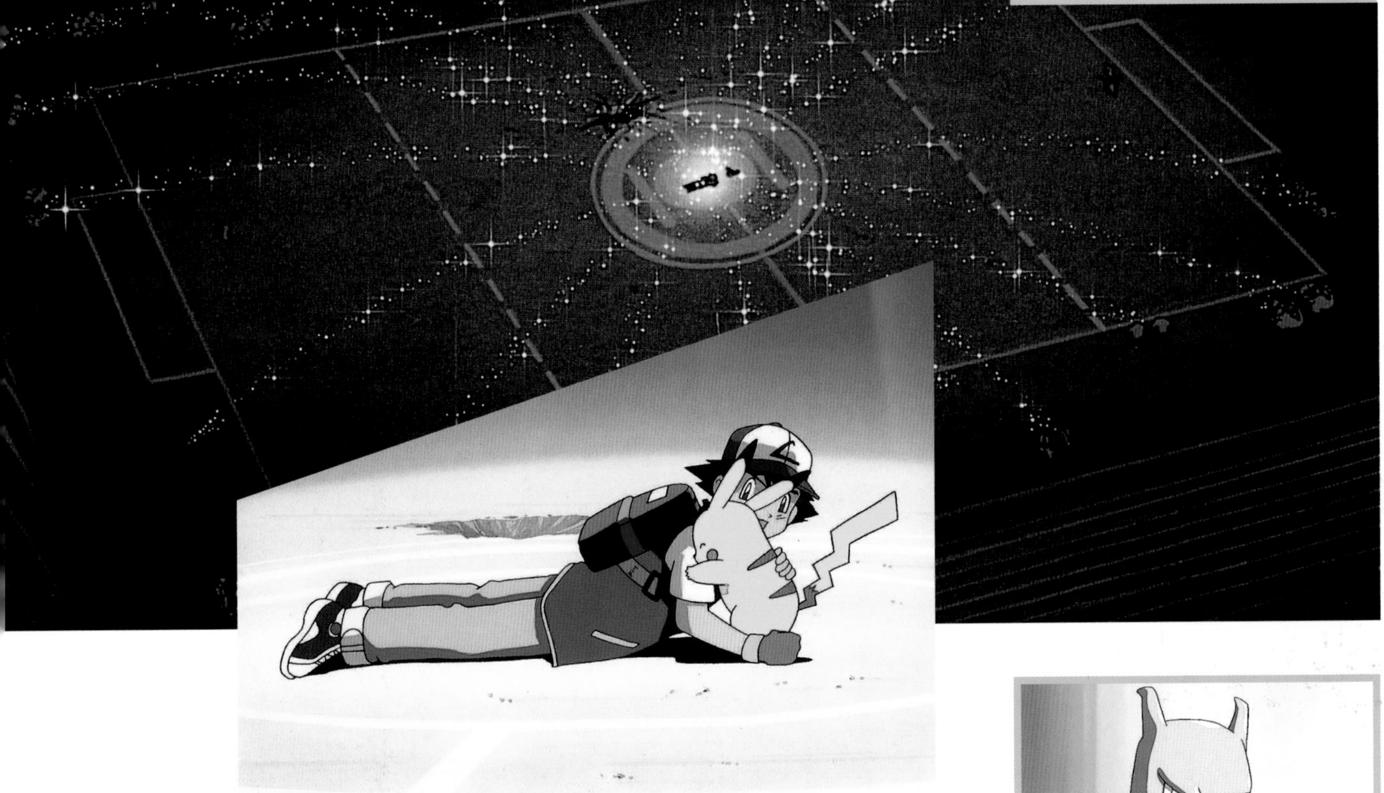

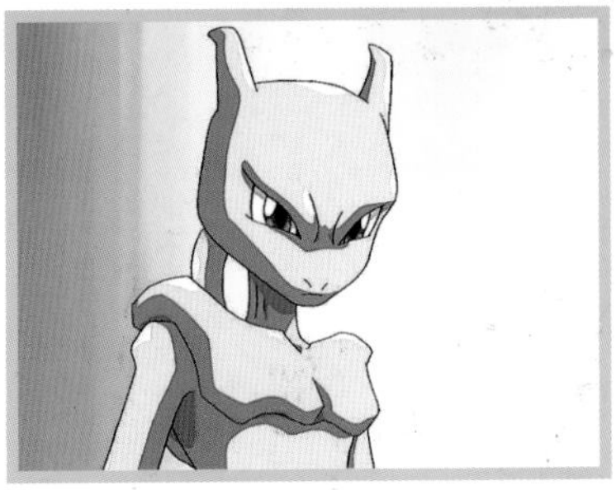

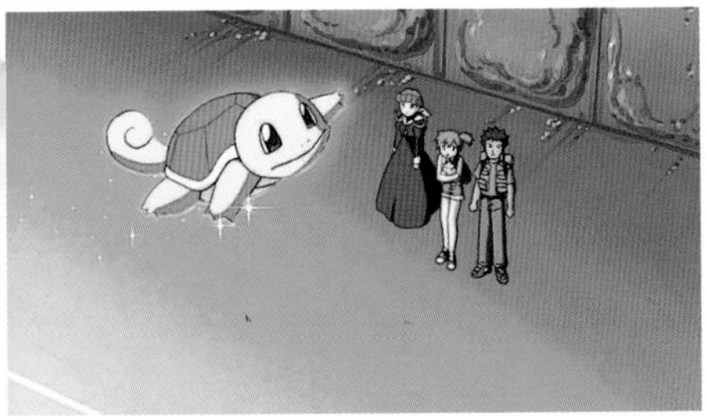

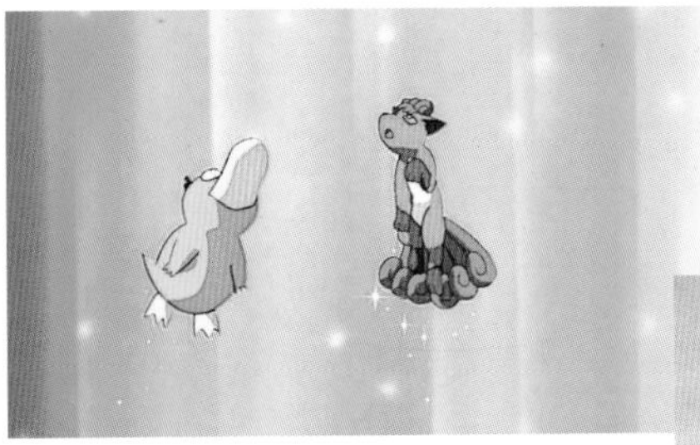

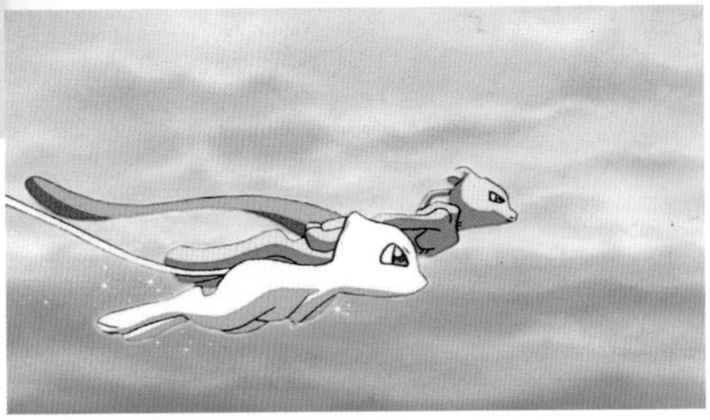

he wakes up. “W-what happened?”

Instead of answering, Pikachu rushes into Ash’s arms.

“No one must know of this battle between the original and the duplicate Pokémon. It is best forgotten,” Mewtwo whispers. Mew nods in agreement.

One by one, the duplicate Pokémon take to the sky.

Mewtwo’s voice echoes through the emptying hall. “We are alive, and we will continue to live…somewhere in the world.”

Suddenly all is engulfed in a blinding light.

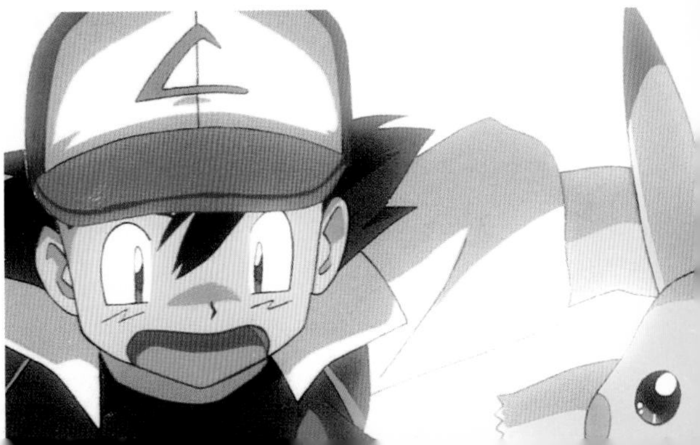

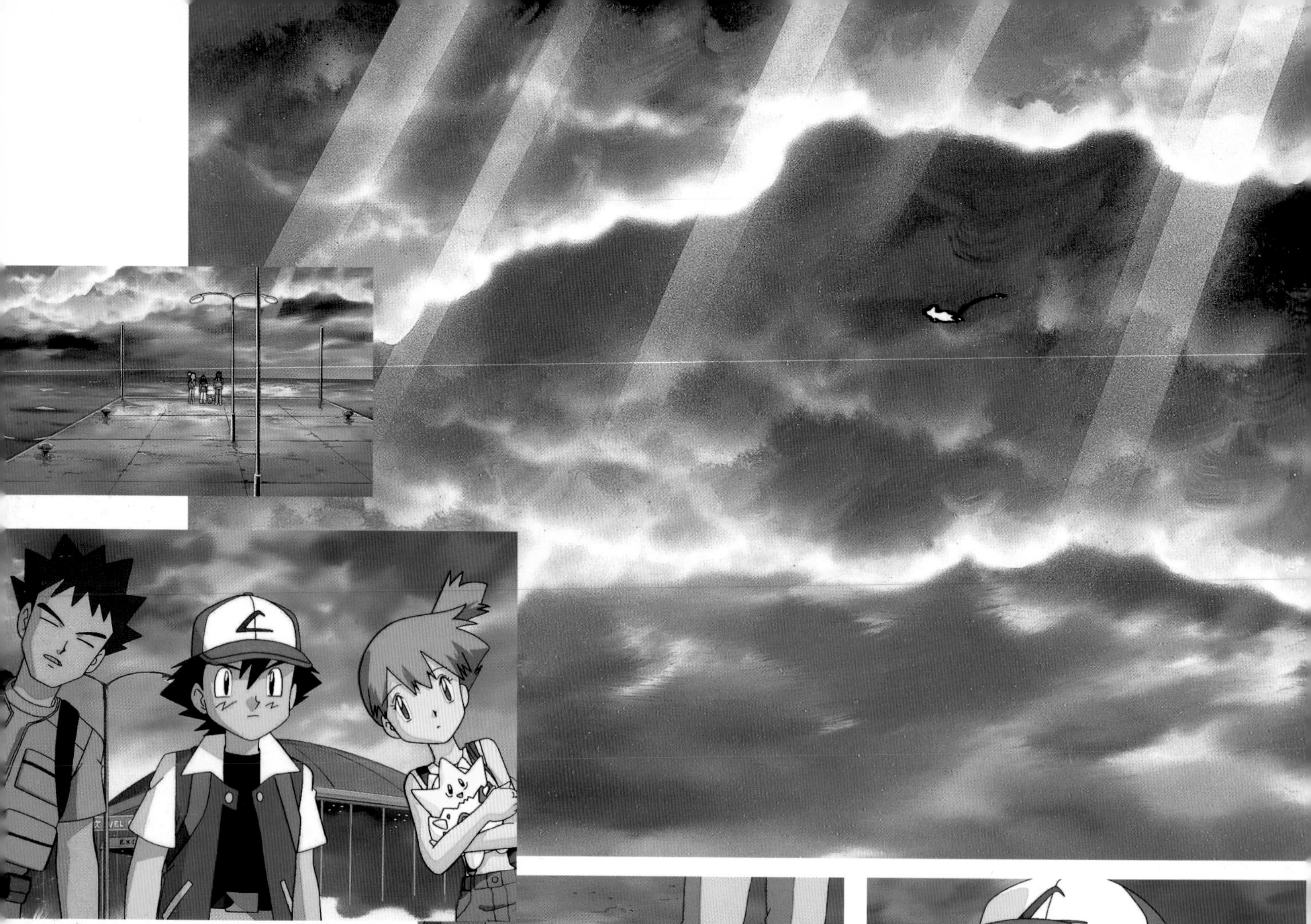

Ash and his friends arrive at the storm-tossed harbor again. But this time they can't for the life of them remember why they are there. Suddenly the shadow of a mysterious Pokémon passes overhead, reminding Ash of the first day of his Pokémon training journey.

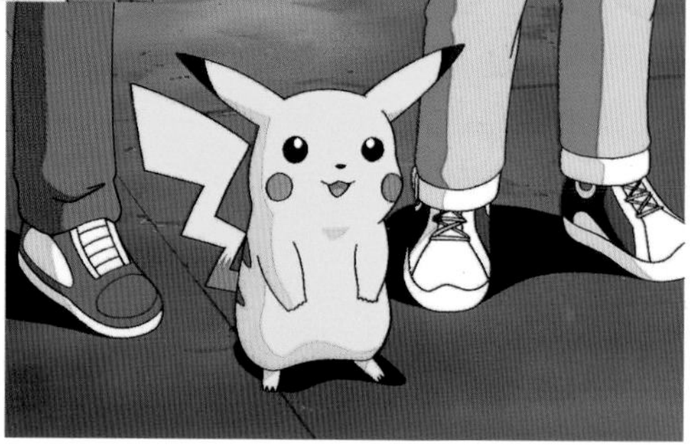

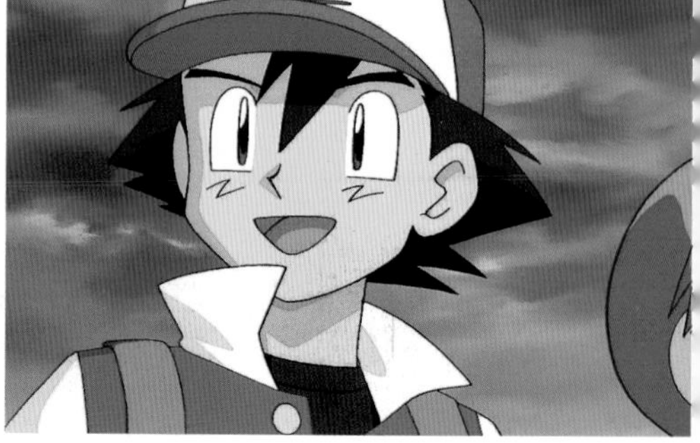

The Storm That Never Was

A storm is brewing over the sea.

The waiting room at the harbor is full of Pokémon trainers and their Pokémon, including Ash, Pikachu, Misty, and Brock.

"What are we doing here?" The three friends wonder.

They're not the only ones. All the other trainers are asking themselves the same thing! And Nurse Joy is standing beside them as if she was never missing.

No one remembers a thing.

Then, right before everyone's eyes, the storm clears up as quickly as it came. High up in the sunny, blue sky, Ash sees something streak past. "What's that?" he shouts.

"What's what?" asks Misty.

As quickly as it appeared, the white streak is gone. It seems to Ash that it was heading

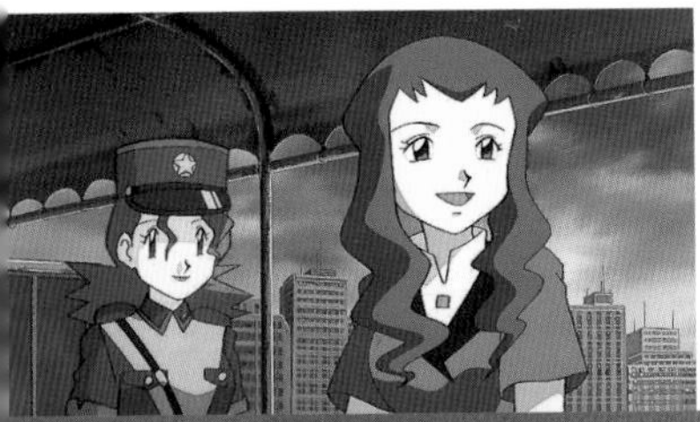

Was it all just a dream? New Island spreads out around them as if nothing had ever happened there. "What a nice island—so quiet and empty!" exclaim the members of Team Rocket.

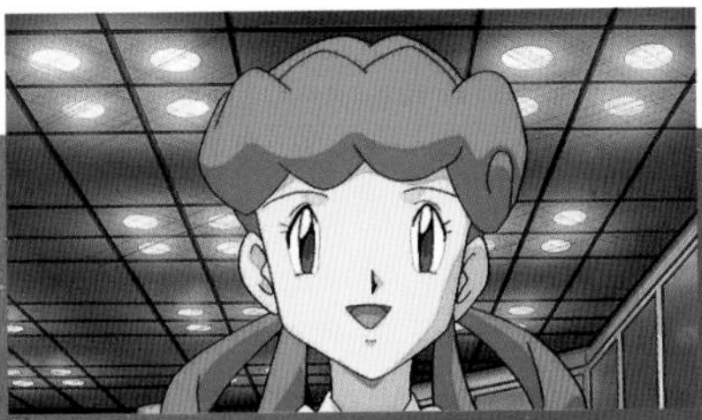

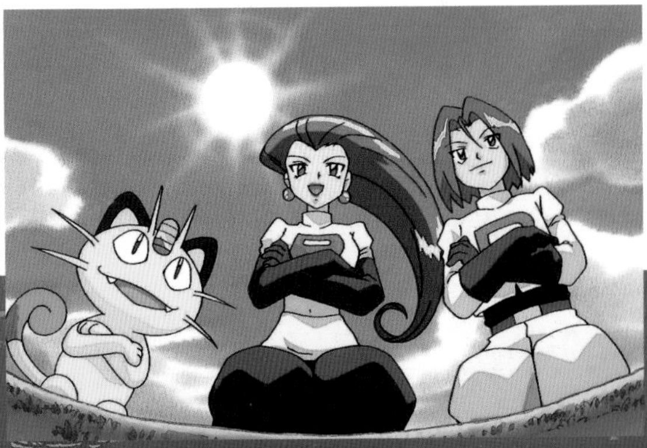

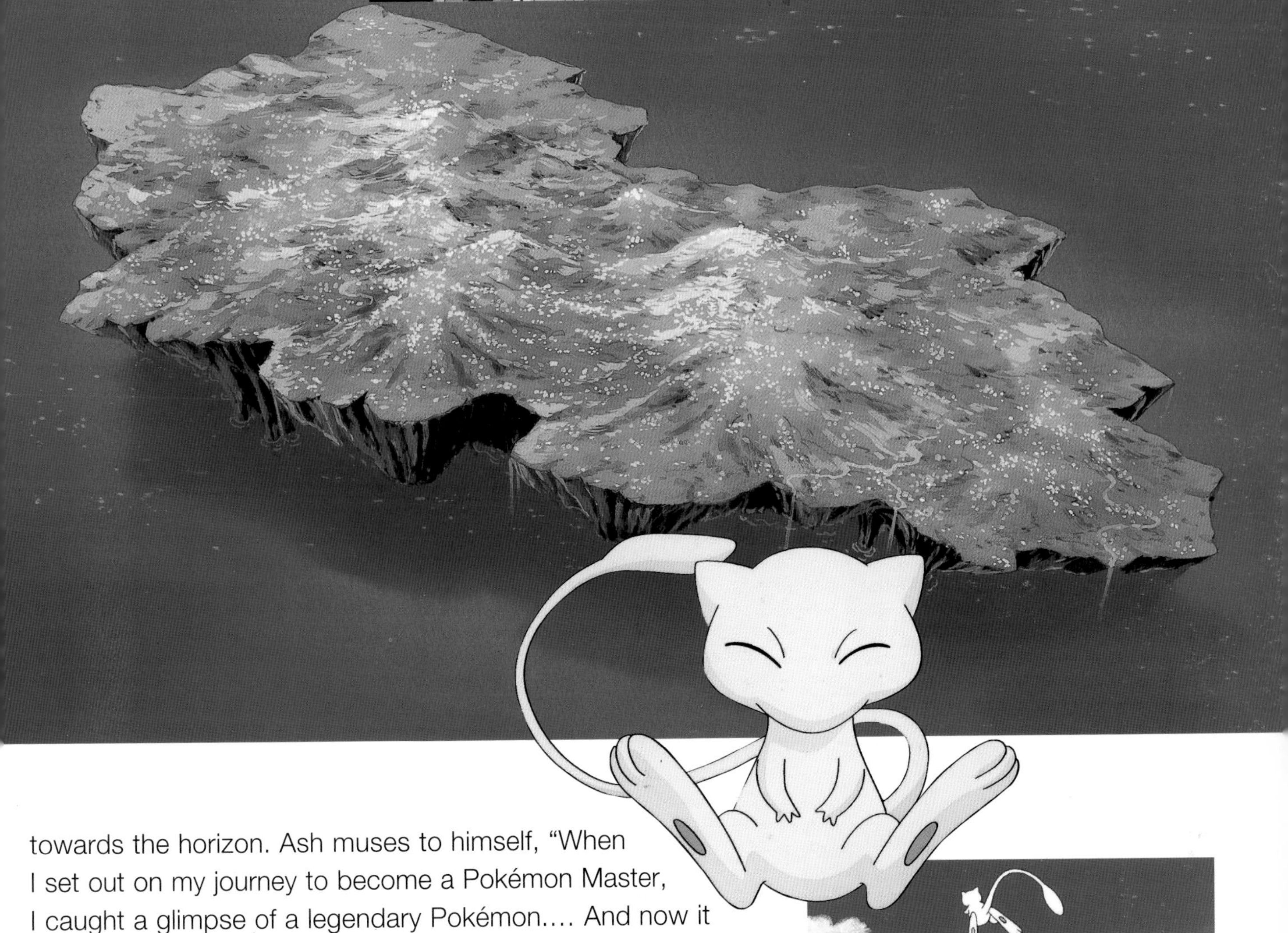

towards the horizon. Ash muses to himself, "When I set out on my journey to become a Pokémon Master, I caught a glimpse of a legendary Pokémon.... And now it seems I just saw one again..."

Ash continues staring up at the sky.

Meanwhile, back at New Island... There's nothing there except Team Rocket. Their voices echo in the nothingness.

"It's empty."

"It's kind of nice like this..."

"Team Rocket's signing off again!"

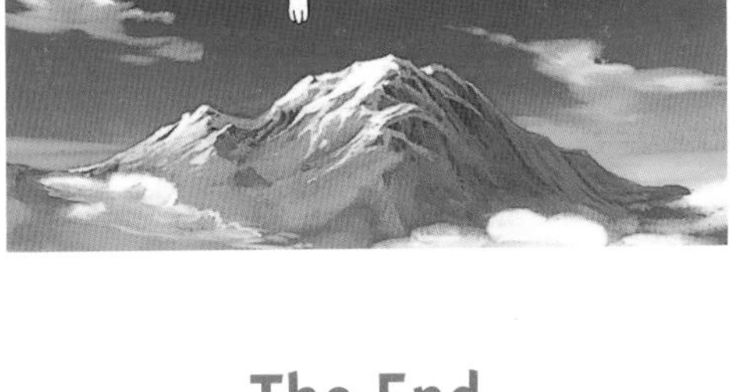

The End

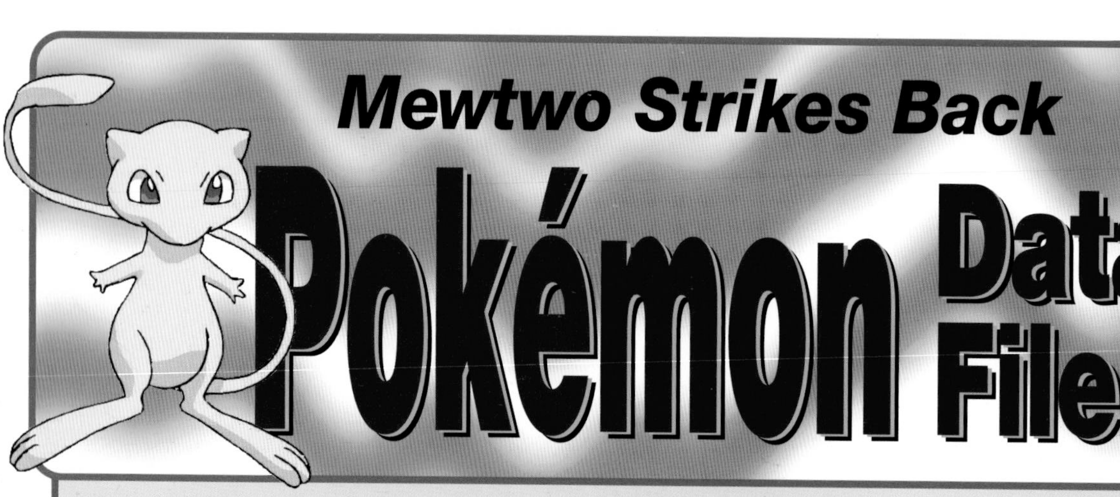

Mewtwo Strikes Back Pokémon Data Files

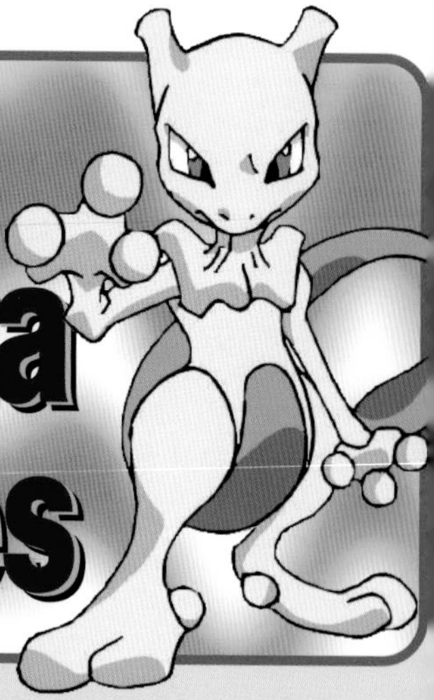

The Pokémon Stars of Mewtwo Strikes Back! Plus Key Action Sequences and Technology Notes From the Movie!

Mew

New Specie Pokémon

Height: 1 foot, 4 inches
Weight: 9 pounds

According to legend, mystical Pokémon Mew lives in hiding somewhere in the world. But no one has actually seen this elusive Pokémon. Mew finally makes an appearance to put a stop to Genetic Pokémon Mewtwo's rampage. A tragic battle ensues between Mew (said to be the most powerful Pokémon in existence) and Mewtwo (who could be thought of as Mew's child). Who will be the victor in this awesome showdown?

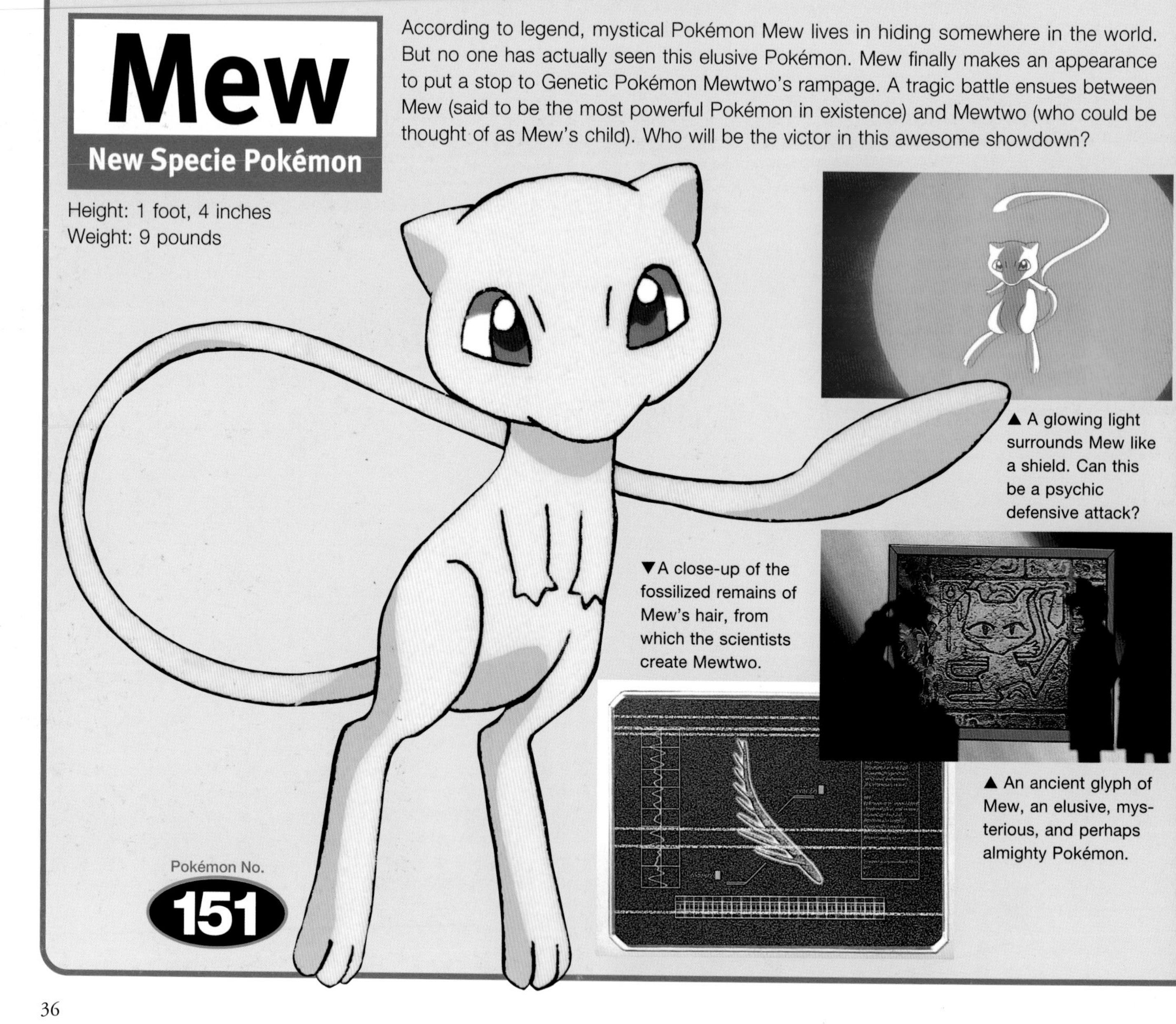

Pokémon No. **151**

▲ A glowing light surrounds Mew like a shield. Can this be a psychic defensive attack?

▼A close-up of the fossilized remains of Mew's hair, from which the scientists create Mewtwo.

▲ An ancient glyph of Mew, an elusive, mysterious, and perhaps almighty Pokémon.

Mewtwo

Genetic Pokémon

A group of scientists create Mew from the genes of the rarest Pokémon in the world: Mew. But the scientists' experiment results in a Mewtwo more powerful than their wildest dreams. Their creation destroys the laboratory where it was brought to life! Then, disillusioned with mankind, Mewtwo resolves to become a Pokémon trainer far surpassing any human trainer. Mewtwo can communicate telepathically with humans and easily control their minds. Faced with Mewtwo's awesome power, Ash and the other trainers go through the worst Pokémon battle they've ever encountered!

Height: 6 feet, 7 inches
Weight: 269 pounds

Pokémon No.
150

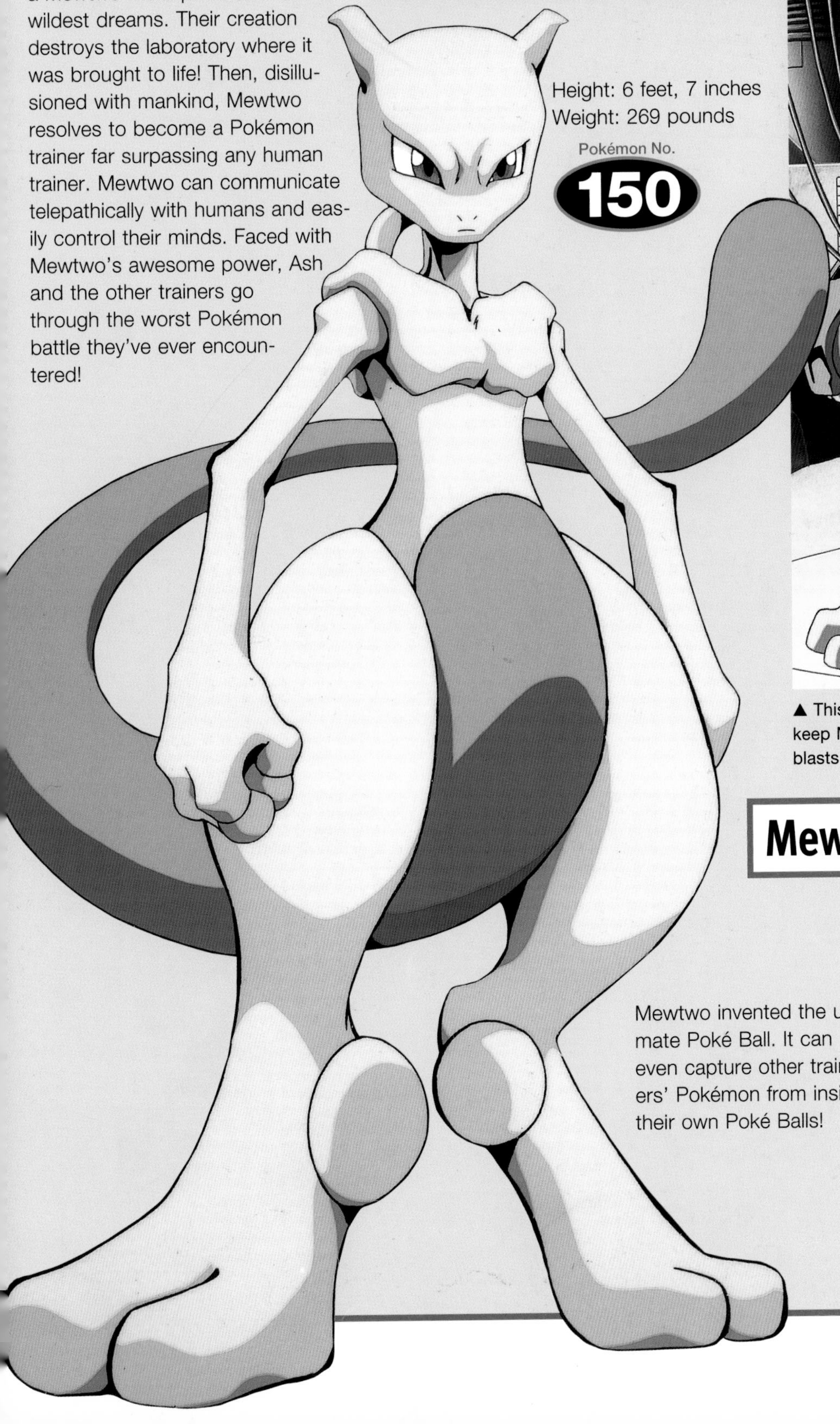

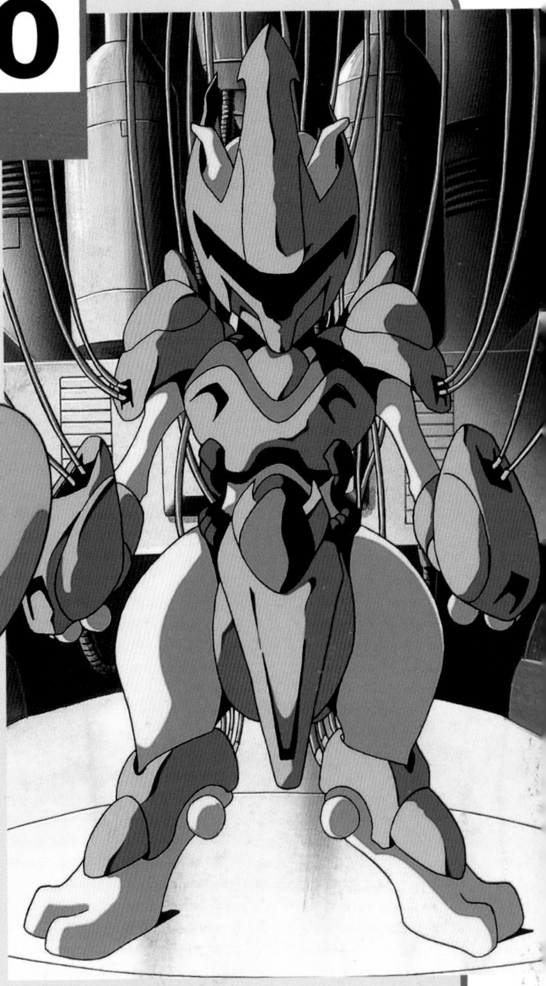

▲ This heavy protective armor is designed to keep Mewtwo's power in check. But Mewtwo blasts it off with a surge of energy!

Mewtwo's Poké Balls

Mewtwo invented the ultimate Poké Ball. It can even capture other trainers' Pokémon from inside their own Poké Balls!

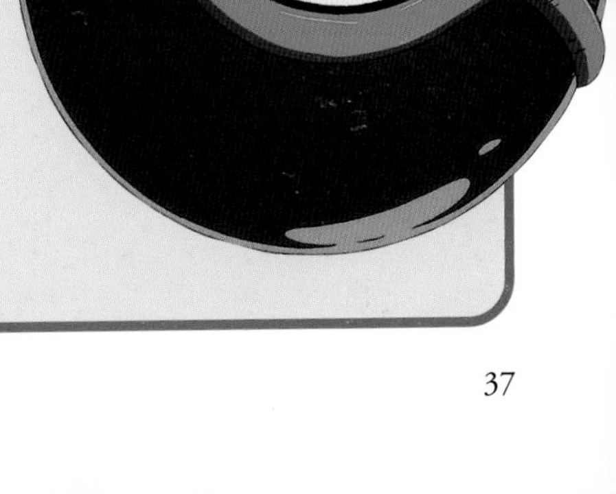

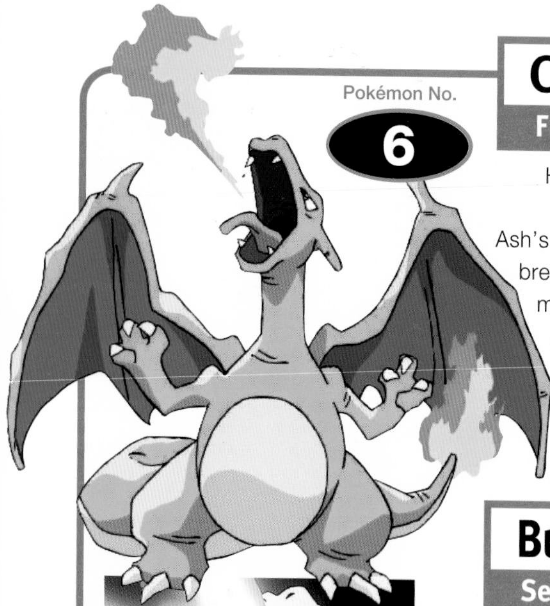

Pokémon No.

6

Charizard

Flame Pokémon

Height: 5 feet, 7 inches
Weight: 200 pounds
Ash's Pokémon Charizard breathes fire and has a massive wing span. A good last resort, this Pokémon occasionally refuses to follow Ash's commands.

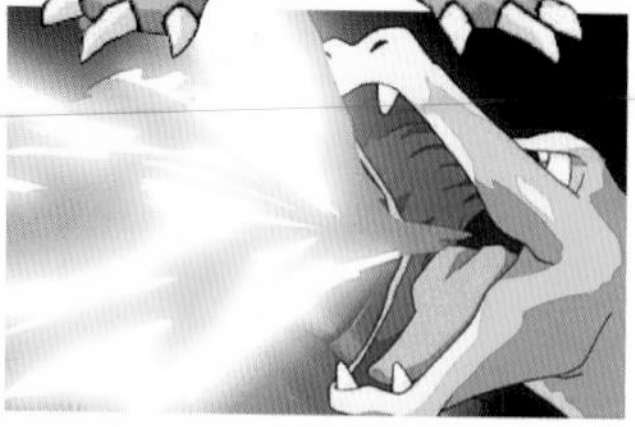

Charizard's "Flamethrower" is so hot it can melt boulders!

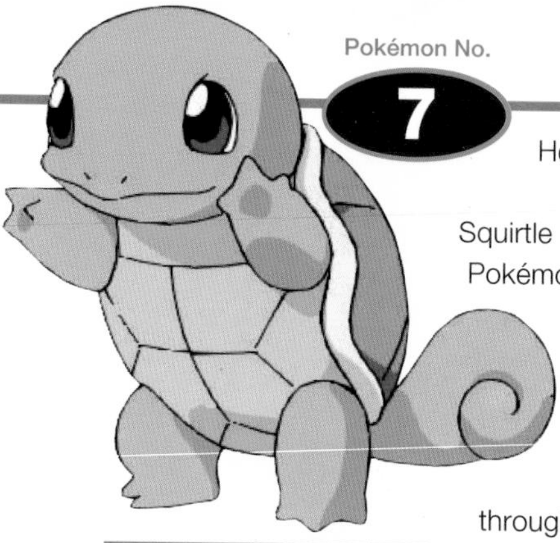

Pokémon No.

7

Height: 1 foot, 8 inches
Weight: 20 pounds
Squirtle is one of Ash's Water Pokémon. When Ash, Brock, and Misty fall into the sea during their attempt to reach Pokémon Palace, Squirtle swims them through the storm to safety.

Squirtle

Tinyturtle Pokémon

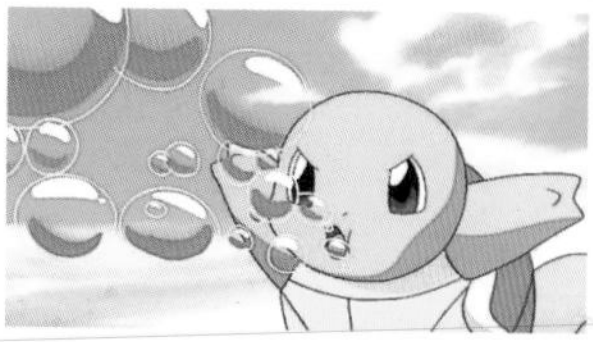

Squirtle's "Bubble" attack slows down its opponent.

Bulbasaur

Seed Pokémon

Pokémon No.

1

Height: 2 feet, 4 inches
Weight: 15 pounds
Ash's Bulbasaur is adept at Grass attacks and has long vines. This cute Pokémon is fiercer than it looks. It gets a lot of action scenes in the movie.

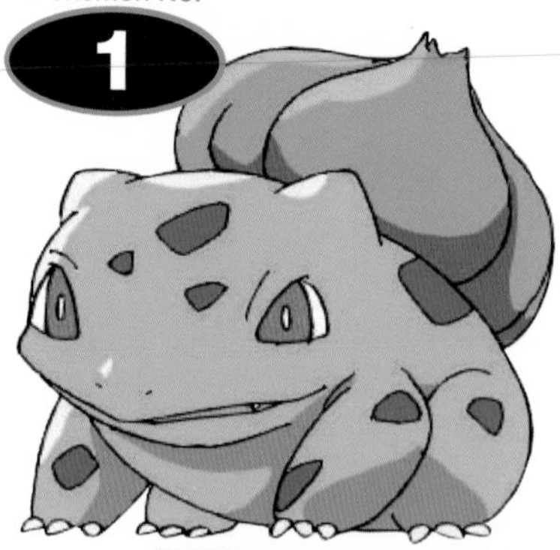

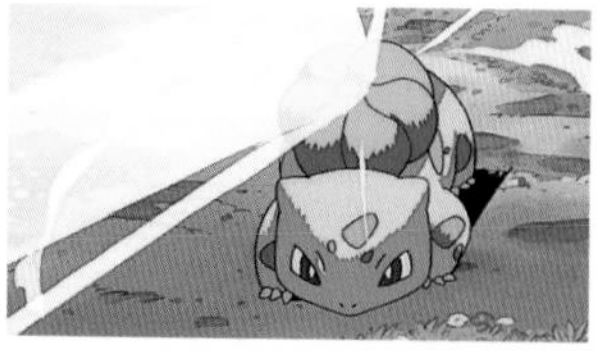

Bulbasaur's greatest weapon is the intense "Solarbeam."

Pokémon No.

120

Staryu

Starshape Pokémon

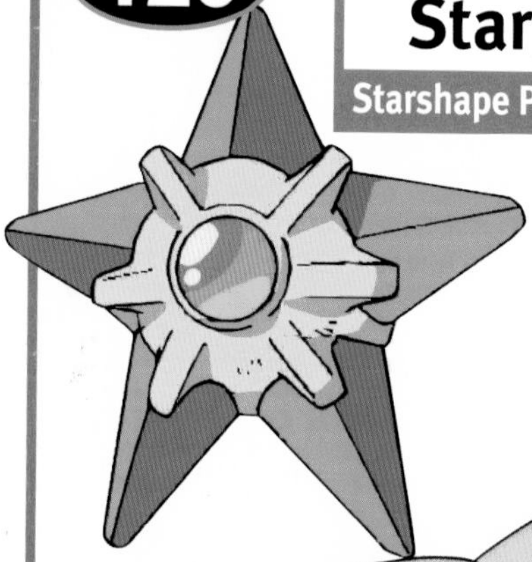

Height: 2 feet, 7 inches
Weight: 76 pounds
Staryu's trainer Misty loves Water Pokémon. Together with Ash's Squirtle, Staryu helps Ash and his friends survive the big storm.

Pikachu

Mouse Pokémon

Height: 1 foot, 4 inches
Weight: 13 pounds
Pikachu is our ever-popular electric Pokémon. Even in the movie, Pikachu ends up the star of the show. Pikachu, you're the only one who can save Ash! Go Pikachu!

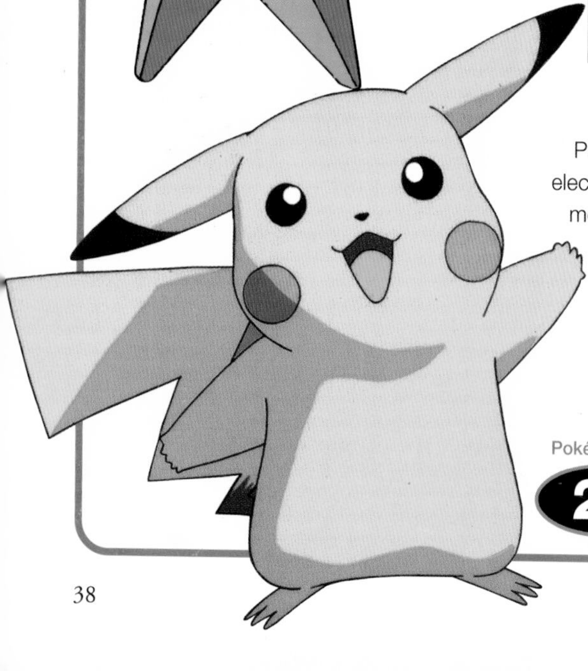

Pokémon No.

25

Pokémon No.

149

Dragonite

Dragon Pokémon

Height: 7 feet, 3 inches
Weight: 463 pounds
Dragonite delivers Mewtwo's invitations to Ash and his friends. Despite its great weight, Dragonite is the fastest flying Pokémon.

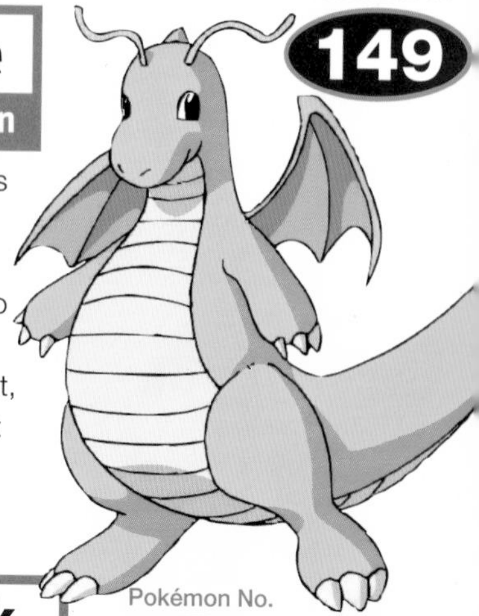

Psyduck

Duck Pokémon

Pokémon No.

54

Height: 2 feet, 7 inches
Weight: 43 pounds
Somewhat short-tempered Misty often yells at this difficult water Pokémon. Good-natured Psyduck is always a little out of it.

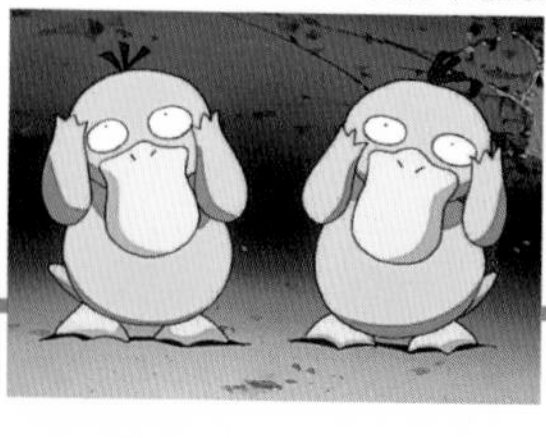

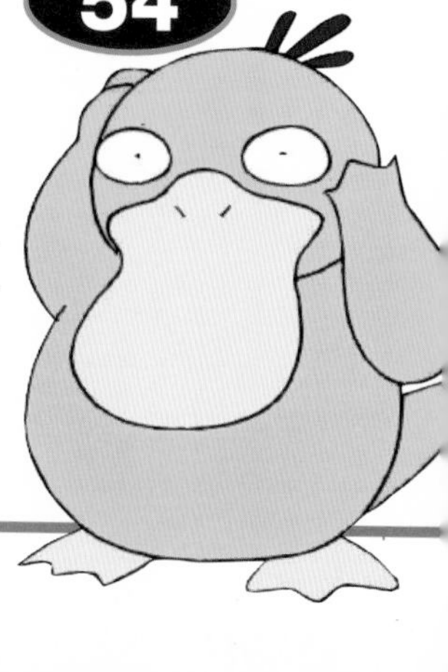

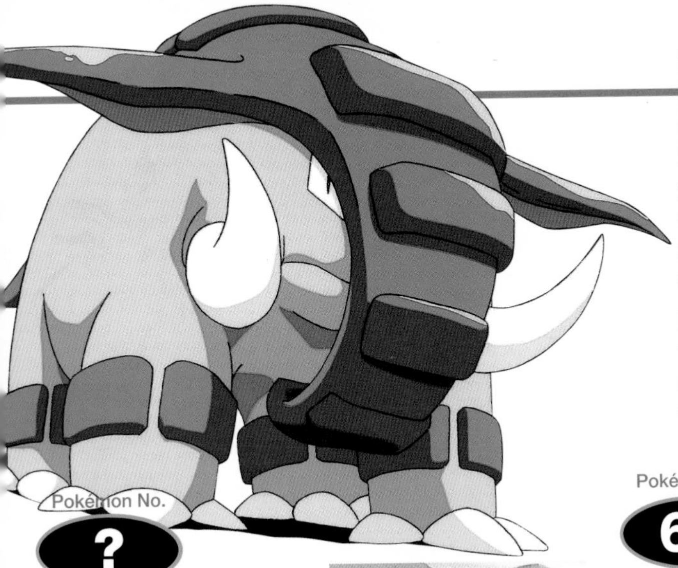

Pokémon No. 37

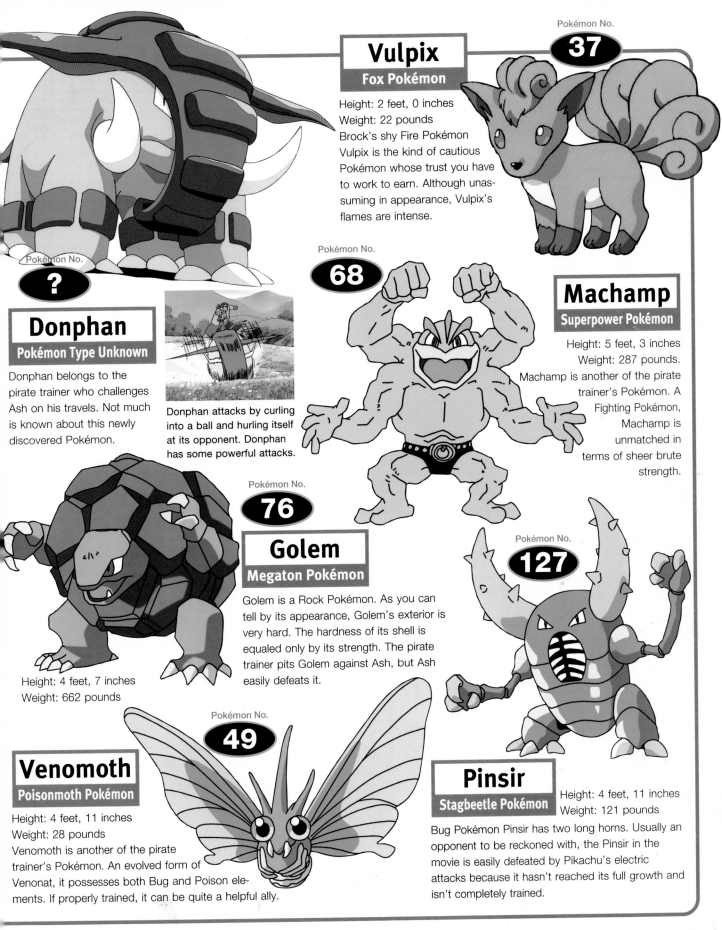

Vulpix

Fox Pokémon

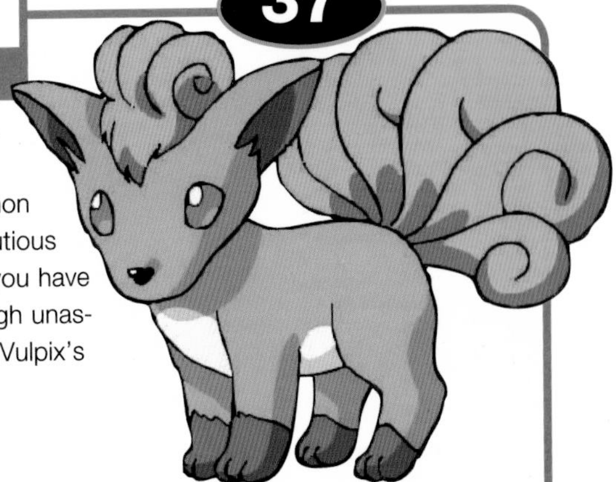

Height: 2 feet, 0 inches
Weight: 22 pounds
Brock's shy Fire Pokémon Vulpix is the kind of cautious Pokémon whose trust you have to work to earn. Although unassuming in appearance, Vulpix's flames are intense.

Pokémon No. ?

Donphan

Pokémon Type Unknown

Donphan belongs to the pirate trainer who challenges Ash on his travels. Not much is known about this newly discovered Pokémon.

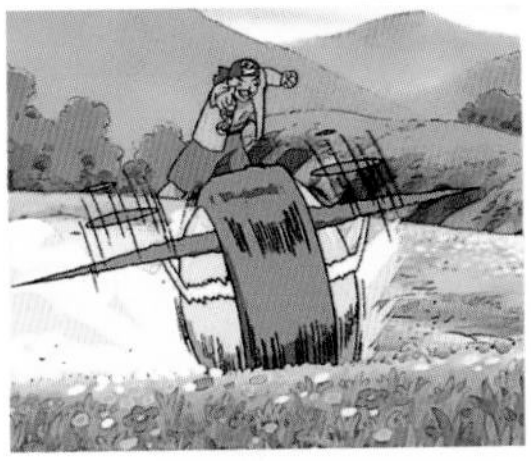

Donphan attacks by curling into a ball and hurling itself at its opponent. Donphan has some powerful attacks.

Pokémon No. 68

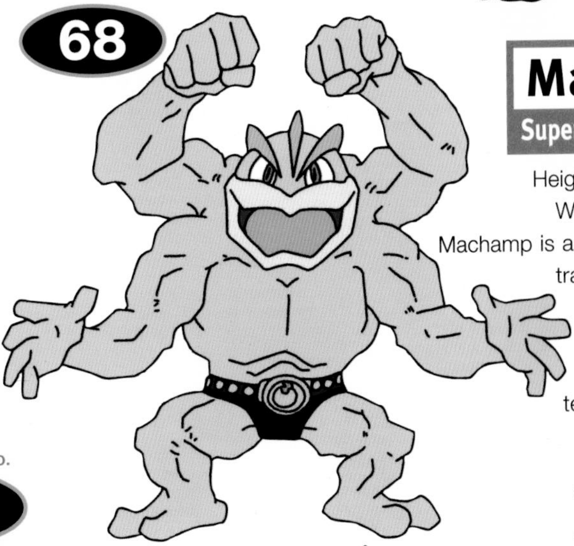

Machamp

Superpower Pokémon

Height: 5 feet, 3 inches
Weight: 287 pounds.
Machamp is another of the pirate trainer's Pokémon. A Fighting Pokémon, Machamp is unmatched in terms of sheer brute strength.

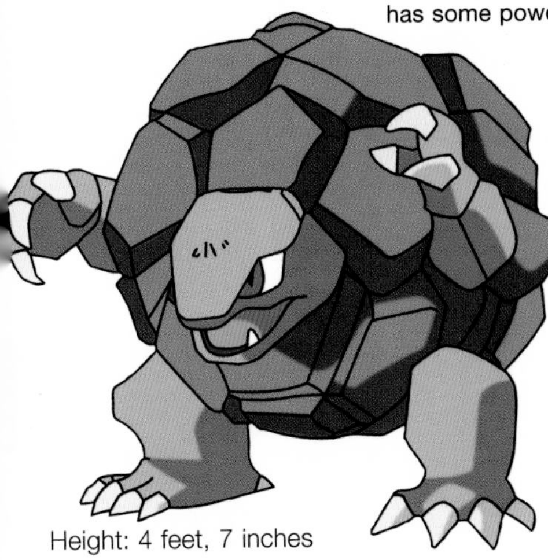

Pokémon No. 76

Golem

Megaton Pokémon

Golem is a Rock Pokémon. As you can tell by its appearance, Golem's exterior is very hard. The hardness of its shell is equaled only by its strength. The pirate trainer pits Golem against Ash, but Ash easily defeats it.

Height: 4 feet, 7 inches
Weight: 662 pounds

Pokémon No. 127

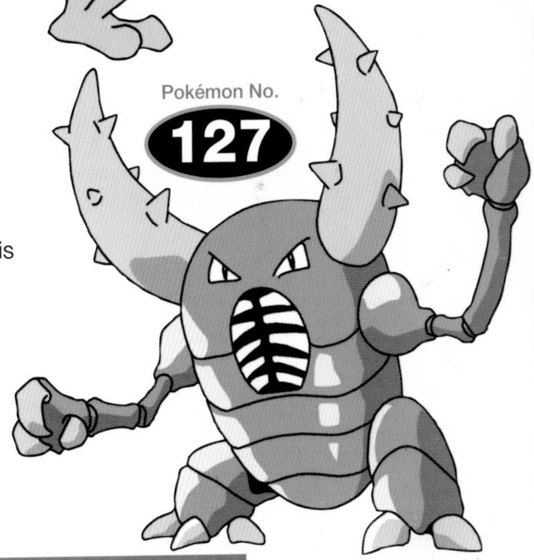

Pinsir

Stagbeetle Pokémon

Height: 4 feet, 11 inches
Weight: 121 pounds
Bug Pokémon Pinsir has two long horns. Usually an opponent to be reckoned with, the Pinsir in the movie is easily defeated by Pikachu's electric attacks because it hasn't reached its full growth and isn't completely trained.

Pokémon No. 49

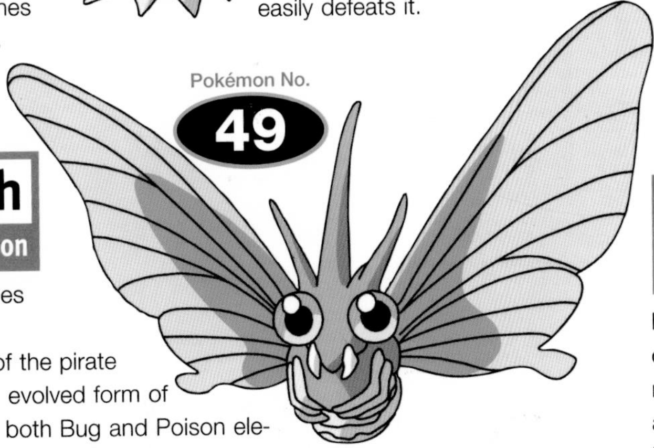

Venomoth

Poisonmoth Pokémon

Height: 4 feet, 11 inches
Weight: 28 pounds
Venomoth is another of the pirate trainer's Pokémon. An evolved form of Venonat, it possesses both Bug and Poison elements. If properly trained, it can be quite a helpful ally.

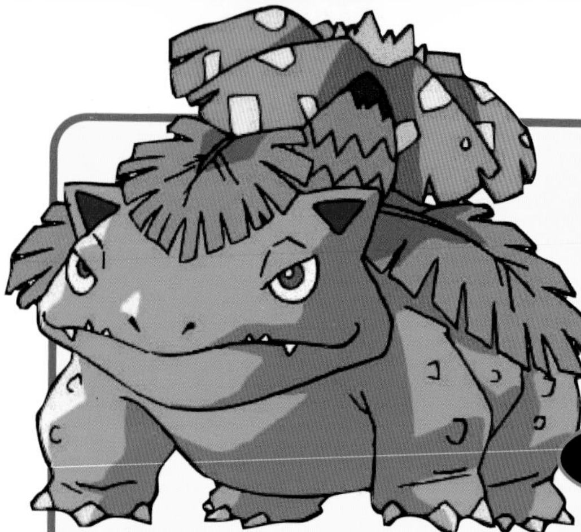

Pokémon No.
3

Venusaur
Seed Pokémon

Height: 6 feet, 7 inches
Weight: 221 pounds

Corey has nicknamed his Venusaur Bruteroot. Venusaur possesses both Grass and Poison elements.

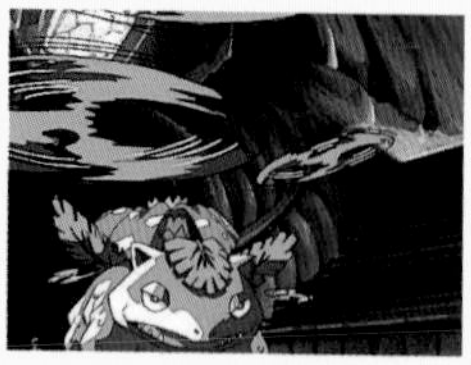

Venusaur's "Leaf Cutter" attack can slice through almost anything like a hot knife through butter!

Pidgeot
Bird Pokémon

Height: 4 feet, 11 inches
Weight: 87 pounds
Pidgeot is the evolved form of Pidgeotto. It is so large, it can carry Corey to the island.

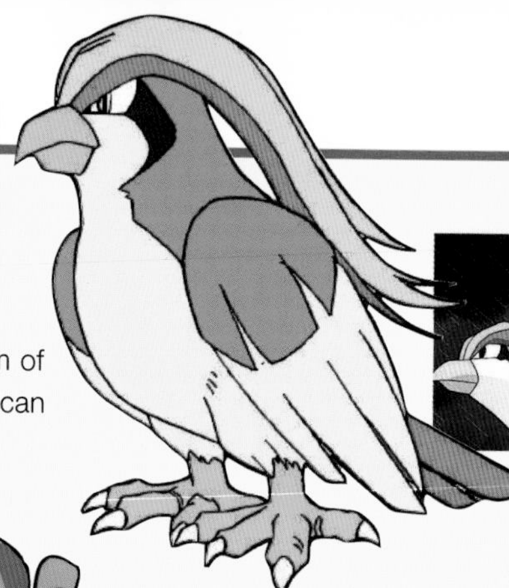

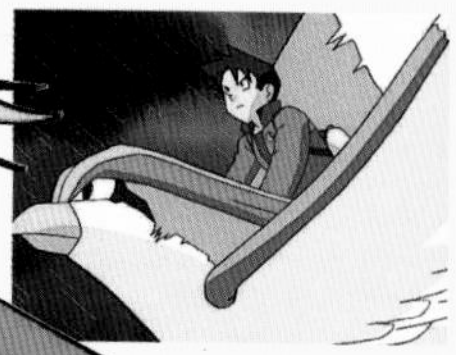

Pokémon No.
18

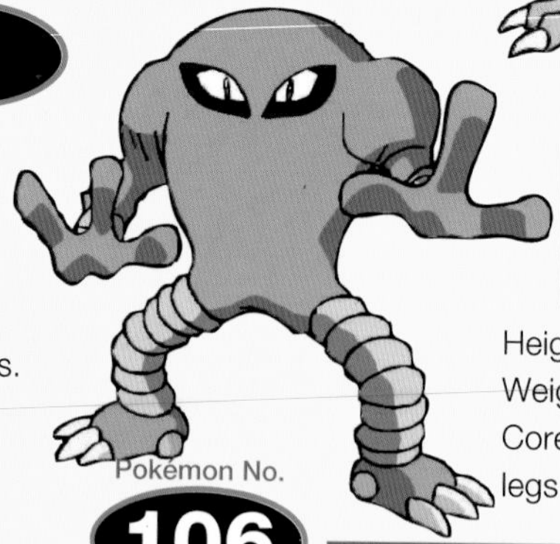

Pokémon No.
106

Hitmonlee
Kicking Pokémon

Height: 4 feet, 11 inches
Weight: 110 pounds
Corey's Hitmonlee is a combat expert. Its flexible legs enable it to deliver powerful kicks.

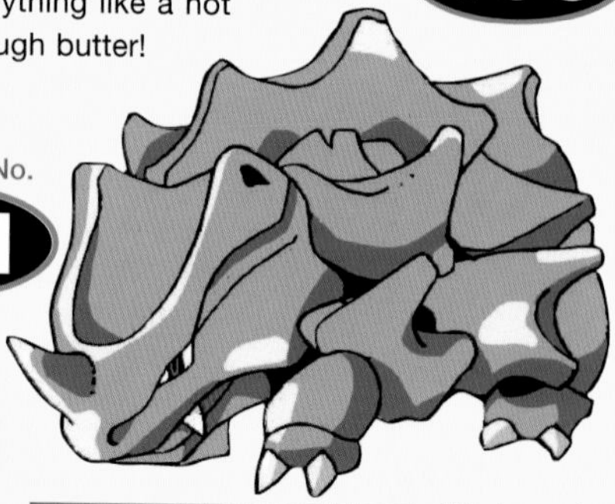

Pokémon No.
111

Rhyhorn
Spikes Pokémon

Height: 3 feet, 3 inches
Weight: 254 pounds

Rhyhorn has both Ground and Rock elements and is capable of great brute force. At Corey's command, Rhyhorn attacks Mewtwo.

Scyther
Mantis Pokémon

Pokémon No.
123

Height: 4 feet, 11 inches
Weight: 123 pounds
Corey's Scyther possesses both Bug and Flying elements. Its razor-sharp arms are its primary weapon.

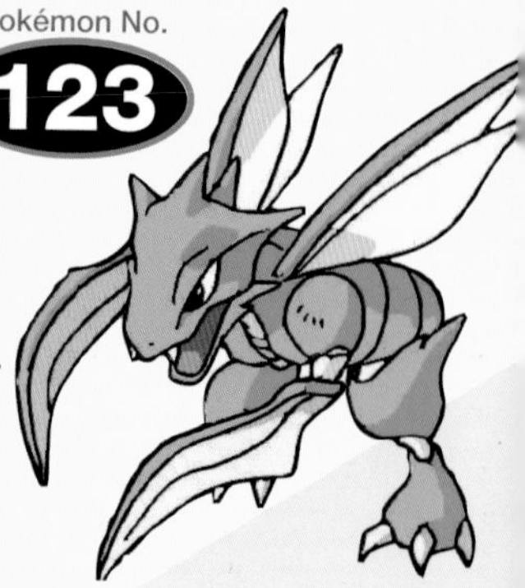

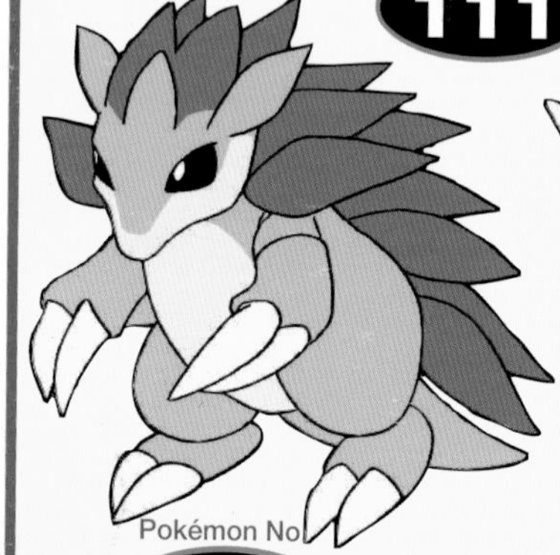

Pokémon No.
28

Sandslash
Mouse Pokémon

Height: 3 feet, 3 inches
Weight: 65 pounds
Corey's Sandslash is a Mouse Pokémon like Pikachu, as well as a Ground Pokémon.

Seadra
Dragon Pokémon

Height: 3 feet, 11 inches
Weight: 55 pounds
Fergus' short-tempered Seadra is the evolved form of Horsea.

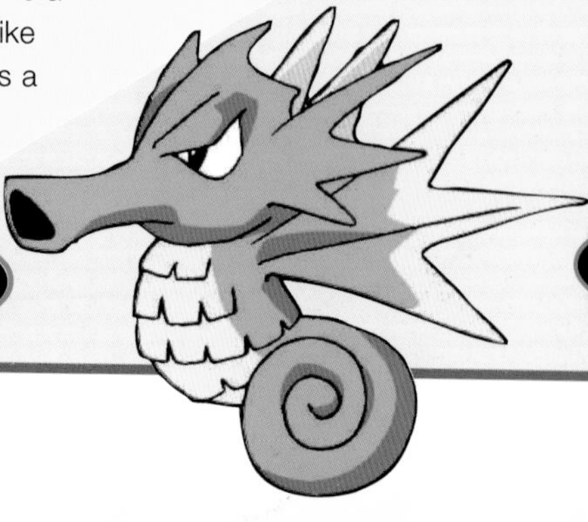

Pokémon No.
117

Vaporeon
Bubble Jet Pokémon

Height: 3 feet, 3 inches
Weight: 64 pounds
Fergus' Vaporeon is an evolved form of Eevee. It can melt in water to make itself invisible.

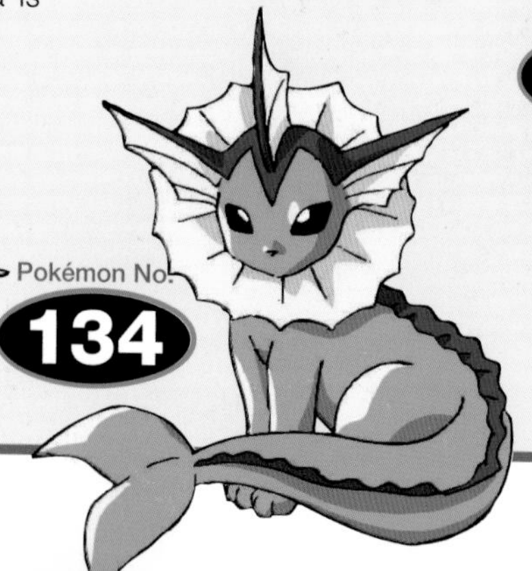

Pokémon No.
134

Golduck
Duck Pokémon

Height: 5 feet, 7 inches
Weight: 169 pounds

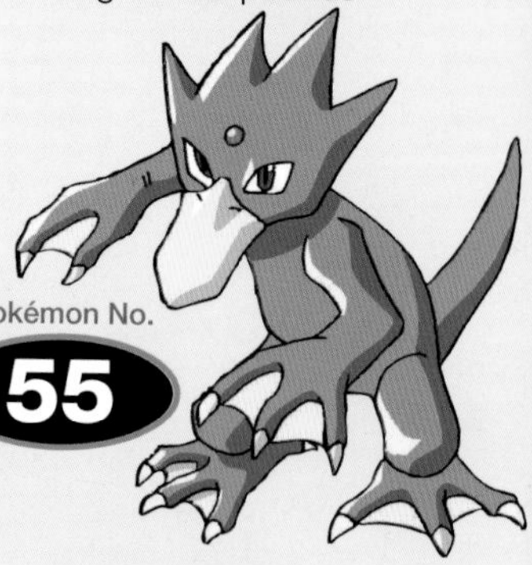

Pokémon No.
55

Fergus' Golduck is a Water Pokémon. An evolved form of Psyduck, Golduck is far more powerful and reliable.

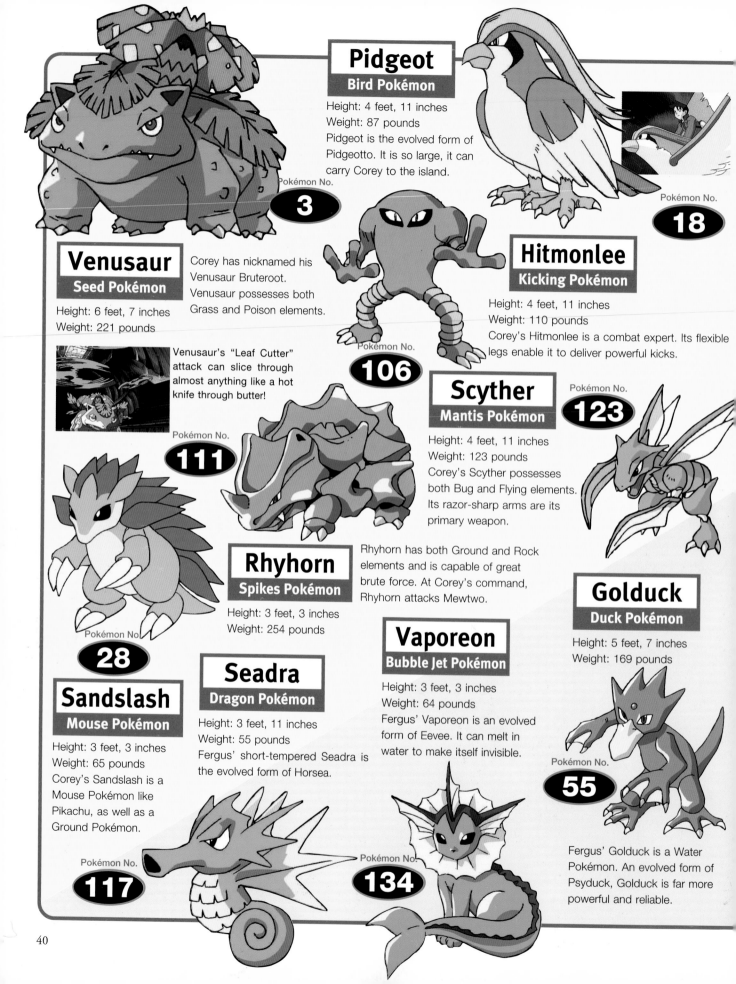

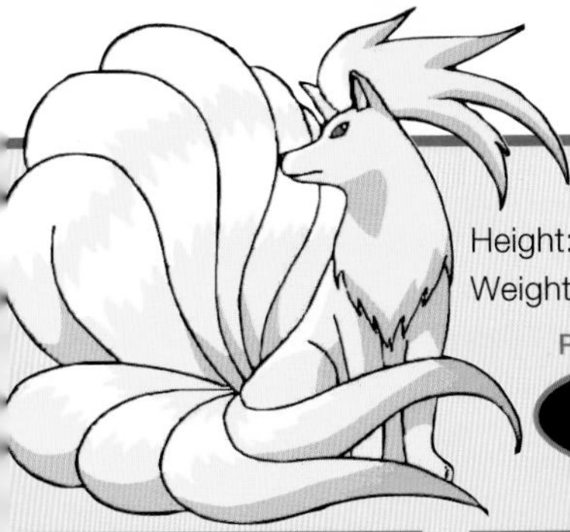

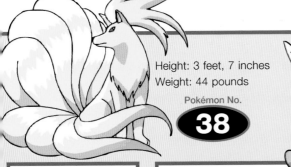

Height: 3 feet, 7 inches
Weight: 44 pounds

Pokémon No.
38

Ninetales
Fox Pokémon

Neesha's Ninetales is an evolved form of Vulpix. In the sunlight, Ninetales' golden fur gleams and its nine soft tails flow luxuriously.

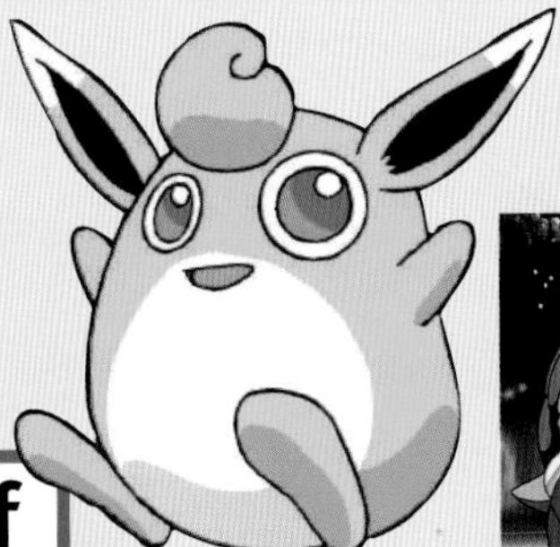

Pokémon No.
40

Wigglytuff
Balloon Pokémon

Height: 3 feet, 3 inches
Weight: 26 pounds
Cute Wigglytuff is tougher than it looks. Wigglytuff is popular with girl trainers.

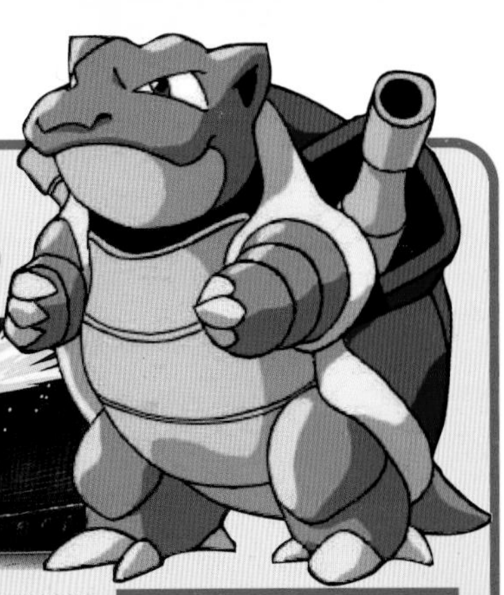

Pokémon No.
9

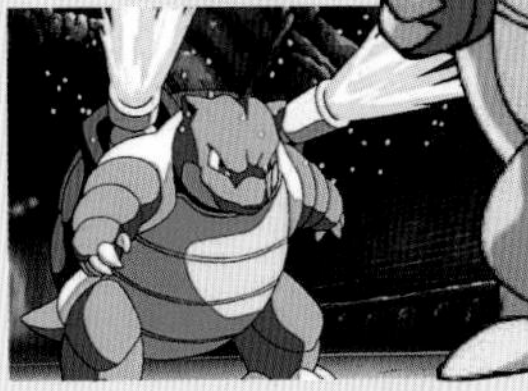

Blastoise's special weapon is the "Hydro Pump."

Blastoise
Shellfish Pokémon

Height: 5 feet, 3 inches
Weight: 189 pounds
Blastoise is the highest evolved form of Squirtle and Wartortle. Neesha has nicknamed this one Shellshocker.

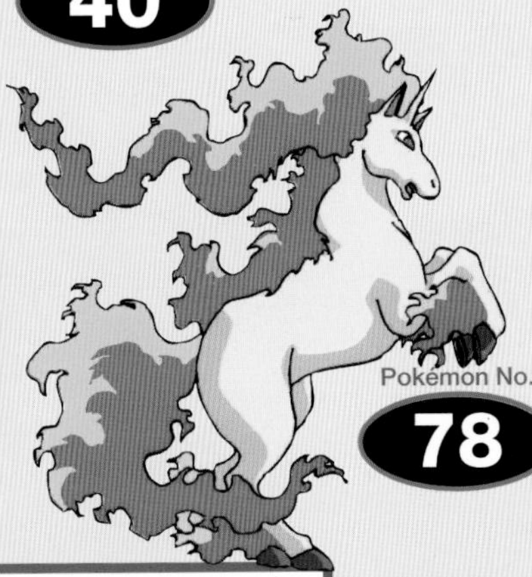

Vileplume
Flower Pokémon

Height: 3 feet, 11 inches
Weight: 41 pounds

Vileplume are popular with girl trainers. Erika of the Celadon City Gym also has one.

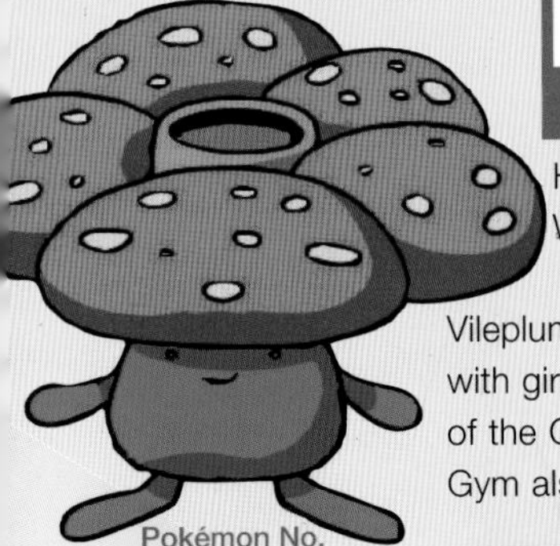

Pokémon No.
45

Pokémon No.
78

Rapidash
Fire Horse Pokémon

Height: 5 feet, 7 inches
Weight: 209 pounds
This Fire Pokémon's special traits include its beautiful fiery appearance and ability to travel at incredible speeds of up to 150 mph. This Rapidash is very close to its trainer, Neesha.

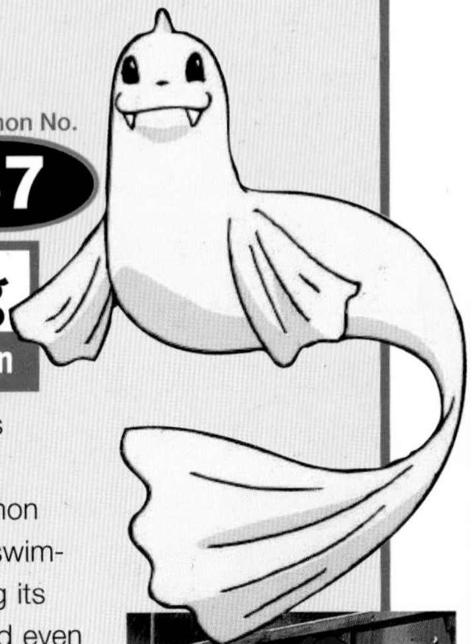

Pokémon No.
87

Dewgong
Sea Lion Pokémon

Height: 5 feet, 7 inches
Weight: 265 pounds
Neesha's Water Pokémon Dewgong is an adept swimmer capable of carrying its trainer across rivers and even oceans.

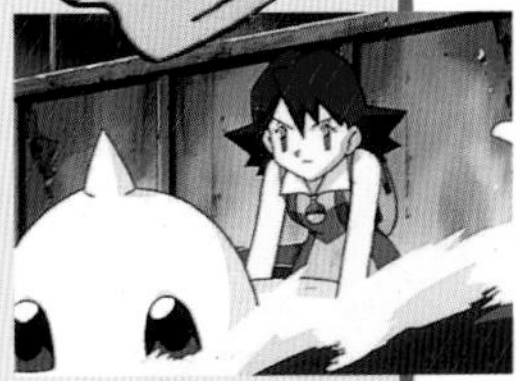

Dewgong is one of the steadiest swimmers, even in rough seas.

Nidoqueen
Drill Pokémon

Height: 4 feet, 3 inches
Weight: 132 pounds

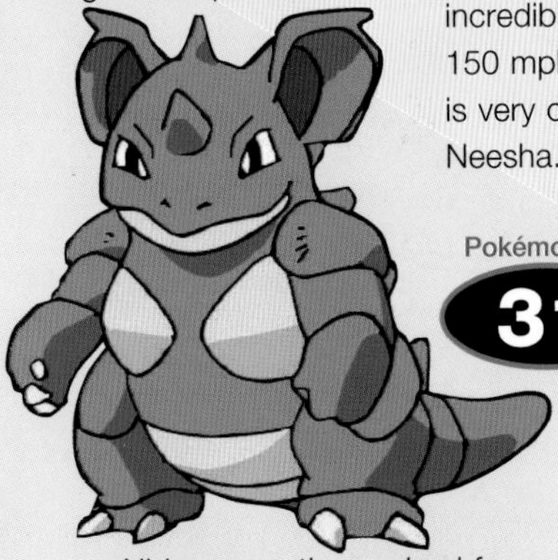

Pokémon No.
31

Nidoqueen, the evolved form of Nidorina, possesses both Poison and Ground elements. Although not a Water Pokémon, its trainer is Fergus.

Tentacruel
Jellyfish Pokémon

Height: 5 feet, 3 inches
Weight: 121 pounds
Fergus' scary-looking Tentacruel possesses both Water and Poison elements.

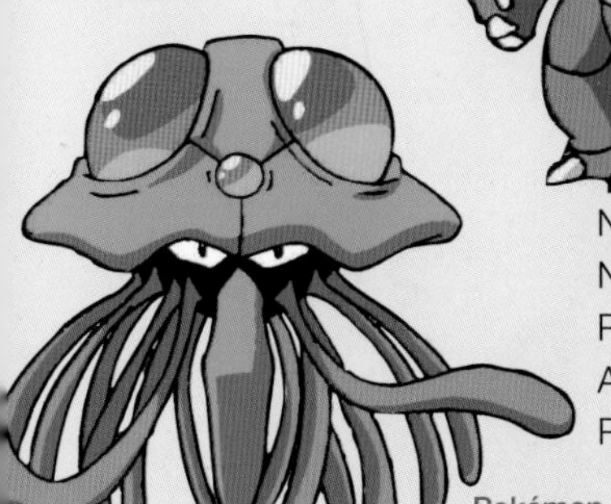

Pokémon No.
73

Gyarados
Atrocious Pokémon

Height: 21 feet, 4 inches / Weight: 518 pounds
Fergus' Gyarados possesses elements of both Water and Flying. Few trainers can handle its ferocious personality.

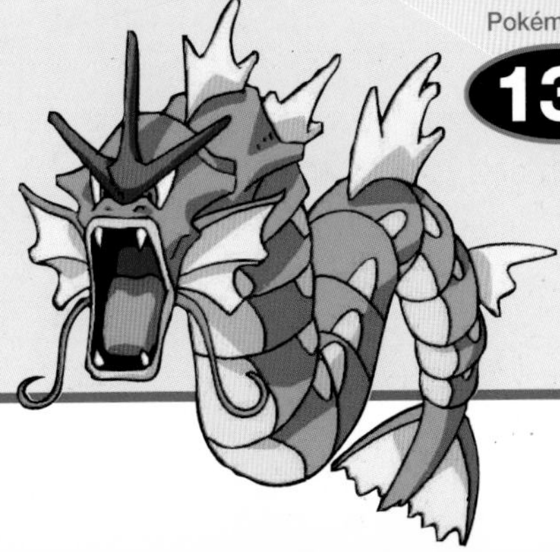

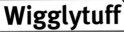

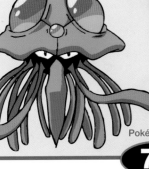

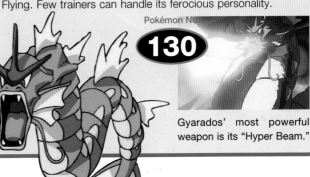

Pokémon No.
130

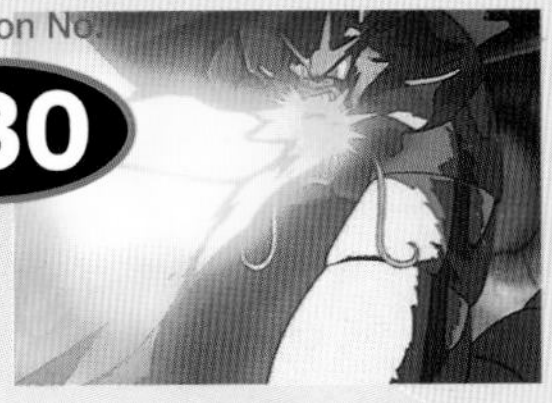

Gyarados' most powerful weapon is its "Hyper Beam."

PIKACHU'S VACATION

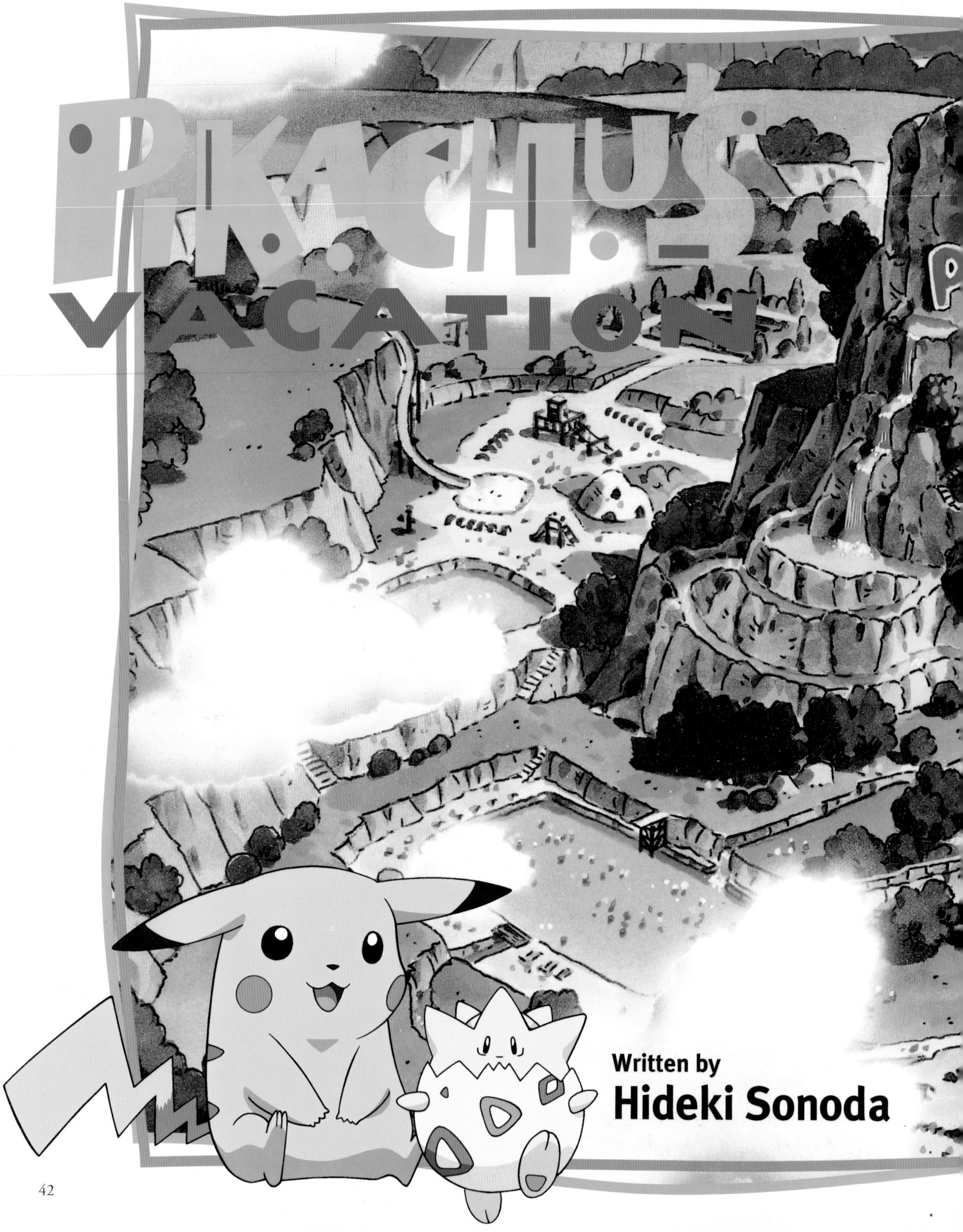

Written by
Hideki Sonoda

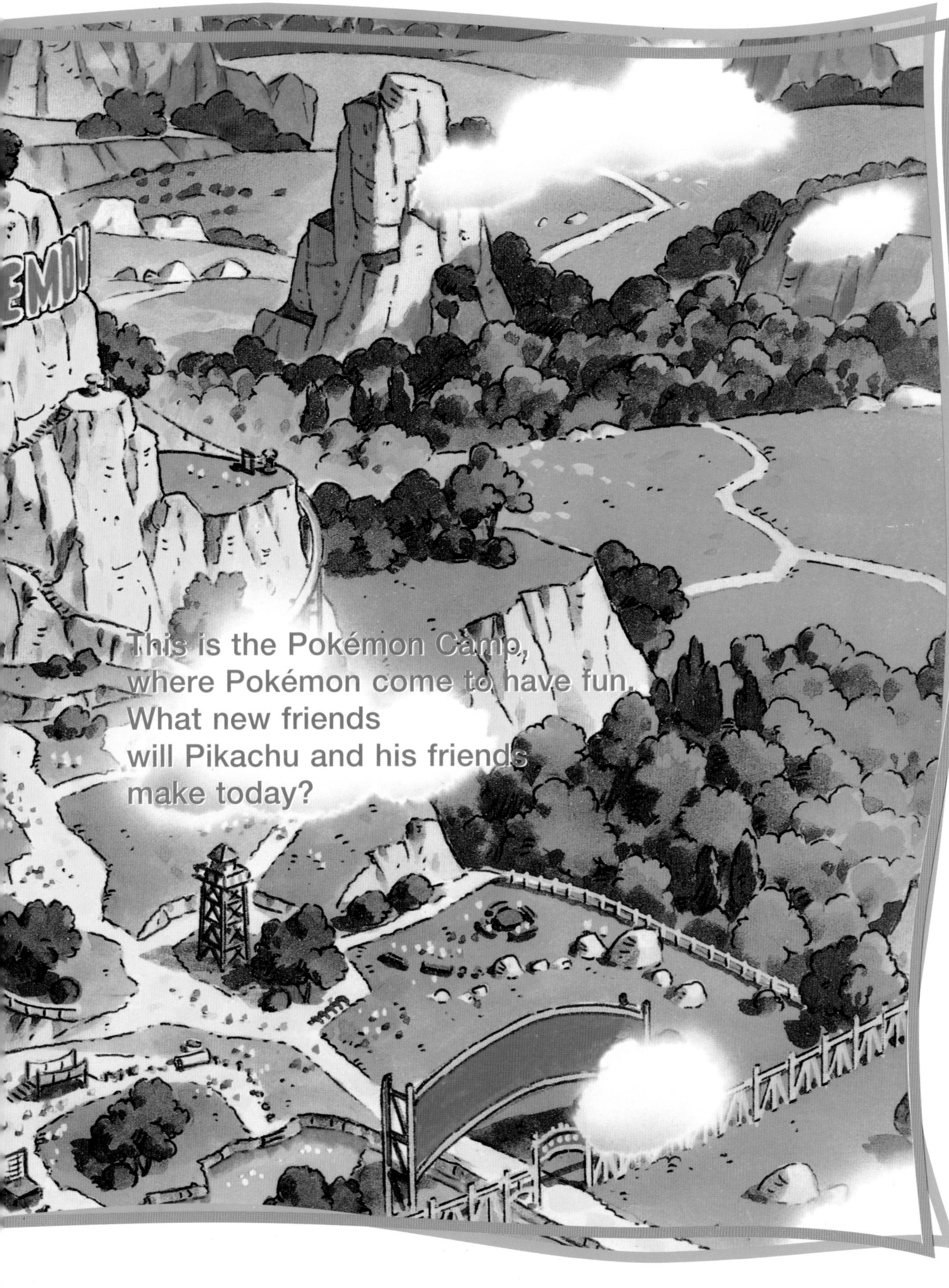

This is the Pokémon Camp,
where Pokémon come to have fun.
What new friends
will Pikachu and his friends
make today?

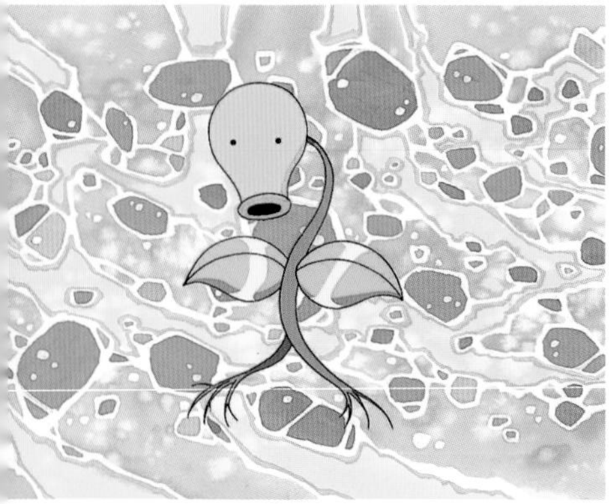

It's time for fun and games at the Pokémon Camp! Pikachu and friends will be all on their own, without Ash and the other trainers, for the whole day.

All the Pokémon dash to the Camp. They can't wait to start playing! But just as they are about to begin, they notice that Togepi is whimpering. Then Togepi begins to cry.

Pikachu and friends are puzzled. What's the matter? They try to cheer Togepi up by making funny faces, but Togepi won't stop bawling. Psyduck, as usual, doesn't

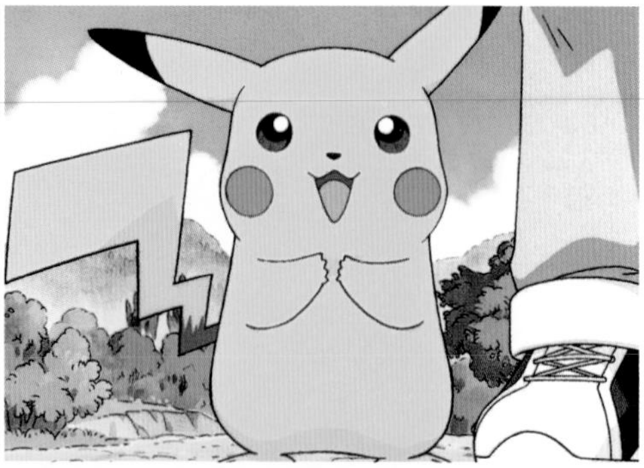

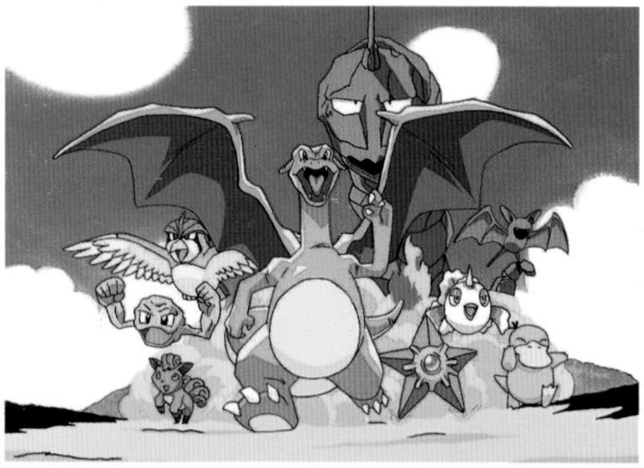

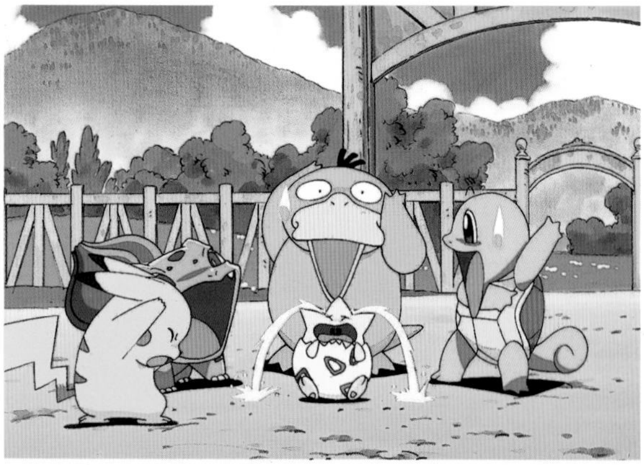

Togepi's sudden tears take everyone by surprise. Pikachu tries to make Togepi laugh with the "Make a Funny Face" attack, but it doesn't work.

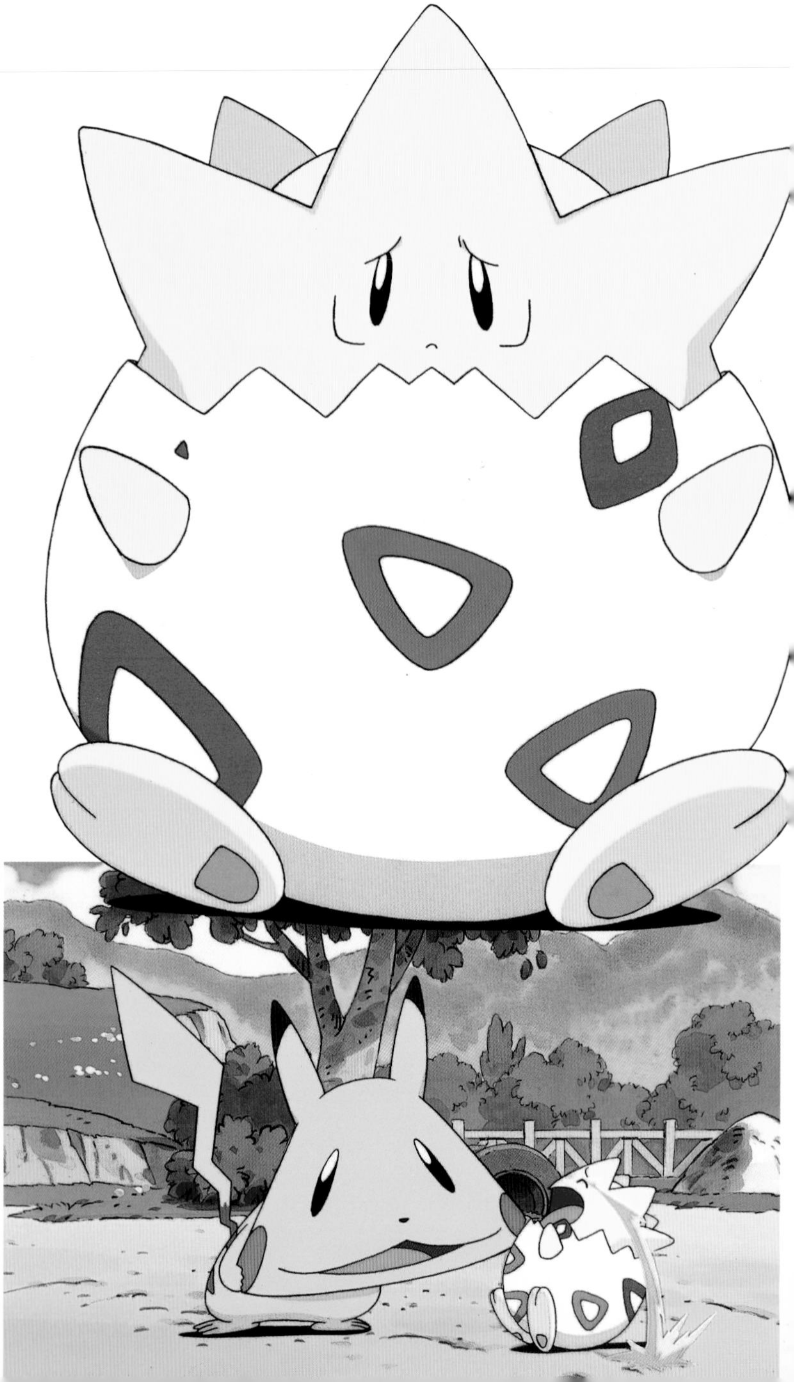

have the foggiest idea what to do, and just scratches its head.

Squirtle is convinced that making funny faces is the answer. But to its dismay, Squirtle's funny face just makes Togepi cry even harder! Squirtle is just about to give up when it gets a bright idea. There is a big, red, juicy apple on a tree. Surely Togepi will stop crying after eating that delicious apple!

Bulbasaur helps by using its "Razor Leaf" to cut the apple down from the branch. But just as they are about to give the apple to Togepi, Psyduck grabs it and eats it in one gulp! Oh no!

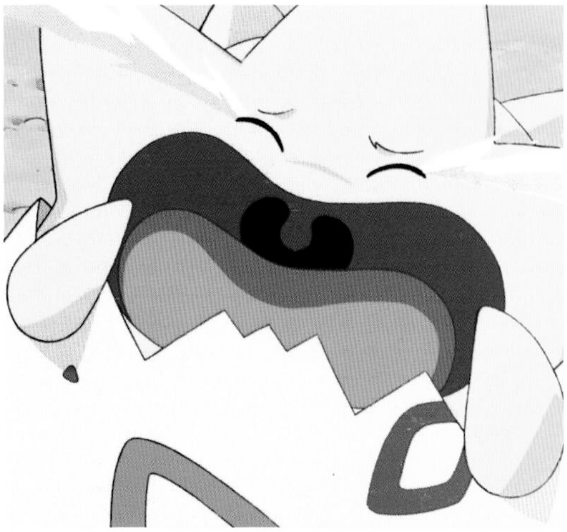

And Togepi just keeps on howling.

Next Bulbasaur tries to comfort Togepi. Rocking Togepi in a "Vine Whip," Bulbasaur sings a lullaby. Finally Togepi falls asleep.

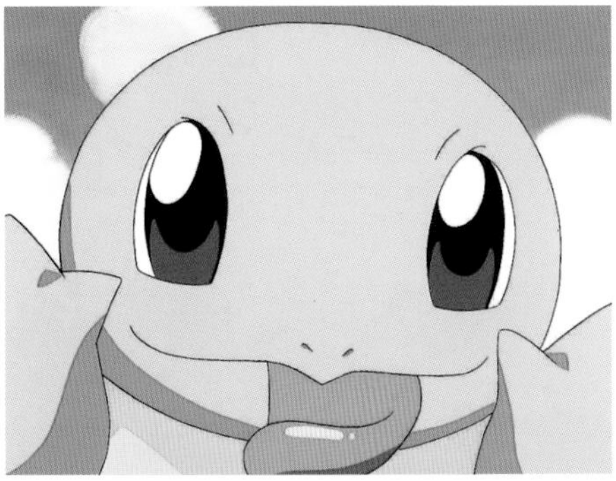

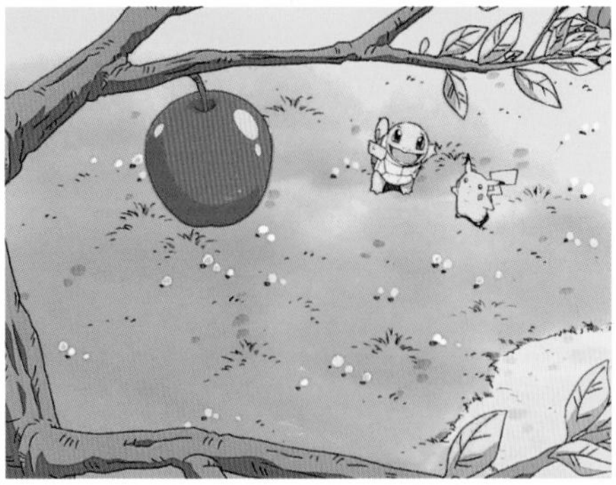

Poor sad Togepi! Psyduck eats Togepi's apple, but Bulbasaur's lullaby does the trick, and now Togepi is all smiles.

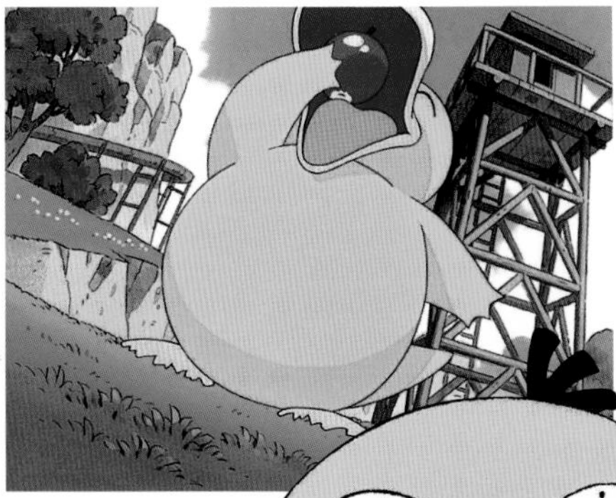

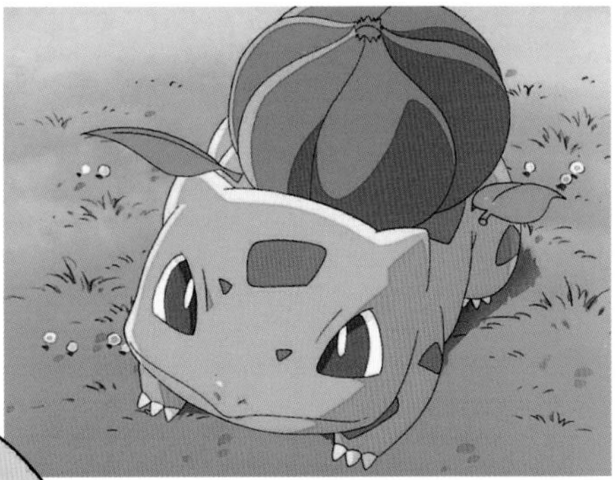

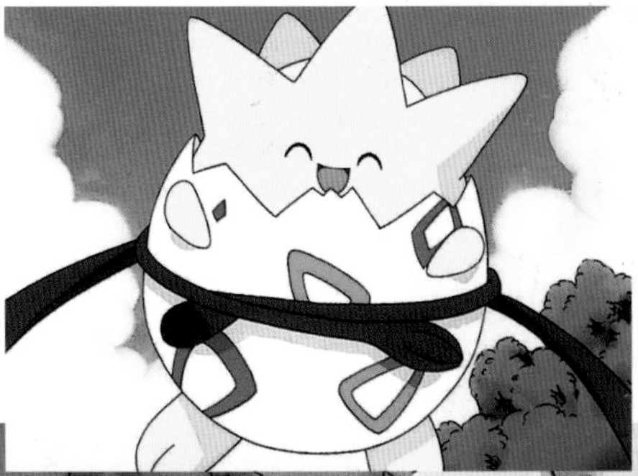

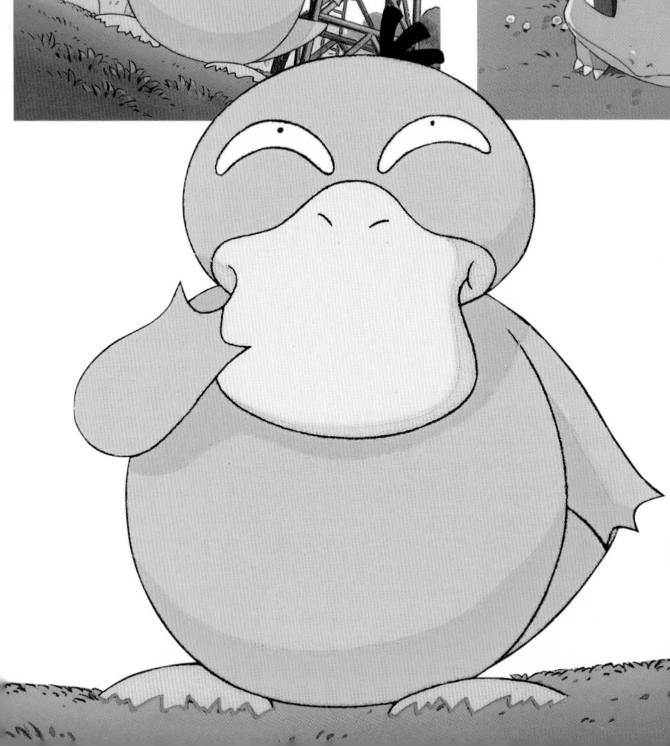

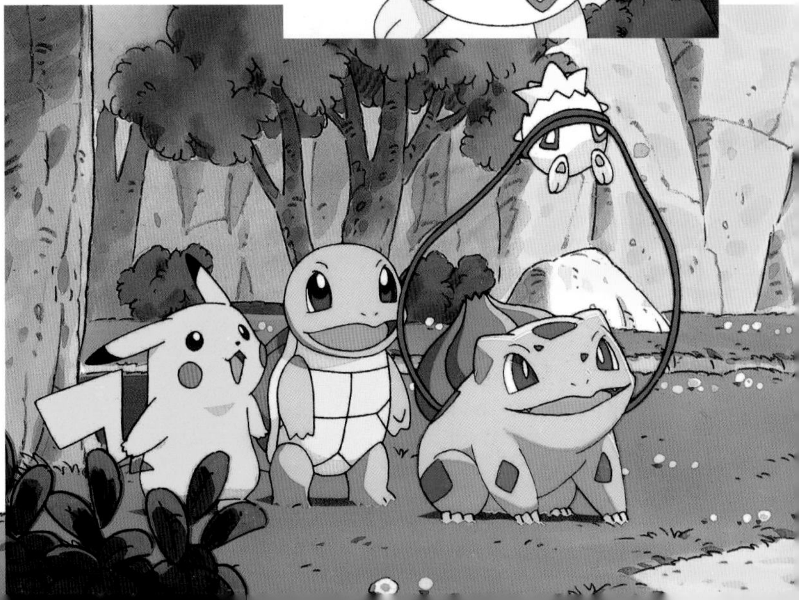

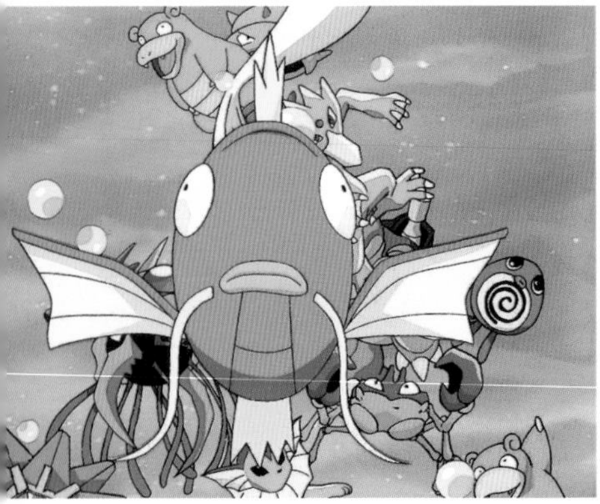

Just then, along come four Pokémon laughing loudly together: Fairy Pokémon Snubble, Lonely Pokémon Cubone, Mouse Pokémon Raichu, and Balloon Pokémon Marril. The four are the best of friends.

Disturbed by the ruckus, Togepi begins to stir. Pikachu pleads with the noisy Pokémon to be quiet, but it's too late. Togepi has woken up and begun to cry again. Seeing all their efforts gone to waste makes Squirtle and Bulbasaur mad.

"Bulba, bulba!" threatens Bulbasaur.

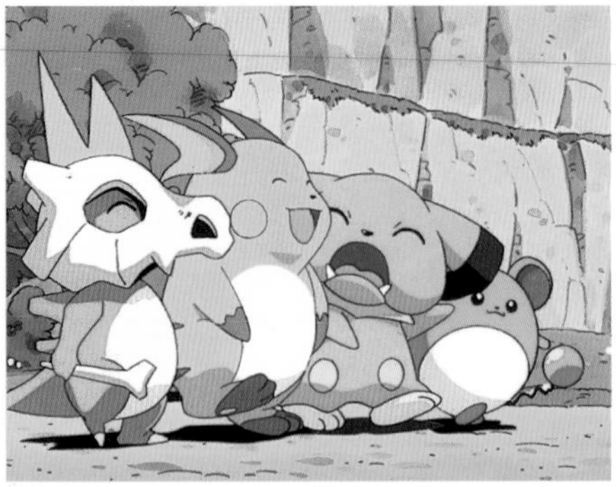

Unaware that Togepi is sleeping, four Pokémon make a loud entrance.

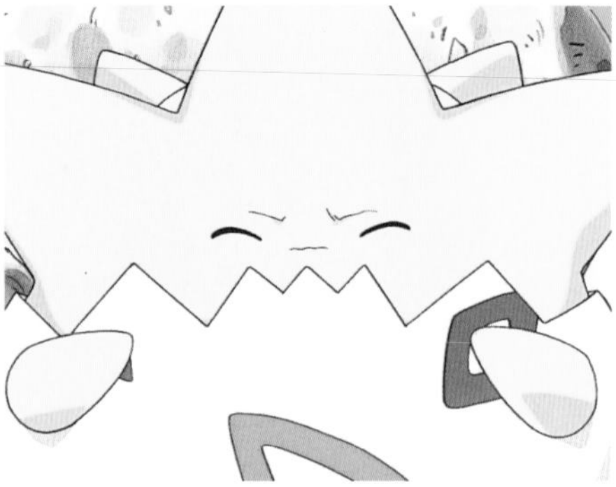

The four strangers' laughter disturbs Togepi's sleep.

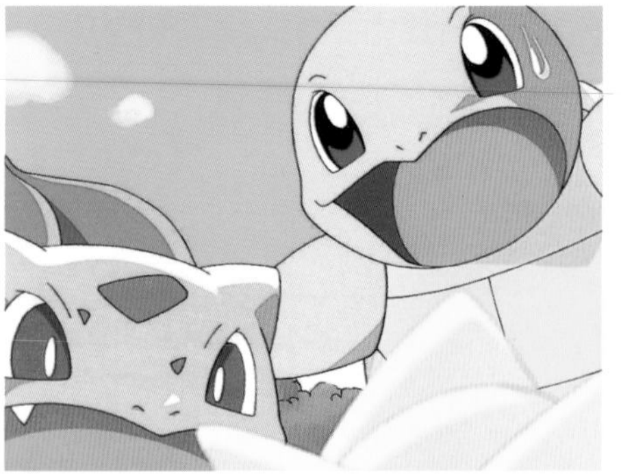

When Togepi starts to wake up, Squirtle and Bulbasaur panic! Quick, do something!

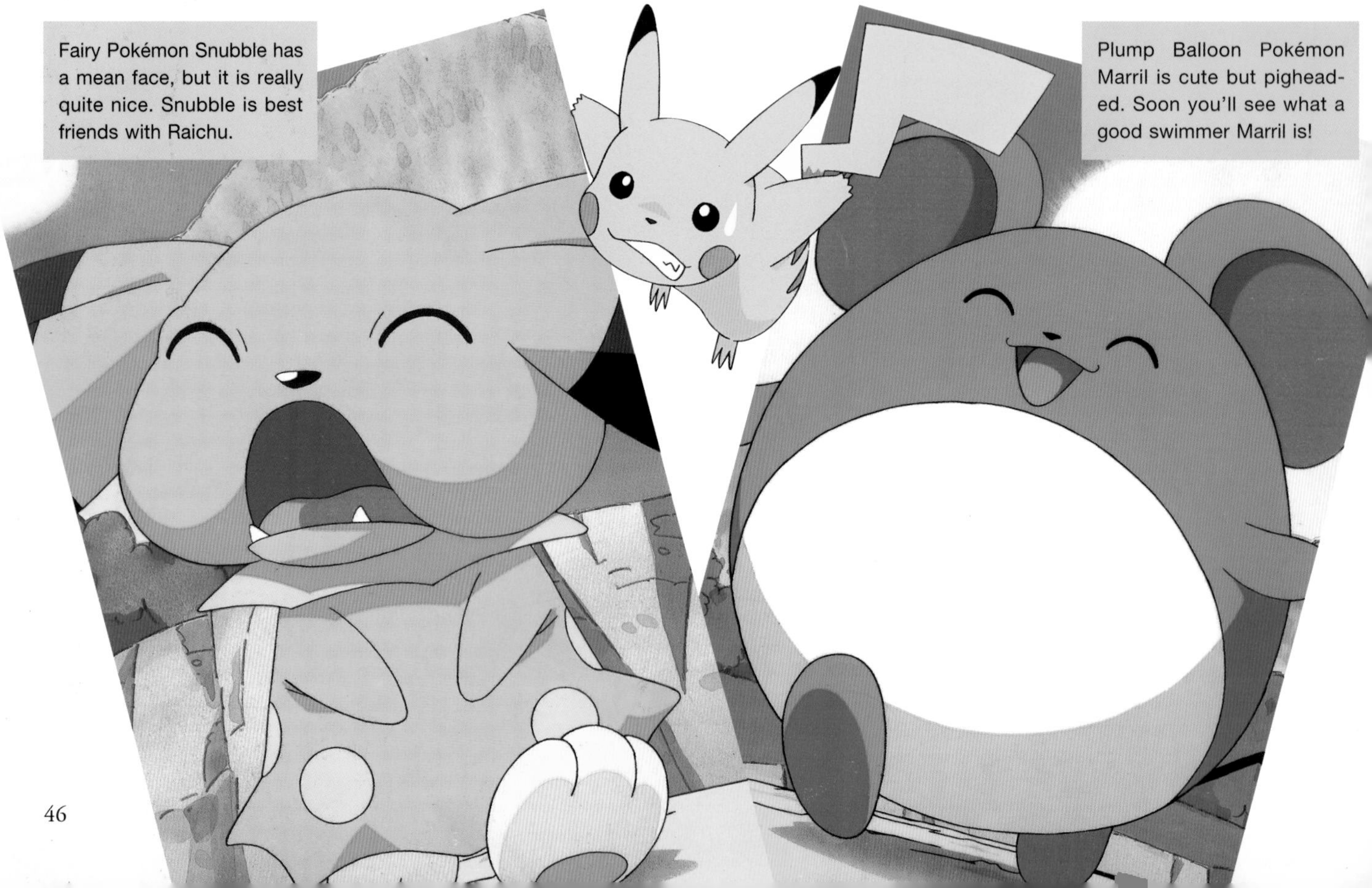

Fairy Pokémon Snubble has a mean face, but it is really quite nice. Snubble is best friends with Raichu.

Plump Balloon Pokémon Marril is cute but pigheaded. Soon you'll see what a good swimmer Marril is!

"Squirtle, squirtle!" complains Squirtle.

Having no idea what they did to deserve such a scolding, Snubble and friends get defensive. "Snubble!"

Pikachu tries to keep the peace by explaining the problem to the four friends. "Pika, pikapikachu...." But Squirtle and Bulbasaur won't give Pikachu a chance.

It looks like a fight is about to break out!

Pikachu desperately tries to make friends by offering to shake Snubble's hand. But meanwhile, some distance away, a catastrophe is about to happen....

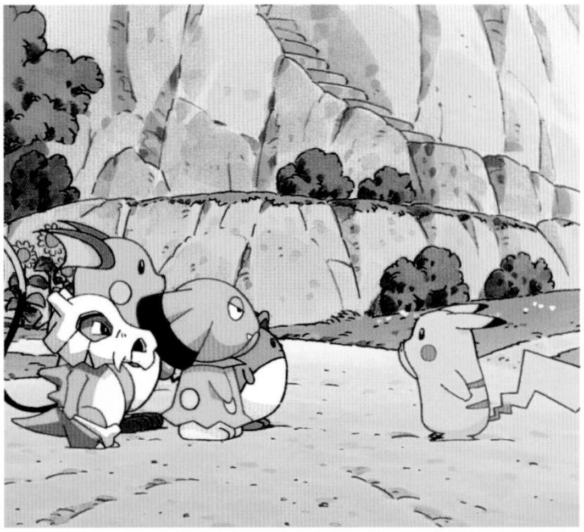

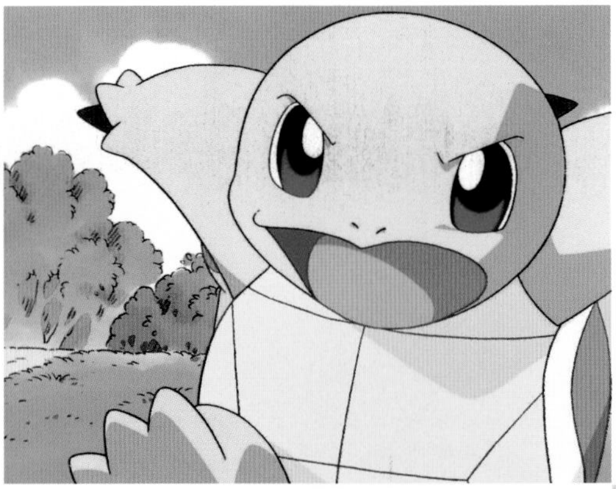

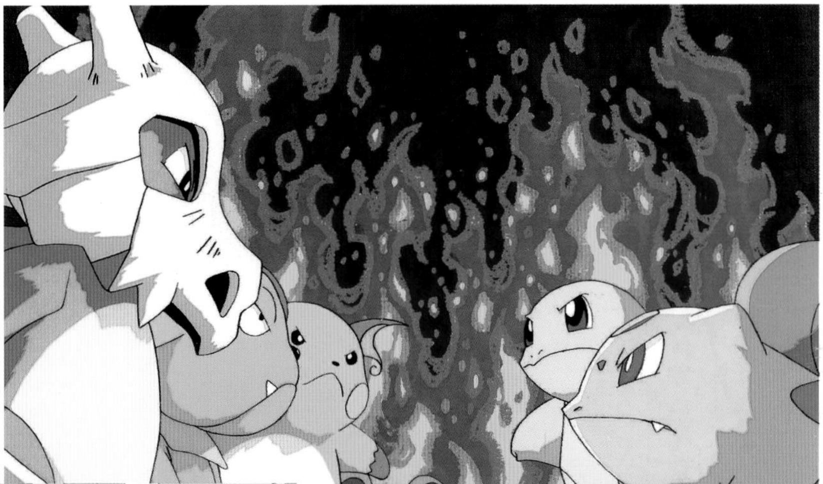

As the four approach, Pikachu pleads with them to be quiet. But when impatient Squirtle jumps into the fray, tempers quickly flare.

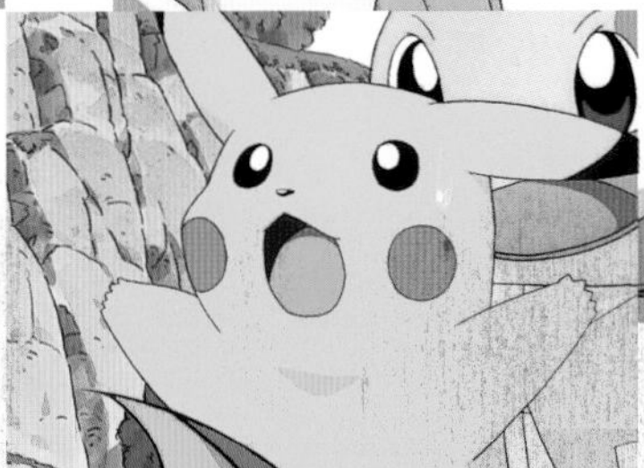

"Pika!" Pikachu tries to smooth things over. In the meantime, Togepi is getting into mischief....

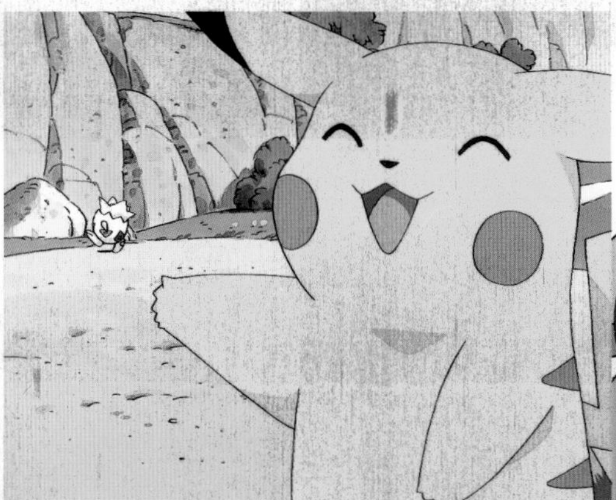

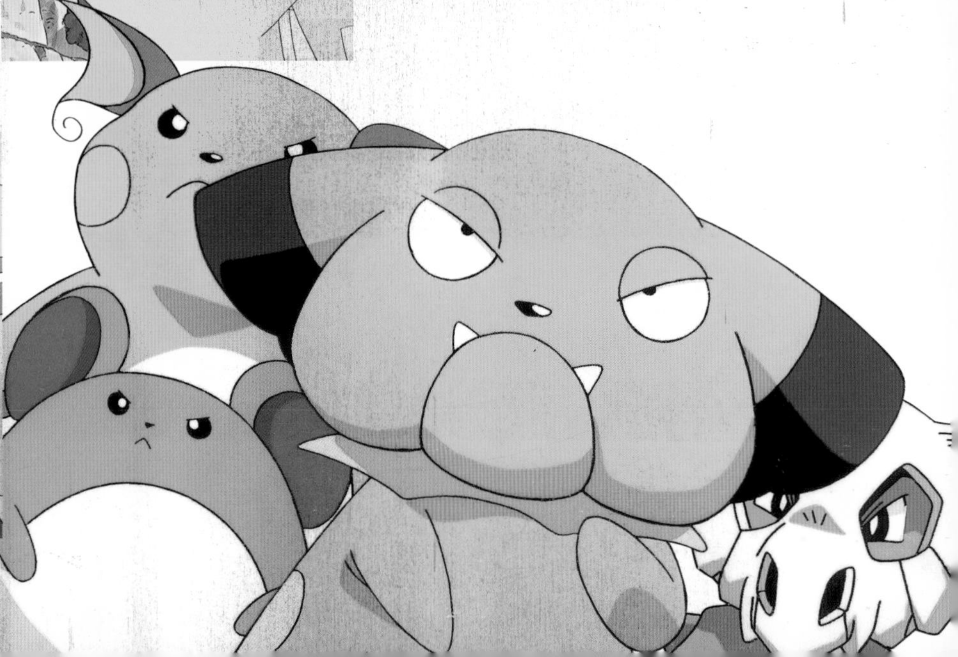

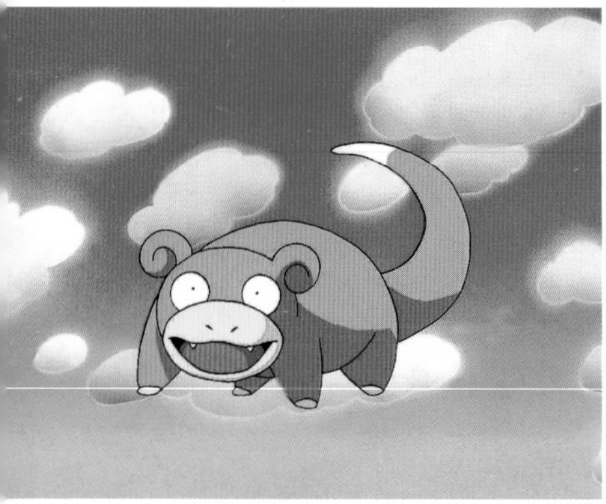

Togepi toddles off by himself towards the log bridge! Chattering happily, Togepi is just stepping unsteadily onto the bridge when....

"Pika!!" Pikachu runs frantically after Togepi. Pikachu has to get there before Togepi falls off! Pikachu follows Togepi onto the bridge, but to Pikachu's dismay, the log begins to roll. Pikachu and Togepi run faster and faster on the rolling log. But in the end, Pikachu falls off the log and straight into the river. "Ker-splash!"

Pikachu lugs Togepi to safety. But when they finally

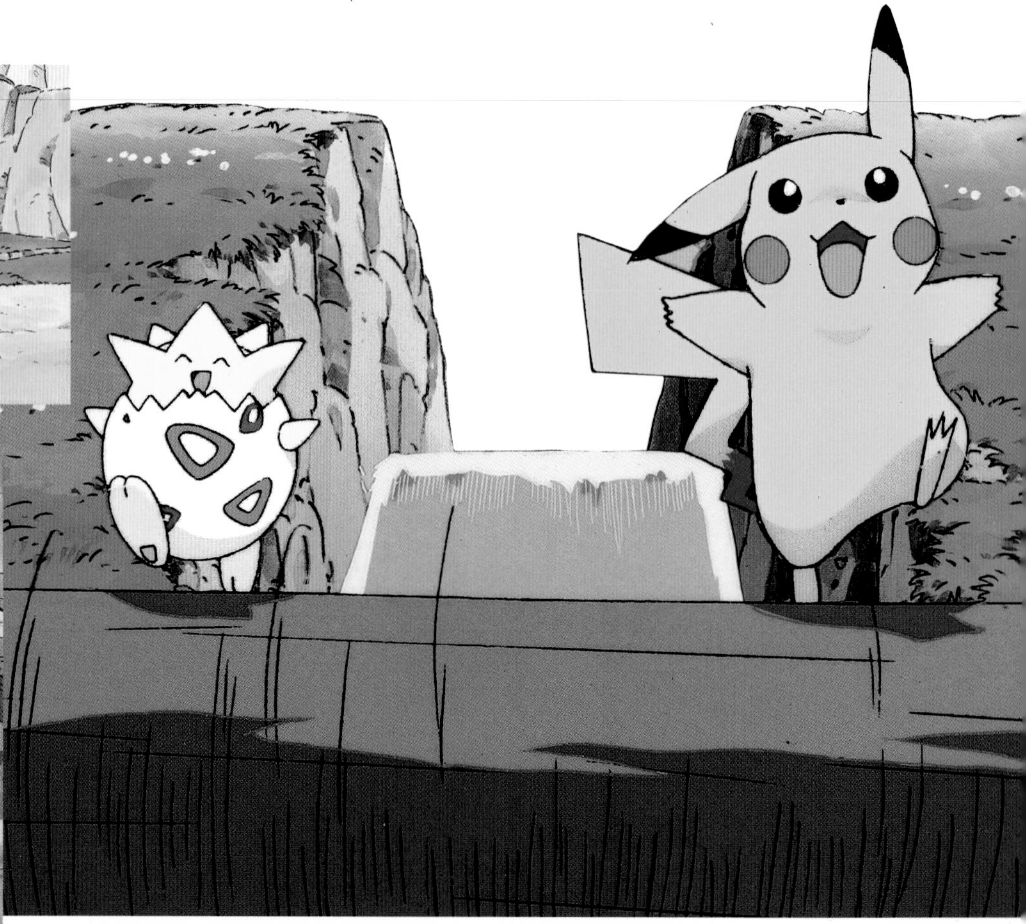

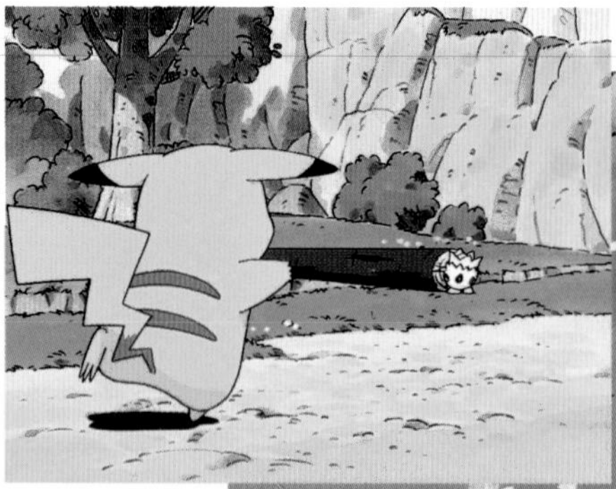

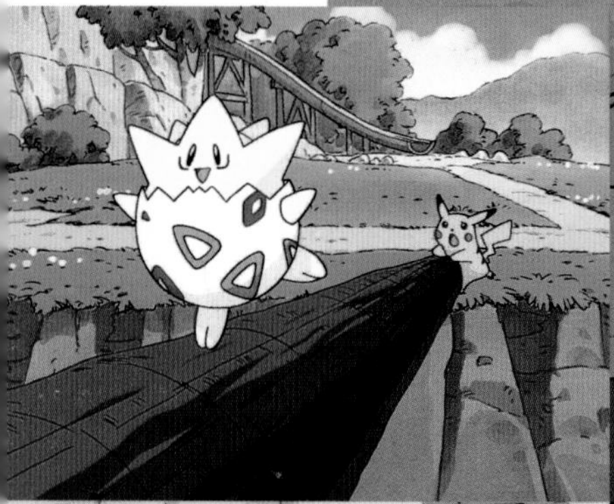

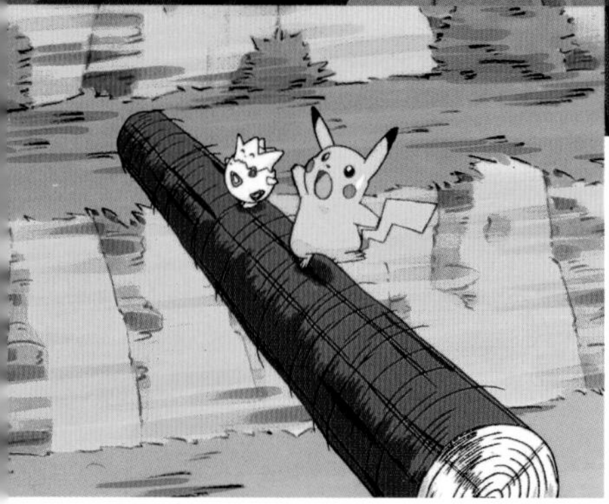

When the log begins to roll, Pikachu is frantic. But Togepi thinks it's all a game!

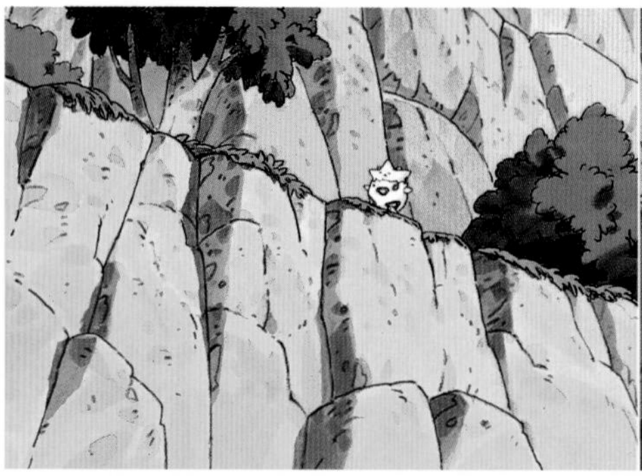

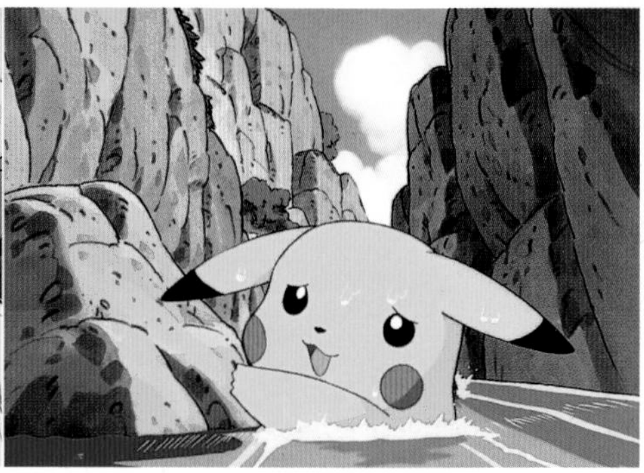

get back to their friends, they find them locked in a bragging contest.

Squirtle boasts that it's stronger than Snubble.

And Snubble boasts that it's stronger than Squirtle.

They brag about everything from who can puff their chests out the furthest, to, oddly enough, who can roll their eyes the best! Neither side shows any sign of backing down.

Pikachu lets out a big sigh.

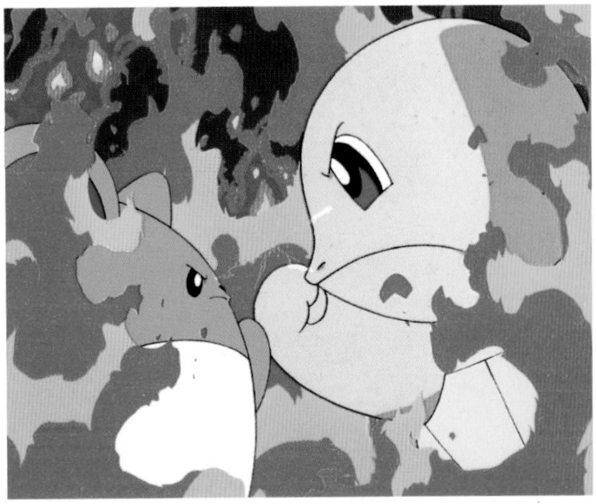

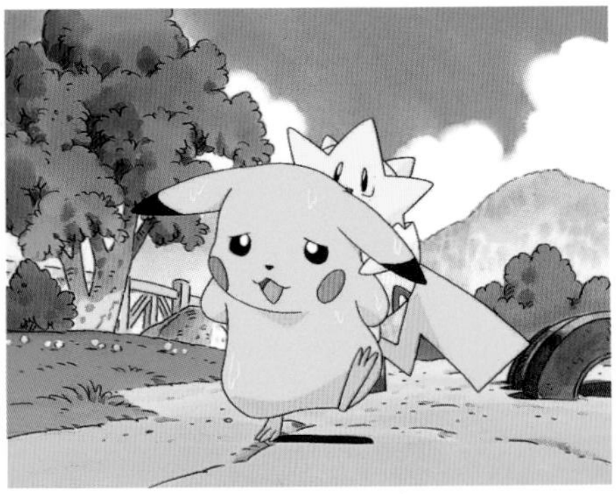

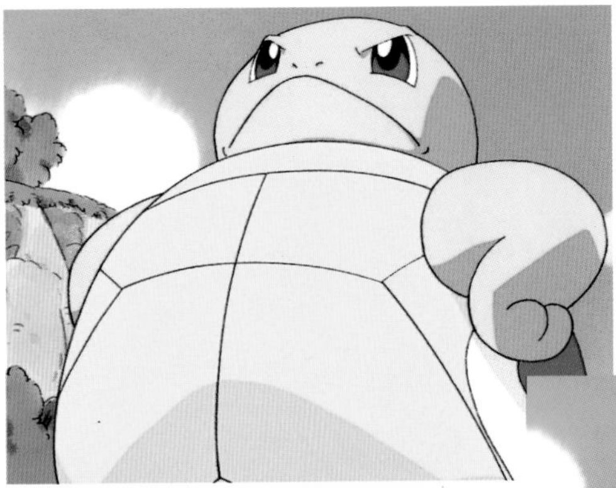

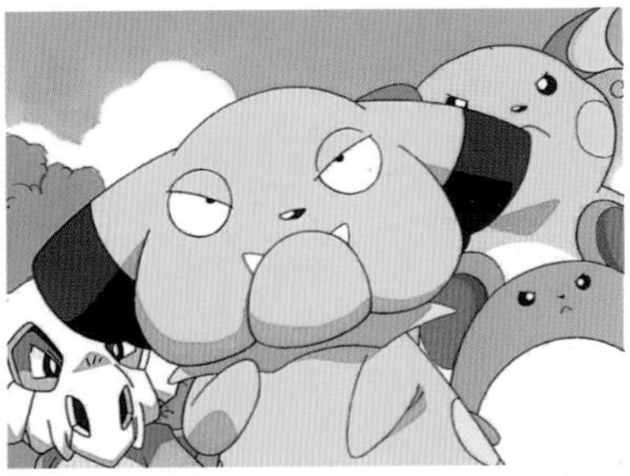

A sopping-wet Pikachu gives Togepi a piggyback ride. Upon their return, they find the other Pokémon in a tense standoff. Looks like a fight is brewing!

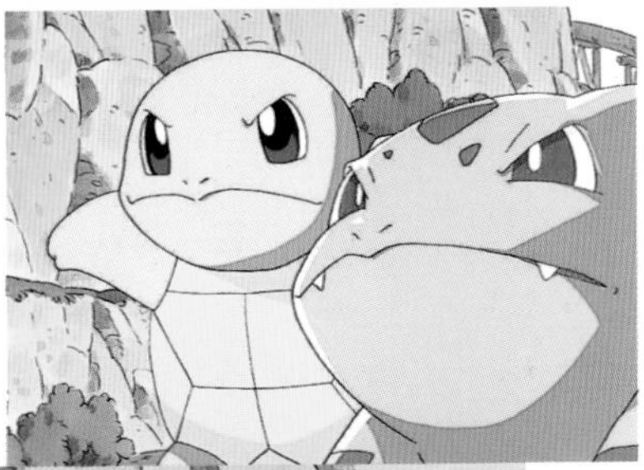

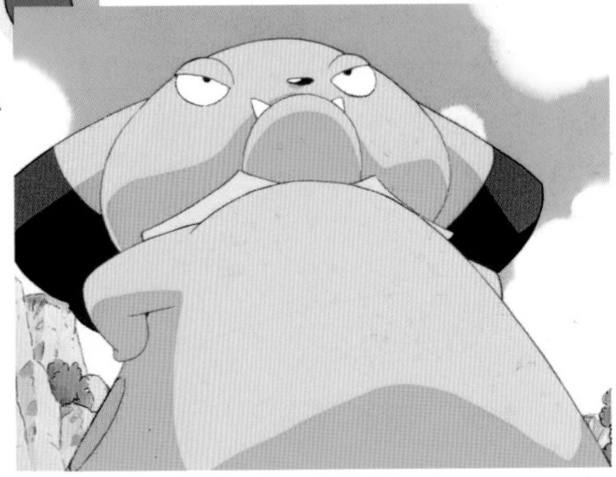

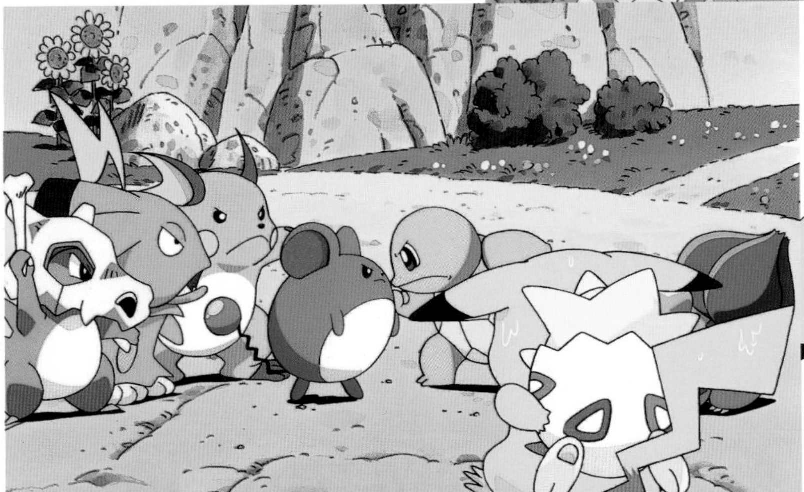

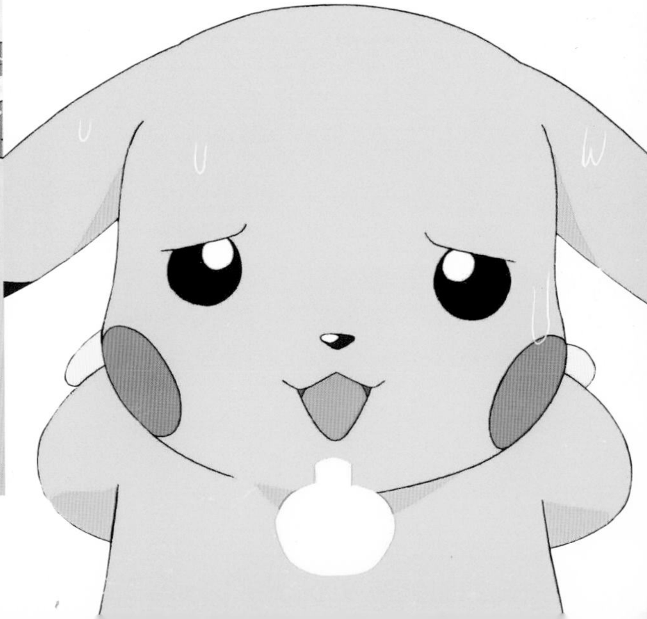

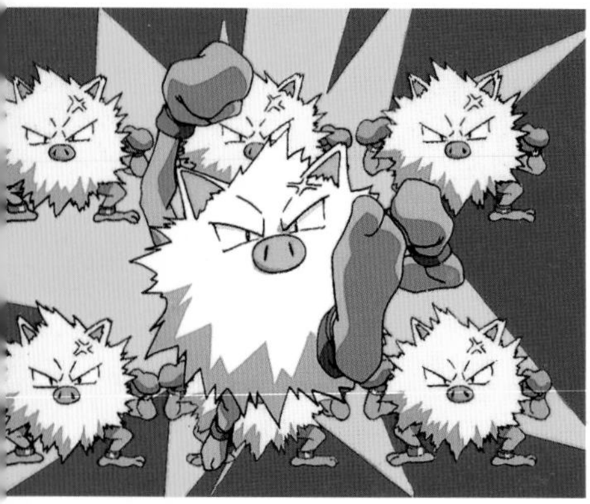

This special, natural swimming pool is perfectly designed for Pokémon. Crystal-clear water flows into it from a beautiful waterfall above.

All the Pokémon in the pool are enjoying a refreshing dip. But the calm is broken by a disturbance. Squirtle and Marril have decided to have a swimming race here.

But before we swim, we need to stretch, right? The two Pokémon finish their stretching and get into position on the diving platforms.

"Pikaaaa!" shouts Pikachu to start the race, just as Electrode sets off a loud explosion. "Boom!" Squirtle and Marril dive into the pool at the same time.

Everyone cheers Squirtle and Marril on. Both Pokémon

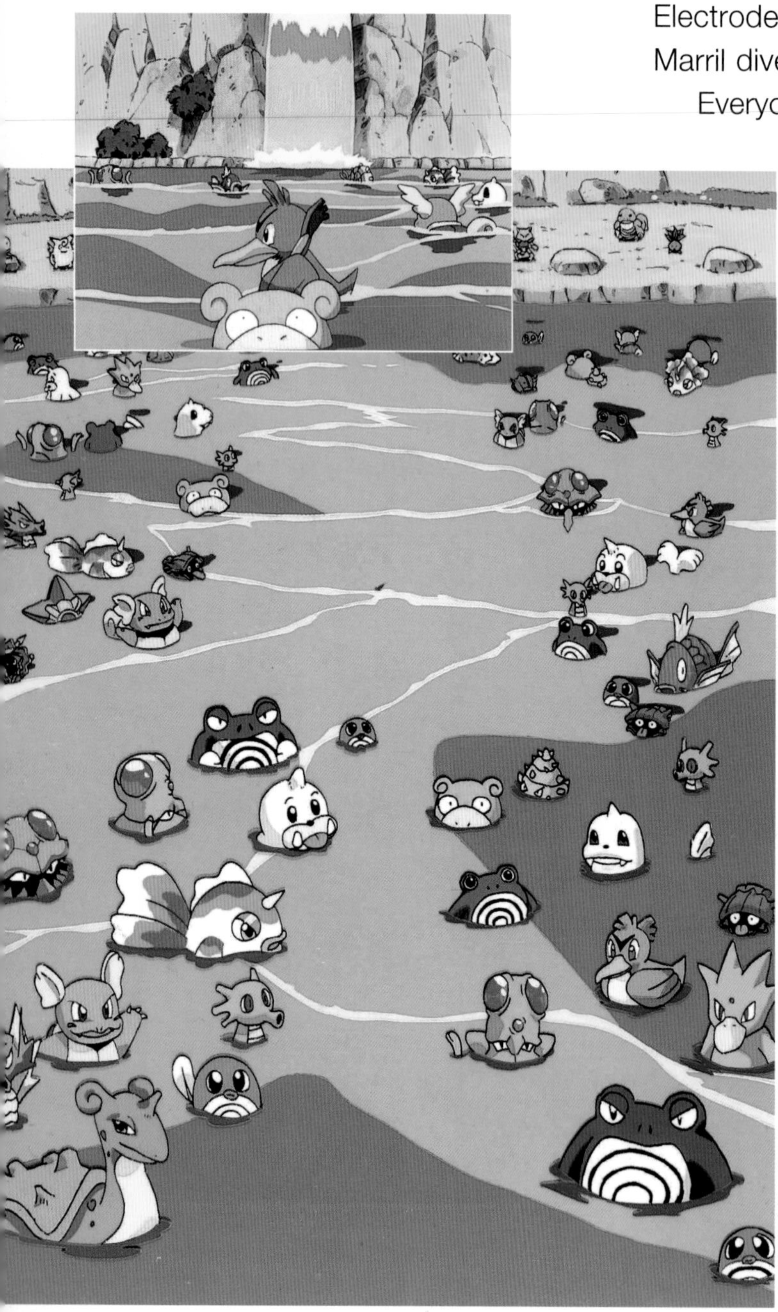

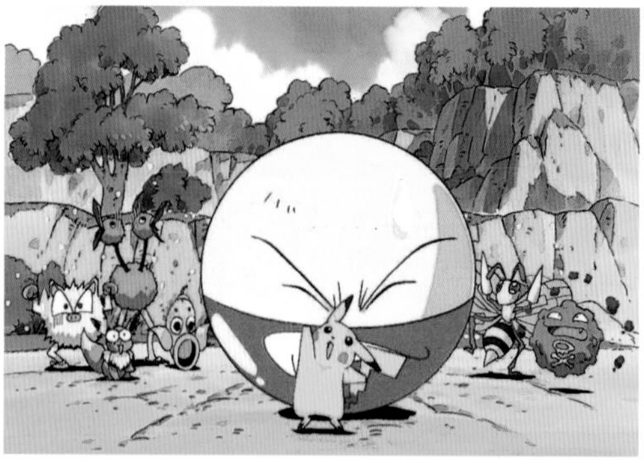

A variety of Water Pokémon are having a great time in the Pokémon Camp Pool, which is about to become Squirtle and Marril's racecourse.

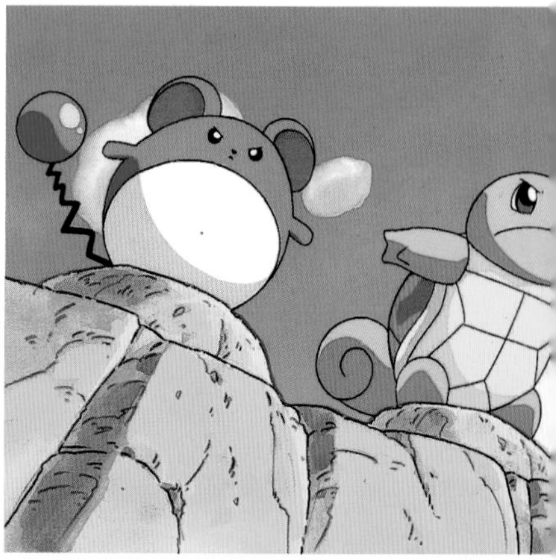

Pikachu and Electrode announce the start of the race together. At their signal, Squirtle and Marril are off!

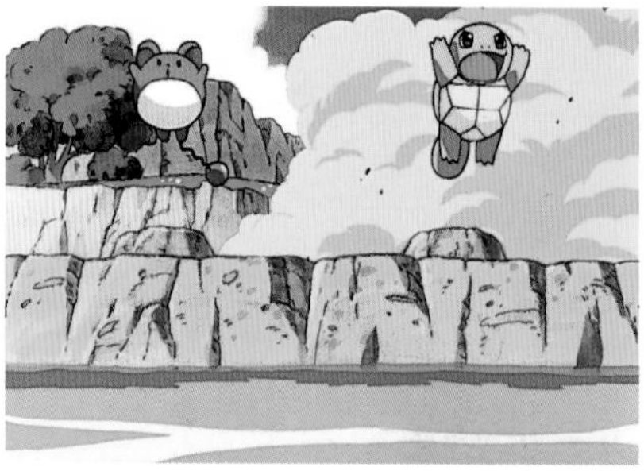

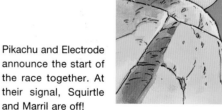

are swimming their hardest—both are determined to win the race. But Marril, swimming face down, isn't looking where its going...and so the Balloon Pokémon veers off the course and crashes right into Starmie!

Squirtle sees an opportunity to take the lead, but suddenly stops. "Squirtle!? Squirtle!?" What's going on?

Suddenly everyone, including Squirtle, realizes what the problem is. Squirtle has swum on top of Goldeen who, unfortunately, is swimming in the opposite direction!

Meanwhile, Marril has gotten back on course. In moments, Marril has reached the finish line. Needless to say, Marril and its friends are very happy about the big win!

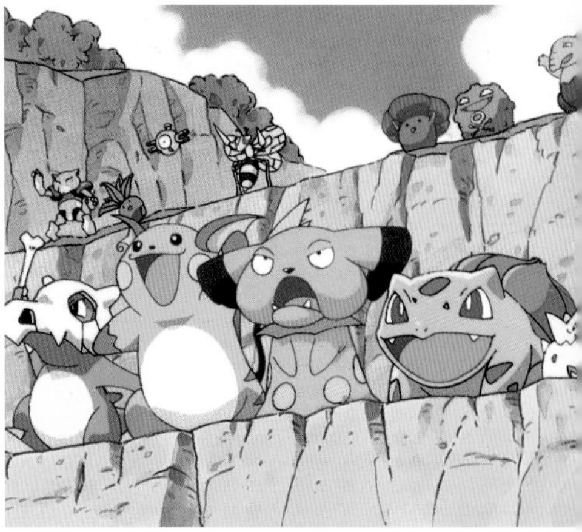

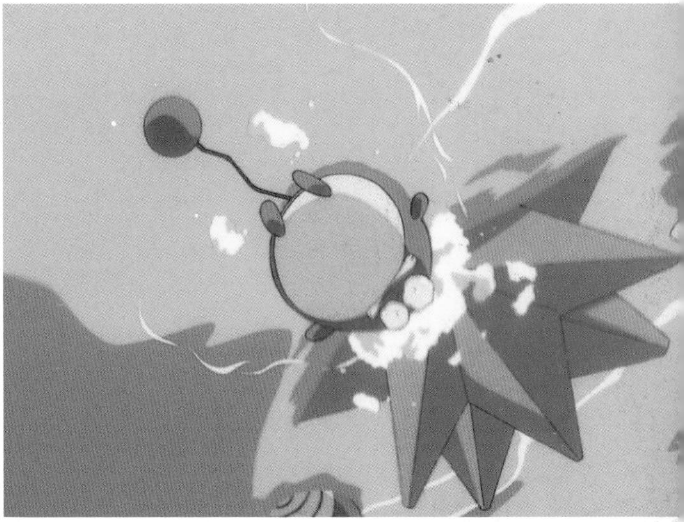

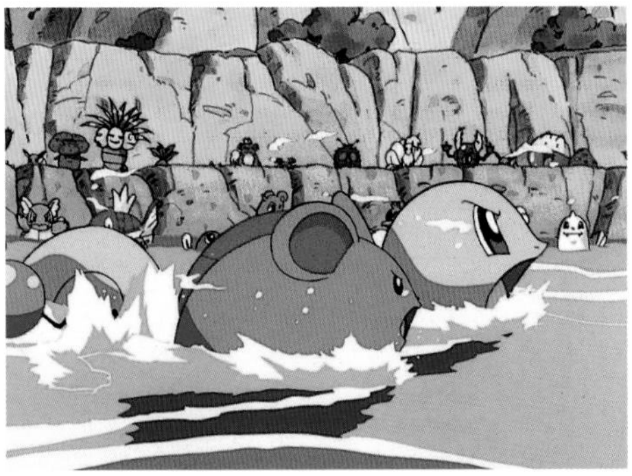

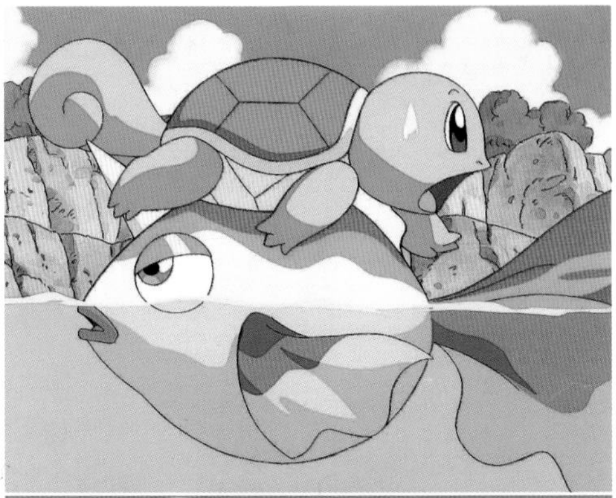

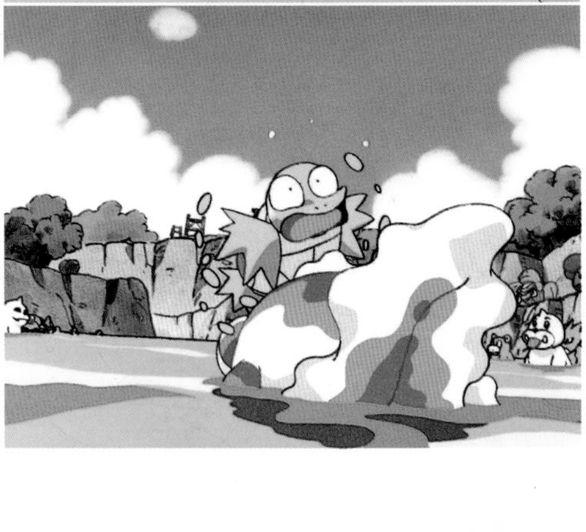

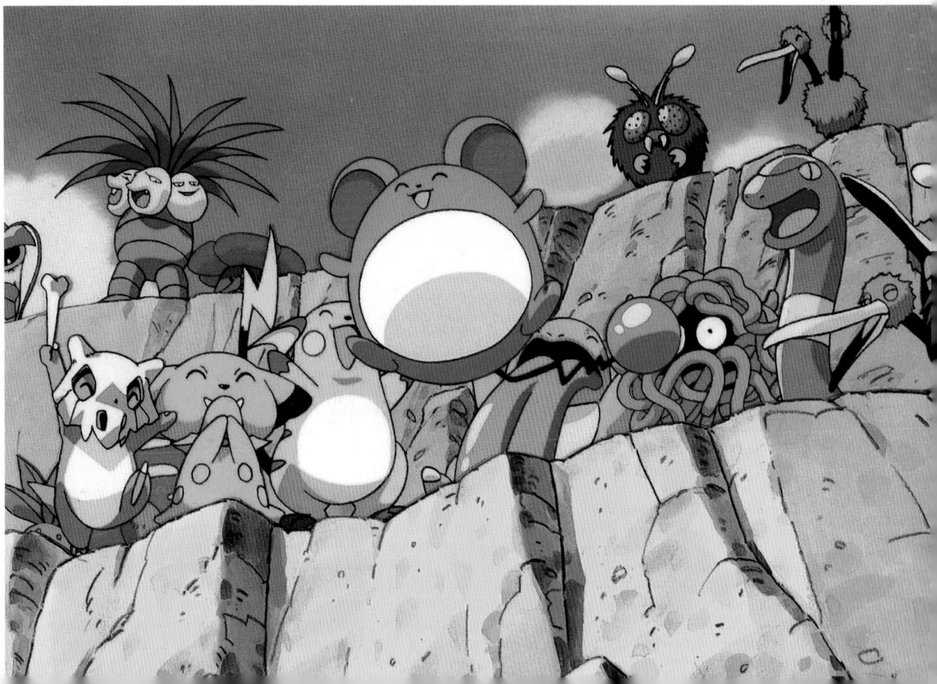

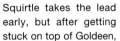

Squirtle takes the lead early, but after getting stuck on top of Goldeen, it's back to the start! Squirtle tries its best, but Marril wins the race. Marril and friends jump for joy.

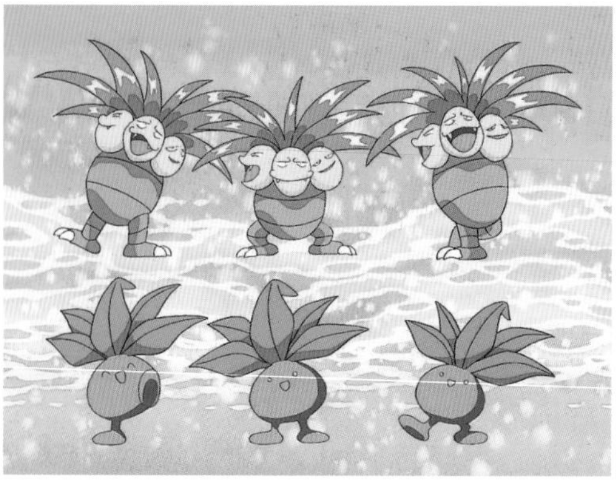

None of Pikachu's efforts to help everyone make friends are working.

"Raaaaaiiii!" Overcome with excitement, Raichu accidentally shoots a bolt of electricity in Togepi's direction. Pikachu jumps to protect Togepi and gets hit with the brunt of the electricity. "Pika, pikachu!!"

Now even mild-mannered Pikachu gets mad. It's like the straw that broke the camel's back. In this case, you could say, "It's the bolt of electricity that broke Pikachu's patience!"

Pikachu and Raichu face off, pushing against each

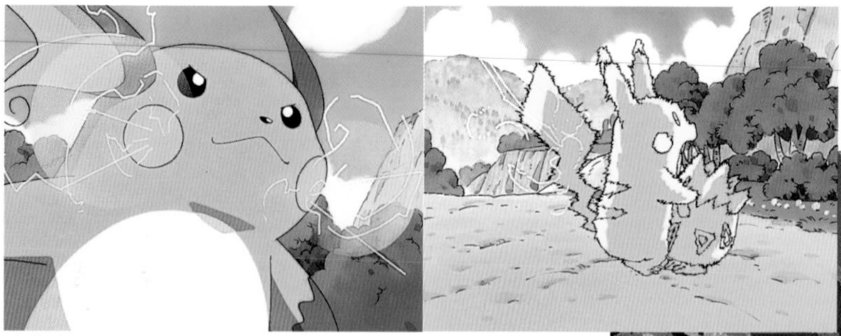

When Pikachu finally loses its temper, Pikachu and Raichu glare at each other fiercely.

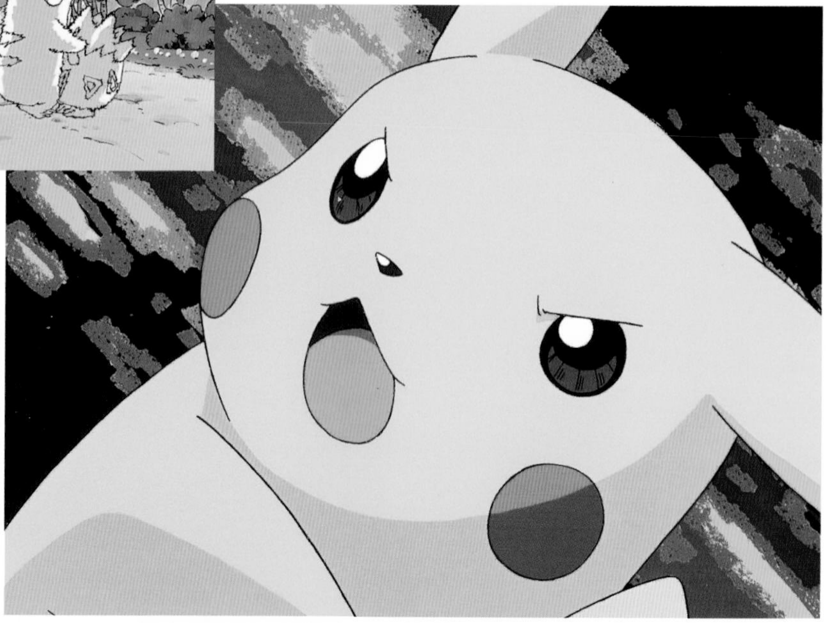

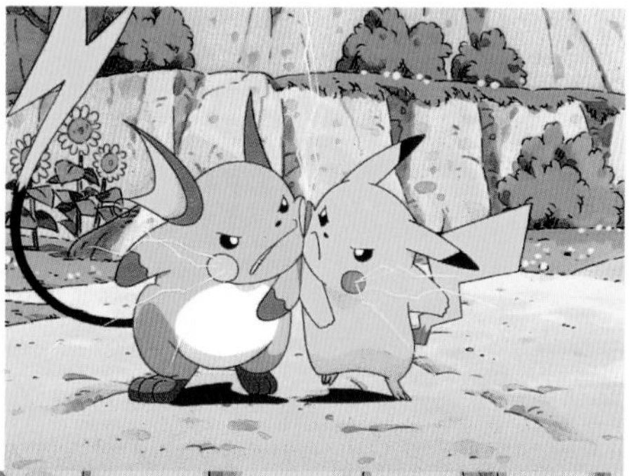

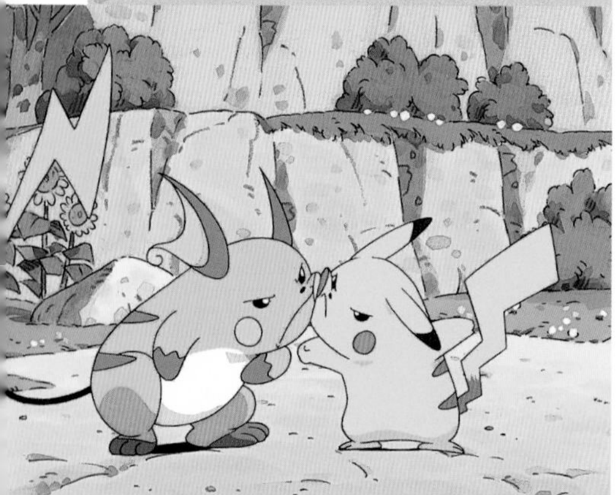

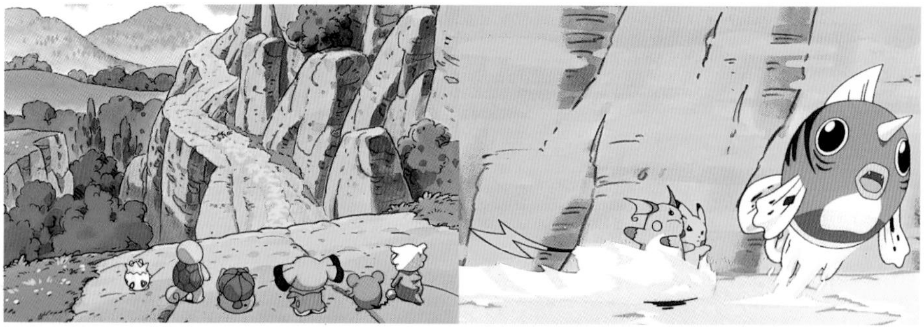

Still frowning, the two Mouse Pokémon race up into the hills, over the water, and all over the vast Pokémon Camp—without a thought to the havoc they cause!

other's electricity pouch. Suddenly, they start to run. Pikachu! Raichu! Watch where you're going...!

Glued together by electricity, the two Pokémon race faster and faster. Up hills, down slides, on and on they run! Neither is willing to back down one bit!

"Boom!" Together they crash through the walls of the maze, and they knock over Jigglypuff who was playing on the logs. "Whoosh!" They slide down a rope in one go, almost running over Mr. Mime. And "Pow!" They knock Hitmonlee and Hitmonchan off their feet! Still, the two keep running!

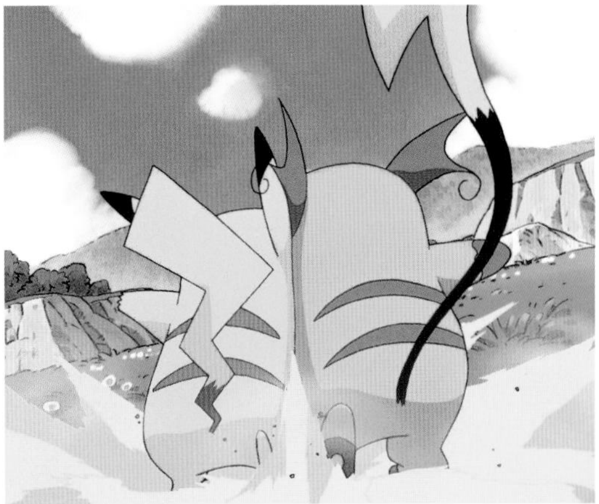

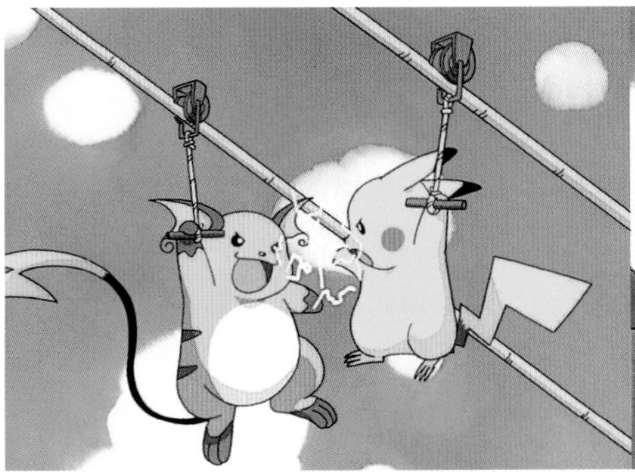

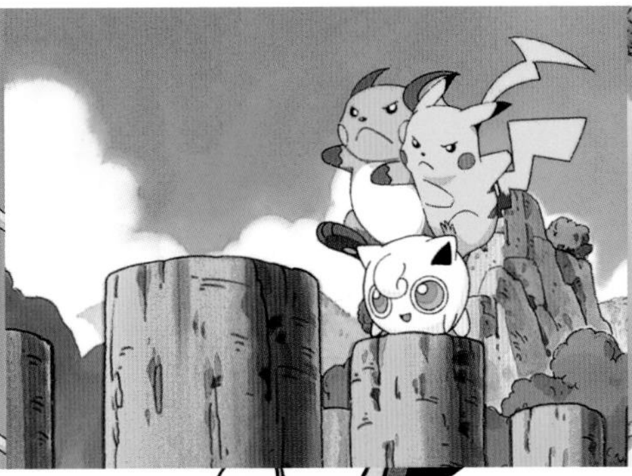

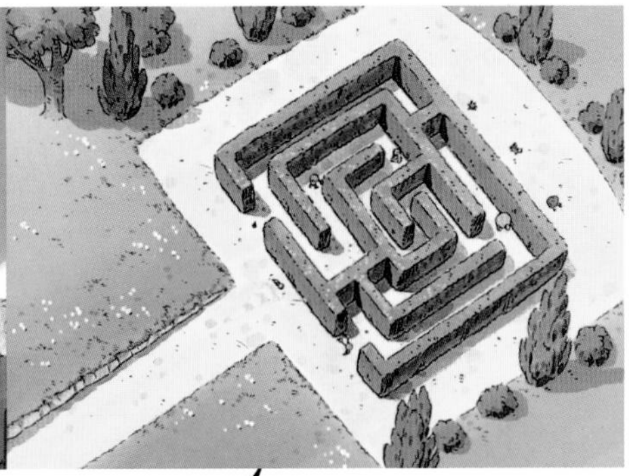

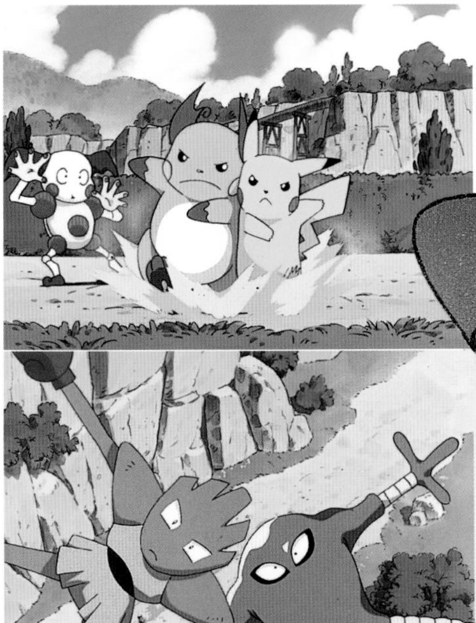

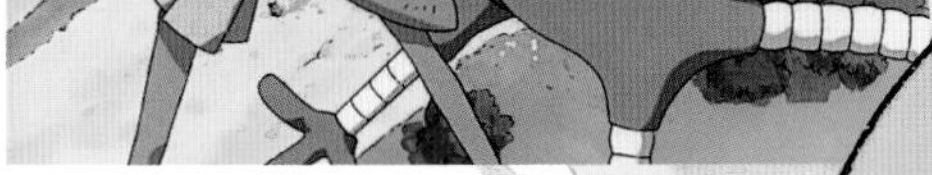

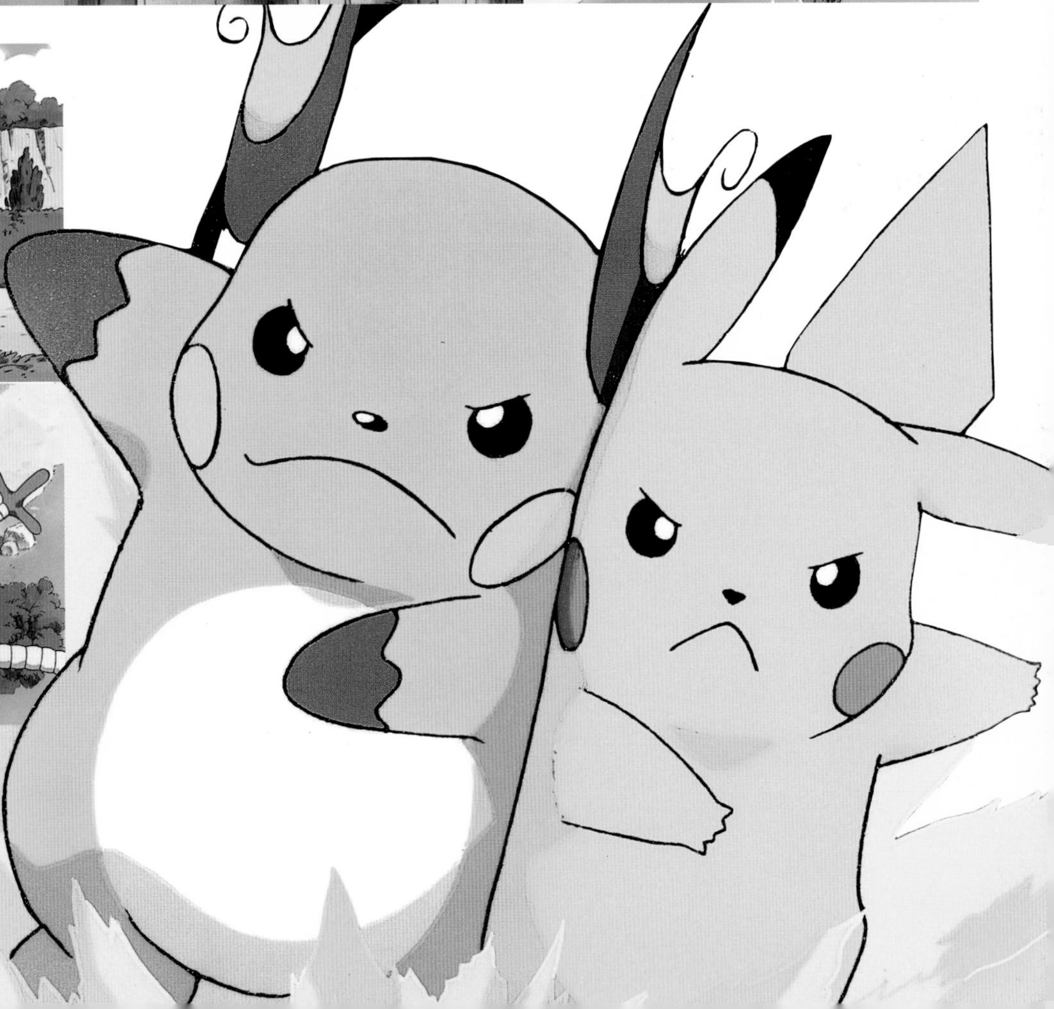

Stubborn Pikachu and Raichu play rough! Even knocking over both Hitmonlee and Hitmonchan doesn't make them stop!

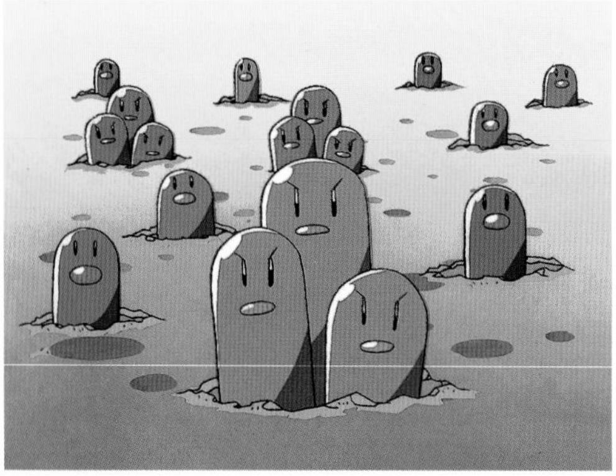

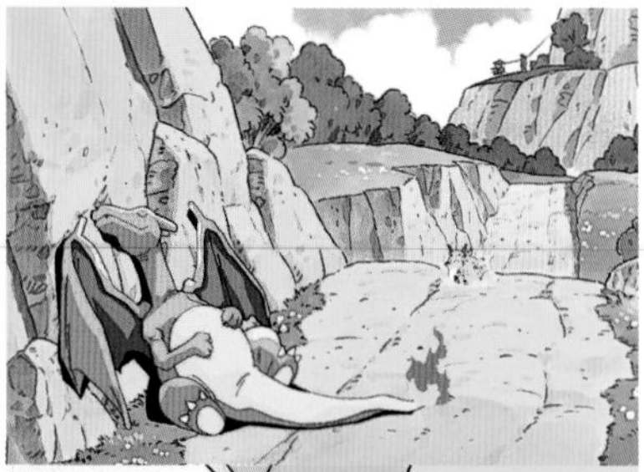

On the mountain road, Charizard is taking a nice little nap. Even the flame flickering on its tail looks relaxed.

Suddenly Pikachu and Raichu appear, racing down the road toward Charizard! Not looking where they're going...the pair accidentally trample over Charizard's tail!

"Zzzzzarrrrrr!" Charizard roars with surprise. Who dares to step on my tail and wake me from my nap? Furious, Charizard rears up, blasting flame from its mouth, and thunders after the two Pokémon.

You're the ones! Charizard screeches, unfurling its wings with a great "Whoosh!" The blast knocks Pikachu and Raichu over!

Pikachu and Raichu get knocked off the edge of the cliff!

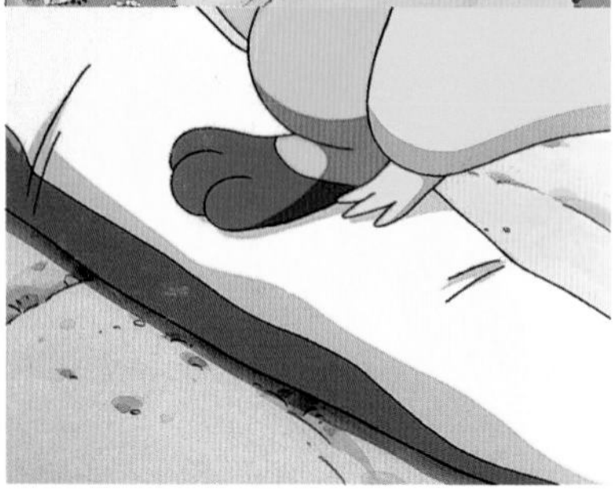

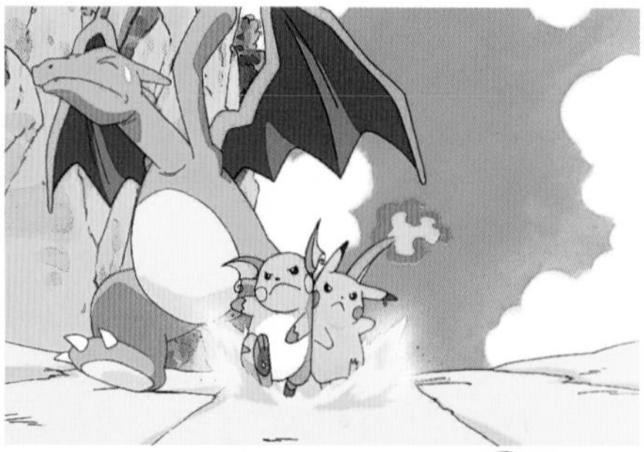

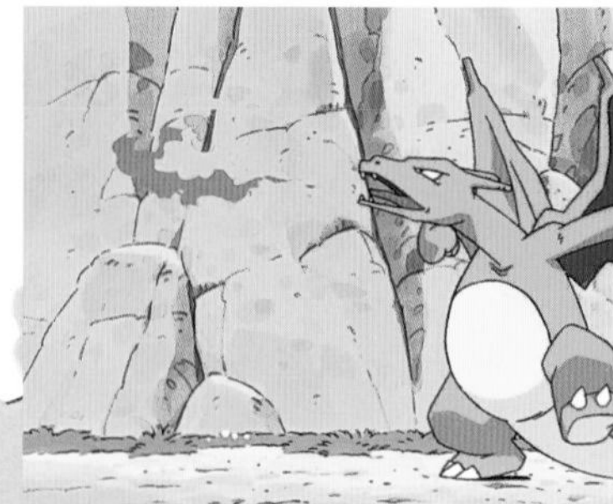

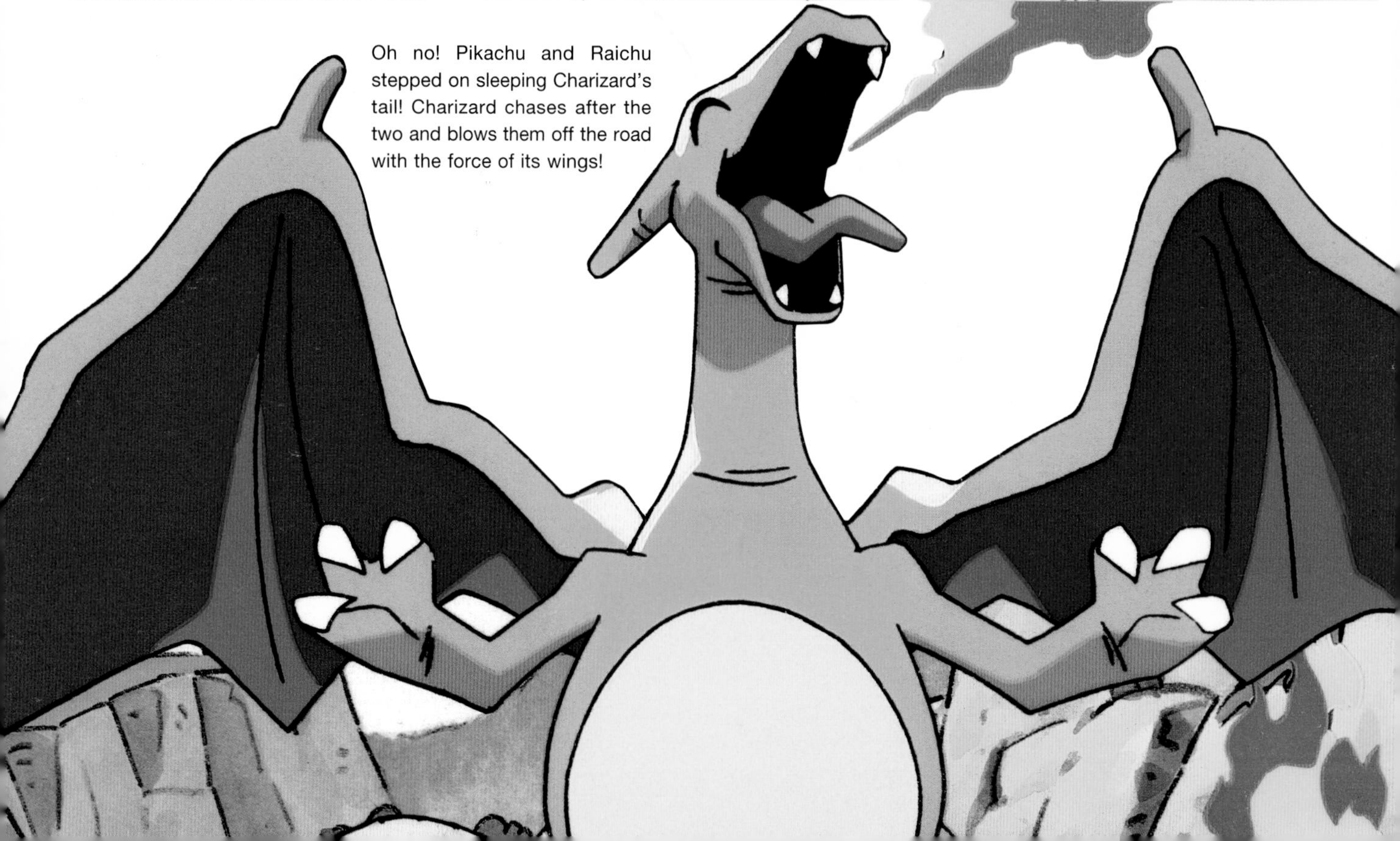

Oh no! Pikachu and Raichu stepped on sleeping Charizard's tail! Charizard chases after the two and blows them off the road with the force of its wings!

"PIKAAAAaaa!" "RAAAiii!" The two yell as they fall.

Fortunately, at the exact spot where they are about to land, big, soft, furry Snorlax is sleeping, its puffy tummy rising up and down with each breath.

"Boing!" Pikachu and Raichu bounce safely onto Snorlax's tummy. But just when they think they've landed safely, Snorlax rolls over—right on top of them!

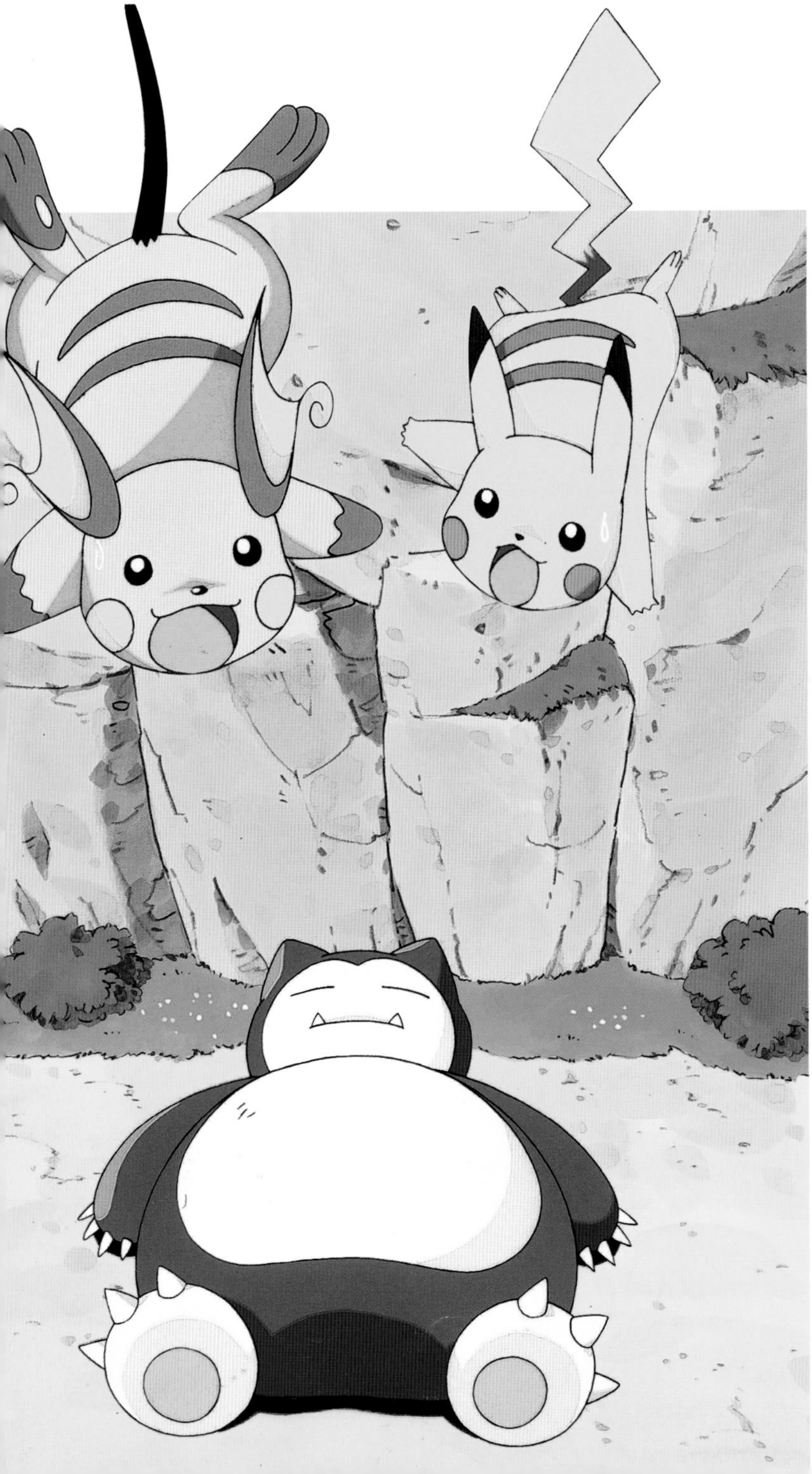

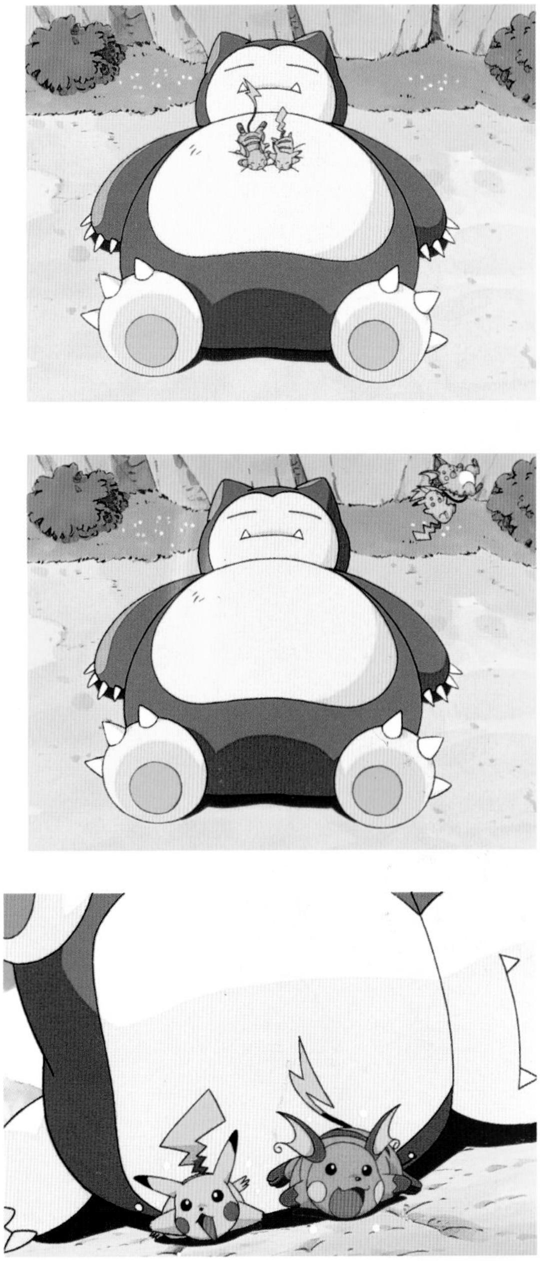

The two fly off a cliff and bounce off sleeping Snorlax!

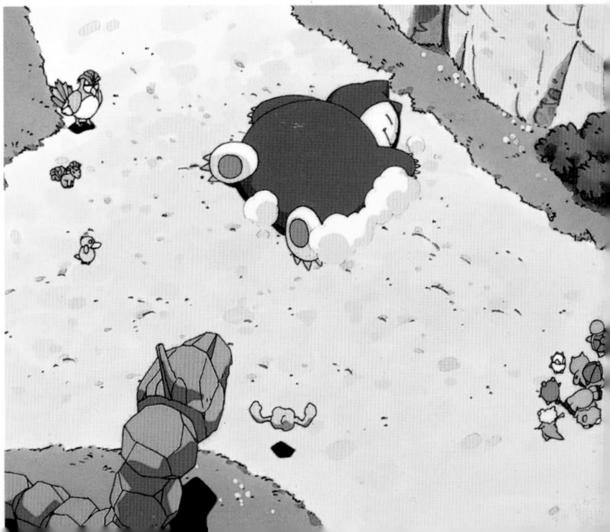

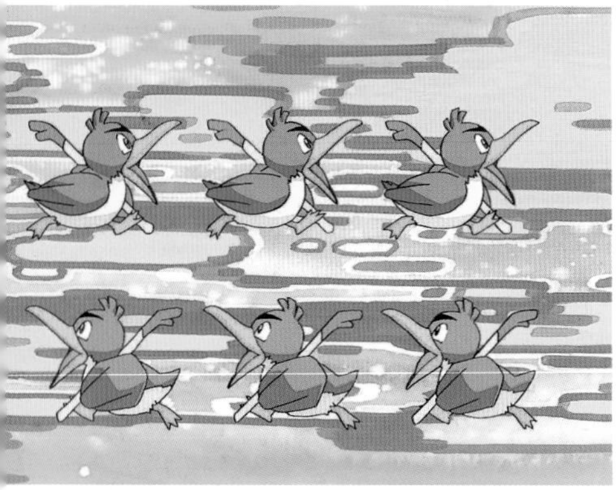

After quite a struggle, Pikachu and Raichu manage to crawl out from under Snorlax, who is still fast asleep. But here comes Charizard, still mad about getting stepped on and woken up! With a great roar, Charizard heads directly for them. Charizard flies so low that the tips of its wings almost graze the ground, and Charizard flies so fast that no one sees it coming.

"Zzzzarrrrrr!" Its sights fixed on Pikachu and Raichu, Charizard swiftly closes in. But Charizard is so intent on its targets that it doesn't look where it's going...and flies headfirst into a pipe! Charizard is quite surprised to find its head caught inside the pipe.

Try as it might, Charizard can't free itself. Charizard roars with frustration, but the flames from its mouth just heat up the inside of the pipe and char the fur of

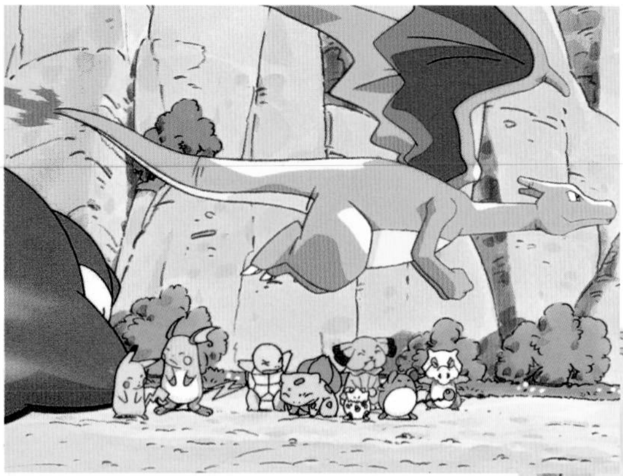

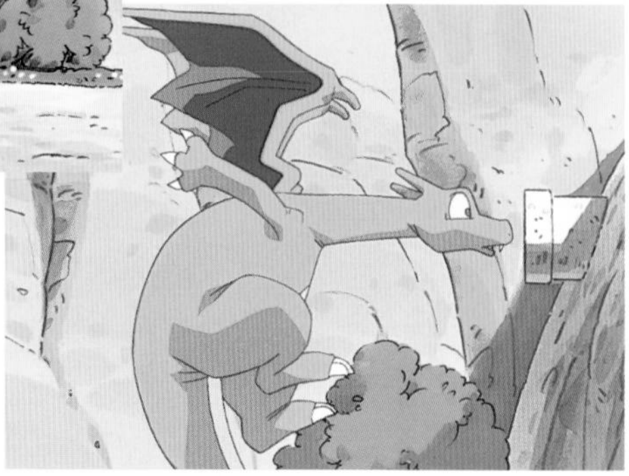

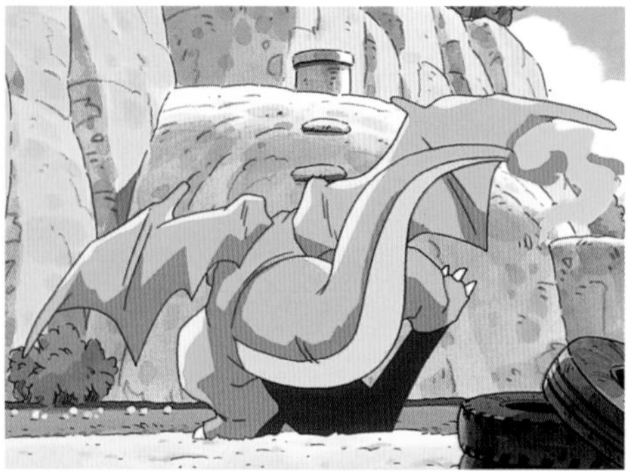

Cocky Charizard zips past everyone's heads and carelessly flies straight into a pipe! Charizard struggles to free itself, but to no avail. Then usually fearless Charizard begins to panic!

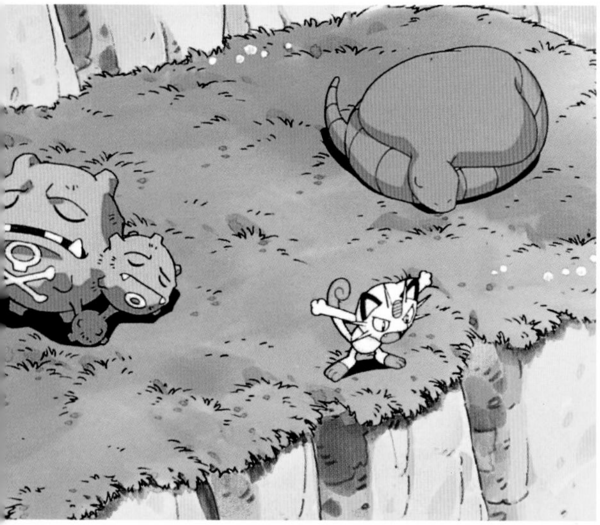

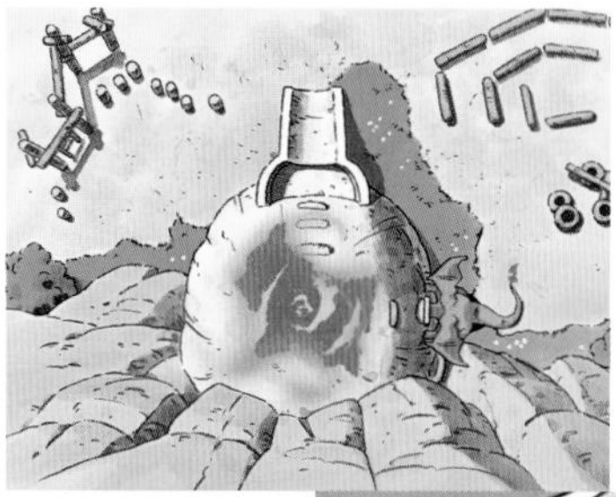

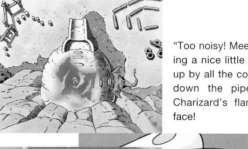

"Too noisy! Mee-owth!" Meowth, who was taking a nice little nap above the pipe, is woken up by all the commotion. When Meowth looks down the pipe to see what's going on, Charizard's flame scorches poor Meowth's face!

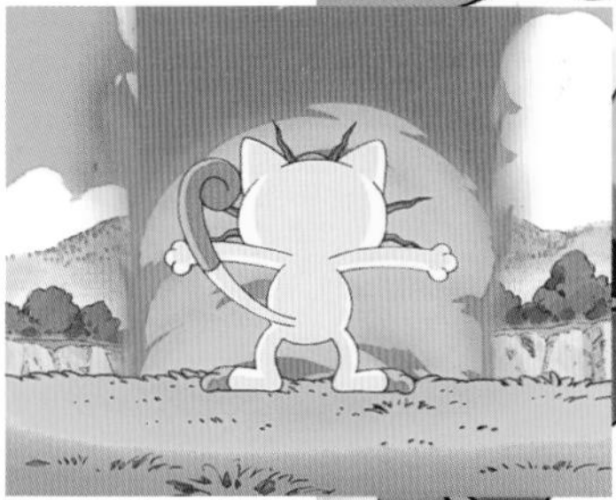

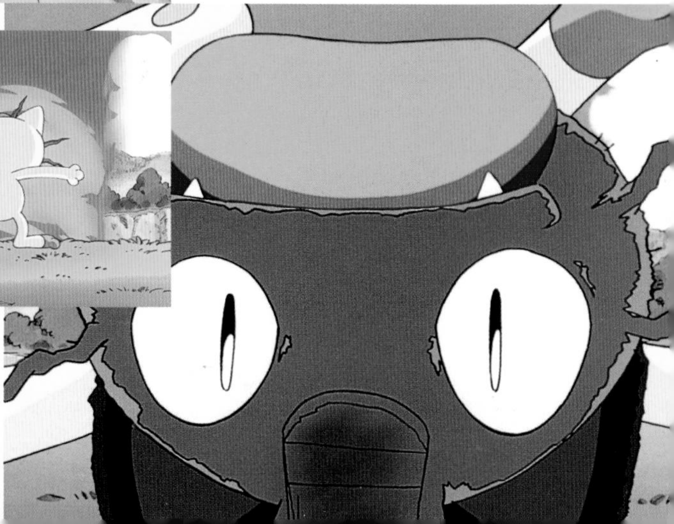

Meowth—who has just looked down the other end of the pipe to see what all the fuss is about!

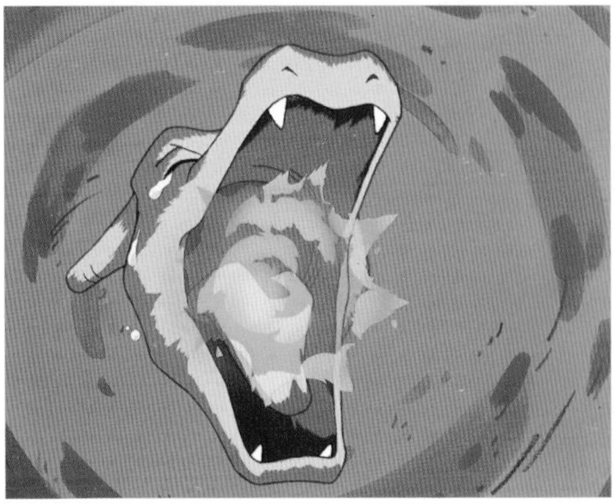

Helpless, its head stuck inside a dark pipe, rambunctious Charizard's spirits begin to falter. Tears spring to Charizard's eyes. Every move only seems to wedge Charizard's head even further into the pipe. Charizard has no idea what to do!

Just then Charizard feels a rope being tied around its leg! Pikachu and the other Pokémon have all teamed up to try to rescue Charizard! Geodude, Vulpix, Pidgeotto, and Onix are all pitching in. But even with all the Pokémon pulling at once, Charizard's head still won't pop out of the pipe.

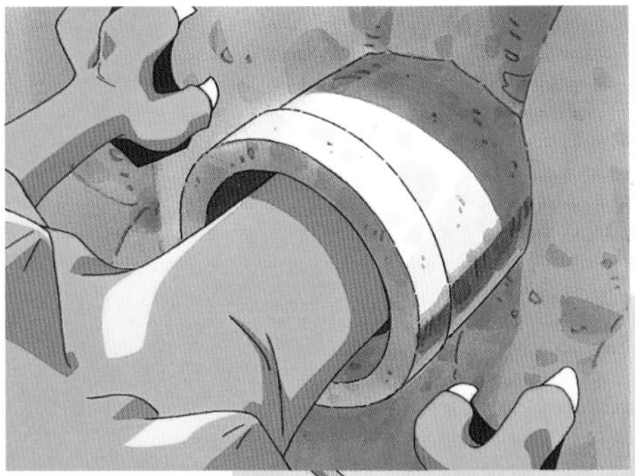

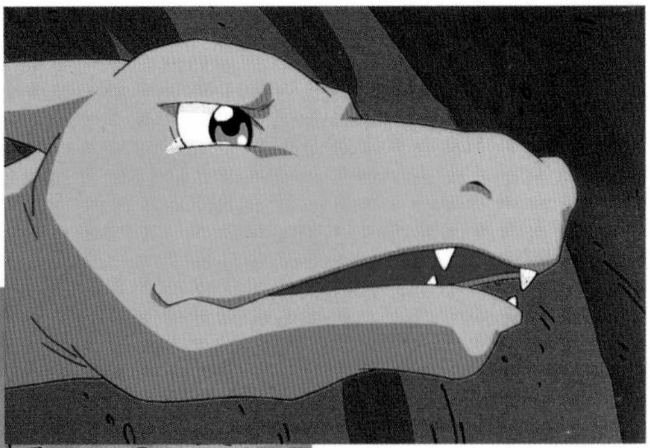

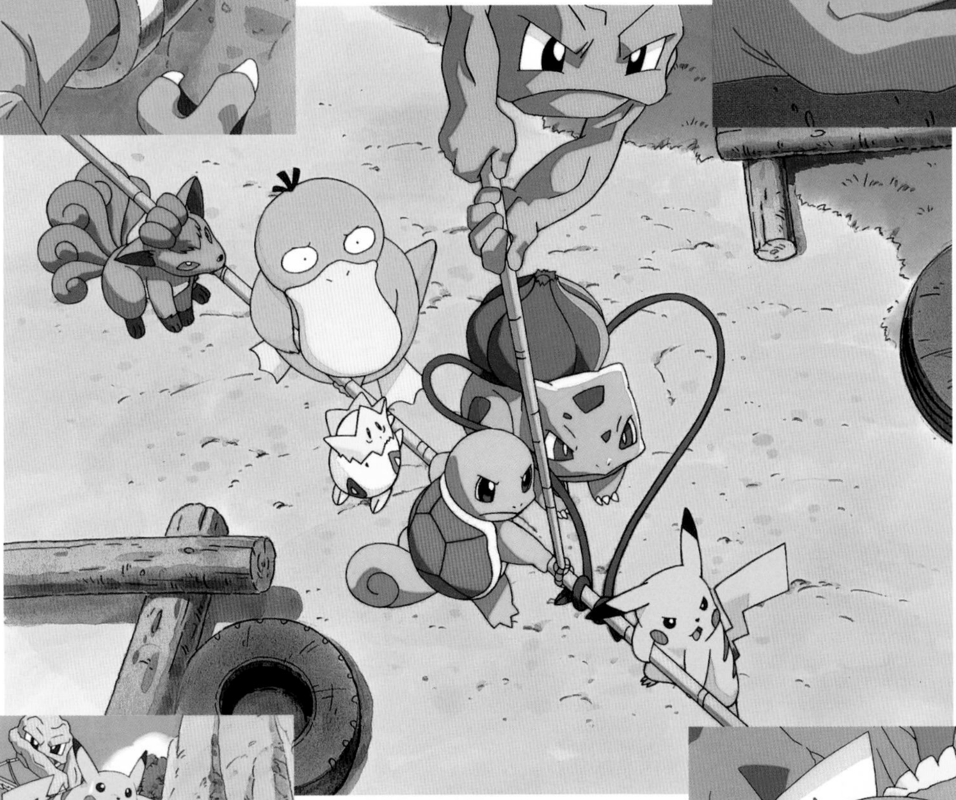

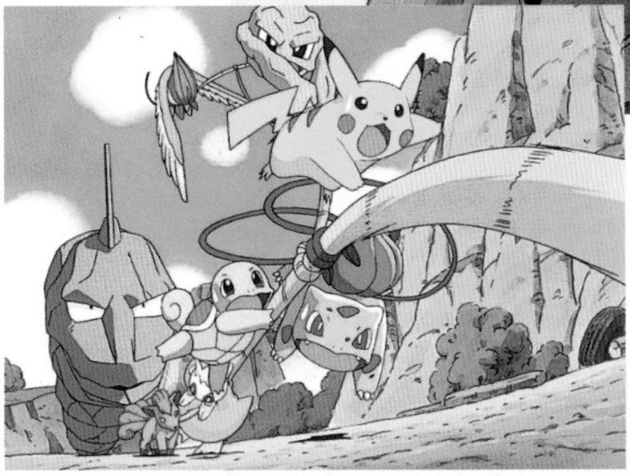

As Charizard begins to cry, the Pokémon pull the rope with all their might. Come on, everyone! We have to rescue Charizard! But heavy Charizard doesn't budge.

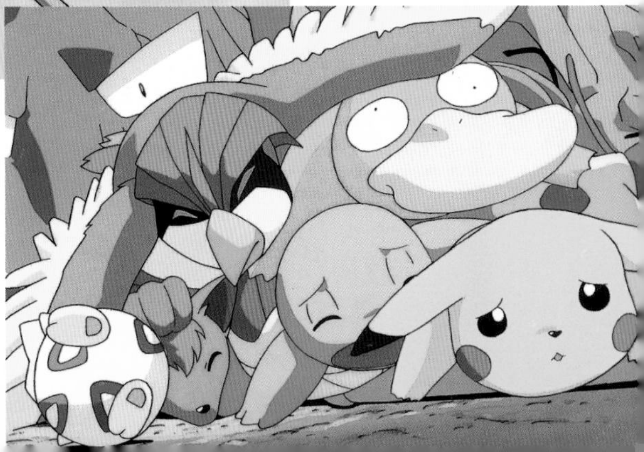

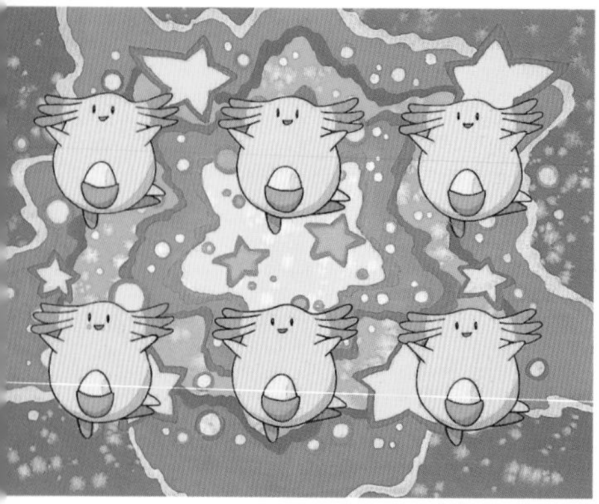

Watching Pikachu and the others fall all over themselves trying to pull Charizard out of the pipe makes Snubble, Raichu, and their friends laugh out loud. They think it's especially funny when Charizard moves its legs and everyone trips and falls down. But this is no time for laughter! Charizard is in serious trouble!

Pikachu realizes that they can't free Charizard by themselves. So Pikachu goes over to Snubble and its three companions and asks them to help with the rescue effort.

Snubble and friends think it over for a moment. Then they agree to lend a hand. After a while, even Cubone joins in. With everyone giving it their all, they finally manage to pull Charizard to safety!

Everyone shouts with excitement!

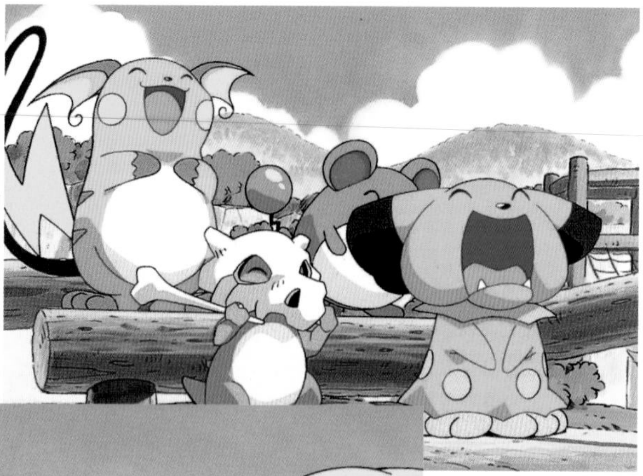

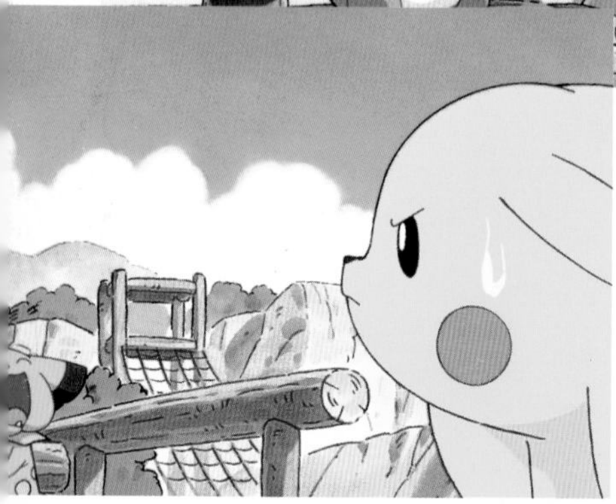

Pikachu is annoyed to see the four friends making fun of the other Pokémon's attempts to rescue Charizard.

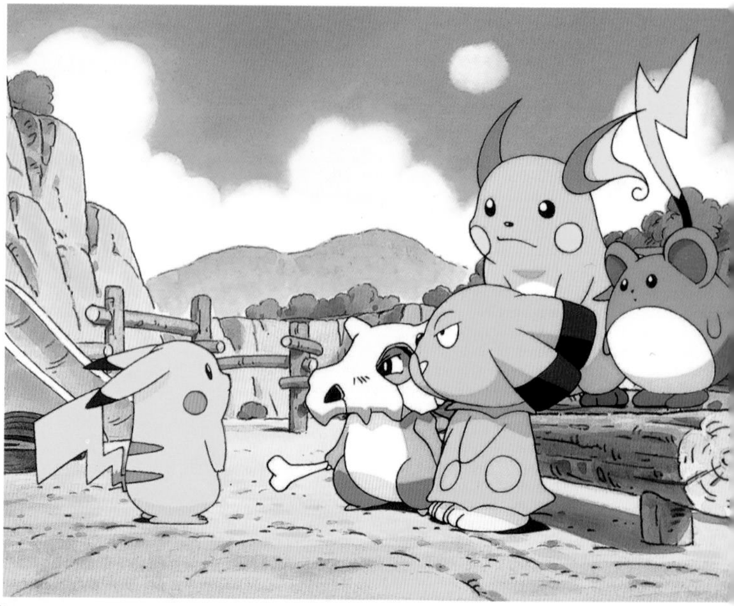

Pikachu asks Snubble and friends for help.

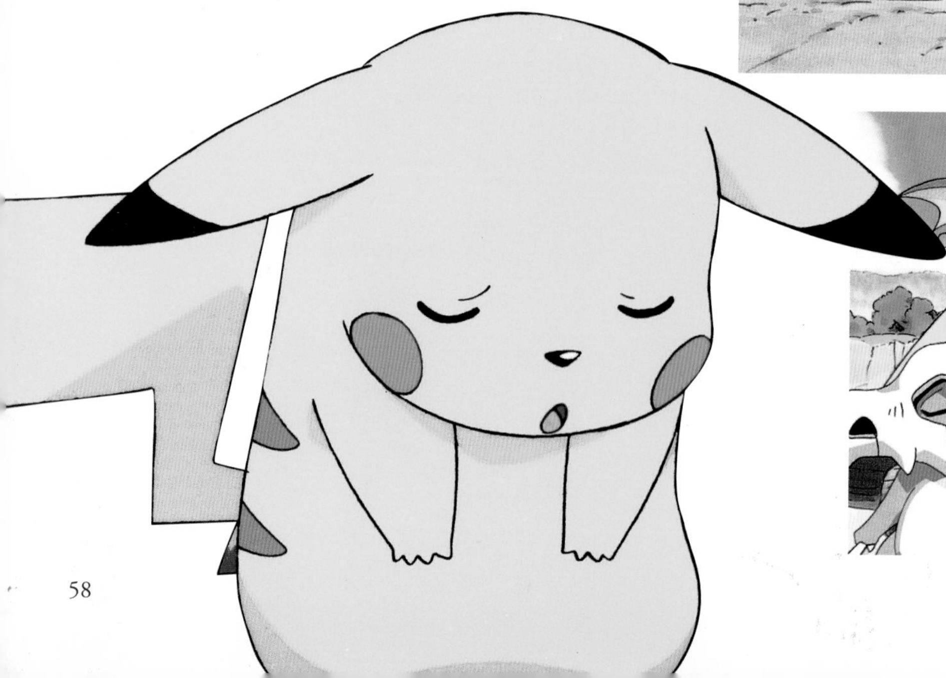

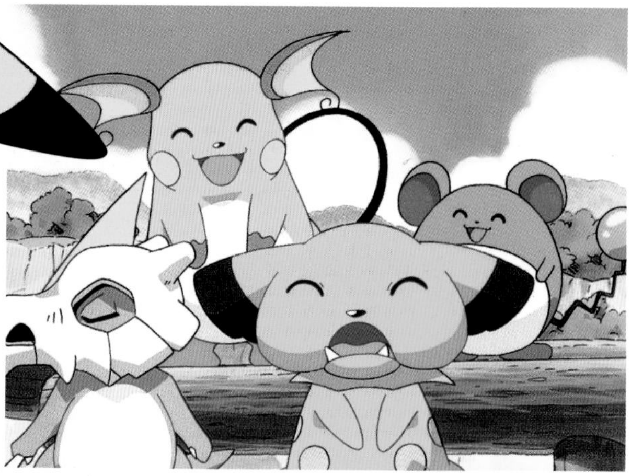

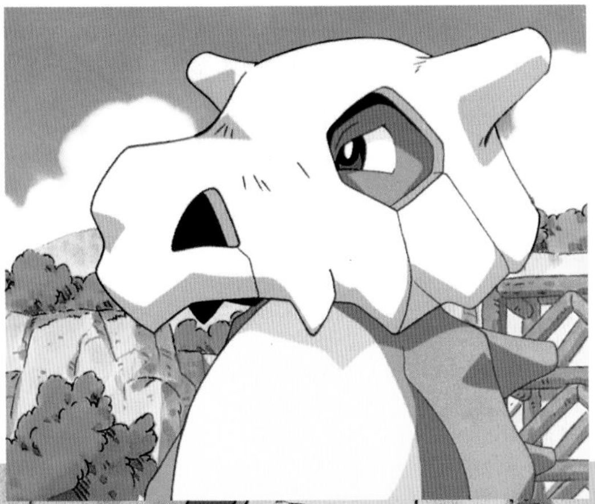

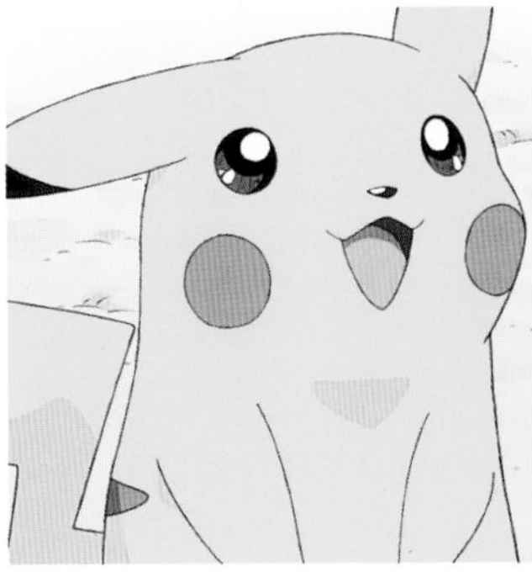

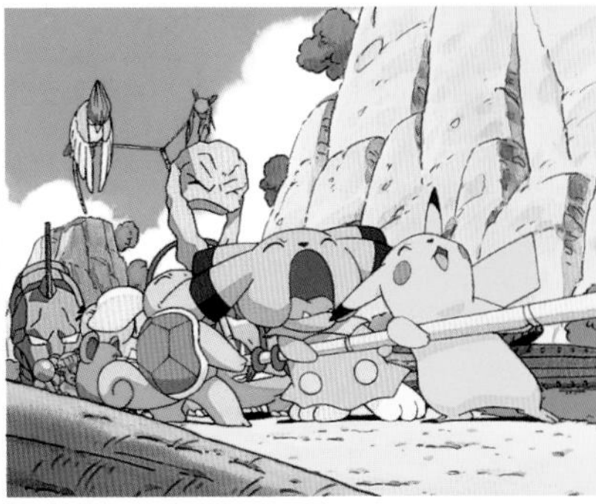

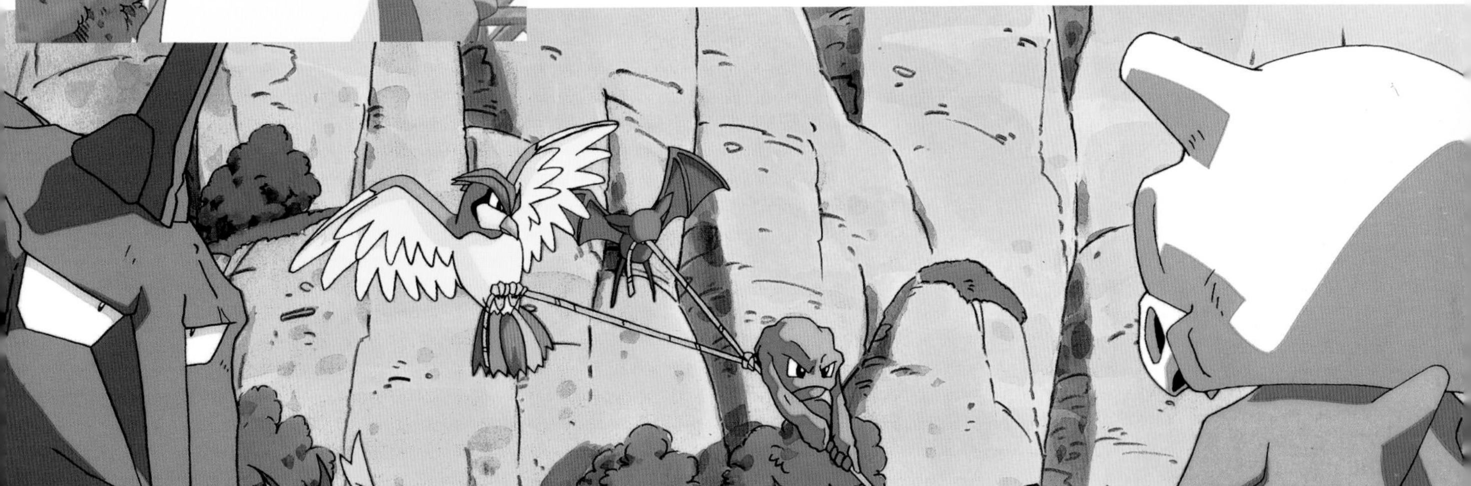

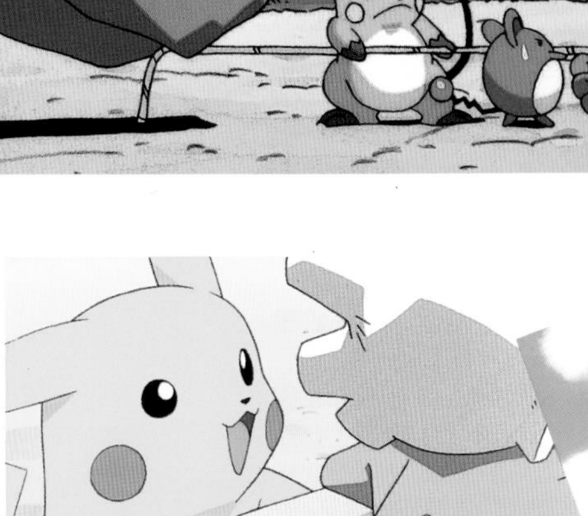

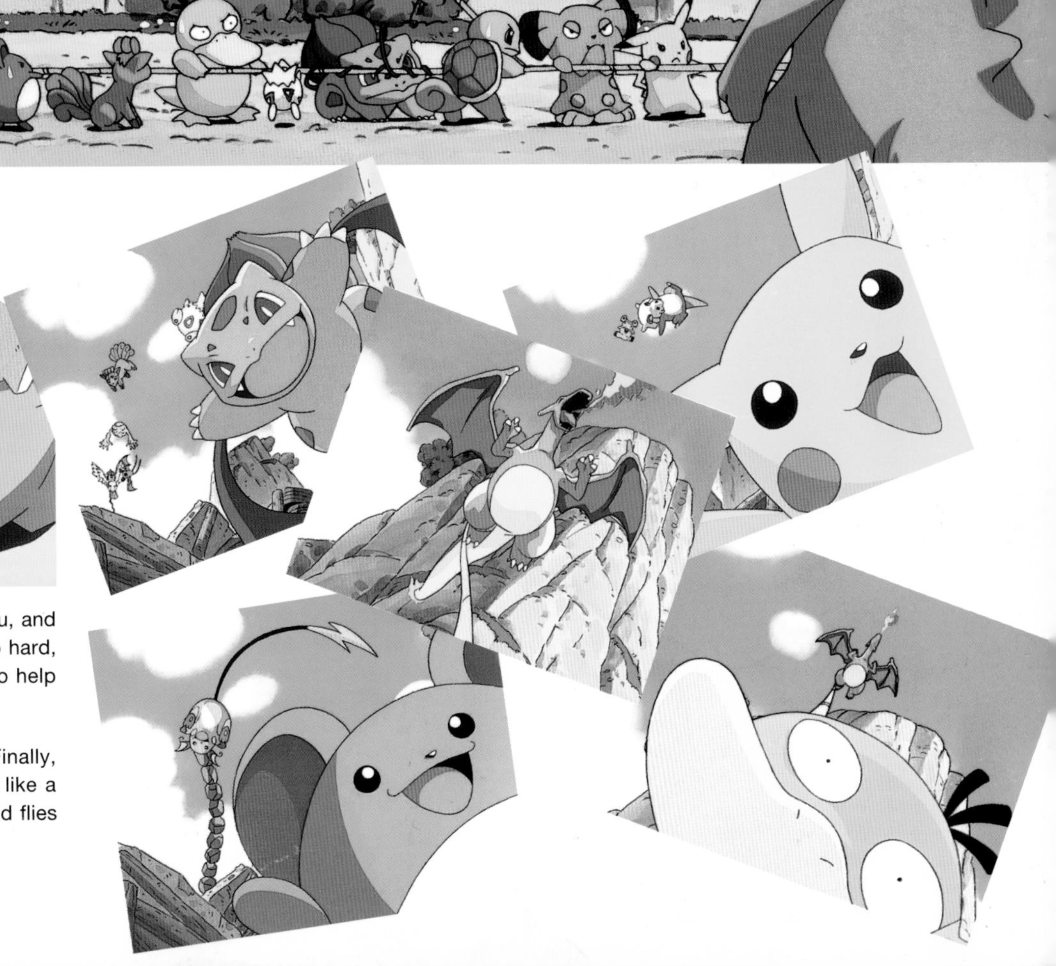

Basically good at heart, Snubble, Raichu, and Merril join in. Seeing everyone trying so hard, Cubone, usually a real loner, decides to help too. Heave ho!

Everyone pulls the rope together. Finally, Charizard's head pops out of the pipe like a cork! Charizard is swung into the air and flies happily away. Everyone jumps for joy!

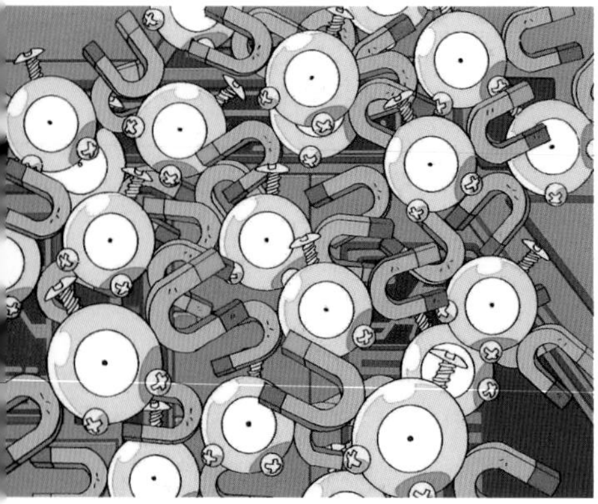

Now it's time for a big cleanup. Here at Pokémon Camp, the rule is: "If it's broken, fix it!"

Everyone carries logs, stacks tires, and so on, and in no time at all, the Camp is all tidied up. To the Pokémon, cleaning up together is like a game.

"Each Pokémon may be small, but together, there's nothing we can't do!" That's probably what Pikachu and friends are thinking as they fix up the Camp. By the time they finish, all the Pokémon have become fast friends.

Now the fun starts! The Pokémon make tunnels in the sandbox, whip down slides, row the rafts, ride the seesaws, and just plain have a great time together.

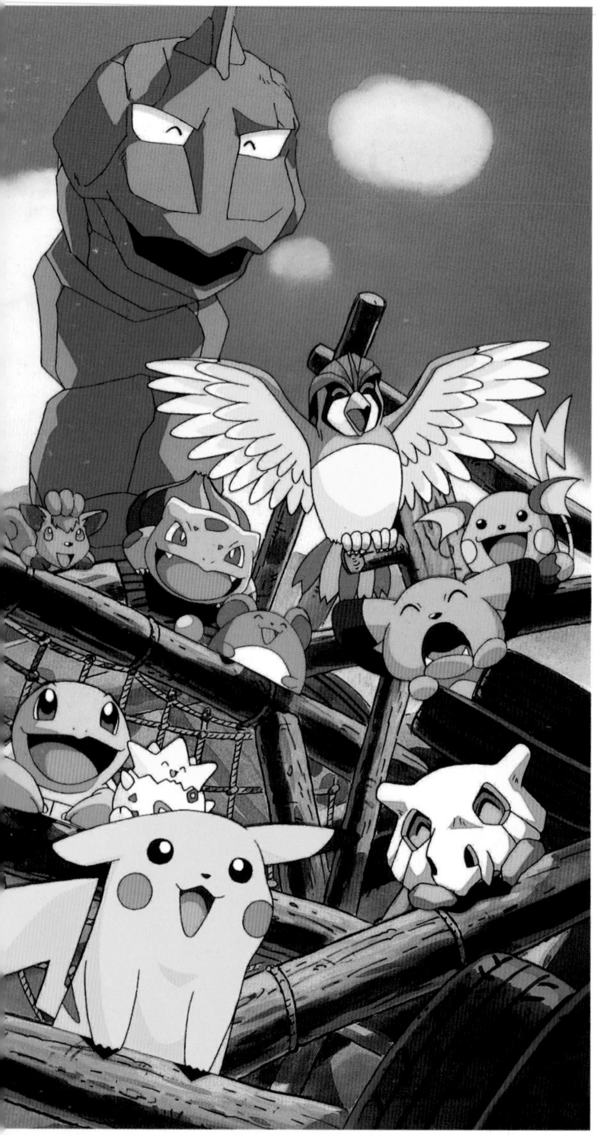

We had a fight, but we worked things out, and now we're all good friends. It's fun to have a lot of friends!

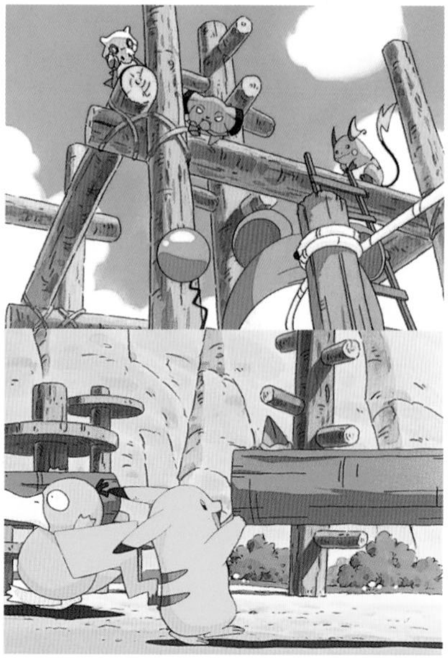

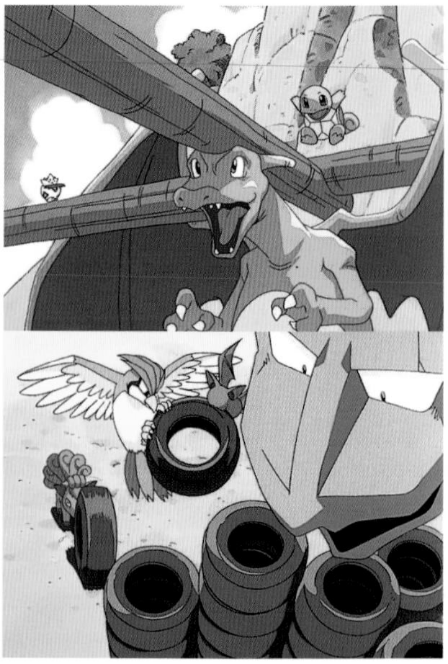

Each Pokémon's power has its limits, but if they all work together, it's amazing what they can accomplish! Fixing up the Camp? With everyone pitching in, it's a cinch!

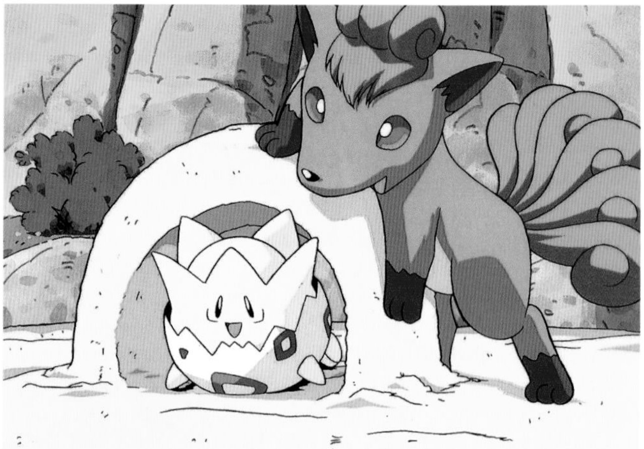

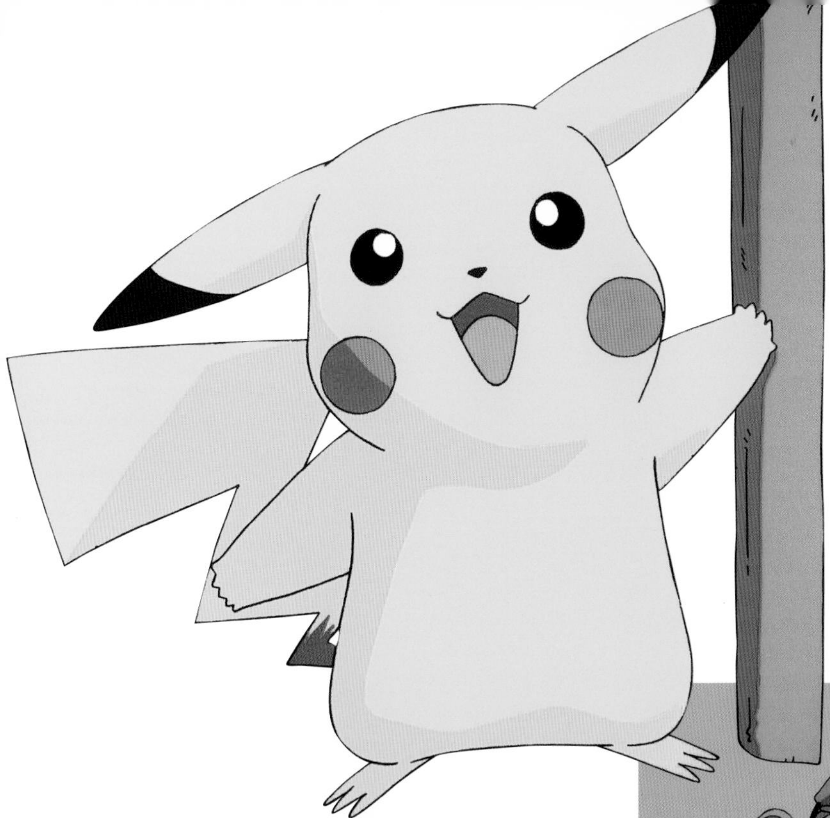

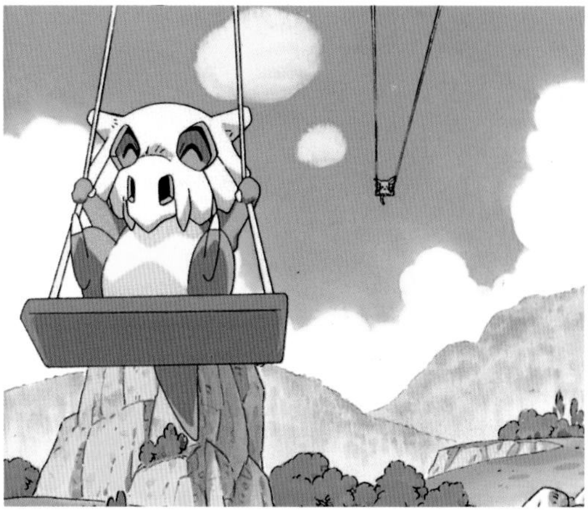

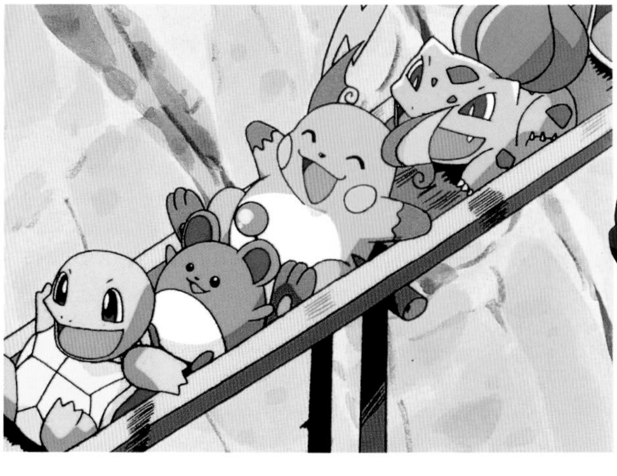

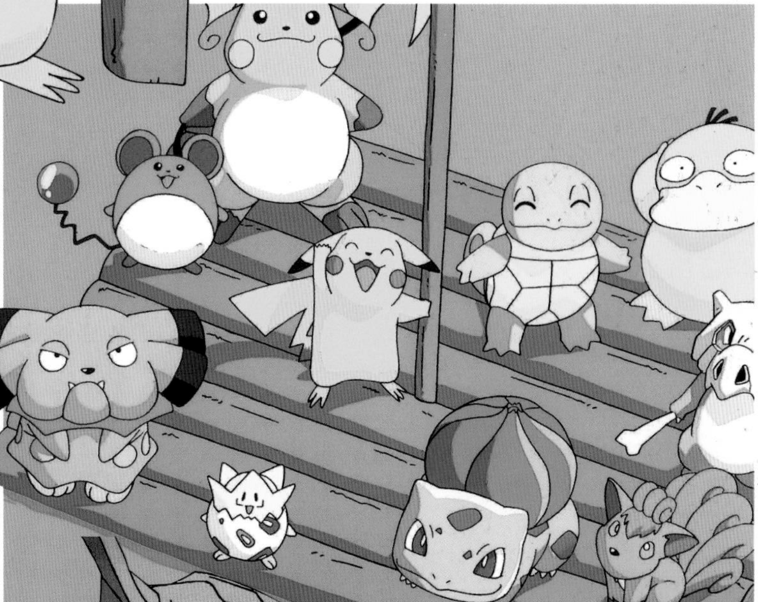

Now that everything's fixed, let's play! Let's ride the seesaw, the slides, and even the rafts! Let's make up for all the lost time we wasted fighting! (But since we got to know each other better, maybe a fight or two is all right sometimes.) At first we didn't get along, but now we're friends!

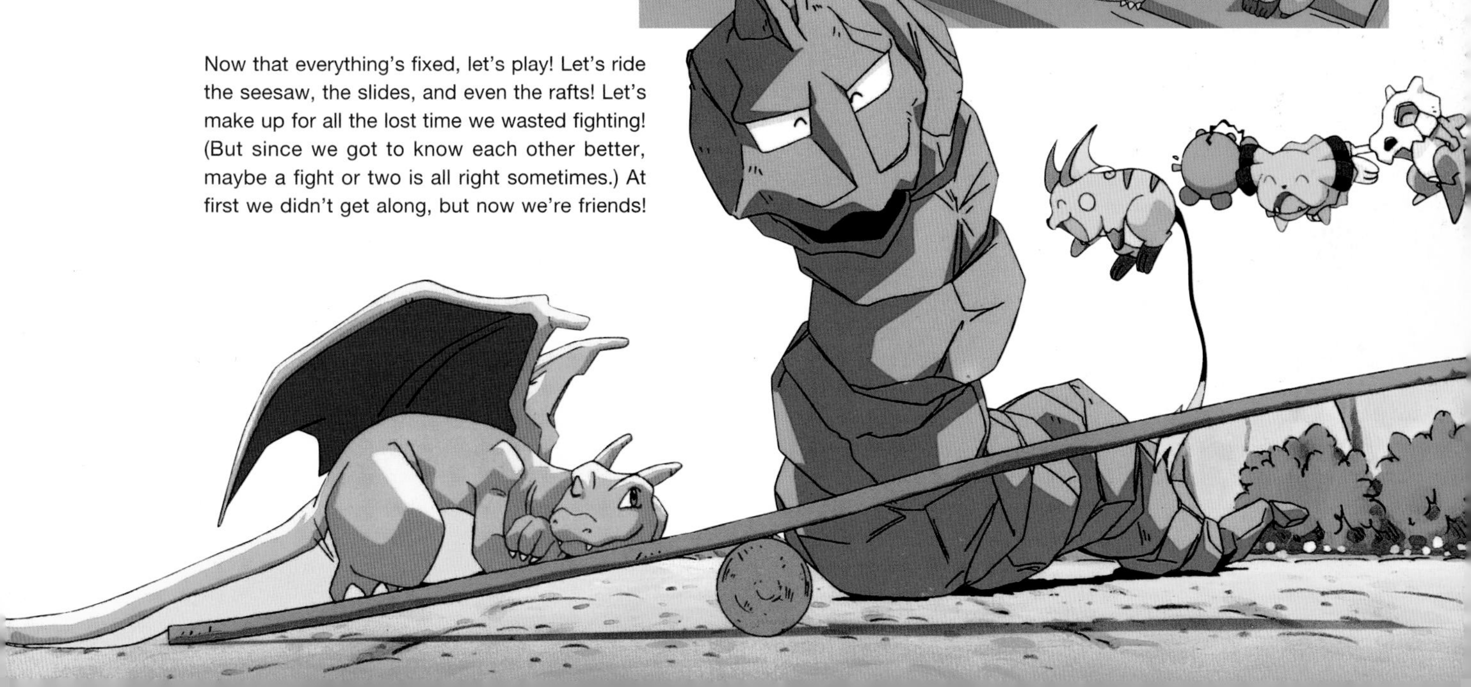

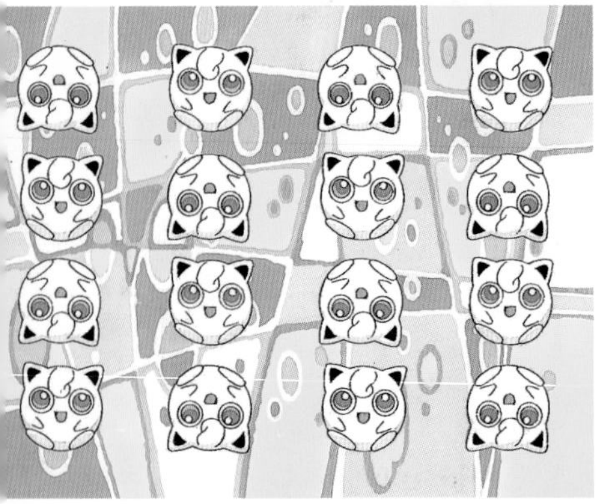

All too soon, the sun begins to set, spreading its bright, fiery hues of gold, orange, and red across the sky. The Pokémon stop to watch the sunset. Warmed by the last rays of sunlight, all the Pokémon turn into Sunset Pokémon!

Summer vacation only comes once a year. Next year, summer vacation will come again. But next year's summer vacation will be different from this year's vacation.

Tomorrow we'll see another sunset. But that sunset will be a slightly different color from today's sunset. Today, too, will never come again. Pikachu remembers Ash saying something like that once.

Let's play again together sometime soon!

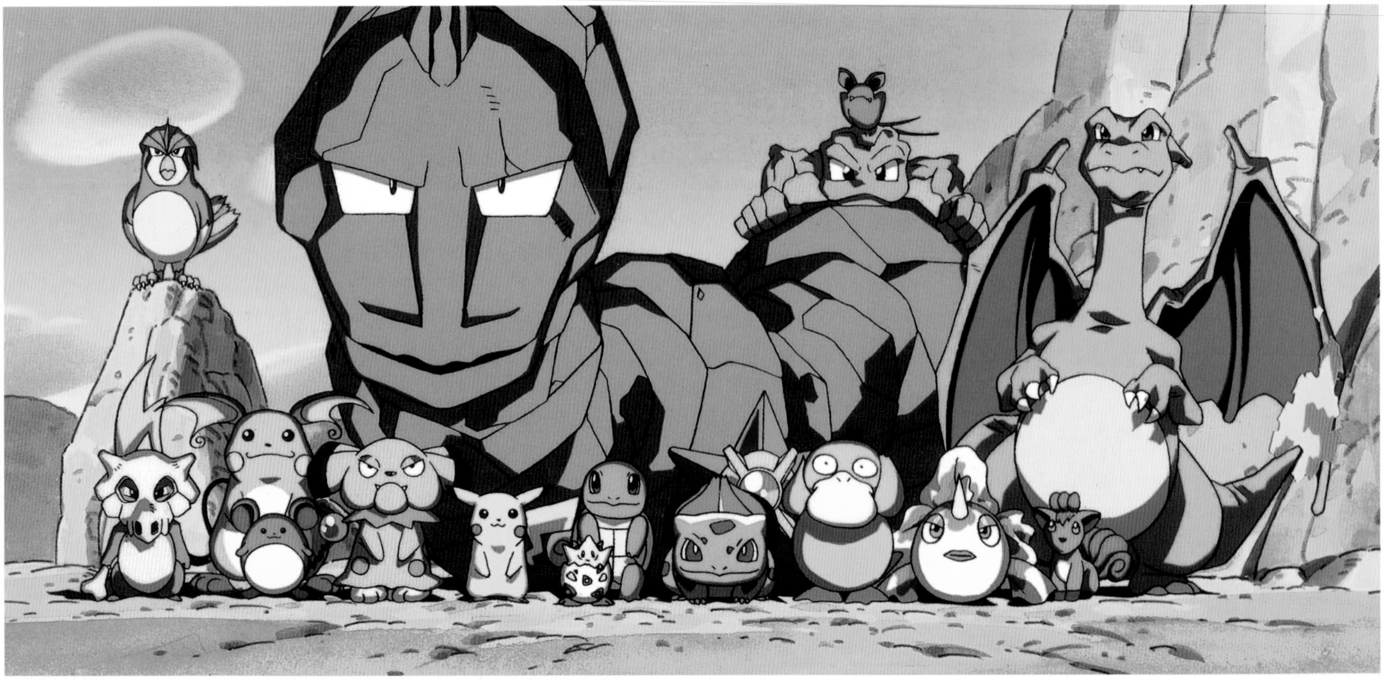

Playtime comes quickly to an end as the day is bathed in the warm glow of the setting sun.

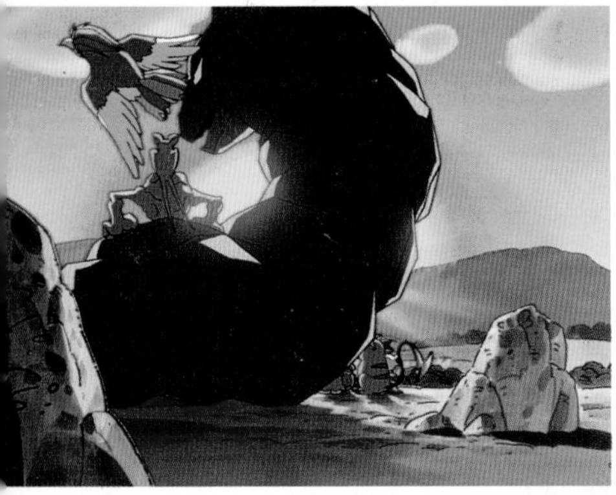

Onix and friends slowly walk home.

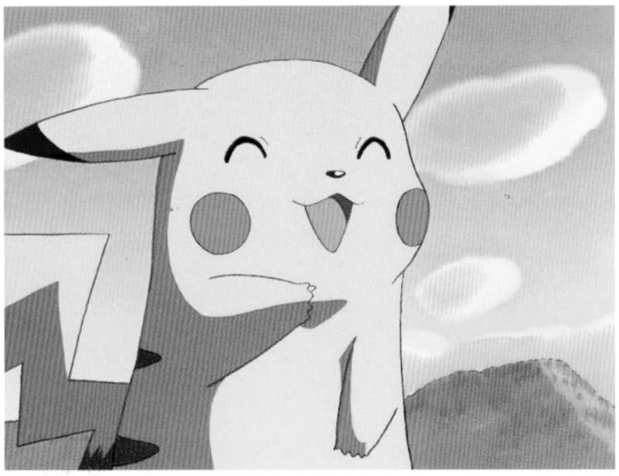

Pikachu says good-bye and reaches out to shake hands.

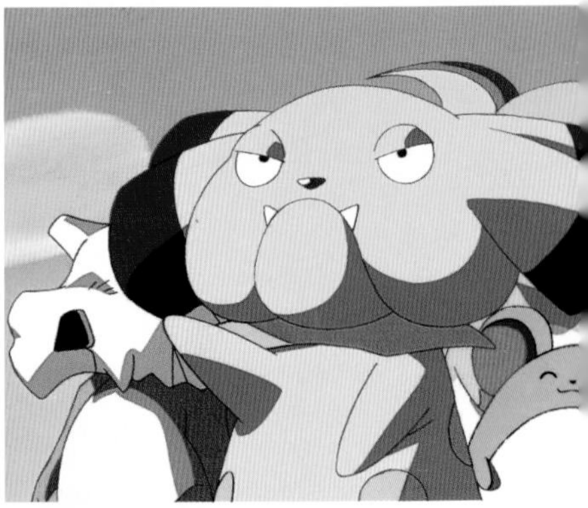

Things didn't go smoothly at first, but now, everyone has become friends. Snubble shakes Pikachu's hand.

Pikachu and Snubble shake hands to cement their friendship. Both promise to see each other again sometime, somewhere.... Running back to Ash, Pikachu thinks, "Wow! What a great day!"

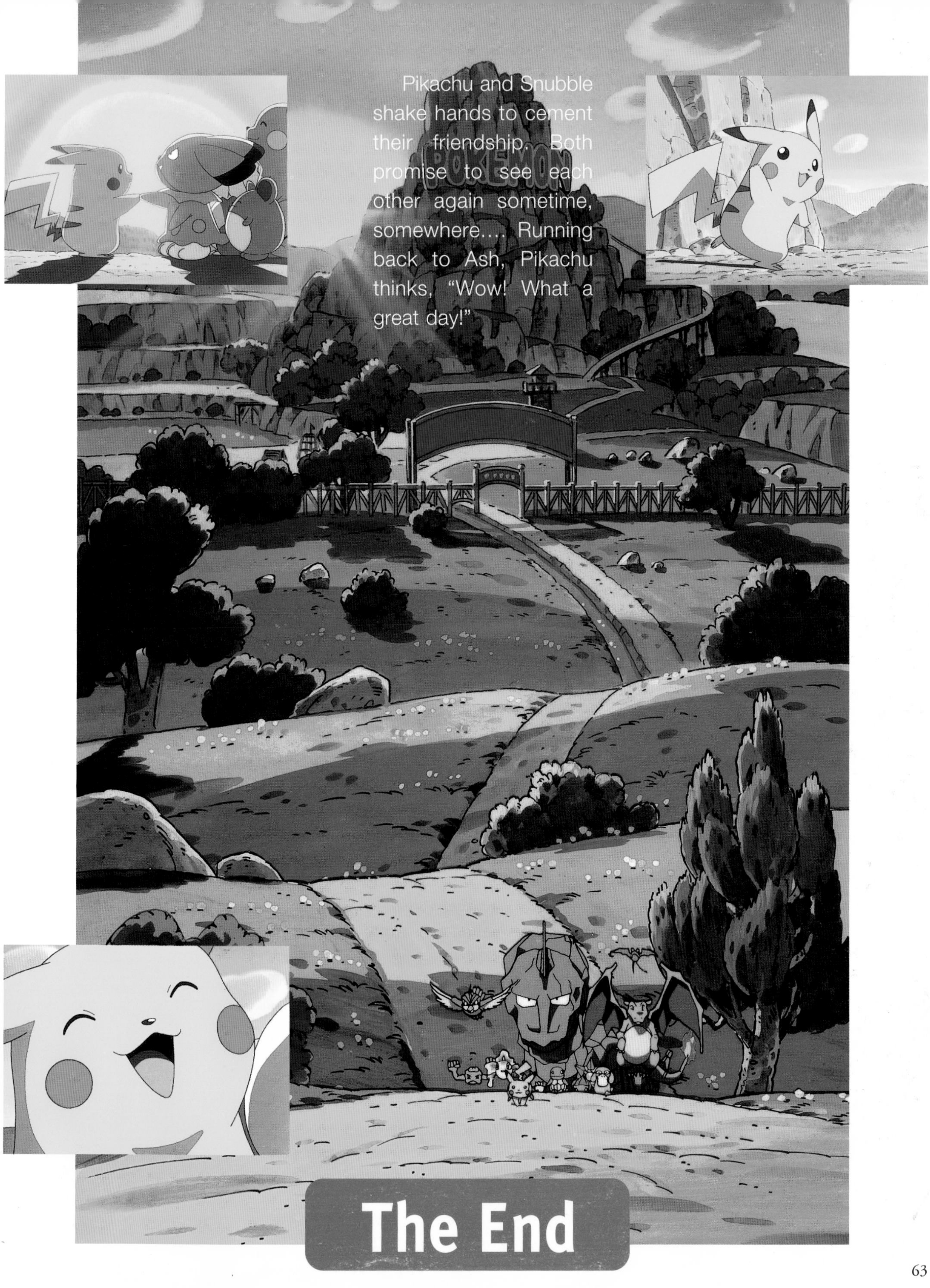
POKEMON

The End